AN IMPRINT OF WHAT BOOKS PRESS | LOS ANGELES

EDENDALE

ALSO BY MICHAEL VENTURA

NON-FICTION

Cassavetes Directs

If I Was A Highway
(photos by Butch Hancock)

*We've Had 100 Years Of Psychotherapy And The World's
Getting Worse* (co-author with James Hillman)

Letters At 3am: Reports On Endarkenment

Marilyn Monroe: From Beginning To End
(photos by Earl Leaf)

Shadow Dancing In The USA

FICTION

The Zoo Where You're Fed To God

The Death Of Frank Sinatra

Night Time Losing Time

EDENDALE

Michael Ventura

ISBN: 979-8-9866258-5-0

Library of Congress Control Number: 2023907838

Cover art: Gronk, *untitled*, 2022
Book design by Ash Good, www.ashgood.com

Giant Claw
363 South Topanga Canyon Boulevard
Topanga, CA 90290

GIANTCLAWPRESS.COM

for
Ginger Varney

We'll always see each other in the movies.

CONTENTS

EXPLANATORY

IN THE KEYSTONE COMEDIES *A Flirt's Mistake, The Face on the Barroom Floor,* and *Those Love Pangs,* our D'Varn usurps roles, costumes, and mannerisms performed by Cecile Arnold, who otherwise bears no responsibility for D'Varn's behavior. The author assumes complete responsibility for not only D'Varn, but also Willie, Esther, Sommie, Brick, Fred, etc., authorial projections all. Historical figures abound in *Edendale,* most importantly Mabel Normand, Mack Sennett, Charles Chaplin, Wyatt Earp, and Ava Gardner; they are not puppets; none act outside the norms of their documented behaviors. In addition to the Keystones named above, silent film aficionados may recognize scenes from *Mabel's Strange Predicament, Tillie's Punctured Romance, Kid Auto Races In Venice,* and *The Clansmen* (aka, *The Birth Of A Nation*). Other motion pictures herein are directed by the author, who emphasizes that no "biz" featuring lions, bears, pigs, cars, bicycles, costumes, jumps, falls, accidents or sensuality, is foreign to, or more extreme than, the American silent cinema on and off the screen circa 1912-1927. "Workpoints" at the far end of this volume details major sources. My intent: to present people of a certain profession, in a certain time and place, as these people experienced themselves, without exaggeration or suppression, and through them, to close in on what Conrad called "that glimpse of truth for which you have forgotten to ask."

With well wishes,
The Author

KEYSTONE PUBLICITY SHOT, CIRCA 1912:
MABEL NORMAND – APPROX. AGE, 17

ANITA LOOS
*In the beginning, Hollywood was a gypsy camp
and everything was fun.*

MABEL NORMAND
*In the beginning, we were golden lads and girls.
We didn't know what to do with our money or ourselves
and we didn't care.*

MACK SENNETT
*In the beginning, we brought box lunches
and picked oranges right off the trees.*

THE KEYSTONE

BLANCHE SWEET
We were all so young. We had to be.

MACK SENNETT
*All jokes are old, and there are only
a few of them.*

1

I LOOSED MY LONGISH HAIR. Put on my sister's favorite thing to wear—the neck-to-foot white nightdress she'd always say she wished she had the nerve to wear all day—then grabbed that beige coat of hers that has the slim waist and fur collar. Folded the coat proper. Shook my hair out more, feelin pretty. Poured oil from our table lamp, a splatter here, a splatter there, struck a match, lit those curtains, watched em catch, then stepped out the back door barefoot. The soles of my feet are tough like my hands—hands and soles are my only parts not silky soft—bet I could dance barefoot on hot coals. I'm resentful of shoes.

Took two long strides, planted my feet wide, my back to the house—enjoyed the flame-throbs hot on my behind. My fire was catchin good, cracklin loud. I held the folded coat to my chest. Through my mouth I took a long breath—tasted wood-smoke on my tongue. Then I ran. I'm all legs. I can really run.

I ran like a deer across Daddy's fallow field—"More a patch than a field," he'd say. I jumped the gulley just for fun, then slid down its side, hopeful the dress wouldn't tear. It didn't. I was out of sight now. Free and clear.

They'd know they couldn't catch me.

My sister would mind about the garment and mind like the dickens about the coat—but as to the house, bet she'll be grateful I had the nerve. My sister's Fred—Winifred, I call her Fred, sometimes Frederica. She calls me Willie. She's my twin but bustier, makes me mad, I'm so flat. I try not to hold it against her. She'll say, "Willie, don't spite me, not my fault I'm built the way I'm built," and I'll say, "My built ain't my fault neither, but I've always gotta be compensatin it." "You could stuff in some hankies." "That don't set with me." And she'd say, as she often says, "I wish you weren't so stubborn." I wish so also, sometimes.

I never worried about Fred getting clear of the fire. She runs near as fast as me.

I didn't know that Mother would want to get out. She might just lie right down in the flames. As for Daddy, he'd get out or not—depends on if his limp was hard or easy—it varies by the hour. I suppose it was mean to set my fire during his afternoon nap. I didn't wish him dead, not exactly, but I also kinda did.

And our boarder—I never wanted him in the house anyway, but he happened to be at his job so I didn't hafta mind about him. He smelled of oil, worked on the big rigs right here in Edendale somewhere down the trolley line. When Daddy decided to take in a boarder I was excited it might be a movie, but his ad in the classified read **NO ANIMALS—NO JEWS—NO MOVIES.**

Now I ran the gulley east and climbed the hill, keeping to cover. Don't know why they call em "hills," they're mountain-steep and at the top you see and see and see. And all the while I climbed I'm hearin fire crackle and folks yellin. Smoke-smell followed me up the slope like the house was saying *Goodbye* and I'm saying *Good riddance.*

When I made the top I didn't stand straight up, but crouchy-stooped to the western slope and looked down from behind a rock through some big bush of some kind. Fred knows the names of all the bushes and trees, and all the flowers and birds, she's real proud of that, and, I suppose, has a right to be. So I let that be hers, and make it my business not to know those things. She lets sewing and such be mine. I let cooking and such be hers. We had kind of an arrangement that way, about this and that—though we're both of us good with animals and with running. When people call us "the twins," well, that wasn't a way to stand on our good side—same time, we're proud of being twins, but only with each other. When I was sure of cover, I looked down at the fire.

There was Fred, front of the house, jerking that pump-handle for all she's worth to fill wood buckets for Daddy and some neighbor-men come to help. Daddy'd raise up a bucket and slosh my fire—useless, completely useless, which Daddy realized as I thought it—he threw his bucket down so hard it busted. He was beat. Bucketing in general stopped right there.

Mother hadn't lain down in the flames like maybe she should have. Just stood apart, watching. It had been a year, no, more than a year since she'd said a word.

I was hoping our outhouse would catch but it didn't.

Why I put my family's house to fire is a why I'll get to later, if at all, except for saying that there's telling the truth and there's doing what's true—I'd told the truth and that did no good so I reckoned to do the truest thing I could. Nothing seemed truer than to set that house afire. It was true and it was fun, and I'm for fun every time.

Smoke rose high and drifted over the hill into the Valley. I stopped watchin the house and watched the smoke—but then, over the Valley, above the river, oh my goodness, an aeroplane. I'd never seen one close. There it was, free on a breeze, like it could be anywhere but it was nice to be here a while. I made out two people seated on the lower wing betwixt slats that held the lower wing to the upper. There was two big spinning fan blades mounted behind the two people. One of them wing-people worked sticks and peddles that stuck out in front of him. That flying machine titled slow and easy on a turn, climbed a bit, headed toward me, got closer, the thump-thump of its motor louder as it neared where I could make out clearer the man who was the operator and beside him a woman, which just knocked me flat. Who ever heard of that, a woman in a flying machine!

They neared and neared more, coming straight at me, till I could make out his goggles and his red cap, and the woman bundled up, though it was warm enough, her hat tied to her chin with a white kerchief like she had a toothache or the way you'd tie a dead person's jaw closed, and they went right over me, sweet as you please. That was a thrill, but bigger yet is when I seen how they turned toward my smoke, to watch my fire. I'm looking out from my perch and they're circling the house, up in the air, and just then some of the north wall fell, throwing lots of sparks. The roof partly caved in. Then I heard the bells.

Even Mother looked up at the thump-thumps and watched the aeroplane that came to my fire, and, with that and them bells, my family members and a gaggle of neighbors were yellin every which thing and lookin every which way till a four-horse water-tank fire wagon galloped round the bend clangin its bells and raisin clouds of road-dust.

Now that was a sight—them reinin in their horses, firemen jumpin to the ground, two of em unreel the hose and two work a long pump handle while one jumps off with a canister cradled in his arms, and they all got helmets while another who wears a cap gives orders.

Big white letters on that red wagon read **Edendale #1.**

Them firemen paid no mind to the house, it was too far gone. They hosed grass that was burning, and the chicken coop, our chickens running every which way bumpin each other down, and, what with flames cracklin and that fireman with his canister sprayin white suds with a fury, and our three dogs jumpin and barkin, Miss Milk Cow moanin and strainin at her tie-rope, firemen hosing the hay bales—well, it was the most excitement I'd yet seen.

Daddy, he'd just sat himself on the ground now, holding his big Good Book. It was smolderin. I got nothin against the Bible, I hate just *that* Bible, but there it was smokin so I felt better, gray smoke-curls oozin out as he held it and opened it and patted down sparks that were eatin the pages. Oh, you know he was deliciously mad.

Served him right. Not that Daddy took a belt to us more so than any daddy I ever heard of, and I guess I deserved it often enough. He fed us regular. Worked us hard, but I never minded work. Gave us more religion than most, but I guess that's good, even if it didn't take. And he never laid an improper hand upon my person like Mother's brother tried. (And oh, what I did to him. Uncle never tried again, never came near us no more.) What it was about Daddy is that Daddy hated me. Daddy plain and simple hated me. So I made it my business to hate him twice back.

As for Mother, what happened to Mother was between Mother and God. One day she was Mother, and then less and less so, and then came the day she refused to say a word—all that day, and ever since. "She's just took silent," is how Daddy put it, and that's where he left it, like it didn't matter. Now she looked up at the aero, how it's flyin circles like a lazy bumblebee, and as it turns she turns her head to see. Now she wouldn't do that if she didn't like to. I can't remember the last thing she was interested in, but here she was likin somethin, because of me. This was a good day so far, the best day ever.

But what happened next was better than anything and beyond my dearest dreams. The word I'd heard was that the Keystone movies had a special phone line to Edendale Fire Station #1, so's they'd know of a fire right off and send their movies to photo that fire for one of their flickers. Now I wanted to prance and dance because it was so. It was so.

One two-seater open-air motor-car, then another, roared in, trailing dust swirls, both motors full of movies. I could tell cause sticking up from the car in front, like the mast of a boat, was a crank-camera settin on three long legs like I'd seen in the illustrateds. Those motors skid to a stop, kick up dirt, and them movies leap off.

Six, maybe seven, wore fire-fighter helmets, but bigger than the real fire-fighter helmets, and the one that didn't wear a helmet, he jumped around yellin through a funnel and waving a flop-hat while the one with the camera pulled out its three legs, set it down, and commenced to crankin. Those movies in fire-gear got in folks' way, ran frantic at the hoses, got soaked, fell down, while one ran straight at the fire—a woman, by God, and she let her dress catch a little, or maybe didn't let it, maybe it just did. The movies rolled her over the ground to smother flames and hosed her down as the camera cranked. Then that Edendale #1 true fireman swung his canister at her and sprayed her all over with white suds. The movie with the flop-hat waved it all around yellin and pointin. Mother didn't take much notice, but Daddy and Fred sure did.

Fred had to, cause a movie grabbed her, scooped her right up, she's yellin and arm-wavin, he drops her, she crawls in dust-mud, he grabs her ankles and pulls her out of harm's way, and Daddy—he'd been just kind of paralyzed by it all—he sees that female movie muddy on the ground, and her garment's stickin to herself kinda lewd, oh-boy-howdy, Daddy springs up like he's gonna fight, but the movie lady, quick as anything, she trips him, all the while that camera's crankin with a terrible racket, but even from way up this hill I heard Fred's ripplin crazy laugh as a movie raises her straight off the ground like she don't weigh nothin and tosses her on a haystack that's still smolderin. Now the real fireman turns his hose on her and on the smoky hay and that blast of water rolls her off onto what was dirt but now's mud. Then, what with this shenanigan and that, and Daddy yellin but nobody pays him mind, it all got over just like it begun, movies piled in their motors and sped away throwin back dust while that cameraman, standin in the rumble seat, he cranks at Daddy who's yellin and throwin stuff after them, anything he could grab, rocks, charred wood, anything.

By the time they left, our home was a pile of burnt. Only the outhouse and our shanty horse-shelter got spared. I never did see those two plow horses, they musta run off before I topped the hill. Not that they were much for runnin, but a fire kind of inspires every livin thing.

The Edendale #1 genuine firemen gathered up their gear. I didn't even notice the aeroplane flying off until I couldn't hear its thump-thumps that I'd gotten kinda accustomed to. There it went, way over the river west up the Valley, shrinkin in my eyes to a speck I could barely see until I couldn't.

I looked back down and everybody—my family and the neighbors—was just standin round, like people do after church when the service is over and they've shaken the pastor's hand and they hang about on the lawn in their Sunday best makin chit-chat.

Me, I was envyin Fred. She was gonna be in a flicker, a Keystone. They're the best. Why, Daddy, he'd be in it too! And he hates flickers. That was rich. That would have made my day even if nothin else had. Daddy in a godless flicker and nothin he could do about it.

And then I was kinda sad. Cause everything had happened that would happen. The fire was in the past. There'd be nothin of interest more to see. It was time to go. I knew where, too—cause I wasn't gonna let Fred have one up, not when it came to flickers. As I thought that, Frederica, she snapped her head around and looked straight up at me. She couldn't rightly see me, I know, but she knew what was true. How she shook her head with a toss that swirled her long hair—a way to say goodbye? I believe so. She'd know it was my fire. Sure she would. Aloud I said, "Ok, my twin. I'll see you again."

I WENT NEAR CROSS-EYED watching these two women at the same time who weren't in the same place. The one was shorter than me by a little, and curvy, and I'd seen her before, but not really. The other I'd never seen anything like. Plus stuff was going on which I was watchin as well, and what with watchin—all at once—this and that and somethin else, it got me dizzied. Didn't help that I'd not eaten since the fire, nor drunk a drop of water. But I'd found what I'd set out for.

The boulevard's sign said "Allesandro," the side street's "Effie," and me, I'm sittin on the sidewalk with my back to a fenced lot, knees up, Fred's coat in the crook of my lap, a little ways from an entrance with one word in a narrow straight-up-and-down frame:

K

E

Y

S

T

O

N

E

The little woman I'd seen before, I'd seen her in flickers. She and me were the only gals in sight not wearin hats. She's goin all frantic with, "We're gonna lose the light!"

You lose your handbag or your senses, you don't lose light.

Now it's, "Where in Hades is that motherless streetcar?!"

That's what everybody's waiting for, to board a streetcar?

The little woman, she was for sure Miss Mable Normand. I was thrilled. But in flickers she didn't seem so tiny. Still, her eyes were just as big, and her lips shined bright with red paint like you see on the covers of the illustrateds—same with all the gals in this bunch and some'a the guys. Their eyelids, and under their eyes, were smudged black and gray, and there was a guy in a ticket-taker's outfit that was too small for him, and I counted six cops of the Keystone type of which none of their uniforms fit, and none of their helmets, some being too big, some too small. Miss Normand called out to them, "Boys, don't know whether I'll use you or not. Be ready to jump in."

That Miss Normand! She bossed folks about, sayin we'll-do-this or you-do-that, and those guys hopped to it, which I'd also never seen—cept at church suppers. Miss Normand stood by the flicker camera—I shoulda said by now that all this buzzin'n'hollerin centered round their crank-camera perched atop three legs—anyhow, she's lookin up at the sky, pacin this-way-that-way, glancing nervous up and down the street, while a bowler-hatted guy stood stock still watchin her and hangin on her every word, the bunch of them tense like they were fixin to run a footrace.

A number of motor-cars came and went on Allesandro, a wide boulevard of hard-packed ground. One junk-wagon pulled by a scrawny horse approached and passed, an old gent at the reins as scrawny as his nag. A crone walked by, a red scarf bound her hair and flowers filled a wood crate that hung on straps around her neck, different-colored different-petaled flowers, and she holds out a flower to one movie and another, asks for them to buy, so Miss Normand says, "Brick, buy em all and get her outa the way." A tall good-looker in a slouch cloth hat says, "Gotchya, Mabel," and he does that. Miss Normand and this Brick person didn't look related, but they were using first names. I know what Daddy would say of such. "Movies are a rough, unmannerly bunch."

That crone grinned at her big sale. She still had all her teeth that I could see. The Brick guy, he's handing out her flowers to just anybody and I go back to watchin that other woman I mentioned. She—well . . . sun blazed on her wide-rimmed white fedora, a man's hat worn a man's way, kinda slanted to the side, but what's under it ain't no man. And she's wearin a man's white dress jacket, and a black tie on a white shirt, and white slacks on her long, long legs, and this is a day for what's brand new because woman-slacks ain't even in the illustrateds. I loved her pearly pointed high-class-lady shoes, with heels liftin her a palm's width off the ground, as though more height was something she needed, which she didn't. She's got a wide mouth and strong nose and big excited eyes, honey-colored hair and creamy skin. Heart-shaped face, but with a toughness to it somehow. I didn't know her name but one day everybody would: D'Varn . . . D'Varn. There's only one. She wasn't who she'd later be. She was even better. But that's me judgin and I'm a "special case," as she would say. That was my first eyeful of D'Varn. That was my life I was seeing.

The Brick person held out a red flower. D'Varn took it, considered it, tossed it over her left shoulder.

Then from north on Allesandro a deep bell clang'a'clanged and folks yelled "Trolly!" and "Big Red!" and all tensed up as it neared. Miss Normand bent her knees like she's about to dive off a board—then shouted out, "Crank that sonofabitch!"

I almost peed. I could not believe, really could not believe, how that lady yelled a curse-word smack in the middle of the street in front of God and everybody. If Daddy's right and there's a Hell, these people don't fear it.

The Big Red trolley's clang'a'clangin and Miss Normand jumps into an open-air automobile parked not far from me. One of her Kops cranks it, it starts with a belch, and she drives it herself right onto the trolley tracks. Stops cross-wise so's the trolley's gotta stop, and stop it does, a'clanging furiouser.

So while she's doing that—here's what about I mean about cross-eyed, you had to watch lots at once to keep track of these movies—that bowler-hat guy and this big gal, big and tall, with flowers on her hat, they jump the rear steps of that trolley, push toward the front, and they make to get off. But now there's Miss Normand standing in their way. Well, the conductor and the ticket-taker yell their brains out but nobody minds them, just like with Daddy earlier, while the passengers are all excited, the bell's clangin, and that camera's crankin with a racket that cuts through yells and bells and what-not.

Miss Normand, she plants herself there and points to Bowler Hat, then jabs at the ground in front of her, and she means business saying, "Mister, down here, right now!"

Bowler's sheepish, shrugs, let's go that big gal's hand, starts to step off the trolley to where Miss Normand said, but Big Gal kicks Bowler's rear so that he rises off his feet and falls straight forward. Miss Normand dodges sideways. Bowler lands smack on his kisser, jeez. Big Gal hops over him, Miss Normand trips her, jumps her, pulls off her hat, pulls at her hair, tiny Mabel

Normand wailing on that big gal who's screamin bloody murder . . . while D'Varn, who I didn't yet know was D'Varn, awaits the opportunity to board the trolley. She can't step over Miss Normand and Big Gal, so she gives Miss Normand one swift kick that rolls her under the Big Red. D'Varn then steps on Big Gal's rump like it's a lump on the sidewalk, those heels dig in and Big Gal yowls while D'Varn boards the Big Red grinnin back at the camera like never-you-mind.

Miss Normand's rolled between the wheels and she's lyin on her back between the rails. I'm worried for her, lain down under a trolley and all. The conductor protests loud as ever, gonna call the law, whereat Miss Normand yells "NOW BOYS!" and them Keystone Kop folk swarm all over everything and steal the conductor's hat and the passengers are happy-as-to-make-themselves-sick, Kops push Miss Normand's car off the track, she's yelling "START ER UP!"—meaning, I guess, the trolley—a guy yells "YOU OK DOWN THERE MABEL" "START ER, KEEP CRANKING, CAMERA PAN RIGHT WITH THE TROLLEY!" and camera guy's saying, "Mr. Sennett don't like me to swivel the frame," and she's' all "SCREW MACK SENNETT!"

There it is again! Bad language! From a female! In the middle of the street.

Trolley rolls over and past her, she calls "Cut!" Camera stops cranking. D'Varn and Kops jump from the trolley as it shoves off. Everybody's waving to everybody, even the conductor, who's got back his hat. Miss Normand tells Camera Guy to set the camera smack in front of her and point it down to where she lays between the rails, then it's "Action," he cranks again. Lying on her back Miss Normand shrugs and looks up with a face that's kinda, "What's a girl to do?"

"We'll snip er there. The End." Crankin stops.

And now everybody's, well, people again—which is sort of disappointin. I'd wanted to see what would happen next, but what happened was that everyone got just work'ish. Like their shift was done.

I'm sittin against that fence, huggin my knees, breathless. Couldn't look at anything more. Buried my face in my knees.

Bigger than I'd bargained for, this was—and me feelin so out of place. In the dark of my closed eyes I knew I had no money, nowhere to be, and no gear but Fred's coat. I didn't regret what I'd done to Daddy's house cause I'd done what I had to, and what I'd seen this day was plenty worth seein, but in my bare feet and white night-dress I didn't look like anybody in this town, which wasn't so bad right here cause neither did these Keystones, but they'd go off and then what? I didn't even have a name—anyway not two. "Willie" was fine, but for a surname I wouldn't go by Daddy's no more.

I was concerned with myself now and not even noticin what these movies were doin. When I looked again they were gathering up stuff and passin this way and that, but it was like I saw without seein, until I had that feeling you get when being stared at. Looking down at me was herself, D'Varn.

I'm sittin on the ground and she's tall as tall. From where I squat she looks like a statue. That all-whiteness of her clothing wasn't as bright. The street had gone to shade—probably what Miss Normand meant by losin light. D'Varn looks down at me with a funny-peculiar smile and lights a cigarette. Well, this was my big day for "I've never seen," cause I'd never seen a woman smoke tobacco cigarettes. Not even in flickers. It's even really and truly *against the law.* My eyes musta bugged out cause she laughed—a short laugh that went all through me. I listen to it still. No sound said trouble like the laughter of D'Varn. Not trouble-terrible, but: Get ready, somethin's comin.

"You fetching little gah'mine," says she.

There's lots of words I don't know.

Says me, "Do I say thanks or throw rocks?"

That got a laugh. Her laughter made my stomach squirmy. I passed gas.

Couldn't tell if she noticed cause she's sayin, like to herself, "Gay-meen or gah-meen? Guh-meen? Gah-mine?" Her eyes flashed. I'm all pins-and-needles. "Must ask Somerset," says she. Looks at me. "Pronunciation is key, according to Somerset." Her voice was kind of tilted, like she was tryin to hold it a certain way. So I'm startled how she yells to no one in particular, "Where's that Somerset!"

Then she kneels at me, like you do to a little kid or some dog.

"Somerset's a good egg," says she. "Only man hereabouts you can trust. Only person who wants nothing."

"To want nothing is still to want," says a voice full of strange.

I don't know where he came from, cause my eyes were all for D'Varn. He looked like his name, "Somerset." Looked like what Mother calls "a proper gentleman," cept he wasn't wearin no hat, the one man not wearin a hat. And there was somethin wrong with his voice.

"Sommie," says she.

"I've requested you not call me that," says he.

"Sommie, I have a question."

"Naturally."

I'm sweatin scared now. These movies are not like actual people. I didn't understand a thing they did nor a word they said. As for trust, I trust just Fred.

She did her askin.

"Depends," he answers, "upon one's pretensions. One does hear gay-mine—I avoid such people. Gay-meen is incorrect as well. Guh-meen—impossible, never say guh-meen. Properly, gamine's *a* has a flat or open sound, while the *i* and final *e*, bridged by *n*, combine to sound a double *ee* or a flat *in*—or possibly the *i* is hard." Is he giving her the runaround? "Both indicate gender as well as inflect sound: *gah*-meen or gah-mine, though American usage sounds to me more natural, somehow, and that, usually, would be gay-min. I see we have one here."

Now they're lookin at me, these two, like I'm somethin in a cage.

That got me riled and it musta showed.

Says D'Varn, "Careful, Sommie, it might bite."

Says he, "It just might."

"Who's biting who? Can I watch?" That was Miss Normand—smoking a cigarette.

To prove I wasn't no puppy I stood bolt up straight but too fast and got airy-headed. Fell back down the way I'd come.

Miss Normand, she says, "Somebody get this kid a sandwich. And water."

I heard me sayin, meaner than I meant it, "Who you callin kid?"

"We're all kids, sweetie. Look what we do for a living."

I started to say "I don't take what I don't work for" but I'd be sayin it to her back, she's walkin off, and just as fast that Brick guy is handin me half a ham sandwich and he's got a wood water bucket with a tin ladle.

Well, then it was like there was just me and that water and ham, I was all over em and damn my pride. And the Brick guy's sayin, "Don't eat so fast, you'll puke. And don't be embarrassed to be hungry. There's not a person on this lot who hasn't had to skip meals for a day or two or three."

Then he was gone and so was that Somerset person. And D'Varn. They were all gone.

I was thinking how Miss Normand looked at me with those big dark sparkly eyes, so kindly. Daddy liked the world "guile," he'd say I was full of guile, but if anybody was *not* full of guile that would be Miss Mabel Normand—a straight shooter she was, you could just know. D'Varn, on the other hand, lookin over Miss Normand's shoulder moments ago, she was fuller of guile than me, eyes laughin like she knows your secret and just might tell.

So there's just me now, sittin on the sidewalk. Two Big Red trolleys passed, one to the north and west, t'other to the east and south. Motor-cars, a few. I'd ridden in trolleys, of course, but never a motor-car. So my mind kinda was wanderin about while my behind felt fixed to the pavement.

Then D'Varn's here of a sudden. These movies come and go just-like-that.

"Mabel wanted me to see if you were still here and if you were alright. She'd've come herself but she had a beef with Mr. Sennett. That's a regular feature this time of day. She's crazy as a bedbug, Mabel, but there ain't a bad bone in her."

And whammo: D'Varn's furious. "*Damn*," she says.

I'm thinkin, What did I do? But she says, to herself not me, "I said *ain't*." And her eyes teared up, so help me. Then she's back to regular. Even happy. How'd she go from one to the next so fast? Wasn't she just the strangest, beautifullest living thing?

I said, "Gotta return this bucket and ladle."

"Wanna see some flickers?" says she.

Before I could say anything she said, "*Want to* see some flickers."

"Shur," says I.

She held out a hand to help me up and I took it. She put her other hand over mine and pulled me to standin. Very warm, her hands. Almost hot. She dropped her one hand but kept holdin mine with the other. She's sayin, "They'll be fresh prints, clean and bright, not like after the exhibitors shred and streak em up."

And there was me, understanding not a word, walkin by D'Varn into the Keystone, hand in hand—D'Varn's so warm, while my free mitt clutched the cool tin rim of that wood bucket.

3

THE KEYSTONE'S GOT A BIG FRONT GATE that kinda looks like a kid's sketch of a Spanish mission, but that's not how we went. We stepped through that door I sat near and got maybe five strides till I knew what I forgot.

"Fred's coat."

"Who's this Fred?"

"It's her coat."

"Fred's a her?"

I let go D'Varn's hand, put down the bucket, turned right around.

"You'll come right back?" She said that funny-like, younger-like. I went and got the coat where it lay on the pavement, then came straight back to D'Varn just where I left her, standing as if posing for her portrait.

"Here you are again," says she in that younger voice. She held out her hand. I took it and then what? Couldn't budge. Just stared.

Says she, "What do you make of it, you?"

Says me, "I smell livestock."

Some kind of putridness cut through it all, but I smelt chickens and pigs and fur—horse-smell too, naturally. Smelt sawdust, kerosene, varnish. Paint, fresh. Lamp oil. Perfume (D'Varn). Sweat. Fresh-washed linens, like when they hang on a line. Outhouse stench. Woman-smell and man-smell. Muddy soil. Road dust.

I sneezed.

"Open your eyes."

Didn't realize they were closed.

There came a great roar. Then another. Made me shudder. A beast.

Bustle of all kinds. Folks moving about.

D'Varn laughed full out. "Hey, you! Open those pretty green eyes."

I was holding her hand tight and opened my eyes lookin up straight into hers, sparkly green too.

"Never have I seen," said she, "a dark-haired lass with eyes so green. Ha. I just said a poem. What else you gonna make me say. *Going to* make me say. By the by—I am called D'Varn."

"I never heard that name, does it go first or come second?

"Both. In one. Just one. Made it up."

"You can do that?"

"You can do even that, yes."

"What's the bad smell?"

"I know! Sommie explained it. There's some kind of silver in the film stock, so—film that they've shot and are not—*going to*—use, they have a way of burning it that—retrieves!—retrieves the silver. Stinks something mighty."

We're standin there, a few steps inside "the lot," is what they call it, and, while she explains an explanation that did me no good, I'm finally really lookin and seein—cause you can look and not see too.

In this late light of day, feeding-time sure enough, across the lot and near a fence a gal cast grain for a flock of chickens. Couldn't see pigs, but heard their snorts as they fed. And there was a well, a good well, the kind where you crank up the pail. Oh, me, this Keystone place—it was a farm!—not for a while, but once it was. Small, about the size of Daddy's. And the oldest building— weathered, but well-kept—was a farm cottage—a nice one, too, built strong. I recognized a barn and a harness shed. The newer buildings mostly looked rough-shod. And a big fantastical building of wood frame, with walls of muslin linen! And here and there were staircases leading nowhere, walls that stuck up not attached to anything, some with doors, some with shelves—and more that I couldn't take in all at once. D'Varn, she enjoyed my surprise. She pointed straight up, where on frames high above the ground gauzy white muslin linen was strung in wide swatches flat overhead, ripplin gently.

"Defusers," she said.

Whatever that means.

People went about every which way, I didn't try to notice them closely, but you couldn't *not* see Big Gal from the trolley head straight for us. She smoked a long thin cigar and wore denim overalls pressed tight against big bouncy boobs. Her walk had force to it. I liked that. Her boots were wide but came to a point, with heels high as D'Varn's—height she didn't need more of either. A red scarf you could see through wrapped round her neck and flowed behind her. Her hat wasn't quite a cowboy hat and wasn't quite not—more an explorer's hat, like in the illustrateds. Thick shiny auburn hair poured out from under that hat darn prettily. A wide mouth, a broke nose, and eyes, well, hard. Hard blue.

She stopped two paces from us, looked me up and down, smiled kind of grim. Said, "Who's the frail?"

"We don't know yet," says D'Varn.

"Taking we-don't-know-yet to the first-shows?"

"Interested?" says D'Varn.

"Is she supposed to be interesting?"

D'Varn struck a pose. "So very much so!"

"So very much so!" Big Gal poses back with a jut of her hip and fluttery fingers.

Them hard eyes looked into mine as though expectin me to look away. I don't look away. She had blubbery lips that managed to be, I don't know, you wouldn't say pretty but you almost would. "Smoochy lips," Fred might call them. The lips smiled. The eyes didn't.

"Little Thing, I'm Big Esther. Big Es—for my big ass." And she slapped her rump.

I laughed because I was supposed to.

"She'll do for a snack," says Es, like I'm not there.

"Let's us go," says D'Varn.

And there I am wondering where I am, holding Fred's coat and D'Varn's hand, walkin between these two, tryin to figure how old they are.

"Ouch!" That was me. And off Big Esther goes, walking strong toward a row of outhouses by the fence, after pinching my—as she would say— ass. Hard.

"What are *her* hobbies?" says I.

"Weepiness. Weeps a lot. Doesn't like to be interrupted at it. Just unlucky in love, I guess."

We're walking slow, like you stroll in a park, holdin hands as gals do, and I don't know what's come over me that even in this strange place D'Varn is really all I can see. With eyes just for her I almost fell over a dwarf.

A plump teeny bit. No-nonsense plain. Gray hair under a Sunday bonnet.

Says to D'Varn, "Thought you'd get away with it?"

"A girl can only try."

"That outfit is Keystone property I'm responsible for."

"Not the shoes."

"Report tomorrow barefoot, then, that's your business, but the rest had best be pressed and spotless. That hat alone is worth two days of your wage."

And she trundles off as D'Varn calls after her, "Thank you, Mrs. Sarbossian!" And to me, "She's not a bad sort. Circus through and through, generations of it. Says here she's finally found a circus that stays put. Mr. Sennett, he pretends not to notice when we gals borrow from Wardrobe. What he cares about is that you work hard, throw yourself into it, all of you into all of it. Remember that and you'll do fine."

Wasn't I just passin through?

Now again I heard it. A great roar. A beast. I don't know why I didn't say anything. Maybe cause D'Varn didn't seem to notice.

We headed for a big'ish plank shed with a peaked roof, all nailed together any old way. Inside were uneven rows of folding wood chairs and every sort of person sittin on them, some I'd noticed and some I'd not yet seen. The chairs faced a screen on the east wall near an upright piano where a piano-lady sat. Lots of people smoked—includin the women—and every few feet, on the floor, was a bright brass spit-bucket. I promptly tripped on one and would have fallen had not D'Varn, holdin my hand, jerked me up so I stumbled into the chest of a very, very tall man. A foot, anyway, taller than me. His shirt was bright white beneath a black vest. A knotted tie—silk. Silver gray hair peaked out under a pricy black hat, shiny velvet-like—"high toned," Fred would say. Sleeves rolled up neatly to the elbows on the longest, longest arms.

"What in the name of sin are you doing here?"

D'Varn pulled me aside and I saw he addressed the character just behind me, a feisty sort in a suit store-bought off-the-rack that almost fit. A straw skimmer on his head, a wire notebook in his left hand, a pencil in his right. The cigarette between his lips wasn't lit.

"Scrounging copy, Mr. Sennett."

"Run it with a still or next time I'll throw you out."

"I'll do my best."

"That doesn't fill me with hope. No photograph, and this is it."

"Napoleon, let the man do his work," says Mabel Normand herself, her little hand tappin Mr. Sennett's shoulder from behind. He stepped aside. I see she's sitting on a high, high stool which brought her almost eye to eye with him. Her legs were crossed, her white boots laced up the front with black ties, and she's wearin a long lavender many-folded outfit of rich fabric, with a hat to match, feather and all.

"Hi, honey," says she to me, "you better now?"

I hardly believed Miss Mabel Normand was talkin to me like she'd known me all my life.

"Much better, Miss Normand. Thank you for askin."

"D'Varn I see you've taken her—in hand, so to speak." There was devilment in Miss Normand's eyes.

"Mr. Sennett?" This notebook fellow looked like to be countin every button on Mr. Sennett's vest. "Is the exhibitor situation improving?"

"New theaters open fast as investors can lease vacant stores and rent chairs from the undertaker."

The fellow writes that down in quick squiggles.

"Nap," says Miss Normand to Mr. Sennett, "you interrupted my interview with this young gentleman. Now, good sir, where were we?"

"The public, Miss Normand, is interested in, fascinated by, your likes —"

"—and dislikes, which I'll keep to myself, thank you. But if anyone wants to know what I enjoy most say I love dark, windy days when trees break and houses blow down, and what I like best is to—don't say 'work,' that's too much like dear Mary Pickford—just say I love to pinch babies and twist their legs."

"Mabel ..." Mr. Sennett shook his head weary-like. "Just tell them Miss Mabel Normand can throw herself into any part instantly, even a part that doesn't exist."

Some man called out, "Does anybody know what day it is?"

"The fourth of February, Anno Domini 1914." That was Somerset's odd voice.

"The *day* is what was asked."

"Wednesday," said about ten people.

"So these flickers open in five days' time, then. All I wanted to know.

Many thanks." The speaker was a huge man, bigger than Mr. Sennett and lots fatter. He sat beside a tiny woman. I'd seen them both in Keystones.

The piano lady plunked loud and lights switched off in a blink. They were electric bulbs, hung from wires wrapped around rafters that kept this shed from falling in on itself. That's why everybody seemed so bright-like. I wasn't used to such light.

Me, I'm just a rag doll, pulled this way and that, cause now I'm yanked down beside D'Varn, and I can't see anything past the huge man who'd asked what day. D'Varn notices my situation, and, like I don't weigh nothin, she sorta flips me up on her lap, where I could see fine over the small gal next to the huge man.

The piano played. The dark felt good. Smelled of all kinds of tobacco, plus somethin sweeter. A big metallic racket started up behind me. A wide beam of light cut through smoke to the screen. D'Varn's lap was warm, cushiony in the sweetest way, and I'm sittin with my dirty bare feet hangin in the air. Me, I had no idea why I wanted to laugh and cry at the same time.

Ok—I guess I had ideas. But I wasn't talkin to myself about them. It's like I knew and I didn't know, and those two parts of me weren't acquainted. But my nipples burnt, which made me nervouser. Way deep inside me was all jelly. I didn't know what to do with myself so thank goodness the flicker started.

D'Varn's one hand rested on my knee. An arm wrapped round my waist, and that hand drummed its fingers on my thigh. I leaned against her bosom with one shoulder. Her hand on my knee clutched hard when the flicker started with a title that said KEYSTONE and A FLIRT'S MISTAKE and A FARCE COMEDY. Then the huge man and little lady sitting right in front of us are down a street and walkin toward us from the screen, and there's D'Varn with her back to them and her face to us, standin in bright sunlight on the corner. She fusses with her gloves like she's got nowhere to be, and what she's wearin! Under a proper enough hat—and that eye-smudge, like right now—a long white dress that's dress enough until just about halfway down the thigh, after which it's gauzy thin, and what with the sunshine you see the outline of her long legs like shadows, but clear and nice.

The huge guy stops to visit with D'Varn while his little lady doesn't realize, walks sprightly on, talkin like he's still by her side, gets to the steps of her house, realizes what's goin on—the guy and D'Varn hittin it off—and she scoots sprightly right back and gives him what for. D'Varn makes a face and huffs away.

"Roscoe, you take that from Minta?" It was Mr. Sennett and folks were laughin.

"You bet he does!" the little gal whoops.

"Every day!" the huge guy, Roscoe, laughs, and everybody laughs more, while I'm hopin to see D'Varn in that get-up again, but turns out she's gone from the flicker.

Minta—now I know her name—turns and is surprised to see me, cause our faces are right close. She gives me a once-over, says to D'Varn, "We're all just being ourselves up there, ain't we, cutey?"

"*You* sure are," says D'Varn.

"Got you there, Minta!" Don't' know who said that, but it got more laughs.

Well, now there's two fellas, well-dressed, in a park—and they're lookin at this "Rajah," a tall number with a beard wearin all kinda robes, the likeness of a drawing in *The Arabian Nights*. He holds a large umbrella over his shoulder for shade. The two well-dressed fellas are behind him a little ways and they're excited at the sight of him. I'm not gettin it. One fella sprints up to him, from behind, still can't see past the umbrella, says some stuff, and the Rajah faces him and our fella gets a bad surprise when he sees Rajah's beard. Rajah blusters, goes to belt the fella with his umbrella but that fella runs off. A title tells us, RAJAH SWEARS DEATH TO FLIRTS.

Still don't get it.

Roscoe and Minta fuss at each other in their house, and there's Roscoe now, got away from Minta. He's on his own in the park. Sees the Rajah from behind and we do too. So now I get it—we see that from behind this Rajah looks like some tall filly in a billowy dress holding an umbrella over her shoulder. Roscoe goes a'flirting, Rajah turns on him and mayhem ensues, more so and more so, all the way back to Roscoe's house, where Minta and some Kops get into the act. Minta beats the stuffin outa Roscoe. The End.

Was it funny ha-ha? Some. Mostly it's kinda wild, seein folks do anything they feel like, and in the dark with all the scents and breaths and shadows it makes me feel kinda nervy and excited. I'm clappin and whoopin like everybody in the shed. Somebody yells, "Is that one of yours, Sommie?"

"You could tell?"

Everybody hoots.

Lights go on, they're settin the next one up, folks talk and smoke and compliment and kid, while I'm feelin a little foolish on D'Varn's lap but I don't want to be anywhere else. I see nobody's lookin twice at me, so I just kinda dangle my feet in the air and let myself be happy. Not silly happy. Serious and a little scary happy. I mean: There I was!

D'Varn talks soft to me. "Look, I gotta go. When this is over. Got someplace to be. But if you hang back and find yourself a shadow to stand in while everybody leaves, there's this building." She told me how to find it. "It's the prop warehouse, there's everything in there, and beds and blankets. Nobody'll mind, I'm almost sure. Then I'll see you in the morning. Ok?"

I hadn't thought ahead, but, if I had, that's about what I'd figure on my own. Find myself a corner, bed down in Fred's coat, and, like it says in the Bible, take no thought of the morrow but let it be sufficient unto itself.

D'Varn whispers hot in my ear, "I think you're gonna be my chicken."

Lights switched off again but I barely paid attention. Folks laughed and cracked wise but I'm concentratin on D'Varn's hand rubbing my knee, then up a little on my thigh, and I know she's gonna feel somethin soon and I'm waitin to see what she'll say.

"What the hell?" She feels some more. "Ain't you somethin!"

See, Fred went to the flickers one day without me cause I was a'bed with fever. Snuck off, of course. We'd steal nickels when our folks weren't looking—not that Mother cared anymore—and we'd sneak off for flickers. Fred comes back all excited about what she liked best, which was how this gal pulled a knife from a garter under her dress. Fred challenged me to make us one apiece. A good garter, I discovered, is hard to sew—and it's harder to fix up a garter-belt that won't hardly show. You need the best clasps, material that won't lose shape, and if it's gonna hold a blade you need strong light leather for the sheath. Of course, you get the knives first, before you cut the sheath, and the blade can't be too long, nor have a bulgy handle—a slim knife, see, razor-sharp on either edge and both edges curvin to a fine point. Took a while, cause we had to filch coins from Daddy little by little, and that leather wasn't cheap, and as for them knives, you don't wanna know. To save, we became no better than thieves. We were dedicated on those knives and "knife-wear," as Fred called it. Now, everywhere we go, we got what she called our "sidekicks" close on our pretty white thighs.

D'Varn's discovering mine slowly with her fingers, which has me ticklish, but it was ok to laugh cause everybody else was, at the flicker.

D'Varn hugged me tight. "You. You!"

Don't think that didn't make me happy.

But, believe it or don't, the next flicker took my mind off D'Varn.

It starts, and Minta says, funny-like, in a voice sorta Somerset'y, "Ah, my flickah begins! Oh! It cawn't be. Is that possible? How extraordinary! Is it really me?"

A voice like Somerset's, but not Somerset's, says, a little fearfully, "My sentiments entirely."

On that screen was the Devil. I was raised to know the Devil. I'm looking at him, glad I got my knife. Small comfort, a knife against the Devil, but small is better than none. Amongst these folk the Devil lives. The Devil lives right here.

I hated for Daddy to be right about anything, even a little bit right. Hated more that he'd be right about flickers. But if I'm honest I got to admit that was the Devil I saw. Didn't have time to think on it. That flicker didn't last but five minutes. Bright went the lights and I had other things to think about.

When you pay a nickel for to watch a program of flickers and it's over, the room gets light but not so bright as all these bulbs hanging off rafters, and when you pay a nickel the folks around you are regular total strangers, but they're not strange, like now, and they're not the very same people as was just behavin crazy in the flicker. Also, when you pay a nickel and it's over you're not sitting on the lap of D'Varn.

But was the flicker over, or did it just kinda slide off the screen? Cause Roscoe, he lets out a whoop, leaps up, Minta screams—more like, squeals—cause Roscoe's grabbed her by the shoulders and lifts her straight up high, her head just missed a rafter, and her kicking feet knocked her chair back on my knee, hard. Roscoe's swingin Minta this way and that, yelling sweet nothins, and that piano lady plunks a tune that folks start carryin on about, singin, dancin, some dancin two-by-two, some dancin alone and some with chairs, a tune even I knew, how *the city is a wicked place*

As anyone can see,
And cruel days round your path may hurl,
But midst the giddy urban swirl
Of temptation, trolleys and follies,
Oh, Heaven—will—protect—the working girl!

Mr. Sennett sang loudest and finest. (D'ya know he wanted to sing opera? I learned that later—learned later what "opera" was too.)

Best was D'Varn. Not her singing, lordy, no. But the rest. On her lap I'd been, I guess, somewhere between a little kid and what she called her "chicken," but with that music I went all chickeny cause of how she moved under me, and I beg your pardon if this sounds dirty but D'Varn's thighs below my bum beat time up and down, and one hand slapped my leg, and her arm hugged me to her so my back felt her front, so, well, I went all rippley inside and didn't mind anythin in this world.

The music stopped, she bounced me off her lap, and I darned near tripped on a fallen chair as she stood up to her full height.

Says she, "You'll be here, right? In the morning? Please, stay."

I was all-at-once too proud to say if I'd go or stay.

She looked at me deep and I looked deep back at her and off she went.

Me, I'm standin on my own amongst these movies.

And, you know, I almost liked it better that way.

So I was scared of D'Varn? Some. Hated that she wasn't there but was kinda glad she'd gone.

And then I'm looking level into the big dark kindness of Miss Mabel Normand's eyes. "Sixteen, right?" I nodded. "I was fifteen when I started—all of four years ago."

Someone offered her the ladle from a beer bucket but she nodded no, still lookin at me.

"Mary, too—sixteen when she started. And that stuck-up Lillian." She saw the question on my face. "Pickford and Gish?" I nodded. "Now we are all old women. Of course, even at fifteen I wore shoes. Your feet are long and thin like mine, I bet we'll find a pair for you. Tomorrow. I can guess your plan tonight. If anyone catches you, including that ungainly and unmannerly Irishman"—she nodded toward Mr. Sennett—"tell em Mabel said it's ok. I'd let you use my dressing-room if I was sure you didn't have fleas or lice or both."

She said that with no sting, just the gorgeousest smile.

Lightly she touched my arm. *"Heaven will protect the working girl—you know not to count on that, right?"*

I winked her.

"Alright, then," says she, and away she went.

The lights flicked off and on.

"Let's call it a night, kids." That was Mr. Sennett.

I knelt to get Fred's coat where it had fell and I pressed its fur collar to my face for her smell. Breathed her deep. Slipped my arms into her sleeves. Let her coat hang open, loose, cause you never know when you'll need to run.

4

I WAS ALL ABOUT ME AGAIN, just kinda standin, not really seein, and folks did what they did as they left. Then the building went black as pitch, all but the open door, where the outside night was lighter than inside. There in the doorway was someone large and strange of shape.

I knew it was a woman cause of a wide-brimmed feathery hat. The strange shape was not so strange when I got what it was—a long coat, open, and under the coat is what they call an evening dress. Too dark under the hat to see the face, but I guessed.

"Come here," said Big Es. "Here to me. D'Varn'll be pissed, she hates when I'm late. Course Miss D'Varn can be late all she wants, but not me, noooooooo." I didn't move. "I said come here."

"Maybe if there's comin-here to be done, you should do it."

At which Big Esther belly-rumbled a laugh. There was no niceness in it—but, anyway, she'd laughed.

"Alright, Little Snack."

It struck me then: not one soul yet did ask my name.

Which I didn't have time to consider, cause Es came at me and didn't stop, grabbed my shoulders, bent toward me as she pulled me up, just my big tippytoe still on the floor, her thick tongue in my mouth movin around. That tongue in me! Squirmin and thrustin and tickly on the roof of my mouth and along my teeth, all forceful and tastin of wine like what Fred and I sipped on holidays before Daddy went teetotaler—that kiss went on a little while. Couldn't help but kiss back a little, only a little. Then my mouth was empty and I was full on my feet again, my shoulders aching where she gripped me. She let go.

Breathy she said, "Did you like it?"

"Beats a poke in the eye with a sharp stick."

I did like it.

But what counted was in my hand.

"Where'd you get that?" asks Es, eyein my knife.

I do not remember whippin out that blade, musta done it as she came at me, cause there it was, in my hand, about a inch from her balloony tits.

"I see why she likes you," Es says. "Had to know how you taste—had to know before D'Varn. She's waiting on me."

And off she went, cause what these movies have in common is comin and goin real quick.

Me, I'm standin in the dark shakin and blubberin. Not because of anybody's thick tongue. I'm shakin cause I don't want to stick somebody, anybody, ever. But I mighta stuck her. Woulda. Does that mean I'm bad?

Daddy says I'm bad and Fred says I'm not, but I'm the one that ought to know and I'm the one that don't.

Just then the door closes and latches and I yell and go for it, knowin where by the dim glow round the doorsill. Knocked over chairs and spit-buckets, barely kept to my feet, hit that door and pounded on it. The door rattled on its hinges, that shed was built so rickety-like. I hear a lock unlatch, the door opened, and I stepped out into what light there was.

Standin ready for whatever came toward him was that guy Brick. He wore his cap pulled down on his eyes, like a tough, and stood like he was game to fight anyone, anytime, for fun, money, or old clothes.

"Mabel said to watch for you as I lock up." He pushed his cap up with a forefinger and gave me a toothy grin. Goofy smile. Smart eyes. "You ain't the frail from the fire this morning."

"That was my sister."

"Yeah, she had—well—more." He made an impolite gesture about breasts, but not in an impolite way.

"Yeah," says me.

"The prop building's that one yonder." He pointed. "Mabel told me, like I said."

He looked me up and down, but frank, not rude.

"You're—different. Can't put my finger on it, but I will."

"Careful that finger don't get bit." I admit his 'different' crack got me sweaty.

"Night," says he. I said "Night" back.

I liked watchin him go. That man had a don't-fool-with-me walk to be trusted.

And there I was, finally, just me, at the Keystone, in the dark. I buttoned Fred's coat against the chill. The sounds of the night felt far off. Where I stood felt quiet as death.

The prop building was long, wide and high. Ramshackle, like that other. No windows. A double door, left ajar. I stepped in tippy-toe, into the dark—some dim light way the other end made for shadows at my end, bulky shadows of shapes and sizes. Took a few steps and klapooey! Clang bang wham slam damn it all.

I couldn't see what fell with me, but lots had.

I lay on my back on something-or-other bumpy beneath me. Then I'm blinded starin straight up at bare electric lights.

"Hullo? Hullo? Is it a person? Please speak up, if so."

"I'm a person!"

"Possums make their way in now and again," the voice was closer, "and cats, of course, and once a coy-O-tey."

I knew that voice. Didn't want to meet him lyin on my back. I scrambled, more things fell, but I got to my feet.

Says his peculiar voice, "Are you—my death?"

"Am I which?"

He points and I see I got that knife in my hand again, and again I don't know how it got there, except that I was rattled from the fall and as I picked myself up it just got there.

I says, "Excuse me," turned, hiked my dress to put it back in its sheath, mumblin sorries.

"We met earlier. I am called Somerset."

"I remember."

"I was told to expect you, so I must apologize for being rather in a state of undress." And he was, just shirt and suspenders, underdraws and socks. "I was changing when you clattered in, so I hope you'll pardon me, I won't be a moment."

Now he's gone and I'm catchin my breath, seein where I am. I never figured it before, but it seems makin flickers takes lots and lots of just plain stuff. Utensils. Drapery. You got your shelves of vases there, all sizes and designs, and shelves packed with pitchers, face-wash basins, glasses, tea sets, liquor bottles, milk bottles. Stacks of chairs of all kinds, tables of all kinds, oilskin table covers, fancy doilies, Tiffany lamps. I'd knocked over three hat-stand-sorta poles where hung ladles, frying pans, stir-spoons, now all scattered on the floor. There's a kid's snow-sled—which I knew only from flickers, cause I never seen snow. Me, I'm strolling through rows and rows and racks and racks of stuff and stuff and stuff, Victrolas with big sound-horns, telephones, telegraphs, buckets (some with wringers), washboards, a roll-top desk or two, patent medicine bottles, dressing screens, free-standing closets, candlesticks, kerosene lamps. Seems Mr. Sennett had stuff enough to outfit a fair-sized little town. And the place was terrific with scents of musty cloth, wood oil, horsehair stuffing, silver polish, brass shiner, cat poop, what-all. There's a row of mirrors and there I am and am and am and am, by the half-dozen.

Now that's a sight. And it's no wonder folks are bein so nice to me, cause as Raggedy Annie as I look it's either be real nice or get your gun and put me outa my misery. And, sure, my hair could use a brush and about a hundred strokes, but I'm pretty even so!

"We'll do fine cause we're more-than-usual pretty," Fred would say, and she'd say, "Pretty's like having a secret that everybody wants to know."

"Admiring ourselves, are we?"

Didn't I blush!

Somerset wore what the illustrateds call a "smoking jacket," and slippers, and he smoked a pipe with tobacco-smell that came straight from someplace wonderful.

"It's my observation that the Keystone person must be an artful exhibitionist and something of a ruffian. You may just do."

"Is there somethin wrong with your throat?" says me. "It's like your voice is made outa half-curdled cream."

"You have a feral quality that, at least thus far, charms. It's clear you've not heard the King's royal tongue, which once was Shakespeare's, as spoken by a loyal subject of His Sovereign Majesty. I am and speak English."

"I speak English."

"Continue to believe that and be happy. Come."

He went and I followed while he's sayin, "I was preparing myself for evening when you so noisily arrived. I sleep little, employing the night for study and to write."

"You live here?"

"I do not think of it in that way. I've prepared a place for you. I hope it will suffice. Mabel was brief but firm in instructing that the situation I prepare for you be, in her word, 'nice.' She is, in my opinion, the finest of souls, but haphazard of character. Wednesday she's your fairy godmother, Friday she's forgotten you exist. The following Tuesday she's your oldest and dearest friend, for perhaps as much as several hours. But angels are bound to be erratic. There's so much need of them, you see."

"Holy Mike!"

"Whom?"

I was struck bug-eyed by a line-up of white statues of every size, in all sorts of outlandish postures, all of them women, all of them naked or just barely not.

"Ah. Haven't you noticed, in the Keystones, when we portray some tastelessly over-decorated home, in the background are one and sometimes more of these vestal virgins, eternally nude? It's quite deliberate. Mr. Sennett insists on it. They've raised no comment, these beauties. To film naked women is gauche but statues of naked women are culture, God bless America. I am quite certain bevies of young boys pay their nickels over and over for the same flicker to see our fair statuary."

I didn't know how to talk to such a person. I kept my trap shut.

He led me on to my "situation." It was fine. There were several kinds of beds in a line against a wall, and he'd screened off one that had an iron frame, made it up nice, and on a night-stand was a wash basin, a water pitcher, a mug, a candle on a fancy silver holder, and matches. And on the floor, a tiger—a rug made outa an actual tiger. And by its head, a chamber pot.

"Do be cautious with the candle. We don't deserve to die like witches. Yet."

"Thank you, Mr. Somerset."

"Here, I'm simply 'Somerset.' 'Mister' is Sennett. And there's a chap called Watson, sometimes he's also a 'mister.' Otherwise, Keystoners are shockingly democratic about names. And yours is, if I may?"

There it was. What's my name now?

"Willie."

"That's first. Last?"

"Both."

"As in, Willie Willie?"

"One's enough. D'Varn's just D'Varn and gets away with it."

"More on what D'Varn gets away with another time." He started to say something else, probably 'goodnight,' but I was pumped and didn't feature bein so soon alone. "Hey, Somerset?"

"Mabel would say 'hay is for horses.' Your question?"

"Around here, what do you do?"

"I'm a scenarist."

"I don't need to hear nothing more."

"Pardon me?"

"I'll keep my sins to me, you keep yours to you."

"A fine plan, and we'll stick to it, but, as I tell D'Varn, pronunciation *is* key. It's pronounced sen-arist, sounding somewhat like sin-arist, but it means scene-arist."

"There are many words I don't know and your mouth is full of em."

"Scenes. I write scenes for Mr. Sennett's comedies. They call that being a scenarist. It worries you, not knowing words?"

"Some."

"Good. That means you'll learn them." He spoke that kindly, like a pastor of the nice sort. "Will you permit a personal question?"

"If I can ask one back."

"Fair bargain. My question is, what do you want? Out of life, I mean. What do you want out of life?"

And, don't you know, it was like he'd handed me a flower. Made me warm inside.

"I want for people to like me as I am."

"Such prodigious ambition."

Two of those words I knew.

But it was like a mask fell off his face when I said what I said. He smiled, and, well, you wouldn't've thought he had such a smile in him. "To like you as you are, is it? I gave up on that so long ago. And yet..." His voice drifted off on a long breath.

"My turn."

"As agreed."

"D'Varn said you don't want nothin."

"A double negative—which I'll explain another time. Your question?"

"Is it true?"

"Not that I don't want anything, but that I want *not* to want."

"That sounds sad."

"Infinitely."

He smiled, as though at himself.

"Willie, I must go now and write my sentence. I write it several times nightly, before I work on Mr. Sennett's scenes, or, as you'd have it, sins. My sentence, as though it has a life of its own, tempts me to write it many more than several times—but that way madness lies."

"So—what's your sentence that you write?"

"We'll work on your grammar one day, shall we?" Then he said, like he was quoting scripture: "The relative and the absolute exist in the same continuum." A pause, then: "The relative and the absolute exist in the same continuum."

"And a Merry Christmas to you, sir!"

"Indeed. Dear child. Goodnight." He turned away, then turned back. "I've told no one. How queer I should tell you."

He went to the nightstand, lit a match off his pipe, then flamed the candle. "I'll be shutting down the electricity in a moment. Remember, caution as to fire. And you'll empty your own chamber pot, won't you?"

And I'm alone, and the electricity disappears, and I've candlelight. I was thirsty, poured water from the pitcher to the mug, then waited just a bit. I still tasted of Es's wine-dipped tongue. I liked that. Mother had a way of saying "honest"; in Mother's way, it was an honest taste. The last of it faded with the water.

Doused the candle, but couldn't imagine sleep. In the dark hung the homey aroma of Somerset's pipe. As though to welcome me to sleepy-bye I heard one more great roar. This time it didn't startle me a nick.

And I'm layin there, and can't get over that Daddy's farm is in Edendale, a few steep hills east and a bit north, and also Mr. Sennett's Keystone is in Edendale. I'm still where I've lived all my life, but it's like a thousand miles beyond. That was some question Somerset asked.

Once I looked straight into Daddy's hate and told him, "All I want is for folks to like me as I am, the me that's really me."

"That'll never happen in this world," he said. "Ain't nobody'll tolerate that 'really me' of you cept Fred."

I repeated "prodigious ambition" a couple times. It felt like chewy taffy.

Daddy plucked down in Edendale before we were born for no reason but the name. He'd say, "That's where we all come from, Eden." He'd say we were the fallen, every last soul of us. But those folks riding in the sky—could people fall upwards? Fred would say, "Willie, times I think you don't know up from down." I gave that thought and decided she was right. Not up from down, nor right from left, nor in from out, cause things seemed to me both or neither or in-between. Not my fault God filled His creation with so much in-betweenness that now we got folks in the sky flyin sittin down. How's a person supposed to get used to that? And what about the birds? How do they feel findin sittin-down human beins way up there? And if I'm in-between, too, stead of good or bad, how's that my fault? Now Fred, with her turn of mind, she'd say, "God didn't create flyin-sittin-down, folks did." Then me, with my turn of mind, I'd say, "If I sew you a dress that don't fit, that's my responsibility, not yours. God sewed each and every one of us, and if somethin about us don't fit that's His responsibility. Same with flyin-sittin-down—He made folks that could do it, so a share of the responsibility is His." "Blame it all on the Lord now, whydon-chya!" she'd say, and I'd say, in my imaginary argument, "I didn't say 'all,' I said 'a share.' The rest is our business, how we do."

Speaking of Eden and such, what do I now smell?

The best smell in the world, is what.

Baking bread.

I swear, I smelt baking bread. From where, who knew? When we were little and Mother was Mother, she'd be baking bread and we'd be hangin about the kitchen for the smell, me and Fred, and Mother'd say, "You got any questions about Heaven just remember the smell of baking bread, and put that together with Forever. That's all you need know about Heaven."

And thinkin of that time and those days I thought of the hawk and my kitten, my pretty grey kitten, when I was little as little, the first animal that was all mine. They said I had to name it and I couldn't think of a name and I was in the yard watchin my grey kitten play and tryin to think of a name when swooped down a big hawk and scooped my kitten up and I watched it fly off, me laughin and laughin that my kitten was flyin. I didn't know, being so little, exactly what that hawk would do with her. Just laughed for happiness at my flyin kitten. So—D'Varn's a hawk. Maybe. I don't care. I'd like bein in the air. ***///***

GHOST BUILDING

GLORIA SWANSON

The Sennett system of making pictures,
strange as it was, was actually fun. You never
knew what the person next to you was going to do.
It was a wonderful way to make a living.

AGNES DEMILLE

There was great excitement and great fervor.
They didn't know what they were working in,
they didn't know what the future would be,
they didn't know what they were doing. They knew
that every new picture broke boundaries,
some one new thing would be done.

1

HOW'S A PERSON SUPPOSED TO FIGURE—talk about in-between-ness!—wakin with the Devil in my head midst smells of Heavenly bread? Stronger now, the smell, like it's risin from the ground. And bells ringin. Three kinds. One's tinny—shepherd dog's collar? No, too steady—a shepherd's staff, the bell hangin on twine from a hole drilled in the grip. But a dog, too, trained good, yappin soft, suggestive-like, not a bark to wake folks. And a happy-like clatter of harness bells, a one-horse rig, and the clip-clop of hooves that for no reason I can think of is the comfortin'est sound, a horse steady at slow trot. Maybe a humble cart, maybe moneyed with frills and brass and lanterns affixed, and in the seat a man, cause it always is, but, hearin it, I imagine it's me. And, from somewhere far, a streetcar's clang, strong and high.

Clip-clop and tinkly harness got softer, farther, the streetcar closer, while the shepherd walked slow, each step makin a sweet double-ring—his sheep musta been a safe space from the tracks or he'da moved faster. I know that's a fine hard-workin dog for that shepherd not to worry at that trolley. And sort of under those clear bells were the muffled-like bleats of the sheep and the dull thud of their hooves on the packed ground of the street.

Which all distracted me good from the Devil in my head, but, soon or late, there'd be no avoidin him. Of a sudden the shepherd was almost as bad cause he brought thoughts of my dear Daddy. I maybe don't have a memory earlier than when City, as Daddy would speak, posted laws about herding—orderin down just how many cows, horses, mules, goats, pigs or sheep may be driven through the city's streets in any one herd, with how many herders required for such-a-much livestock. Daddy screamed of socialists, socialists, socialists takin over God's free country, socialists, socialists, natural sworn enemies of the decent farmer-man, which was himself, God-sworn opponent of godless red socialists. That was some memorable tantrum, cause Fred and me were wee, little as little, but that mysterious "socialist" word stuck on us like a burn-scar, so's I couldn't help discomfort ever after when Daddy read a paper and anything he disagreed with was them godless red socialists, who, if he feared them so, had to be even meaner than he.

When I got through rememberin, streetcar and herd had gone beyond hearin. Just me and the Devil now, me lyin here chilly, feelin all Mr. Sennett's props hulk round me in the dark. No choice now but to follow my mind where it didn't want to go, but had to, cause a mind's got no control over itself, which, saith Daddy, "is how it's the Devil's instrument! That old Devil ken get in yer mind anytime!"

I lay still but for rubbin one cold foot against the other under the covers, and I tried to feel protection breathin that Heavenly smell, and got to considerin how sitting on the lap of D'Varn, while folks laughed amidst tobacco-scent, I seen the Devil on that screen. I can't get over it. I'm feelin D'Varn's front against my back, her thighs under my rump, she's holding me hard and I'm feeling her laughter all through me, I'm happy and scared. Then there's a skinny imp, walkin quick and funny, waddle-like, and you see by the way he puffs his cigarette he's mean as spit. Twirlin a cane he was, tippin his bowler hat at this and that, pants and shoes some sizes too big, vest a size too small, the Devil don't need to care how he looks, no, he cares for nothin but trouble and disruption, curlin his lip under that little moustachio. The Devil, he can't take a stroll for the sake of a stroll but that he's gotta make someone unhappy.

It all began so normal, like those flickers they call "actualities," about real stuff, that run maybe five minutes—at the flicker theater, usually two or three actualities begin a program. The crowd in this flicker is real people, not movies. What's goin on is real—in this one it's kids racin kid-size cars that go like real cars, pretty fast, and you don't see that the Devil is the Devil right off, cause he's just a guy smokin a butt, cept he's too far out on the track and a cop, not a Keystone, a real cop, tells him to shove off, at which he tips his bowler hat. He walks off some, waddlin—it's the walk that clues you first, you see he's strange, he don't walk like no one real. Then he looks at us. That ain't right, not for a flicker, not like that. He looks at us, interested, walks off, comes back, looks again, real interested. And the kids are racin their cars and the crowds are yellin and then it's him again and you start to get it, he ain't so much lookin at us as at the camera that's making the actuality-flicker. He don't want that camera to crank at nothin but him. He keeps goadin that camera to crank at him, and the boss of the camera tries to fight him off, thinkin he's dealin with just a man, but there's nothin just-a-man about this imp, you can't fight him off. And he does an annoyance and another annoyance and you can't get rid of him. The Devil struts and looks down his nose on all the goings on, cause he knows what's important here, which ain't the common people nor the race nor the kids—and it's nothin to him to slap a kid, he swings at one kinda hard—no, he knows what's important is that *he's* shown up, *he's* here, amongst us, and we'd better know it, and the camera is how we'll know. Oh, the Devil has discovered that camera! Where that Devil comes from, there ain't no cameras, it's like he's never heard of one—he ain't God, after all, he doesn't know everything—but now he's seen one and he claims it. It's gotta watch him or else. On that point he's all meanness. You can just see he's indestructible. Knock him down, he's up again. Throw him around, kick him, threaten, he ain't fazed. Try to reason with him, he listens all polite-like, tips his bowler at you, swings his cane like a toff, but that's just to make mockery, he's listenin just to prove he won't listen. That boss is out-matched and finally knows it, allows for the Devil to look straight into that lens, claiming it as his own, and the meanness of his face is big on the screen scrunchin itself up into more meanness, writhin his lips in meanness, twistin his nose, raisin his eyebrows, squintin those I-don't-care eyes right at me.

Everybody was laughin. Not me. I see what I see.

I'm not very smart. Fred got the smarts. But I know the Devil's found the flickers and there's no tellin what's comin. And it's to Keystone the Devil came, same as me, breathin deep of Heaven.

I'm bothered that I'm not more bothered. I see it all again on a screen in my mind and see why they thought it was funny. It is. Kinda. Kinda funny.

I breathed Fred's smell on the fur collar of her coat wrapped round me and wished that she was here to tell her about it. She'd say some comfort, clear and sensible. First time in my life I woke without Fred near.

Paw scamper! Then another. Not scurry-fast—that would be rats. Delib-erate-fast. Gotta be cats. Maybe two, maybe just one moving swift to catch some breakfast. A rooster crowed, real close—that chicken coop I seen. Then birdcall, and another, and more. It'll get light soon. A thump on the roof I could just barely hear. Bird, maybe. No—squirrel, I'd guess, from its pitter-patt to the edge where it musta jumped. Too light of step for a raccoon, which are all over these hills, like the deer. A raccoon would be headed home, but the squirrels are comin out. Time for raccoons to call it a day, time for cats, squirrels and birds to get a move on and make their living. Cougars hunt these hills night or day but they mostly stay away from folks, cept once we lost a cow to one—that was an awful howlin. I like to lie still and appreci-ate how dawn-light stirs the critters before it arrives, and you can't quite mark the instant—I know, cause I've tried—when dark's no longer full-dark. The stirrins increase gradual-like, till you hear it's tomorrow before you see.

A motor rolled by, big, gotta be a truck with how its heavy noisiness bullied over the little and delicate sounds.

Lay there some more, listenin. Keystone was comin awake, slow, like the land does. Someone's footsteps, then chicken-cluckin—feedin the coop. A growlin farther off, somethin else being fed, somethin big. That well-handle's crankin, creakin. Voices, just a few, morning-soft, sleepy. So I upped out of the covers, swung my feet over the bedside, stared at em, like I like to, first thing full awake. These feet, my feet, they're slim, high-arched, long-toed, and toed right, you know? The littlest was littlest, the next longer, the next longer still, like it's supposed to be. Fred jokes how toes are the only thing about me that's how it's supposed to be. My feet, so pretty you can't imagine. That morning, so dirty you can't imagine. Grubby. Grubby can be cute but I wasn't feelin cute. I was feelin the want of a hairbrush and soap, and salt for my wetted finger to scrub my teeth, clean the sleep outa my mouth. (Daddy wouldn't spend for flavored canned tooth powder.)

My pretty, grubby feet, right and left on either side of the head of that I'm-a-rug-now tiger. Tigers have big heads

A scratchy sound! Then a voice. I had an idea from where—a Victrola with a long wide horn, like Fred and me saw demonstrated in a downtown store on one of what Fred called our "voyages." Somerset taking advantage of the props, I guessed. But this tune… kinda talkin while kinda singin, how life is all cloudy and full of rain but this gent is full of nothin and who's to soothe his thumpin brain? *Nobody.* Then I'm confused. First verse he sounds like, well, a gent—says his "Nobody" almost like Somerset might, but sly. But then he sounds colored. Then white again. Till that's all kinda mixed together, while always comin back to "Nobody" and him saying "Nobody" each time some different way. Then scratchy, scratchy, slower and lower, gettin aggravatin, till Somerset, in that smoking jacket—blearier than earlier but otherwise the same—he comes to my "bedroom" holding, with both hands, a steaming mug.

"They let the darky sing. Terribly good of them, to let the darky sing. So terribly, terribly considerate and good."

He was strange in the eyes and not really talkin to me.

"Physics," says he, "is fascinating, harmless, useless. Meaningfully so!"

"Good mornin—I suppose."

"Your baseball sport appears useless but functions socially to a purpose. Flickers are not harmless. Altogether too much of life randomly, pointlessly fascinates. Physics. Professor Einstein's physics…"

I point to the mug. "Do I get to drink that or stare at it?"

He hands it over oh so politely.

Smelled funny, but felt good in the chill to hold a warm mug.

"A rather inferior tea in blend with a truly inferior brandy. Serves for a spot of inner warmth. Brewed with paraphernalia from la-bor-atory props! Clever of me. Frightfully. So much is frightful."

First sip scrunched my face up, second sip was better, third was alright. Somerset's eyes were unnatural bright.

"I bid you a fair morning, lass."

"Thank you, fair good sir."

"How ever did you know to speak in that way?"

"Fourth grade play. My one line. Fourth was as far as I got fore Daddy pulled me out t'doin full-time chores. Sister's smarter'n me at readin and figures. Mother insisted she stay all the way through sixth. Used to be Mother might do that now and again—insist."

"Did you mind leaving school? Did you resent?"

"Never minded work. Never much minded anything my sister did."

"Families are snakepits."

And he makes a little bow and leaves, saying "Physics" in a whisper, and all the while was that scratchy-scratchy sound, lower and slower, through the horn of the Victrola.

2

I'M OUTSIDE, IT'S NOT FULL LIGHT, and there's nothin for me to do. I'd employed the chamber pot, emptied it as ordered, rinsed it with water from the pitcher, and that was the finish of anything for doing. I'm used to doing, all through daylight. Milk somethin, feed somethin, churn butter, fix biscuits, stir up a stew. Dig in the vegetable garden. Tend that fruit-tree that's ailin. When it rains you darn, can, pickle, cut a pattern for a shirt or dress or overalls, cause it was mine to keep track of needs in the way of clothing. Rain or shine you can always draw water, so you'll have it by. Chop firewood. Scrub the outhouse, if it comes to that. Yesterday was a "voyage," as Fred would say, but what was today?

It unsettled me how Keystone still looked some like the farm that had been. Some family made a stand here till they quit or died or sold up. They were doing pretty well when they built that farmhouse—nicer than ours, though Daddy could carpenter pretty good. And it hit me like a slap how I'd burned down his work. Not sorry for that. Only the feeling you get when something is done and done and done for, like the farm here that ain't no more a farm, and all the work that made it a farm was gone, as though that work had never been.

It ain't only the living that dies. Work dies too, in its way. The work my family done, it had died. I killed it.

I guess, yes, I was sorry a bit.

But not enough to let sorryness hang on me.

Me, I'm strollin here and there in the Keystone, thinkin as I'm strollin, while that smell of Heaven's coatin the air like a sheen. At the coop I visited with the chickens, at the pen I visited with the pigs. Did you know you can teach a pig to wink? I taught one once. Fred has the touch with animals too but she couldn't match that and oh it burned her.

Folks are showing up by ones and twos. It's lighter but no warmer, me bundled in Fred's coat and my grubby pretty feet freezing.

The folks mostly gathered at the far end of a building that was not even really a building. But, for being not really something, it's really big. Maybe a block square, maybe more. The sides are plank walls maybe five feet high, buttressed with polls stuck in the ground and propped against the planks. And long polls, maybe three stories high, driven in the ground four feet or so apart, and nailed to the polls are great swathes of white muslin canvas sewn together with sail-twine to make a smooth cloth wall. If you scrunched your eyes you might think a building once stood there and this was its ghost.

"That's where we shoot flickers."

The Brick fellow had stepped up behind, to watch me stare.

"We shoot em ever where, but here's where we shoot 'interiors,' as they call em. I'll show ya."

I guess movies don't say good morning.

He walked on and I followed. Counted eight steps up to the floor of the Ghost Building.

"Look sharp for your bare feet. Liable to be nails and tacks and shards lyin about."

He had a red flannel sack hanging from a stick over his shoulder. Whatever was in it had lots of angles that pressed against the cloth.

I ask, "What's in your bindle?"

"Books. Surprised a bindlestiff like me reads a book?"

"Nothin surprises me around here."

"Keep that viewpoint and you'll do."

Inside felt almost as much "outside" as outside, get me? See, about every twenty feet, above, there's this double cross-beam arrangement that you'll just have to take my word on, and strung tween the beams is more canvas— the canvas is "defusers," like D'Varn said, and like this Brick said, explainin how sunlight spreads evenly and casts no shadows when it shines through a canvas-ceiling or canvas-wall. "That," says he, "is how you can shoot all the day but your shadows don't move, so you can match your shots." So the outside light is inside, but different than it is outside. Now you get me?

While he's explaining I'm seeing. Laid out across this huge painted-yellow board floor are two walls of a saloon here, and three walls of a bedroom there, with all their fixins in proper place. And lots more. Spread across this hall—if "hall" it is—is a kind of maze of, I suppose, "interiors": a drawing room, a prison cell, balconies, staircases, Chinese laundry, railroad station, hallway, dry-goods counter, each with just two or three walls, cept the walls ain't real—they're pretend-walls, propped from behind or nailed to the floor. Some were solid "sets," he called them, which didn't move, but most sets looked temporary, and there was something rough about it all, hard-edged, make-shift, splintery, and, well, fragile-like, dangerous-fragile, like a none-too-mighty wind could blow this whole not-all-there affair to Kingdom Come.

We stop in the prison cell. Brick says, "I been in a few a these."

"Prison-proud, are ya? If you robbed a bank, mister, you ain't wearin the money."

"Beating up on scabs and goons till I'm outnumbered and arrested. Used to be kinda my hobby." Oh Brick, he was man-proud, he was.

He takes a small sack of tobacco from his jacket pocket, pulls out the paper, and rolls himself a homemade, then produces a match and lights it off his fingernail and puffs while lookin me up and down with those savvy eyes.

"Wonder what they'll do with you. You're pretty enough—prettier if you'd do somethin girly with that mop."

"Got a hairbrush?"

"Not on me. You'll not be a Keystone Bathing Beauty. Too flat."

"Watch it. I'm sensitive to that."

"Too flat, as I say, and too slim. Those gals are buxom and meaty. You're built kinda like Minta—cept, as I say, flat."

"Wanna stop with bein so frank with a lady?"

Smilin goofy again, Brick is. I glared at him, but without spite. Ain't often you meet a man that's a man.

Says he, "I'm a frank sort of person. You?"

"When it suits me."

"That means you ain't." Which disappointed him I could see. "Mabel wants you here, you'll be here—whether Mr. Sennett likes it or not, cause he can't deny her a thing. Hungry?"

Lordy, I was hungry. All I admitted was, "Thirsty."

"We can fix that."

He walks and I get in step, saying, "What do you do around here?"

"Some'a everything. But I'll be a director yet."

"And that is?"

"What Mabel was doin when you showed up, when she was telling everybody what-all to do—that's a director."

"Enjoy bossin folks, do ya?"

"Just a natural leader, I guess," and he laughed to himself in a private way. "Better here than a coal mine."

Couple'a steps later Brick says, "He does deny her one thing, Mr. Sennett. Mabel wants to marry. Mr. Sennett, he's a hesitator on that. Me, too—so don't get any ideas."

"Look at the big man dream."

"I forgot—you're kinda lavender, I saw. D'Varn's favorite color."

Lavender's nice enough but I wasn't wearing a stitch, nor D'Varn last night, so what's he talkin about? Got all nervous to hear her name.

And all the while I'm lookin and wonderin what in this Keystone could I do. Cause Mother didn't raise no daughters couldn't account for themselves.

Steppin in and around sets—a rich lady's bedroom, a poor family's kitchen, a variety store—all abutted together at this angle and that. "That's so if you're shooting this one set there's no other set picked up by your lens," Brick says, and I says, "There seems a lot to remember just to shoot a little flicker," and him, "You can say that twice."

Of a sudden a terrible greasy stink kinda slicked all over us.

"Breeze turned with the sun-up," says Brick. "That odor is developer and fixer on wet film shot yesterday, drying out on drums yonder in that barn. It's where they cut and splice the footage."

He spake with authority and not as one of the scribes, but it was Greek to me.

He dropped his cigarette and stepped on it. Says, "There you go," pointing at a gaggle of folks by a table just outside at the far end of the ghost-building—and, as movies seem to, he walked off in his own direction, for his own reasons, without a nod.

I'm hungry and thirsty and I see donuts and a water bucket on the table and a coffee pot over a pit-fire. Smells of coffee and the sweet scent of milk when a cow just gave it up.

I consider myself as a shy person. It's one thing to do as I'd been doin and, brother, it's another to step by your lonesome into a group of people who know each other and pick up a donut as if I had a right to, and ladle up some gulps of water from the same bucket-and-ladle they drank of, grab a tin mug from a stack on the table and hold it out to the gent who commanded that big ranch-style pot.

"What they got you doin, dolly?" A shorty with a walrus moustache and big eyes spoke through a mouth fulla donut.

"Dunno." Which was only true.

"Ain't that the way? Might tell us to hang off a roof or climb a pole or kick a cop—a real one—and there we'd be doin it, obedient monkeys to a man."

"I look like a man to you?"

"Sure not."

Saying which, he pinched my butt.

Couldn't feel it much through the coat and couldn't help but grunt a laugh, making coffee squirt up my nose, making me sneeze, making him laugh. All in all I took it as a compliment and gave him a curtsy.

There's them that pinch like gentlemen and there's them that pinch crude. Walrus Moustache, he did it like a gentleman, and now he tipped his derby.

"That's the way," says he.

So there I was amongst em.

And now again the roar of the beast. And another.

"What the Sam Hill was that!" one tall number wanted urgently to know.

Walrus Moustache snickered and poked me with his elbow, like to mean, "This guy's a rube."

The commander of the coffee didn't answer the tall number except to say, "Bet there wasn't one coyote within two miles of here last night. No, nor raccoon, nor deer."

Leastways someone heard that roar sides me.

Brick walks up, gets his coffee'n'donut, says to Walrus Moustache, "Chester, see where in the paper the Ford Motor Company announced an eight-hour workday? An eight-hour workday! Imagine. And a minimum wage of five dollars for one day's honest labor, five dollars for just eight hours, guaranteed. Twenty-five dollars a week, by God! That's the progress of the workin man."

Chester looked respectful but opined, "Folks workin just eight hours ain't gonna make many flickers."

"It'll come one day here too. Union'll come."

"Damn you for a socialist, Brick." It was the coffee commander.

Daddy, I'm sippin mornin coffee with a godless red socialist!

Says Brick, "You make fine coffee, Jake, but knowledgeable you ain't. The I.W.W. is not socialist."

"Naw, they're worse. Don't they let even the colored in?"

"They'd let even you in, if you'd wise up."

"Mr. Mack Sennett allows for a man to make an honest dollar. Don't need no union here at the Keystone. Bet he's got an eye on you, you and your red prideful Wobbly ways."

Cook says that smiling tough, but Brick ain't smilin at all. Some change come over him. The fight rose up in him, the need to hit, and as he swallowed that fight back down I liked him more.

"You don't wanna badmouth Wobblies too much, Jake. Not to me."

No one knew where to look. Cigarettes got lit, handmades and store-bought. I reached for that pitcher of fresh milk and filled my mug. That cow hadn't fed on fine grass but under the circumstances it savored good. Missed how Mother'd say, "Milk's best when you can taste the moo."

Brick drifted off. Talk sorta lagged. I coulda ate five more donuts but no longer felt so bold. Put my mug down on the table, set to walk off myself, when Jake says, "Spect me t'deposit your mug in the pail, little lady?"

"I don't expect nuthin," says me. I took the mug and dropped it so it clanked into the pail that I hadn't seen till Jake nodded at it, decidin as I did so that it was time to climb a roof.

3

BY NOW THE MORNIN'S BUZZIN, traffic's loud on Alessandro with street-car bells and horse clip-clops and engines shifting gears, while a line of folks formed at the main gate—looking to be hired, it appeared—and others walked in like they had a place to be and a thing to do, and one shift of donut people left and another formed as shamelessly I grabbed two donuts more, cause I couldn't help it, then wandered off to find my place to be. A roof seemed a nice out-of-the-way idea.

Once I got that in my head I had a purpose and could walk around like anybody. The biggest building would have the most interesting roof, and here that would be the building that looked like a bad sketch of a Spanish mission, hard beside the mission-type gate. Over two stories high was that roof, where I'd see down into the street and back into the Keystone.

From the base of its back wall that roof looked even higher. I unbuttoned Fred's coat to climb, antsy now about wearin this thin white nothin of a night-dress, which I don't know how I had the nerve to step out in yesterday, and really, what must these people think of me? No help for that now, so I concentrated on my climbin problem, spotted a barrel standing free, rolled that barrel near the wall (which wasn't any more queer than other folks doing their what-all), scrambled atop it, boosted up from there to a window sill, took good hold on a drain-pipe that seemed fastened solid, then, toes digging into stucco, I monkeyed up that pipe.

Fresh as spit, that stucco, sharp to my feet.

Some older gal, by the voice, yelled, "You there! Get offa there!" I didn't look back and she didn't call again, then I was at the roof-lip, which was the hardest part, cause the pipe naturally stopped at the top. I swung up a heel, got a footing on the rim, and then I'm up, and then I'm over.

Alright. I'd done something. It's always worth your time to climb a roof.

Didn't think till I stood up that when I swung my leg to hook my heel over that roof-lip, well, anyone mighta looked up my dress and seen stuff. That flushed me to the roots. But, looking about, seems no one noticed.

The sun warmed that rooftop some, for which my feet were grateful.

I looked about to see what I could learn. Across the street was a sign above an awning on a building small-ish in wideness but it went back a ways. The sign signified, in green letters with red trim, GREENBERG'S BAKED GOODS'N'SUNDRIES. That's where they cooked up that Heavenness. That's where came those donuts out-of-the-oven fresh and milk straight from a cow without anybody foolin with it. Saw the roof of a stall behind the store, and a small corral, and stacks of hay, and a high fence where I expect vegetables were gardened. Barrels lined the store-front. Maybe flour, sugar, sour pickles. We'd had a local sundries store—Fred and me, when we were little, would run to that pickle barrel, knock off the wood lid, hoist our-selves to the rim, dip our heads into that pickle juice, gulp it, eyes tight shut against stinging, and run off. Daddy made us quit it with a whipping—well deserved, I must admit.

A breeze came up stiff, ruffled my hair, the kind of breeze that don't go away—somethin you know from its first puff. Across the yard, how the ghost-building took the wind was that its canvas ceiling and walls kinda slapped all at once, like a real hard clap, then kept clappin quietier so's you forgot to notice. White wind-smooth clouds moved fast and high from the west and south and the scent let you know rain's on the way, later in the day, and I'd bet lots of it. The breeze flickered leaves on the hills, every leaf catching and losing its little fleck of sun, making the trees to sparkle. Daddy'd be out prepping for a storm and barkin orders for chores—cept his lone farmhand's gone, along with farmhouse, sheds and critters—but anyway most times he's right about weather: breeze like this, scent like this, rain pours by nightfall if not before. I reckon the same holds for today.

Lookin down into the Keystone, folks were movin about—but not as purposeful, and there was Mr. Sennett, dressed more expensive than others, a head and more taller than almost everyone, cigar clamped in his teeth, and he's all agitated about something with another tallish sort in a beret. And there was Big Es in overalls and a straw sombrero—peculiar to see her, cause last time I saw her she had her tongue down my throat, and near got stabbed. Seemed everyone down there's agitated and antsy. Not me. I was peaceful and alone where folks don't think to look up and see.

Now as to the general agitation, I discovered the why of it, which was on the street of Alessandro, where no one knew what to do. It was all about three wagons, each half again as long and wide as your normal haulin wagon, stacked three tiers high with barrels of who-knows-what fastened round and round with rope, and each wagon with a four-horse team and one teamster up on the board seat. Four horses was two too few to haul loads like those at any pace comfortable for such a thoroughfare, specially here, headed northerly, the grade steadily steeper. Motor-cars honked, trolley bells clanged, folks raised their voices and a spooked cab-horse whinnied panicky so's the cabbie jumped off his perch and held that nag's bridle down hard. Those long wide haulin wagons squeezed to the side of the street best they could, but it was no good, traffic from downtown backed up behind em, and traffic goin downtown had it not much better. It was all just kind of one long slow swaying-back-and-forth bunch of I-don't-know-what-to-do angriness.

A cinch the Keystone Company was not complete and ready for work on time, what with traffic bunching up as far as I could see.

And look, there's a Keystone camera-cranker settin up, just in front, as Walrus Moustache Chester dashes across the street admidst the vehicles, and he's chased by Keystone Kops, who make a show of tripping over each other as they fail to tackle him, then all dash back toward the camera—I figured they'd use the footage, as they say, for some flicker yet to be. Normal folks barely noticed cause those movies didn't strike anyone unusual in the general discombobulation.

After a while four real cops come up, mounted on tall horses, making no great speed through the confusion on their way to take charge.

And there's Miss Mabel Normand steppin angry-fast from downtown's direction—I guessed she run her car up on a curb, disgusted, and decided on walkin. Her stride ain't like anybody's. Her left foot steps out straight but her right follows with a pigeon-toed curve—pigeon-toed on one side only! For no reason at all, it's kinda sweet. She's wearin an any-old hat, an any-old dress, and any-old jacket, lookin like anybody—yet not. I'd notice her walk if I'd never heard of her.

Then, across the street, stepping out from Greenberg's bakery—herself, D'Varn. No idea where she came from. Guess I couldn't see her for the wagons and vehicles all bunched up, what with me trying to see everything at once, which seemed my new habit. On a farm you look at one thing at a time—plus the weather.

D'Varn's hat was again a man's hat, dark, and she wears it aslant. But that velvet jacket, and its satin collar, how prettily they catch light. A white blouse open at the top, neck exposed wide in a V—which just ain't done, anybody would notice that anywhere. A belt at the waist, and her dress cut to swirl at any move, exposin lots of ankle and calf each step, and guys are noticin, steppin as she does with her sashay, in shoes of soft gray with wedge heels, every inch of her sayin, "I'm somebody!"

And I think, of a sudden, *why* does she like *me*?

As I ask that of myself, from across the street she sees me.

I went all blank. I'd kept her from my thoughts all morning, knowin if I thought on her I'd think on nothing else, when there was so much here to notice and think on. One day Mother, way into her strangeness but not all the way in, she stares at me fierce-like and she whisper-shouts, "Think—and you'll survive. Or anyway you'll have a chance. Fred don't need to. Willie, you do."

I try. I'm not much good at it but that don't stop me.

Seeing me, D'Varn waves and laughs, throwin her head back, and I wave, and she gives a kinda jump, little-kid-like, how you'd never expect her to. I see somehow she's proud of me, that I'm on this roof.

As for me, oh, brother. D'Varn, she was so pretty and beautiful and gorgeous and lovely—all those kinda words scooped in a pile that you light on fire and D'Varn's that fire.

Swift as possible she crosses that crazy street while I go where the façade dips nearest the gate and lean over. D'Varn, I forgot to say, holds a paper bundle in each hand—the smaller is store-bag paper, the larger is laundry-paper wrapped with twine. She'd waved with the small-bag hand.

I'm leanin out over the façade.

"Don't fall!" yelps she, all happy.

"Not me."

"Can you catch?"

"A natural shortstop."

She gives the small store-bag a shake. "For you!"

Tosses it up, throwin like a girl, and I grab it outa the air. Open it. Smells heavenly. Fresh rolls and a jelly donut.

"Breakfast!" says she, like she just invented breakfast.

I go from the front of the roof to the side, for to see her come through the gate, but I didn't think to think that's where all'a Keystone could see me as I leaned over the wall behind that false mission front over Keystone's gateway, more'n two stories.

D'Varn's down there, feet spread wide, hands on hips, hat pushed back, beamin up at me.

"How'd you get up there!" She's shoutin, though I could hear fine if she didn't.

"I got agility!" Only nice thing Daddy ever said about me, and that was grudgin—"You got agility, no denyin."

Oops. We're attractin an audience.

"Get down offa there!" shouts a man in a stiff, starched uniform-kinda suit.

"You ain't the boss of me."

"I'm the boss of everything on this lot, including you." That's Mr. Sennett's large voice.

Where'd he come from? Where'd they all come from! It's like all Keystone's crowdin in.

And there's Brick, walkin with a ladder held vertical in front of him so as not to swipe anybody down, which takes some muscle—it's a long well-made ladder. But Miss Mabel's right behind him with, "Oh, no, Brick, no you don't!"

Lookin straight up at me but talkin to everyone, like the Queen of Keystone that she is: "She got up there somehow, let's see can she get down."

I'm thinkin, Ain't you on my side? But her big dark smilin eyes were bright with good nature, and I see she's makin play of it all as she says, "I dare ya, girlie! I double-d dare ya!"

I'm a person you should not dare. Same as I'll bet she is. You dare a certain kind of person, best be ready to live it out.

Seems I gotta prove somethin to her, and right away, or else I bet I'm outa here.

And I'm not the only one who knows it. Everybody's eyes are on me, a lot of upturned faces under all kinda hats, wide-brimmed, short-brimmed, stiff-brimmed, with and without feathers (and the feathers bend in the breeze), bowlers, derbies, skimmers, straw, beaver, felt, bowls peaked and bowls creased and bowls round, hats cheap and hats moneyed. And there's that plump tiny bit of a gal herding a flock of children dressed scruffy, and they're all starin too, with wide kid-eyes. Never had so many folks looked at me all at once.

Didn't then know the term yet but I "milked it," as they say. Reached into my bag for that jelly-donut and took a big deliberate bite while struttin, and then another bite, and then there's fiddle music! Am I a crazy person? No, there's the fiddler, a gal, bowin a circus'y tune. And I seen then that there was only one thing to do.

Took off Fred's coat to their whoopin and hollerin, and I just let it float-like drop to the ground. Then I struck a pose and tossed my little bag to D'Varn, who caught it.

"A lavender bouquet?" I hear some guy say, and people laugh rude at what's not funny, but I'm concentratin, lookin for tall men. Roscoe, no. Mr. Sennett, sure no. Brick? Bad idea. Then there's the real large fella who acted the Rajah in last night's flicker, and I'd heard him called "Pasha."

It was him I picked. Pointed straight at him so he'd know.

"You they call 'Pasha'!"

"Me?"

"You. Catch!"

Never again would there be anything like the feeling that first time I lit up and out, high, so's to point my toes to the sky and flatten my back at the peak of my leap, then down—on what I hoped was Mr. Pasha, since I'm descendin backwards.

Never again would there be that day, with its bright sky in my eyes, me and those swift-movin white clouds for just moments bein the same, and not even thinkin—as I would next time—to check if my blade-sheath's secure on my thigh and check the security of my specially-designed-and-sewn-by-me "tighties," as I call em, so folks don't see what's there to see, not even carin about that for once, just that I'm in the air that loves me and that I love and that I'd love more and more.

Never again this thought that thrilled, no words for it cept maybe "I've just decided out my whole life!" Cause that's something to happen once, if at all, since I know now most folks never decide a damn thing, just bump and get bumped from one day to the next like bowlin pins and call their bumpin "bein respectable."

Never again the knowin for the first time that I was a somethin, I was a movie, and even if they threw me outa here I'd go be a movie somewhere else, now that I knew what I could do.

Of course that was stuff I thought later, goin back to those moments over and over, as I always would, cause there was so much in them to go back to, they'd never fail me, just the little time it took to leap and point my toes and flatten my back and catch-me-or-don't-Mr.-Pasha.

He caught me sure. He grunted, staggered, nearly fell, but held to me and kept his stance, an arm under my thighs, t'other under my shoulders. Perfect landing.

And Pasha's starin into my face, bug-eyed, shakin his head.

"I declare," he said. "I do declare."

Then he kind of rolled me out so's I'd land on my rump, and there was all their laughter. And their applause.

All present whoop, holler, clap, guffaw, and generally admire.

I got to standin, wobbly, lookin around, me in my long white piece'a nuthin to below my knees, hair untidy, dirty feet, and all these Keystoners lookin at me, and, I imagine, wonderin what ragamuffin specter had fell into their midst.

Mr. Sennett had his hat off and was scratchin his head and puffin that cigar. He bit down on his cigar and spat a wad of tobacco juice that landed so close to my left foot I felt the dusty splash.

Miss Mabel came to me and kissed my cheek and was about to speak but Mr. Sennett bellows, "Where's that damned Englisher?"

"Present!"

"Not you, Charlie. My *damned* Englisher."

"Equally present. Ineluctably present. Present, but not accounted for."

"You're drunk."

"But present."

"You seen that?"

"It was eloquent."

"Compose a scenario for it."

"A perfectly jolly idea."

"Stay drunk if you have to, Sommie, but I want it tomorrow. Pasha, can you catch her from a roof maybe ten feet higher?"

"Why not?"

"Mack!" That was Mabel.

"She's game, ain't you, kid?"

Kid is me, without a lick of sense, happily nodding, "Sure am, Mr. Sennett."

"Sure she's game. You can fall, can't you kid? Pratfall?"

"My Daddy says I'm fallen."

That got a chuckle out of him.

"Can you run like hell?"

"Depends who's chasin."

"You'll do. Three dollars a day, to start. Paper money, but it buys same as silver or gold."

"And three dollars extra for each jump off a building." That was Mabel.

"Fair is fair. But not today's jump, understand—I didn't commission that one."

"For today's," Mabel said, "girlie here gets shoes— two, no, three pair— worth a consideration more than three dollars."

Me, I say to myself, not knowing it's aloud, "Three dollars a day!"

Mr. Sennett grinned. The look on my face musta told all present that three whole dollars a day was unheard of in my life.

"I see," says he, "I got someone here who appreciates our little set-up. Unlike those I might name. You did it how we do it, kid. All these roaring extroverts"— another'a them words—"are purely devoted to turmoil, cause we shoot every fool thing we can think of under influence of hashish or hangover. Get me?"

Hardly, but, "Yes, sir."

"Now someone get her washed, combed and clothed decent, before she gets us all arrested." Then he grabs the guy in the beret, "Pathé, I wanna shoot the jump tomorrow. Make it two jumps, different buildings. We'll see how they play, then figure the before and after. Sommie, the trick to this is she's not the featured player, but she's the jumper."

"Understood. Comprehended. Got it."

"Odd thing is," Mr. Sennett's talking to me, "Sorry Sommie, as I call im, is a first-rate gag man—for an intellectual."

Miss Mabel's pulling my arm, tuggin me somewhere. D'Varn's beamin, even Es has a grin, shakin her head, while Miss Mabel's saying as we walk, "Napoleon respects grit above all. That was a big speech for him. Usually the ape only barks and growls."

"But you love im anyhow," says Minta, suddenly alongside us, small as Mabel and thinner.

"Mack and me are stuck with each other, if that's what you mean by love."

"What else does it ever mean, honey," and off goes Minta, while Mabel's sayin, "You picked your catcher well. Pasha's circus, born and bred, he's spent his life doing that stuff. My shoes will suit you, our feet could be twins. Then I'll hand you over to your friend there," nodding back to D'Varn, "for the fine touches. She'll get you looking like a Christian. You about bested Roscoe's audition. We're walking up that flight of stairs"—she points to a stairway up the side of a two-story shed at the far end—"and Mack asks what can he do, and Roscoe back flips down the stairway head over tail and comes up at the bottom with a pirouette like a chubby ballerina. But from Roscoe something was expected. You"—Mabel stops and looks me up and down, not kindly or unkindly, but like she was figurin how I fit together. "Girlie, seriously—working with Mack or Pathé, don't do *everything* they say, cause they'll keep pushing it and get you broken or killed. I'm serious. You've got to know when to put that pretty foot down and keep it planted—on their necks, preferably."

"Yes, Miss Mabel."

She smiled like to melt me. "You're not listening to a word I say. Come on."

And we went on. Naturally I wished Fred was here to see. She'd agree that jumpin off buildings is a suitable job of work for one such as me.

ONLY SOMMIE HAD ASKED MY NAME, but I didn't mind. I may not have a name but I'm a movie.

I spent a full half hour, maybe more, in Miss Mabel Normand's private dressing room, which I learned later Mr. Sennett had wanted to nail to its door a star—but she wouldn't have it. Said, "It's enough that I've got the only kerosene stove on the premises." I paid hard attention during that privacy with Miss Mabel, saving it up to one day tell Fred, until we heard Mr. Sennett bellow just outside, "*Now* let's get some work done!" Then it's me and Miss Mabel out in the lot, me holdin a checker-patterned canvas valise which is now all mine—in it, three pairs of shoes that each had little heels, plus two dresses, two blouses, two skirts, panties, and a hair brush—and now Miss Mabel Normand is pointing me toward a long shed across the yard. "There's the ladies' dressing room." And that was that.

I walked slow to that shed. Teary-eyed scared. Scared bad enough to drop that checkered canvas valise and run through that gate to don't-know-where. Anywhere that's not this next step.

When Mother was Mother she'd say, "Take a deep breath, cause you always know a little more after a deep breath than you did before."

I took that breath. Jumping off a building is easier than some things.

"We permit no tits at the Keystone," says a brunette. "Plenty of leg, no tit. How I'm built, that's a problem."

"Not a problem I got," says I, standin at the door I'd opened.

"Shut that, honey," says a blond, "fore we have all kinda problems."

I shut it and stepped in. D'Varn's not there and I'm more scared.

What's in front of me is somethin to see.

The door I'd opened is on the side of a building that's no more than a shack. No windows, no other door. It's shaped like a shoebox, long and narrow'ish. On the two longer walls are hooks and nails aplenty from which hang all manner of dresses, garters, hats, wigs, and dainties. A carpenter's table runs down the middle—it's draped with oil-cloth checkered white and yellow, and down its center from one end to the other is a double-sided mirror maybe a foot high. Fastened to the mirror's top, a foot or so apart, there's a rod of maybe four inches where hangs, one electric bulb after another, each shaded in metal-mesh. Wires for the bulbs are strung all over like their arrangement ain't yet complete, and those bulbs cast shadows every which way, and the shadows of those wires crisscross walls and ceiling like webbing. To top it all, fastened to the narrow walls at either end there's two tall, wide mirrors lined with littler bulbs, each facing the other with the room squeezed in between, so's everythin's reflected in everythin.

Either side of the table, lookin at themselves in its two-sided mirror, there's women on low stools, kiddie-height but wide, so the table-top comes to about the rise of a gal's chest. In front of each stool, on that oil-cloth, there's jars and pitchers and porcelain bowls, vials of stuff'n'stuff, and pastes and powders, wigs and scissors, needles and thread, brushes, hairpins, hatpins, wooden combs, and smudge-sticks white and black and rouge. I smelt wom-anness, and smelt perfumes that didn't like each other, sawdust on the board floor, and something kinda like kerosene. Five women to one side of the table, six to the other, in states of almost-nothing-on, lots-of-something-on, and in-betwixt. A quantity of femininity! But with an air of thuggery, what with cigarettes hangin from their lips or trailin smoke on ashtrays of tin. And, like I say, everythin's reflected in somethin.

And what some of these women at the moment are doin is, they're bindin their bosoms.

Wrappin their chests flat as they can with swathes of linen, and tyin the wrap tight with metal clips.

"The Chine'ee bind their feet. At the Keystone we bind titties." That was the brunette.

"Mummies." It's Minta, too flat to need bindin. "Not a Mommy in the bunch, justa buncha mummies."

."With all the runnin and fallin we do, the Boss don't want us floppin." That was the blond.

"Wait'll he buys off the Decency Committee," says Minta, "you'll flop plenty."

One clutches her abdomen and slams down a hairbrush so the table shakes. "I got the curse."

"Alert the press!" Minta again. "Louise got the curse."

This Louise looks straight at me. "Doesn't it just kill you?"

"Don't bother me at all," says me.

"Lucky thee," says this Louise.

"Anything," says Minta, "bother thee?"

"My bothers is my business." Daddy was right again. A rough bunch.

"Guess a gal who jumps off rooftops don't bother about much. *Doesn't* bother." That was D'Varn.

I turn and she's there in the doorway, grinnin at me like I'm a Christmas present.

"What bothers you, D'Varn—besides faulty grammar, I mean?" That's Minta.

"Oh, she's bothered by interest rates," says the Louise person. "Dating a banker."

"Bank president, dearie." D'Varn, mock-haughty. "Chairman of the board."

"I'm bored already," says the brunette, who's met with laughter, and "Nice crack," and "Not as nice as some cracks I could name," and more laughter, D'Varn joining in. I never heard the like. Movies'll say anything. Me, I'm standin still, pleased and shy, hopin I learn their knack so's I can say anything too.

"Well," says D'Varn to me, "let's get those things off you and these things on you." I neglected to say she carried an armful of garments and a feather hat. "Come on. Strip down."

"Do what?"

"Get nekkid." Minta buttin in.

Since I'm a little kid no one's seen me naked cept Fred.

"I ain't takin off nothin in front of strangers."

"Don't see why not?" That was the brunette. "And there I was admiring your nerve. Silly me. You're wearing next to nothing under that coat. Not much to take off."

Just then the one door swings open and in steps a large—but not tall—older gal I'd noticed before. No bindin her bosom! It stuck out in front of her a ways.

And the gals fun some more, to her, about my modesty.

"Ah, she blushes!" That's the older gal, about me. "Absolutely darling, aren't you? My dear, a blush around here is as rare as a raise in pay."

"I want a screen. For undressin."

Well that set off howls and, "Like she's got what we ain't seen!"

"Ladies," says the older gal, "innocence is not to be mocked in my presence."

But she winks em, then goes to a shiny new hand-pump by a basin near me and pumps water into a tin ladle, sippin as the gang carries on with their cracks.

D'Varn turns to the older gal with a pleading look. "Mother?"

"She's your mother?!" That's me.

"I'm everybody's mother," says the buxom older gal. "I debuted on the stage"—

Gals join in, "in *my* mother's arms, thirteen months/nine days of age,"

Buxom gal continues, "April the 9th, 1865,"

The gals again with her, "the day they ended that terrible war."

"Alice Davenport," says she, and presents her hand for me to take, "actress."

Applause-in-fun all around. Says she, "A mature presence is needed in this playpen."

Amidst their funnin most of the gals had readied their costumes and were bound for work.

Mother Davenport addressed them grandly, looking at each as she named them.

"Mrs. Arbuckle," that was Minta, "Miss Haver," that was the brunette, "Miss Fazenda," the one with the curse, "and et cetera, did you darlings volunteer to dive off rooftops? If this gumptious child wants a dressing-screen, she gets a dressing-screen."

And a dressing-screen was got faster than you can say Ty Cobb.

Moments later they're all gone. Now it's just me and D'Varn.

"I still require my privacy," I warn.

"Sure you do. Gals'll be comin in'n'outa here." Then, carefully: "In *and* out of here."

"Tryin t'gussey-up your talk?"

"Trying hard."

She said that grim, then put her armful of costuming onto an empty stool and leaned against the table. Lit a cigarette. Stared like I wasn't there.

Then recalled I was. "Go on, you!"

The screen was taller than me, which ain't hard to be, and fancy. Two dark wood panels, hinged, each panel standing on two feet carved like claws. It could stand free only if it was bent at the hinge, and was painted on both sides with bright Chinee dragons against a dark varnished background. They were winged, those dragons, and they breathed fire.

So Fred's coat comes off, then the no-longer-very-white nightdress I'd been wearing. The screen is in front of the mirror-with-little-bulbs at the room's far end, a mirror bigger than ever I'd seen, and there I am, a little shocked at my slim self so stark. The bulbs on the mirror made me bright as bright. I'm standin in nothin but my blade-sheath and my tighties, sewed by myself so carefully to fit how I need em. I squeezed outa my rigs just to see me whole. I never seen my whole naked self before.

So this is me.

Which is when D'Varn, without askin or announcin, steps behind that screen.

She looks at me and I get all jellied-feelin.

"Why am I not surprised?" Her voice husky. "Ain't you the cat's meow."

"You like me? Flat strange me?"

"Petal-nipples floating on a pond." She said it softer than soft. "And that tush! Pure sculpture. And your legs—purrrrr'fect."

Her face went dark. A little scary. "You're right to be secretive. Gifted is what you are."

Can't stand it no more and I pull up my tighties and squeeze into em, which is difficult in this situation, a situation that's never been, I'm so trembly.

And she kneels and spread her hands near, but not touching, my thighs, sayin, "It's okay, it's okay, sweetie," like you say to calm a pony. "You don't even need to shave your legs."

"People do that?"

"Around here we do. Stand real still." She runs her hands up and down my legs—hands so warm, even hot—and me, I'm wonderin how I can stand up any longer, cause I sure don't want to. "It's okay, it's okay." My legs twitched like I wanted to run, which I also did not want to.

"Just a moment," says she, and I heard her pumping water, then she's back with a wet cloth, and she's daubin my face, scrubbin a little, and she's down at my dirty feet scrubbin.

She's back standin up, her smilin face atilt.

"You must be made of moonlight, you're a crazy-making person, you are."

"It's Willie."

"What's Willie?"

"My name. I'm Willie."

"Sure you're Willie. Give me the willies. Spooky-yum-yum willies."

"D'Varn, is this part over yet?"

She goes, comes back with the clothes, puts them in a neat pile, lights a cigarette.

"Learn our wicked ways," says she, and gently puts it tween my lips.

I cough and take it outa my mouth. "What am I supposed to do?'

"Puff easy and inhale slow. Coughs'll soon stop."

I near jump two feet straight up at the rattle of that the door opening, and footsteps, fast, and chatter, different voices from before except for Mother, who says, "How goes it back there?"

"I'm dressing Cinderella for the ball," calls D'Varn. "She's gonna be a princess."

"A lady-in-waiting will do. They want you two for a centerpiece. Very visible. It's Pathé."

"Tell him what he needs to hear."

"Always, with the menfolk," says Mother. The door rattles again and I guess she's gone while the others wise-crack and do their makins.

What with gals on the other side of the screen, D'Varn and me take to whispering.

She's helping me into garments I don't understand—seen em on respectable folk but never thought I'd wear them—and it feels like she's tyin me up in something tight and fluffy at once, fancy-lady stuff, and I won't even try to tell what-all it was and how she did, cept I felt like her Christmas doll and it made me happy, scary-happy, which was gettin to be a familiar way to feel.

"Funny about you," D'Varn says. "People hard to please take a right-away shine to you, don't they? You just walk in, and Mrs. Davenport—that's Mother—Mabel, Mr. Sennett, Sommie—and me!—right away we're interested. You make an impression, you do."

Nobody liked me all my life but Fred and our mother, yet now I make an impression!

"Those gals in here before hadn't much use for me."

"They give a hard time to anyone new. And I make em itch where they can't scratch."

"These clothes stink like kerosene."

"Fumigant. So we don't catch each other's cooties."

She steps back, gives me the once over, shakes her head, takes a pair of Miss Mabel's shoes from the valise, holds em near my dress to match the color, fits em to me—and they felt gentle on my feet, the first shoes of my life I didn't bristle at.

D'Varn starts again to taking things off me, putting things on, adjusting, tucking, tugging, tries a belt, decides it's all fine.

"We have no time to deal with your hair. We'll bunch it under a hat."

Does this and that with my hair and several hats, and chooses a wide-brim. As she works we whisper-talk like Fred and me after bedtime.

"True about that banker?" I ask.

"He's trying to be a politician."

"True, then."

"True. But you. First look, I knew I was in trouble. And now, brother, I really am. You're a little monster, you are."

She lit up with that and slapped my "tush."

"I know about that kiss," says she. "Big Es just burst to tell me."

"So?"

"Your first?"

"No."

"First with a girl?"

"No."

"Gonna tell me?"

"No!"

Just as I'm thinking she'll never guess, she went and did. "It's that Fred person, I'll bet. She of the coat. Look at the vixen blush!"

Not for shame was I blushin, but for her so easily knowin.

Then I go to volunteerin what, at the very same moment, I resolved never to tell her.

"Fred's my twin. Frederica."

"You kissed your twin!"

"She kissed me first."

"And then you kissed some more, you two?"

"Lots."

I only ever saw D'Varn shocked but this once. She steps back, feet wide apart, hands on hips, and looks me up and down. Lights a cigarette. Her face is dark, like she's decidin on somethin. Shakes her head. And again. Kinda smiles, like she's decided.

And I'm, "What?!"

"What? Do they all jump off rooftops in your family?"

"Nother cigarette, please."

"Course. This first."

Then I'm on my tippy-toes and we're kissin. Soft like you wouldn't believe, her lips. Sweet, her breath, and her tongue oughta be in the Song of Songs That Is Solomon's. That was one Bathsheba kiss. D'Varn all over. Maybe that kiss went on for a hundred years. Maybe, somewhere in the ether, it's still goin on.

Then she steps back, lights another cigarette—when we kissed she'd held the previous cig in her hand, the hand that held the back of my head for the kiss, so I felt cigarette-burn near the back of my neck. Now she lights me one and puts it tween my lips, then gets back to work with a faraway look. Seems with D'Varn, she'd kinda leave while she's still there.

And I'm rememberin Fred reading to me, late at night, from books we weren't supposed to know about. She got em from a book-rent store, I don't know how. Her secret. People kissed in those books, and did things, and people kissed in flickers. But Mother and Daddy? If they ever kissed, we never seen it. So Fred, she wants to figure out kissing, and who else was there but me? Which was good, cause I wanted to know too. So we figured it out and, well, it was even better than it was cracked up to be—and that don't happen so often—so if we were blue sometimes we'd smooch. If Daddy'd caught us he'd've unbelted his black strap and beat us with the buckle end, which made it all more fun, us so quiet not to be caught, and we weren't caught but once and that was by Mother, after she'd gone silent, and she for just a sec seemed not to know if she'd laugh or cry. She did neither, just that her face got kinda dreamy, and she stepped away quietly and shut the door behind her so delicate you didn't hear the latch catch.

"There's nothin in the Bible," says I to D'Varn, "gainst twins kissing."

"I'll keep that in mind."

"I can recite every verse in the Bible about twins."

"Be a dear and don't. Now keep your face still."

She's "highlighting," she says, on my face, and she calls that the "finishing touch," and as she's fastening the hat with hairpins I'm wondering for the umpteenth time why, twice in the Song of Songs That Is Solomon's—verses 4:2 and 6:6—Bathsheba's teeth *are like a flock of sheep that are even shorn, whereof every one beareth twins.* Fred and me could never figure that.

"Why you so quiet?" says she.

"Thinkin on scripture," says me.

"Think out loud."

"You said not."

"I say to."

"It's just strange how in the Song of Songs That Is Solomon's it says Bathsheba's teeth are like sheep."

"Says which?"

"They didn't raise you on the Bible?" says me.

"They didn't raise me. Teeth like sheep? Sounds smelly. What were they thinking?"

"No 'they' about it. Word of God. Don't even ask what God's thinkin."

"Not I, dearie."

And she spins me to face the mirror, which I'd had my back to.

I see a Not-Me me.

She in the mirror, we ain't even been introduced.

5

I STEPPED OUTA THAT SHACK AND LOOKED UP straight into that sky where I'd been and wanted to go again—high clouds scuddin fast to east and south. Breathed deep, D'Varn-taste in my mouth, mixin with storm-smell, a ways off still, but closer. Daddy'd say, "It's comin a gulley-washer."

"What's up there?" says D'Varn, with this way she had of remindin how if you thought anything was more important than D'Varn you had another think comin.

"Up there," says me, "is what you'll find out about, come early afternoon."

"Any more surprises for me?"

"I hope lots."

Now I'm tryin to stay in step with D'Varn's long-legged sashay.

Me-Not-Me moves different! It's like these clothes and shoes do the walking, not Willie, and they know how to step classy.

I'm deciding I like Miss Me-Not-Me. And as I feel a likin for her, Not-Me gets more like me, or I get more like her—or somethin.

And all's it is, is different clothes. Plus fumigant topped with perfume and rouge, and the wig and a feather-hat weighin more on my head than I'm used to, so my neck is straighter and my head moves carefuler. And lookin down there's a pair of Miss Mabel's elegant shoes like none I ever wore. I feel ritzy. A ritzy frail keepin a secret. And D'Varn notices.

"You're getting the hang," says she, "you're a natural," soundin like she invented me, which I suppose she has.

"And hey you," says D'Varn. "Es said you pulled that blade on her, and fast as anything."

"In these duds that'd be some job."

"So society at large is safe for now?" says she.

"Just for now," says me.

Closer we get to the Ghost Building the more I don't wanna. It looks bigger than before. I see from where we are that it's an ant-hill fulla people makin the biggest racket that ever I heard. And me, of a sudden, it's like there's somethin sticky on my feet.

Did I mention that this Brick fellow has brick-red hair and that's why they call him Brick? Well, if I haven't, there it is.

And there he is, kinda dancin at us—as you would *not* expect of him—holding a big gilt-framed oval mirror, and that's the point: He's holdin it at me, now high, now low, now shakin it, now anglin it, and I'm seeing Miss Me-Not-Me—but kinda *me*, you know? I'm seein me or her or who-the-damn, and she floats in that reflection as Brick moves it every which way while laughin, "Looka you, Missy! Looka you!"

I am lookin.

She's pretty, this Missy. Ritzy-pretty and—scuse my French—bitchy pretty. Looks like she knows what's goin on. Makes me wanna talk to her. Ain't that somethin? It's like she's bobbin all round with Brick's boyishness, but she's also very still, in a quick kind of way. I am one confused farmhand.

From the Ghost Building there's a bellow bout "Bring that damned mirror!" But Brick, he's saying, goofy-like, "Should have picked me for catchin ya!"

"Pasha's bigger."

"I wouldn'ta dropped ya," and he turns for to deliver his mirror while I'm sayin to his back, louder than I'd've liked, "You might nota put me down! Mighta walked off with me like I was a sacka potatoes!"

Brick, over his shoulder, "You got a point there!"

D'Varn says low, "Oh, brother, you are dangerous. Brick's too serious to be dangerous with, sugar. Mind your Auntie D'Varn."

"Ain't you a flirt?"

"Not with a man who's lookin for love."

"What's your banker lookin for?"

"What he wants, he gets buckets of."

Which I didn't like to hear any more than she liked for me to flirt.

Anyhow was it me flirtin, or Me-Not-Me?

We stand at the steps of the Ghost Building like we're waitin for an invitation.

We got one.

He loomed above us, on the floor of the Ghost Building's entryway—it was eight steps up, where he was standin, the stage's wood floor being raised above the ground so's it wouldn't warp (even the shacks were a step off the ground, I've forgot to say). Anyway, he's up there, a suited number, his hat a straw skimmer. He's unhappy as hell. And I see he's the flicker-fellow at the racetrack fighting with the Devil! Which takes me aback some, like I'm not aback enough already.

"Took your time gettin here. What are youse, society dames? Youse are dressed like society dames, but society dames you ain't."

"Get off it, Pathé," D'Varn gives back. "Look what I did! The waif's a princess."

"Shop-girl-dressed-for-Sunday woulda done it fah me."

Now he looks me up and down. He grins. This guy couldn'ta grinned much in life, cause it liked to crack his face.

"Some job, baby, I'll give ya that. Anyway, youse actually is early—by mistake. My wranglers ain't wranglin right."

Off he goes.

Now D'Varn gives me the once over. "You're a caution, you are."

"What'd I do?"

"Pathé didn't yell his head off just for the pure meanness of it, once he got his fill of you."

"Why don't you start in to dislikin me—just, you know, for balance, so all this likin of me don't make me walk tipped over to one side."

"I'll consider it." And she pinched me. Sweetly. "A good director, that Pathé, but he's a real stinker. Irritates the snot outa me." She was just getting warmed up. "The guy's a Brooklyn Jew who wears a beret and pretends he's French. I generally enjoy Jewish men, because they talk smart even when they're not, but this ball-buster"—I didn't hear the next part for thinkin how if Daddy knew I was consortin with Jews, and with a gal who liked Jews, the top of his head woulda blown right off. A Jew and a godless red socialist in one day—was I happy or what?

And up the steps we go.

The Ghost Building—*they* call it The Stage, and you see KEEP OFF THE STAGE signs nailed to beams here and there, but it's an impossibility to tell who should keep off what cause everybody's everywhere. Lots—lots and lots—of people. And over in this corner is men in this-and-that costume—Kop, waiter, toff, thug—they're shootin dice and calling bets. And around some tables by them, in every sort of chair, are gals in every sort of garb—rich, poor, fast, prim, waitresses with white aprons and white caps, maid duds, and a gal in nothin but tights—and they're playin cards and callin bets. And everybody's smokin cigarettes or chewin gum, and the guys (and one gal) also smoke cigars, and some guys got their cheeks wadded with tobacco chaws and they spew into brass spit-buckets or right on the floor. The women don't spit. The guys cuss every other word while they're dicin. And that's all just in one corner where folks appear to be waitin for somethin.

Smells of fresh-cut lumber, fumigant, tobacco, perfumes, grease and gunpowder.

Talk about all-at-onceness, Keystone takes the cake. Pay good attention now, cause everythin I'm fixin to say is just like it was, and it was like this every day, cept for rain. When Mr. Sennett said, "Let's go to work," he meant exactly what I'll relate, and it's ok if you don't believe me cause that just means you're regular, and regular won't do in the Ghost Building at the Keystone, which is circus, zoo, girlie show, loony-bin, ragtime, stampede, and throw in a train wreck—every day, all the days cept Sunday, for the goin pay of eighteen bucks a week, which darned sure beats farmin.

So there's the Kops in the Kop station, which is three walls, and they're all trying to cram out the door together, and ashes-ashes-all-fall-down—and up again, and down again—while the camera's crankin up a racket and the "director" (I guess that's what he was) is a'yellin "More light next time!" as the Kops spring up and "more light" must mean "jump higher" cause that's what they do next, while this director also says, "More pace, more pace," speakin to a derby-hatted harmonica player beside him who plays crazily faster at "more pace," and when that harmonica finishes its tune the crankin and jumpin and fallin is over. Course when you see it at the picture-show you don't hear no crankin but for the projector, nor thuddin, nor mouth-harp, nor screamin, nor any racket at all but the piano player down in front of the theatre.

When you see it in flickers it seems, well, almost natural, cause that's what you expect of the Kops, but you're not seein how high they really jump, and you don't hear how hard they come down, the thuds and oofs as they hit, and the curses when it's over, and they get up rubbin this and that part of themselves. And one says, "How's that, skipper?" And the director says, "Let's go, we got a deadline," and all of em pick up and hightail out.

But right by them—right there, two feet off—there's a livin room, I guess it is. "A drawin room," the fancy call it, though what they draw I don't know. It's got two walls, one of which has a window with painted trees behind it, and earnest guys—wearin mostly white shirts, suspenders, ties, and pants of course, and hats—are layin down rugs and puttin up pictures and carryin a big potted palm and placin a table and chairs, and the director talks to Minta, who's dressed to the nines in ruffles and wavin her cigarette in the director's face, and there's a schoolmarm-lookin gal wearin a hat so full of shrubbery you expect a squirrel to pop out anytime, and she's sitting at a harmonium like you see at tent revivals, the kind of instrument you can pick up and carry, and you play it pumpin pedals with your feet, and this gal looks like she awaits a signal.

Meanwhile, hammers are hammerin and saws are sawin—I don't see where, just yet, cause'a all the sets—and different musical instruments in different directions play different snatches of music that stop and go without sense.

A guy in a cook's uniform, cap and all, he comes straight up to me and sticks out his tongue. I swear. Does some jig-steps for my benefit. And off he goes.

D'Varn, she's right beside me lookin at me lookin at everything.

I say, "This-all goes on round here all the time?"

"All the time."

All-the-timeness is kinda what movies do. These movies, anyhow.

D'Varn walks me a few steps this'a way, so I can see where all the sawin and hammerin is happenin, and amongst the men is Big Es in overalls and a floppy straw hat, and she's geared up like these carpenters and sawin at a board. Es does a double-take when she sees me, and spits tobacco juice right there on the floor, then saws some more, harder, and as she bends and saws her big butt sways.

In all this racket if you speak soft and close, nobody two feet away'll hear a word you say.

Says D'Varn, "Big Es has a secret. Can you keep a secret?"

"Are you kidding?"

"Well. Es is from the quality. Arabella Esther Heinz. Went to college. Got a 'degree'—it's just a diploma but they call it a degree. Bet no one else in this joint has one, except maybe Sommie. Es gets lotsa money from her snooty family—to stay clear of them. Oh our Big Esther is rich as Christmas."

Now D'Varn goes red and looks worried rotten. Says, "I just did a bad thing. I did not mean to. I really did not. You can't let on you know her full name. Ever. Promise?"

I dislike to promise cause I keep a promise. Promises fence you in. I promised.

We strolled some more.

Through all that racket of crankin cameras and hammerin and musicians playin different tunes not ten feet from each other, and directors bawlin directions, and thuds of folks fallin and knockin things over, we hear Mr. Sennett and Pathé yell somethin awful about "inept goddamn wranglers" and "expensive delays." D'Varn opined that maybe they'd scrap our scene, whatever our scene was, and that it was just as well to stay away from their argument, so we went opposite it, through clothes hangin on a line, pants folded over the line, jackets and shirts on hangers that hung from hooks on beams, and there seemed no end to the Ghost Building, what with sections of stairs leading nowhere and all the sets like I've already said.

Then, placed on and about an ordinary park bench, are mirrors. An oval one and some small ones and that big gilt-framed mirror Brick had funned me with, and more. And I'm in all of them, fascinated with myself, me and Miss Not-Me both. I'm thinking that, as I look at everything, I'm who I was when I woke this morning, but people lookin at me now—they see *her.*

Then in a mirror I see D'Varn look at me-lookin-at-me.

"You gotta mean what you wear," says she. "Yesterday you got away with wearing practically nothing because what little you wore was like a part of you, so that's what we saw—you, not your clothes. Now this outfit's like a part of you. On just any gal, it might not look real, but it looks real on you. That's a trick no one can teach."

"How many parts a'me you think I got?"

"Lots, or you couldn't look as real today in this as you did yesterday in that other."

Then I feel eyes on me. And I turn. And it's Brick, yards away, starin hard. Just when I turned he looked off, pretendin he hadn't been lookin. Made me feel peculiar. So I took D'Varn's hand and we strolled some, till a man called, "Get back, you two!"

"Dreadful sorry," says me.

We're in front of a hallway set and there's Miss Mabel Normand in pajamas and bare feet, goin real fast through her gestures like a flicker sped up.

She says to the camera guy, "I'll do like that, George."

"It's: Turkey in the straw, turkey in the hay," says he, fanning himself with his fedora. "Dee-dee dah-dah do, dah-day dee-dee day, twice, and you finish on the second 'day.'"

"O-day-K!" says Miss Mabel.

George says "Action!" and the camera cranks and the fiddler plays and she, lookin flustered now, does all those same gestures but slower and with more personality, if you know what I mean—pounds the door, turns, looks shocked, crosses her arms in front of her chest and in front of her other parts like she's coverin nakedness, all to "Turkey in the straw, turkey in the hay." She and the fiddler stop on the same note.

Miss Mabel, straight from lookin flustered to lookin pleased, sees me and says, "Hiya, Catch."

"Miss Normand?"

"Catch. That's you. From this morning. I am the official Keystone baptizer, and I baptize thee Catch. Now, Catch, watch."

And outa one pajama pocket she pulls a firecracker and from the other she pulls a wood match, strikes the match on the door, lights the cracker, tosses it over the wall.

BOOM!

Yells and screams aplenty from the other side of the wall, with much masculine profanity.

Mabel's laughin like the dickens and folks are comin from the other side of the fake wall complainin of maybe bein blinded or gettin their hair caught afire, but Miss Mabel's so delighted with herself and the commotion that no one can stay mad, like I would be, even at her, and everybody starts to laughin and gets back to work.

"Mabel and her firecrackers," says D'Varn under her breath. "Keeps you on your toes."

"So you're 'Catch,' are you?" It's Sommie. He was one of them behind the wall.

He steps back, looks me up and down. Somehow when these movies do that it's not rude.

Sommie says, "*There is no beauty that hath not some strangeness in the proportion*—I quote Bacon."

"'N'eggs," says me. "Sunny-side? Over easy?" I winked him.

"Scrambled, very." He winked me! Didn't seem the type, drunk or sober. "Look at you," he says, like Brick did, but serious. "How smart you look! A regular chancer. You'll give them a game."

"Relative and absolute exist in the same continuum, all's I say to that."

"Have you the shred of an idea what 'continuum' means?"

"Somethin that continues?"

"Not too shabby, for a stab."

He bows. Walks on. Still pixilated.

Then it's Brick in front of us handin us each a tin pail brim-full of water.

"Need some idle folk," says he.

"We didn't mean to be idle," D'Varn says, aggravated-like.

"You'll earn your pay today, believe me."

Off he goes and we follow, carryin them pails arms' length in front of us. It's a job not to slosh our duds.

"You," D'Varn hisses, "can be a real pain in the ass."

"Wha'd I do!"

"That chump wouldn'ta picked me to carry a pail. Just his excuse to be near you."

I blush. "He ain't a chump."

"Oh, brother."

We come to a set that's a hotel lobby with a sofa near a fake window in a fake wall. Behind the camera there's more water-carriers—Big Es is one—with wood buckets and tin pails.

"I hope," D'Varn says, "your arms are killing you, cause mine are me."

I tell her mine are, but they ain't. Hard work I'm used to.

Everybody with pails is told to put the fire out, but there's no fire.

A buncha Kops are lining up to the side of the wall and D'Varn points out the last one. "That's Hank Mann. Watch him. He knows biz."

Says me, "Biz is?"

She shushes me, two fiddlers start to hillbillyin, and Mr. Sennett is behind the camera and yells out, "You first two, second one through dots the first on the book!"

Brick lights the sofa afire and it starts to catch and Mr. Sennett yells "Action!" and one Kop jumps through the window over the flames onto the floor, the second Kop follows and lands beside the first, and as he lands he belts the first Kop's head with the side of his elbow and the guy's head bobs around and he slumps, which I guess is what "dot him on the book" means, which I'm figurin as this line of Kops jumps through that sofa-fire, which is bad dangerous, cause there's curtains and a wood wall and sawdust on the floor and I'm nervouser and nervouser, and that Hank Mann fella is the last. He barrels through the window feet first, lands *on* the fire! On his butt! Slides off, sittin just in front of the fire when, calm as all get out, he fishes in his pocket, then another pocket, pulls out a cigarette, lights it on the fire, takes a puff, passes out.

"That's biz," says D'Varn, as Brick yells "Now!" and everybody sloshes their pails at the fire, dousin the sofa and Hank Mann, and Mr. Sennett yells "Cut!" and the hillbilly fiddles stop and two guys empty pails on Mr. Sennett.

He stands there soakin wet, and surprised, and laughin, and everybody laughs.

"Watch now," D'Varn whispers, "he'll say it."

He can hardly speak for laughin but he chokes out, "We live our art."

Says D'Varn, "That's what he always says when they catch him one like that."

"Lookin good, Catch," Mr. Sennett says at me. "Welcome to the Keystone University of Philosophy and Culture."

Never saw a man happier than he was at that very moment.

Mr. Sennett, he spits a wad of tobacco juice bout ten feet to that soaked smolderin sofa.

A gal with a notepad appears beside him like from out of nowhere, he tells her, "Sommie and Roscoe," and off she goes.

"Catch," says he to me, "Sommie came up with something for you. In record time, too. It's the kind of thing that'll work for you till we see can you act."

And here's the notepad gal with Sommie and Roscoe, and Mr. Sennett pulls a folded sheet from his soaked pocket, and it's soaked too, and he says at them, "I like it. We'll shoot her jumps first, then the before and after—cause I'm dying to see that jump. Then we top it, Roscoe, with a bigger jump for you. Catch'll point, then there's a card: 'YOU THERE!' Then a bigger card with wavy letters and exclamation points: 'CATCH!' Audience won't expect it any more than we did. Thrills and spills."

"It'll take a day to work my fall," says Roscoe. "I ain't no frail."

I'm distracted by Brick lookin at me pained-like. I curtsey. He blushes.

D'Varn's standin by me, not liking one bit that she's invisible in this conversation.

Of a sudden there's Miss Mabel's voice, big and hollow.

Mabel's out of those pajamas and dressed regular and ridin Pasha's shoulders and yellin through a megaphone.

"Catch gets a fiver for the cards! She invented the line."

"She gets a three'er," says Mr. Sennett. "Three simolians for one line? I'm gonna go broke."

You'd think Mr. Sennett coulda got away with disrememberin those three dollars, but that man never forgot anything about money. Pay-time, I got my three bucks extra. A cheapskate, Mr. Sennett, but a straight shooter.

And Mabel bellows through her megaphone, "Ladies and gonifs! I, Mabel Ethelreid Normand, of the Ethelreids of Georgia and the Normands of Alaska"—she'd never been to either place, turns out—"I herebye announce the incorporation on this date and in this place of The Ladies' Dirty-Mouth and Community Aid Society! Our mission: To prove gals ken cuss as bad as any paunchy, punchy prick of a man!"

"Mabel!" That was Mr. Sennett.

"You dangling dicks"—

"Mabel!"

—"are gonna get an earful. A fucking earful."

"MABEL!"

"And you, my good fellow"—she's pointin at Mr. Sennett and I swear she bursts into tears like a little kid—"you get offa my set, you welchin lyin Mick, and to think you were an altar boy"—and she bursts into worse tears.

Mr. Sennett hunches his shoulders and bows his head and stuffs those big hands at the end of those long arms deep in his pockets and slouches off. Never saw a man in more misery than he was at that very moment.

Miss Mabel swings herself offa Pasha's shoulders easy as you please, kicks at whatever stuff is handy, yellin, like the world's endin, "Piss, shit and corruption!"

A tall'ish number, one of the Kops, he sidles up to D'Varn and says, "Bet she heard what I heard?"

"And that is?"

"Listen, I never repeat gossip—so I'll tell you just once."

And he stage-whispers something nasty bout Mr. Mack Sennett and a certain Bathing Beauty on the lot. Says he heard it from Pathé, who's tellin all and sundry.

"If it comes from Pathé," D'Varn snorts, "I don't believe it."

"Mabel doesn't either. Cept a little bit. Just enough."

"Have a Juicy Fruit, Catch?" Brick's by my side. He hands me a stick of gum, and by the time I unwrap it he's gone.

Someone calls, "Ready, Mabel?"

"Ain't I always?"

She heads off and we follow, cause why not, we ain't workin yet.

It's a parlor set with a piano and she says to the guy beside the camera, "George, I do this and this," and her face lights up like the happiest of people and she plunks that piano like she knows how and rolls those big dark eyes and looks over at something or someone that ain't there and jumps up in delight. Then does it again while the camera cranks.

I whisper to D'Varn, "How can she do that? After being so weepy blue? It's spooky."

"I'm looking and learning," says D'Varn.

"You wanna be spooky?" says me.

"Very," says she.

When the camera stops cranking Mabel steps right up to me. "Joining my Dirty Mouth and Community Aid Society?"

I hear myself say what I've never said: "Shit, sure."

She laughs like a rose flower would laugh. And that's spooky too.

"That's my Catch, a real game kid." Then a different voice, man'ish almost: "When you get in front of that camera, girlie, no big broad gestures. Short quick moves. They register. You, too, D'Varn. I see you studying me." And her eyes tear a little. "I'm worth a study, I am."

And she's off.

And a little guy dances by doin a soft shoe, elegant.

Es closes in with that man-stride of hers and somethin smokin in her eyes.

I pipe up, "Say something college."

"She told you about that? The cunt."

So much for college.

She closes her hand around D'Varn's forearm. "With me a minute."

"Sugaree, we gotta work."

"With. Me."

They step off, Es whispering in a heat.

So I'm mindin my own beeswax midst the hammerin and fiddlin and shoutin and thumpin and crankin and cussin, lookin this way and that, trying not to be in the way, when the Devil caught my eye as I caught his.

I did not flinch. That same small bowler's on his head, he holds that same cane, wears those big shoes, and his eyes are fulla mischief. I'm wishing I was Catholic, cause they got the Sign of the Cross, but us Baptists, we got nothin cept not flinchin.

"What you lookin at?" says I to the Devil.

"Something fetching but—not—quite—there."

He burped, or pretended to, and covered his mouth. "Such odd things do pop out of one!"

Stuck my tongue out at him.

Stuck his back at me, tipped his bowler, then he smiled like I never seen, for just a sec, then he's moony, he's silly, he's sad, and he laughs at all that, purely delighted with himself, lookin sweet as any girl. Then his face is still.

"You're the Devil," says me. "That's the Devil's way. He can be anything."

"Devil, is it? Nothing so grand. A minion, merely—but eager to do my part."

"Is that you? You smell!"

"I know."

"You like to?"

"Clever wench. It makes people decide about one."

"Devil's got a stink."

"Does he?"

Some guy calls out, "Chaplin!"

"Pardon. I'm up."

"Action!" someone yells. A camera cranks.

Devil tips his bowler to me and goes, but how he goes—charges into a hallway, knocks a fellow down with a mighty slap—that gentleman rises into the air and lands on his duff with a thump and a groan—and the Devil or Chaplin or whatever his name is, he faces Walrus-Moustache who pinched me at breakfast and they butt chests and the Devil rears back and kicks Walrus full in the chest with the flat of his big shoe, his leg straight out, I thought the man'd die, stead Walrus sorta flew backward through a doorway, the Devil's after him but the door slams so hard in his face his head shoulda come off, but he just pushes the door like nothin happened and goes on in and that's the biz. Crankin stops.

The Devil, he became the most famous person in the world. I got to like him too. That's a trick he had, he made you like him. But never did I forget he is the Devil.

And it's Brick beside me. In the Ghost Building folks behave like ghosts, showin up and disappearin in a great confusion that they swim in fine as fish.

"Ain't it something," says Brick, "how he does that with the door? I've been watching, to figure it. From here, we see the left side of his face and his left hand. He keeps his body between the camera and his right hand. With that hand, his right, he stops the door just at his nose as he rears back his head like he's been slammed. Some trick, hey?"

"Practicin on bein a director, Mr. Brick?"

"All the time. Want another Juicy Fruit?"

"Still with the first, thanks."

Off he goes.

"Miss Catch!" It's that Pathé. "Get D'Varn. Five minutes, ya get me? Other side of the stage, on the big set. Five minutes, not four and a half."

My charm's wore off on him, that was plain.

I didn't rush off. Didn't move a muscle.

"Your début." It was Sommie. "You appear to be thinking, my dear. I am pleased. Are you? Thinking?"

"My Mother said I had to."

"Really!"

"Regular folks eat these flickers up, but I wonder how they swallow em down. Cause these here movies who make the flickers—regular folks wouldn't stand their gaff, not for a minute, not even at a church picnic."

"The relative and the absolute exist in the same continuum—is my sole comment, for the moment."

And don't you know he winked me once more? Then walked off kinda satisfied-like, while I was warm in my heart with the feeling that maybe Sommie liked me as I am.

Off I go, hurryin now, to interrupt the confab Big Es and D'Varn are havin at each other.

Then Es is at me. "Renaissance! Enlightenment! *No man is an island, entire of itself*—unless she's a woman. That's college."

Says me, "Bottom of the ninth, D'Varn. We're at bat."

D'Varn and I make tracks as we straighten ourselves and set our hats just right and I put on the white lace gloves D'Varn told me not to wear until it was time case they'd get blemished. Even my hands have gone over to Miss Me-Not-Me.

It's like there's a stillness—when really there's anything but. There's all sounds of cussin and hammerin, fiddles and harmoniums, folks at odds. But that's all behind the camera.

In front of the camera, on this widest of sets, there's all us fancy-dressed folk standin where Pathé placed us, with me at the front, in the center. We're supposed to be hoitsy-toitsy people arrivin at a function in a grand hall. Behind me is a stairway to a balcony. The stairway has banisters and the balcony has a railin. Pathé's particular that I'm directly in front of the stairway, maybe five yards, and that there's no one between the stairway and me.

"You ain't a scaredy cat," says he as he places me, "so I want ya here."

D'Varn he places to my left and maybe a footstep away.

The set is ripe with a naked lady statue on a pedestal, big potted plants, nice tablecloths on small tables off to one side, a big bear rug, and that tiger rug that felt so good under my feet after I woke up.

I'm not supposed to look at the camera. Pathé was firm about that. He'll say "Action," and we're supposed to have just arrived, me and D'Varn, and we're to gab about anything, easy as you please. That's all.

There's a terrible commotion and shouts and growls and bustlin very near, but that noise seems like it has nothin to do with us. We're waiting in this stillness for "Action."

D'Varn says, "Some directors tell 'background'—that's us—what the scene is, some don't. A scene like this, comedians will do their stuff while we just react naturally. You'll do fine."

I'm noticing for the first time that through the Ghost Building's canvas walls the world outside kind of wavers as the canvas sighs in and out with the breeze, and I see trees and the barn and the like, but as though they're shadows, waverin. That world looks ghostly from inside the Ghost Building!

I'm startled outa my formulatin when Pathé bellows, "Action!"

What happened next happened much quicker than I can say—and slow, too, slower than anything.

Happened about as fast as I said what I just said.

There's the bear that's a rug and the tiger that's a rug, but of a sudden there's a lion, and another, and they ain't rugs. They're yellow-furred, white-pawed, enormous and runnin like fury.

Straight at me.

Didn't see them at first, cause I'm not looking toward the camera.

What I see first is Walrus chargin right by me, and I feel another guy run betwixt me and D'Varn, jostlin us, and those gentlemen are plenty scared, for real, and I look to see what they're runnin from—just naturally, like D'Varn said to be. I look and, like I said, I see lions.

Their heads are bigger than you'd think. Bigger than they look in pictures.

I'm figurin—not really figurin, there's no time—but I'm feelin: That's not right, that can't be. Two big-headed lions runnin straight at me.

As I'm seein and feelin I reach and clutch D'Varn's hand—like to mean, Don't move! Raised to farm-work, I can really clutch. She stayed put.

In half a heartbeat, those lions pass D'Varn and me, one on either side, the thumps of their paws vibratin the floorboards, their beast-smell rank and heady, and did you know a lion's tail is harder than a teamster's whip? It's so. That lion's tail slapped my shin so hard I near lost my footing. Swelled up a purple bruise in no time.

Heard the men pound up those stairs, with the lions just behind as I turned to see. I do not know how those men outrun em. I wouldn'ta believed it, had I not seen. Them lions were two heartbeats behind em, then one heartbeat.

Top of the stairs, the men break to the right on the balcony and dive through a curtain, the beasts on their heels.

Then a bigger racket and roarin and an awful sound of iron rattlin, and I'm imagining those lions got tricked into a cage that can barely hold em.

Me, I'm starin after what I just saw as though I'm seein it again and again. Only reason I'd not been scared is there'd been no time.

But I was shakin some now, and felt D'Varn's tremblin through her hand, while she says low, like it's a long note in a song, "Fuuuuuuuuuuuck."

As though I'd been deaf but can suddenly hear, the noise is terrific. There's a lotta "What the hell was that all about?!"—"Are you outa your fuckin mind!"—"Somebody help us, this gal's wet herself and she can't stand up"—I'm guessin that if D'Varn and me had moved a muscle those lions might have turned on us, we bein straight in front of them and all.

Started in to breathin again. Guess I hadn't since "Action!"

Other "background," who weren't in the path of the charge—well, they hadn't stayed still, they'd run and tumbled and fell and got the hell'n'dickens outa the way. All except this one gent near the stair, who's standin frozen stiff, even now, starin straight ahead, but like he can't see a thing.

And there's Brick with a pistol stuck in Pathé's gut.

Brick's in Pathé's face whisperin somethin fierce, and now it's Pathé that's scared.

Mr. Sennett runs in to break them up, and still all this "I don't believe it"—"Oh my god"—"Will somebody please help us?"

Sommie's by the fallen wet-herself gal, waving a vial under her nose, and he's saying, "Calm yourself, calm yourself," and she goes, "Get your goddamn hands outa my face."

I'm still clutching the hand of D'Varn, and I turn to her, and she's lookin like—well, like she's been run at by two lions.

And Miss Mabel's run in, and Roscoe, and everybody. Was kinda funny when the Kops run in, cause that's like they do in their flickers—cept there was really no place for them amongst all these people in confusion, and they were bumpin into stuff and folks. Mr. Sennett's calmin down Brick, but Brick still has that pistol stuck in Pathé's gut, saying, "It's a goodness nothin happened to"—and he takes a breath—"anyone. I'da killed ya. Keep that in mind every day for the rest of your sorry life."

He stuffs the pistol in his belt. It's an old-timey Colt like Daddy's. Guess he had it out cause of the lions.

Brick turns and looks at me hard. I look back harder. I saw the fury in the flame of his soul, and I let him see that's what I saw.

He coughed a nervous cough and made to fumble for his matches and cigarette fixins.

Then everyone jumps and yelps at an enormous-soundin rifle shot from up the balcony behind that curtain. Another shot. A pitiful whimper. Another shot.

Poor dumb beasts.

If they'd roared since morning I guess I'd got so used to it I'd not noticed.

"Thanks," says D'Varn. Squeezes my hand. Hers is ice cold. Only time ever.

Now Pathé stands in front of me, throws a glance over his shoulder to Brick, says to me, "Pluck. That's what you got. And you know what it rhymes with."

Too chicken-livered to talk back to Brick, so he's gotta crack wise at me.

He stomps off yelling "It's gonna look great on the screen!" (It did, too.)

Now Mr. Sennett's yowling at two cowed men, how he'll not pay a cent for animals they couldn't control.

That about stopped everybody's work, we was all so shook. I guessed lions was over the wall, even for such as these movies. There was at least *something* that was too much for them. I figured I'd seen my last lion at the Keystone. Silly me.

6

WORK WOULDA STOPPED in half an hour anyhow, what with how the rains came, pourin buckets from low black clouds. In no time the canvas overhead soaked through and we might's well been outdoors, what with everybody scramblin to protect what needed protectin—cameras, film canisters, what-all. And everybody means everybody, Miss Mabel, Mr. Sennett, Sommie, the Devil, they lugged what needed luggin along with us common folk, coverin cameras with whatever cloth ain't been soaked and runnin em to the sheds.

The lot was mud, sticky sucky mud, and I'm carryin my Mabel-shoes in one hand and a couple'a canisters wrapped in a blanket under my arm, sloshin through, with D'Varn right behind holdin her shoes to her chest like they's a baby. Then everybody's huddlin in what shelter they'd found, with rain poundin somethin murderous on the roofs.

Seemed it poured like that forever, or as much as an hour. Brick and Hank Mann and Mr. Sennett, flustered as wet cats, ran from shed to shack to shed, tellin folks over and over to don't turn on any electric light "or the whole damned lot'll short out," what with all those wires hanging every which way in dressing rooms and such, and with water streamin through roof-leaks into fixtures.

I stood in the door of the props shed with Sommie and D'Varn to watch the sky fall down. And there's a chicken drownin in the mud. Farm girl me, I lit out for her, but by the time I reached her she'd succumbed, and my ritzy duds clung to and hung on me like sackcloth, weighty with soakin. My fine-lady hat hadn't even made it outa the Ghost Building.

I'm back in the props shed and Sommie and D'Varn are talkin about how when it rains Mr. Sennett has folks do other stuff, build sets, paint sets, what-all, but nothin could be done in this that was like Noah's own flood.

Even when it eased off the company, as they called it, was trapped at the Keystone. Those with cars would only get mud-stuck. Those who'd come on horseback knew not to risk a horse in such muddy uncertain footing. And we heard no streetcar bells.

Sommie says, "You're native to this area, are you not?"

"All my life."

"Notwithstanding that all your life is not a great span of time, does this happen regularly?"

"Every few years. Daddy's got a sayin, that any rube farmer knows no question is more important than *How's the weather?*"

"Wisdom, of a kind."

"My Daddy? Not even a little. Just practical."

D'Varn's fumin like this storm is a personal insult. "It has *ruined* my hair!"

"Quite right, my dear," says Sommie. "Bedraggled will never do. It unsettles your pose."

"I'll give ya a pose right in the nose."

Just then there were sounds I'm not used to. Happy children, a bunch of em. Laughter like you forget when you grow up. And, yeah, I'm young, but as of today I make more'n three bucks daily, which is grown up and then some where I come from. That laughter kinda tinkled through the rain-sound, and, what with both sounds pitched together, I never heard anything prettier.

Then we saw them, twenty or so kids, comin through the gate, playing in the mud, throwin mud-balls at each other, lovin the rain, which had eased some, but just some. The kids were herded by three women quick as sheep-dogs, keeping those kids movin in one direction while they played.

"The Boss calls them The Keystone Kids," says D'Varn. "Built a stage across the street to shoot their flickers. Locals, mostly, and children of some who work here, the carpenters and such."

"Our actors don't seem to have children," Sommie says. "With how you lot carry on, I wonder how you manage that."

"With difficulty," says D'Varn.

As the kids got herded into what I guess was their own dressing-shed, it was like they swept the rain away cause it lightened considerable. Now clouds overhead were pearly gray. Little raindrops, the kind you hardly feel, and enough light shinin through so's those droplets sparkled in the air.

Something come over D'Varn at the sight.

She looked at me and in her eyes I see that, of a sudden, her heart's opened fresh as a flower.

"Hey, you," says she.

"You, too," says me.

"Let's us go. This is a special rain for walking."

It was fun, walkin cross the lot ankle deep in squish-your-toes mud, "bedraggled," like Sommie said, in our fine-lady duds. Miss Me-Not-Me had kinda melted with the rain.

We got our stuff from the women's shed, cause D'Varn didn't trust em not to be "borrowed," what with Miss Mabel's fine shoes and Fred's good coat. Found twine, tied it all in a bundle. "We'll leave our things with Mr. Walker," was D'Varn's plan.

This Mr. Walker was the little gate man. I'd seen him, leaning back in his chair in front of the main gate, gray pants, gray shirt, gray cap, and gray hair, a big gray handlebar moustache all over his kind face, lookin like a man who didn't want to be or do one damn other thing.

But not just now. His cap was soaked outa shape, his neat gray apparel was mud-splattered, and that long gray moustache drooped sorrowfully, though he couldn't have been less so.

"Miss D'Varn, Miss Catch," says Mr. Walker as he sparks a smile and he raises his finger to his cap brim like everythin was normal.

"Mr. Walker," says D'Varn, "would you kindly mind our things while we go for a stroll?"

"In my billet they'll be safe and dry, ladies. I plan on staying the night, no point slogging in this gump, so may you pick up yer stuff when ya like."

"Many thanks," and D'Varn bends to kiss the little man on the cheek.

"Know why I like my job, Miss Catch?"

"No, but I'd like to know."

"It's a great job for cheek-kissin."

I took that as my signal and even I had to bend a bit to kiss his cheek.

"Don'tchya know, I'm kissed more, now I'm old, than ever in my youth. That's the Keystone for ya."

That moment hung there a bit, us-all smilin pleasantly as you please.

Now there came this wagon, leavin the Keystone—four horses pulled its bulk against the mud, and how they braced their hind legs to pull, all together, you saw they knew their business good. In the wagon was a lumpy tarp, and, sticking out from the tarp, this way and that, was a paw here, a paw there, those great pounding paws of the lions. And a stretch of tail. Fifty-fifty it was the tail that hit my shin, which still hurt.

Such squeakin and rattlin as that wagon strained to stay in one piece when those horses heaved it unstuck from mud, to be stuck again and in need of another heave. Their teamster yelled em on and shook his reins, but didn't need a whip. Good horses. Beside the teamster on his wood seat was, I suppose, those wranglers that no one had a good word for, lookin lost-like, and across the knees of one was a buffalo gun.

We watched them pass, feelin—I don't know. A wrong had been done. That was the feel.

Alessandro Street afforded harder ground, not much harder but some, and the wagon caught traction. We watched it turn north toward Glendale.

"Don't that beat all," sighs Mr. Walker.

I thought we was all lookin at the wagon, but now I see D'Varn's head is pitched toward the sky. She's smilin gentle, with her eyes kinda closed against the little droplets fallin.

Still lookin up, she reaches out her hand toward me and I take it, and, still lookin up, she starts to walkin, and I with her, and now she looks at me with all her heart.

I must have looked at her the same, cause D'Varn grinned. When she smiled you could take her picture, her smiles were that perfect, but this was a grin that didn't care what it looked like.

She said, "Smells like the first day of the world, don't you think?"

Not really, but I didn't say so. This street mud smelt oily from autos, wet beast-smell still hung strong in the air, but right with that was the cleanliness of rain, and on the breeze were fragrances of flowers, flowers that are always here all times of year, one kind and another, and wood-burn smell from chimneys, and a glow'y pearly light over all—storm-glow.

"Funny about clouds," says she. "Clouds don't hardly film at all. Isn't that strange? The film stock doesn't pick them up. Heard they're inventing new stock that'll see clouds."

"There's folks can invent most anything nowadays," says me.

"And bless their hearts! We work for the *best* invention."

Rain picked up a little. Made us happier.

She stopped and crooked her head to the side, giving the once-over to a phone-box on a pole for callin in fires and such.

"Do you play 'Do you?'" says she.

She knew by my look that I did not.

"I say, 'I want to talk on that phone, do you?' Then you say, 'I do, I do, I do.' And then we're dare-bound to do it. So—I want to talk on that phone, do you?"

"I do, I do, I do," says I, when I sure don't. I never spoke on a telephone, Daddy had no need of the instrument.

She opens the box, puts one funnel to her ear, talks into another.

"I am calling to you," says she in a lady's voice, "to do something about this rain, it's just awful. But—you're the authorities, are you not? Well! I like that! Some authority you have!"

Hangs up. Arches an eyebrow at me.

I'm all goosy, but I pick up the phone.

A rough voice says, "Now, look, lady."

"Excuse me, sir," says I, high as I can manage, "I'm reportin the person who just made that call. She's one'a them movie trouble-makers and must be stopped and—" Couldn't think. Lost my nerve. Hung up. Sheepish I tell her, "That's my first phone."

"It really is?"

I nod yes and D'Varn gives me a big old great hug.

Then says, "Look!"

Let's me go, points, and before I know what she's pointin at she's off across muddy Alessandro and I'm after her, splashin oily mud all up and down our legs and our dresses, splashin like the dickens—toward a flower.

A tall purple flower sheltered under a small thick tree.

"Trying so hard, pretty iris!" D'Varn says hushed. "Here all alone. Just this one purple iris giving the world all she's got."

I stoop to pick it for her and she yelps, "Don't!"

"You don't want it?"

"I *have* it. Seeing it is having it. You know, baby?"

I didn't, not at all, cept I liked her face-glow as she said so. Liked "baby," too.

Says she, "Ask why I love flowers?"

I did so.

"Cause how can you be angry at a flower?"

Rain picked up more. We stood there in stillness, poured upon.

Her eyes got wide, excited. "Race you back!"

And she's off.

Mud-runnin's fun and slippery and we fell some, laughin, helpin each other up, racin on, and she's lovin being in the lead so I let her be. Her long legs or no, I was hardly tryin.

We're comin on the Keystone gate and I pull up with her, just a half a stride behind, and we turn sharp into the gate and run Miss Mabel Normand down.

Us three in a pile in the mud. We untangle, laughin, but Miss Mabel's also, at the same time, cryin.

"Thank you, my dears. Precisely what I needed."

We're sorryin through laugh-coughs, but she says, "Cause what I needed—was to come down to earth."

So she splashes mud at us, and we at her, and there's Mr. Walker out the door of his station with, "Ladies!"

"You, sir, Mr. Walker," says Miss Mabel, "use the term loosely."

"Miss Normand, not I. A real lady's a lady period, even on er butt in the mud."

We splash him. He bows politely and returns to his office. We splash each other.

"Like the Boss says, we live our art." That was D'Varn.

"The boss, our resident genius, is a goddamn waffling hypocrite," says Miss Mabel. Then she says, "D'Varn! Your dress hiked itself up to your hips and I can see your kitty."

D'Varn scrambled to pull her muddy dress down.

Miss Mabel's sayin, "Where'd you lose yer panties, girlie? None of my business, right?"

"Didn't lose anything. I don't smother my kitty. Like it airy up there."

"Live our art, huh?" snorts Miss Mabel. "Mack don't like for *me* to live it. I say an occasional firecracker is good for the developing room, nitrate film or no nitrate film. Highly flammable is the developing room? Well, so—am—I!"

"You did that *really*?" D'Varn says. "Did you blow it up?"

"No such luck," says Miss Mabel, "but I stood close enough to blow up with them if they blew—cause I'm a good sport." Miss Mabel's eyes are tearing, her lips aquiver. "One thing I know is to be a good sport." She fishes her hands in the mud and comes up with a flask. "Have a nip."

When it comes to me I swig like they did. Tastes like apricots, burns like crazy.

"Live our art," Miss Mabel says. "I'm a good sport. Stood close enough to blow up. *That's* livin your art. His nibs had fits. Serves im right. Engaged for marriage three years, won't set a date." She takes another nip and passes it round. "Don't you know if that shed blew, he'd've had cameras rolling in seconds flat."

Sky's pouring hard again. Minta's running at us, holding a newspaper over her head.

I say to Miss Mabel, quiet, "Do you ever stop?"

"Why would I?"

Oh those big dark eyes.

Minta calls, "Mabel!"

"Araminta! Join us. Feels good in the cracks."

"It's Madcap Mabel, just like in the magazines."

"I'd like to be that person," says Mabel.

"Dear," says Minta, "so would we all."

"Come to make an honest woman of me?"

"Can't be done. Come to get you out of the rain."

"Oh, alright," says Mabel. "Up we go, honeys. Minta, D'Varn don't wear undies."

"Alert the press."

"I might."

D'Varn was right, you can't see clouds. I looked for them as this and that passed on the screen, but skies in these flickers are blank sheets of paper.

I'd got bold and taken D'Varn by the hand and led her past the rows of foldin chairs to the very front, cause, of a sudden, I didn't want to see anyone more. My eyes had filled up with all they could take. Three flickers screened and I barely noticed their frolics, lookin only at sky and background, furniture, wallpaper, statues, shrubbery. I heard laughter behind us but I didn't laugh, nor did D'Varn. We sat holdin hands. It came upon me that not only had my life changed but D'Varn's also. I wasn't gonna be able to shake her and she wasn't gonna be able to shake me. And there was a solemnness to this that my little heart just sorta wept at.

The shack got thick with smoke of cigarettes and cigars. People laughed and coughed and talked as they watched, voices particular as signatures, Mr. Sennett's, Minta's, Roscoe's, Sommie's, the Devil's, Alice Mother Davenport, Chester Walrus Moustache who'd pinched me in a gentlemanly fashion and in no time was runnin from lions. Before us, silent movement on the screen; behind us, voices and projector racket—every voice but Miss Mabel's. She'd gone straight to the piano against the wall near the screen to start plunkin. She plunked good. The piano sounded bigger than when that church-lookin lady played. Miss Mabel drifted off into a lullaby-like melody and Mr. Sennett shouted, "Mabel, play the action!"—but she played lullaby-like no matter what and he gave up. Whispered D'Varn, "That's one sad lady."

Miss Mabel's piano, their voices, the projector's rattle and the rain on the roof blended like a kind of orchestra into something that had nothing to do with Keystone Kops running this way and that, nor with Roscoe pinching Mother Davenport and her arms flail and she slaps him and he rises his bulk into the air and lands plumb on his enormous bum and grabs at her dress as he falls and her dress tears off so's she's exposed in her corset and undies, the picture of mortification—the rain and the voices and the piano together made a music that had nothin to do with such goins on.

Then there was me. On the screen. What musta happened is, those fellows filmin the Kops and Chester in that traffic mix-up, they musta noticed the commotion of the Keystones gatherin to see me on the roof and they turned their camera my way, tilted up, and there's me, I point down—I know I'm sayin, "You they call Pasha!" before a title card comes up with "YOU THEY CALL PASHA?" Then I see me sayin "Catch"—and a title card says "CATCH!"—then off I go into the air. Surprised it went by so fast. There am I in the air, then I'm not. They couldn't move the camera fast enough for the whole shot. It's like I fell somewhere off the screen and was still fallin.

Well, all present broke into claps and yells and whistles while Mr. Sennett says in a big voice, "We're working that into a picture, Catch—so, yeah, you'll be paid for it." And Miss Mabel says, "Catch, take a bow!" I get up and as I do the rain comes down like fury on the roof, so loud, and they're cheering and I'm bowing and boom! The light gives out. The projector is all sparks. Rain pours through the roof there. Then there's no sparks, just bobbing lit ends of cigarettes and cigars.

Lots of confusion until someone lights a lantern. That was Brick. It would be. It's the kind of thing a guy like him would know to do—know where the lantern lay, know to find it in the black, and know to have dry matches in a zipper pocket maybe.

Nothin for it but to leave. Brick stands at the door lightin the way. When I pass him he looks up at the ceilin, I look down at the floor.

Sommie says softly to me, "Mind how you go."

7

I'D NEVER VENTURED SO FAR TO THE WEST, nor seen a palace. D'Varn said Hotel Hollywood's rooms numbered one hundred and forty-four, not counting lobbies and halls. That building shone bright in the dark, many windows still alight so late at night. The steps to the porch were wide as wide, and pillars held up a porch-roof. Hotel Hollywood sported a Mission front topped by *Arabian Nights* minarets. I swear this one building looked bigger than the whole of the Keystone. It fronted on what used to be Prospect Avenue and was now the Hollywood Boulevard, maybe three, maybe four miles toward the sea from Edendale—hard to figure distance, what with how the ride took so long, gettin stuck and unstuck in mud. Mr. Sennett arranged for coach-wagons to haul us all wherever, cussin the expense, promisin to push us harder for work when rain quit, if ever it did.

On the porch of Hotel Hollywood I paused and took a breath. Muddy bare feet, muddy dress, wet Fred-coat, a yellow-checked canvas valise with Miss Mabel Normand's gifts. No money yet, but if I'm correct keepin track— regular day's wage, leapin fee, writin fee—I've nine bucks' comin already. That's a darned respectable week's pay for most folks. But Hotel Hollywood? Said I, "How do the likes of us dare enter somewhere the likes of this?"

"Like we own the place," says D'Varn, and sashays on, me followin.

Plush chairs, silver ashtrays on shiny steel stands, bellboys in tight-butt uniforms with caps that strap under their chins, brass spit-buckets bright as mirrors.

She arranges at the desk that I'm her guest, and I see it don't matter how we look cause anyone who'd been outdoors looked the same, and the desk-folks joked about that, while me, I'm gawkin at hallways and staircases headin in every direction, and actual chandeliers, and all sorts of fixtures I'd seen only in flickers.

I was eager for the elevator, cause I never been in one, but D'Varn chose stairs cause she wanted to give the desk time to make a call.

"What call is that?"

"You'll see."

We're up the stairs and down one hallway, then another, and a door opens. Big Es. In a willowy lavender nighty, and her shiny auburn hair done proper, smilin cruel with her wide mouth as her eyes laughed angry. I hadn't seen her since it started raining. How'd she get here before us?

D'Varn opens with, "You gonna start?"

"I want my share. Of you."

"We'll work that out."

Es at me: "What you starin at, Snatch?"

"Catch."

"Snatch."

"I stare at what I want to. I'm enjoying your frills. Guess you do come from wealth."

"A wealth of bullshit."

Her eyes kind of quivered. I felt bad for her all of a sudden. She saw that and toughed up. I toughed back. It was like a conversation.

D'Varn laughed in her sorta tilted voice, "I believe you two shall become fast friends."

Es closed her door.

Says me, "Your banker must like you a lot."

"You can say that twice."

"I didn't like sayin it once."

D'Varn's room was rooms—a suite, she called it. Fancy sofa, plush, which she called a "divan." Gold-tipped cigarettes in glass "vessels" on a "coffee table." Embroidery draped on chairs, almost as good as Mother's or mine, and of better material. A rug to wiggle your toes in. The colors of everything all bright whites, soft reds, light beiges. Knick-knacks and this-n-thats of porcelain, and a Tiffany lamp lit by electricity like in the illustrateds.

"Approve of my drawing room?" says she.

"And they call it that why?"

"Cause they do. Money doesn't need reasons. That's what I like about money."

"Where's your banker's spit-bucket?"

"It's called a *cuspidor*. And he don't spit. *Doesn't* spit. And he can't come here. He'd be recognized. This hotel is respectable. They're very strict—about *men*."

She sits me on the sofa. Runs her hands up my legs and gets me feelin peaceful and excited all at once.

"Silky-smooth, so smooth." She's rubbin her palms up under my dress on my thighs. "Makes me greedy."

Made me dizzy.

Says she, "Need the bathroom?"

Says me, "The who room?"

"Go look."

She pointed. I went.

It's not that I never heard of em, just that I'd never given them thought. But to turn on a faucet in the sink and see clear water run—lordy! Beats pumpin and haulin. And tile cool underfoot. And a long tub, white as white, settin front and back and middle on three sets of pedestals, I guess they were, bright brass shaped like paws, with claws—compare that to our tin tub out back.

The toilet flat-out embarrassed me. I knew the word from the illustrateds, and how they looked, but to see one actually—it can't be right to poop in your house. And it all smelled so clean. A shit-house *should* smell like shit. Shit and lye.

"Out the way," says she, "I need to tinkle."

I got out the way and turned my head. I listened as her pissy whispered with the waters. A sweet sound really. And a little smell. Then a rush of runnin water and it's all perfume again, cause there was that, a scent in the air, flowery and light.

I step back into the drawing room. I mention how we're muddyin stuff up and she says from the bathroom how maids will clean it all tomorrow.

Maids.

"Look at me," says she.

And she steps out in the altogether, tall as tall, legs so long, a shape to her like an hourglass, pretty pink titties with nipples pointing up and blond fleece on her thing that Miss Mabel called a "kitty." Mud-stained shins and feet. In that lamplight D'Varn fairly glowed.

I was so scared I coulda cried. Crybaby scared. Also very happy.

I'd seen no one but Frederica in the altogether, and, Fred being a modest sort, I hadn't seen much of her since she'd bloomed.

My eyes full of D'Varn, if I'd put words to what I felt they woulda been: Now I know beauty. *Beauty.* Glowing *beauty.* And me, I'd never gave thought to beauty before today. It was nice to be pretty but—this was different.

I was gawkin, couldn't help that, and she liked it, but it made me shy.

Felt myself blush. "I reckon I'm just a silly."

D'Varn, her voice all lush, she says, "Love is silly, and it has to be, or it wouldn't be love."

Love?

"Your face," says she.

"What about it?"

"Two-three-four-seven-eight expressions flowing into each other. Willie, Willie, you are so beautiful."

Beautiful?! What the . . .

My legs wanted to run. My nipples burned so hot. She opened her arms and I run three steps to her and just held on, shakin, my face in her bosom, like I never again wanted to open my eyes. D'Varn's pattin down my hair and sayin "There, there" and "Me too, me too," and I'm smelling something strong that I don't know about and I'm thinkin it's comin from the bathroom but I feel it fume from between D'Varn's legs and that turned it from bad-smell to good-smell somehow. I had feelins all over my skin, on my skin, in my skin. Everything was so strange.

She's holdin me sayin, "I'll draw you a bath, we'll bathe, I'll wash your hair and comb it out, and then we'll make each other so happy."

"I am happy."

"Happier."

And that happened, like we was high in a tower in a fairy tale, and she turns on a electric fan to dry our hair, and brushes my dark long mop, and I brush her honey-colored waves, and there's a mirror in the bathroom I keep tryin not to look at, shut my eyes when I turn its way, like I can't stand to see what's there, myself, this naked way, and she keeps sayin I'm beautiful and I'm this and I'm that and "You have absolutely and utterly the most perfect tush in Christendom."

I hear a very small voice inside of me sayin nothin. Sayin nothin, but I hear it anyway.

"And legs like heaven," says she.

It's too much. Too much for me. Now I don't need that mirror, it's like I'm on the ceiling lookin down at us, like it's happenin to some other Willie, down there, far down, like the ceiling's so high, higher than the building I flew from, and I'm up there watchin.

It was all kind of terrible. And gorgeous. I didn't know what to do so I did nothing. She did things.

I watched us from the ceiling and didn't believe or understand what I saw.

And all of a sudden I'm back. My eyes are where they're supposed to be, in my head.

She'd lain me on that drawing room rug and the weight of her upon me was awful and grand, poundin her kitty against my thigh so hard it hurt, hurt a lot, and like to raise a bruise, and she moaned like she was hurtin, and louder, till she stopped. Then lay on me in a heap, breathing soft but hard too. We was slick with sweat. We smelled wonderful-gamey.

She rolled over. "That's three." She'd done that moanin twice already, what with this and that.

Did I mention the rain? It had started up again, hard.

Lyin beside me, lookin up, she says, "How do you feel, baby?"

"Like the rain is inside me. Like I'm some cloud that's rainin."

It was such a relief not to be on the ceiling anymore. I turned and held her and felt of her.

Maybe we slept a little.

She got up and poured water from a pitcher into a tumbler, one for her and one for me, and brought them to me. The water went down splendid. Got up again, she did, and poured somethin amber from a "carafe," poured into two more tumblers. Handed one to me and clinked glasses.

Says she, "*Salud*, pretty you."

The amber liquid burned good in my throat all the way down. Mixed with tastes of her mouth and skin.

She lit a cigarette and gave it to me and lit one for herself, and on the coffee table was an ashtray shaped like a black swan. I inhaled the smoke. Delicious.

"Tired?" says D'Varn.

"In a way. But not."

"Good."

It was like we were talkin but we didn't. It was like we were havin a long, long conversation somehow while sittin quiet smokin.

D'Varn didn't laugh much. Not really. She'd laugh a burst sometimes, but not really, really laugh. But now she let out the longest, prettiest laugh, like she was spillin all her secrets, and I started to laughin too, and we laughed till we couldn't, about what? I still don't know.

She's bright-eyed and soft-voiced, saying, "I believe happiness lasts forever. Happiness that's *really* happiness, it goes on and on and on, into the stars. Us, we're happy, then sad, always changing, but a true moment of happiness is something that lives on its own ever after."

Then she says, "Come."

She stands, I watch her stand, and watching her move so makes me glad. She opens a door she hadn't opened.

"Come, you!"

"Bossy, ain't ya?"

"Come."

I stand.

Says she, "If my face could flow with expressions like yours, so—what's the word?—'subtle' is the word! If my face could do like you, I'd be the greatest actress in the world. I'm gonna learn you."

"I ain't actin."

"Oh, I know."

Pleased me, that she wanted to 'learn' me. Not sure what it meant, however.

What it was, with me, is that I just wanted to please D'Varn, and she just wanted to please herself, which was fine with me, cause I just wanted to please D'Varn.

"Come," and she takes my hands in hers and kind of pulls me through that doorway.

Flicks on the wall-light.

There is the biggest, most glorious bed.

I hopped on it like a kid. She liked that. Then she goes back for cigarettes and tumblers and the black swan ashtray—though there were white swan ashtrays on the tables by the bed—and it's like we're somewhere inside a big secret.

"Let's play the 'I do' game," says she.

Uh oh, thinks I.

"I want—nipples in my mouth. Do you?"

"I—do."

"Twice more."

"I-do-I-do."

I'm not for talkin dirty, but it's "Do you? I do" this and "Do you? I do" that, playful but oh my, yum, yum, me, now, I'm a kitten, all purr and meow, what with mouths and hands doin this and that, here and there, but not like before, now it's me doin too, and she doin better, and she's got me moanin now, moanin all over, delicious, scrumptious, yum-yum, I know I sound like a dolt but anyway yum.

"Hey! You!" says she.

"Now what?"

"Lay on your belly."

I did so.

"Spread em."

I did so.

Well, her mouth, tongue and all, made its way slow where I never imagined any mouth goes, tongue and all, down slow between my bum's crack and on into the hole.

Jeepers.

THE PALISADES

ROSCOE "FATTY" ARBUCKLE
Our stuff cannot be faked.
When people see it they know
they are seeing real stunts.

1

FIELDS OF STRAWBERRIES just across Hollywood Boulevard. Citrus groves east to Vine. Roses everywhere, growin wild. It's like the breezes that spread our curtains carry flowers in their arms.

Says she one night, "Smell those roses," me on my belly on the bed, spent silly with what-all we'd done. "You," she said, "you all petal-soft, you—your scents—your thorns."

She'd talk frilly like that when we was alone.

She's asleep. Hotel Hollywood's quiet as church. I breathe deep of the night. Wrapped cozy I am, in my bright wool shawls, a blue and a white. I knit em for the chills that flow in from the sea at this hour. My mouth's warm, tangy with a cigarette, Egyptian, gold-tipped—D'Varn smokes em cause Miss Mabel does. I flick a long ash into the bowl of the glass black swan. Got the divan all to myself, in candlelight.

One candle only, in a might-be-real silver candlestick settin on the coffee table's glass top—the flame jumps as the wick flares and its glow reflects on the glass here'n'there. Tobacco all the way from Egypt and a breeze off the sea from who knows where, sweetened on the air of Hollywood's own strawberries and its roses that bloom all year.

How I love this sitting room—or drawin room or livin room, whatever D'Varn calls it on any day—and our bedroom and our bathroom, our suite, our three rooms where I may be as I am, any way I am. Sometimes I sit me down and weep with the relief of it all.

"Silk on my nipples," D'Varn likes to say, "I'll never get used to that. That's a whole world."

True even for flat-as-flat me, sheathed under my shawls in a silken silver negligee, bought with my very own leap-off-rooftops money. Leap off a roof, leap from a tree, leap and leap, in this costume and that, and buy what I please, then needlework some doodles on em so's my stuff is like nobody's.

This dark quiet is different from quiet in the light. Light kinda makes a noise of its own, but in these dark wee hours the quiet fairly sings.

A farm girl don't know much about wee hours. You're doin and doin from first light till dark. Guess I'm gettin cityfied, up late so often as I am now. My habit's become sleep a little, wake, be alone, then sleep more.

The hard-packed ground of Hollywood Boulevard, it's got fallow land on either side where life is all-the-time growin—but there's talk the boulevard'll soon be paved. Lots of pavin going on. Herders of sheep and pigs won't like that. Livestock don't go with pavement. Hard on horses, too. I've taken to movie-ways but have some Daddy in me still, flarin suspicious at pavement talk.

I've come to know these rooms like I knew our farm's each peg and rut. How whites and beiges and rust-reds of rugs and upholstery and pillows blend with vanilla walls that have plaster moldin where they meet the ceilin. Hard brightness of the bathroom. Thick embroidered curtains of the bedroom, always drawn—always shadowy, the bedroom. How differently our lamps throw light. The Tiffany, its many-colored dome, spreads light evenly all around, and you turn it off and on with a switch that's like a key. The standin electric lamp has a prettily stitched cloth shade and throws light hard straight up and down—it plugs in the wall and you turn it on with a push-button near the door, and that's how you do the bathroom lights, with a push-button over the sink, those bathroom bulbs around the mirror squinty bright, and under the sink a kerosene lantern seeming far from home, there for when the power fails, as it does regular. Candlesticks, swan ashtrays, cigarette "vessels" (gold tips standin straight up and bright). Vases of purple and red glass. The bureau in the bedroom for folding things and the built-in closet for hanging things, and on its two doors there's D'Varn-length mirrors. And her vanity bureau, and its mirror. Electric chandelier in the bedroom. Not many such rooms in Hotel Hollywood. They let Mr. Billy Banker, D'Varn's fella, fit it for his "Venus," as he calls her, all smarmy smiles, thinkin he's charmin. I cordially hate his insides. "He's spoiling me," says she, "and I'm spoiling you."

Not true. I ain't spoilt if every day and night these rooms feel to me fresh as new paint.

"Our suite is all 20th Century," D'Varn bragged, "and we deserve it."

"Any special reason why?"

"Beauty, Miss Willie—and my willingness to share it."

She'd say stuff like that, then laugh a laugh I didn't like.

"Look at the little hypocrite!" says she. "All disapproving of what she can't help but love."

"20th Century" is the telephone, shiny black, on its own stand in the bedroom so's the front desk'll wake us.

On the divan I'm likin the candlelight's flicker upon the crystal face of the prettiest clock—crystal that plinks if you tap it with your nail, the clock-face, in a mahogany case on its own shelf on the wall. I like its quiet ticks, but need no clock to know the hour.

Funny how you leave home but home never leaves you. The more things weren't like the farm, the more I thought of the farm. No electricity, no phone, no bathroom, nothin of the fancy. "Nothin but you," I hear Fred say in my mind, though she never said that really. I hear Fred say, "You musta been fancy-at-heart all along to be sittin in all this fanciness now and breathin easy as you please -- and *smoking,* I declare!"

I light another Egyptian by flicking the head of a wood match with my fingernail like Brick taught me.

"This is only the beginning," D'Varn would say. "I mean to have a house one day as big as this hotel, and every room nicer than these." I don't let on how it hurts me when she says that, cause I can't figure likin anywhere better than right here.

No sound anywhere now but that pretty clock's tick. Clock-time doesn't mean much to a farmhand girl. There's sunrise, sunset, and the weather. There's Sundays and regular days. Hereabouts, there's the rainy time and the rest of the time. There's what you plant and harvest at what phase of what moon. And every year there's the new catalogue of the Sears & Roebuck's, and it sits by the family Bible, and we leaf through that catalogue in idle moments to dream on how it would be to order this or that—even Daddy, studyin tools and implements he'll never afford. And there's birthdays, especially your own, and there's Christmas and the Fourth. Thanksgiving means that it's almost Christmas and Easter means you're midway tween Christmas and the Fourth. And the spring and harvest fairs. The days, the months, the year, that's how they pass on a farm, almost without countin. Only that your age changes and the past gets larger.

But at the Keystone? At the Keystone time blurs and goes back and forth like nobody's ever seen. You watch somethin one day that's you as you were two days back, then you watch it again at a flicker-theater weeks later. You shoot the end of a story before the middle or shoot two endings and the middle before they figure the beginnin. Or you shoot somethin for one story that goes instead into another. And maybe one day you wear six outfits and the next three days you wear only one. And you're a good girl in the mornin and a bad girl in the afternoon, a rich girl on one set and a poor girl on the next. Runnin from a villain one day, in cahoots with a villain the next. Turnin out two, three, even four Keystones in a week, so's they've takin to calling it "The Fun Factory," though our fun is ever so much hard work that at the same time ain't work at all. At the Keystone everything happens at once, or it rains. Then it's payday, then it's Sunday, when time behaves like it should before it goes blurry again Monday.

D'Varn's snorin her murmur of a snore.

I raise myself up and tippy-toe to the bedroom door. There's D'Varn on that big white bed, covers all a'tussle, and still as still, and it's like she's floatin through the night on her very own cloud.

I curl back on the divan and watch my cigarette smoke, like I can for hours.

Dozed a bit. Just a bit—the candle barely melted. If I dreamed I didn't know it, but it seemed I'd returned from some far place. This was the way with me now, a come-from-afar feel when I opened my eyes that made every waking in our suite taste some like the first time I woke there… oh, that first time, that mornin of scents all rain-fresh, D'Varn heavy asleep, her arm across my shoulders, how our bodies smelt of each other with a kind of oneness I'd not known—me shocked at what-all we'd done, shocked at myself. Wonderful-scared, and nervy. I breathed deep gulps of storm-charged air. Stayed half afraid of my own body for days after, cause of what it wanted and what she wanted from it. But in all that confusion of wonderful-scaredness there was a kind of laughter, like someone laughin who you can't see, and that someone was somewhere inside me.

Funny to think of it now, how that first morning I'd set myself to lyin still so as not to wake D'Varn—funny, cause D'Varn is tough to wake at best, cept I didn't know that then. Funny, too, what came to mind as I lay there feelin so new: Miss Mabel Normand's globe—the whole world bright and round as a balloon.

Miss Mabel had the Keystone's only private dressing room. After what she called my "audition," the leap that got me called "Catch," she'd taken me off with her.

"Come to my igloo," she said.

I knew enough to know igloos are made of ice, but she unlocked the door and woof! The heat near pushed us back.

"My ice cream!" she screams.

And into that stifling room she goes, with me followin, as she flicks on an electric light by a switch on the wall that's got wires runnin into it from the ceilin. Rushes straight to a big tin pot and lifts the lid, and there's what's left of chipped ice-wedges and a paper box, which she retrieves and opens.

"Soft," says she, "but not *so* melted. Like some ice cream?"

There's a spoon on a linen napkin on her dressing table with its big mirror and its this'n'thats for makin up, and we sit on a narrow bed, and she spoons out soft ice cream and feeds it to me like I'm a kid, while I'm watchin us in the mirror, me and Miss Mabel Normand, sippin vanilla with a shared spoon. Then she springs up to tamp down her little stove, throws ice-chips on the flames, which hiss and steam as kerosene-stink fills the room—all the while tellin me it's the only stove at the Keystone, and Mr. Walker is the only one cept her with a key to her room, and chilly mornins he lights her fire early so's the room's cozy when she gets in. But with all the delay and commotion that mornin, the room had got hot. Also, Mr. Walker fills her tin with chipped ice and an ice cream box from Greenberg's across the street. That's her breakfast, "with an apricot brandy chaser. Want some?"

"Thank you, no."

She has some while I stare at her things.

On a night-stand there's a painted plaster statue of a woman in a blue shawl with her bare foot steppin on a snake. And, in front of the woman, a small red glass candle holder.

Daddy hated Catholics almost like he hated Jews, but you can't help but know the look of their Holy Mother Virgin Mary. Miss Mabel's watching me study it, smilin a little.

"You're a watcher," says she. "You watch things hard. That's important for an actress, watching."

There's books, there's magazines, there's her Mabel-things, there's dresses and hats on hooks on the walls, and make-up stuff on the vanity, and a hair-brush with an engraved looked-like-silver handle, and she lights a gold-tipped cigarette with a tiny wood match from a tiny silver box, and she watches me as I take in her room, about as little as our bedroom at the farm, mine and Fred's, and in a corner, on its own wrought-iron stand, there's a bright globe of the whole world gleamin from the ceiling-light.

Says she, "Ask me anything about geography!"

"Ma'am?"

"Never call me that."

"Miss Mabel, I don't know the first thing to ask."

"Ask me about Tunis."

"I'll bite. So what about it?"

"It's here," and she moves the globe and puts her finger on what even I know is the tippy-top of Africa. "The Jewish girls of Tunis are thought to be beautiful and marriageable only if they are fat and very fat! Big as Roscoe. Three hundred pounds! I don't weigh but a hundred, and you weigh maybe less, so we'd not find husbands were we Jewish in Tunis. How's that?"

Ok, this alarmed me. Not Jewish girls in Tunis, but that we were speakin of them, or she was.

"It was all in last month's *National Geographic* magazine, that's sitting right over there too close to the stove. Too close! Those fat girls could light this whole place up."

She bends to pick up the magazine and reads me about the dress-up costumes of those Jewish Tunis gals, satin breeches, pink silk jackets embroidered in gold thread, tall sugar-loaf caps, *"and,"* she reads, *"curious slippers ending under the instep."*

She got the biggest kick out of it.

"I'd hate to be so large," says she, "but, oh, to wear such clothes!"

She showed me the photograph. Not an illustration, a photograph. A huge pillow'y gal, so big I wondered could she walk.

Says Miss Mabel, "Ask me something else."

"Miss Mabel..."

"You just jumped off a roof."

"Yes."

"Ever do it before?"

"Nope."

"You like to read?"

"Billboards. Street signs. Illustrateds."

"Don't blame you. I am reading *The Psychopathology of Everyday Life* by Professor Sigmund Freud of Vienna, who uses words that aren't in my dictionary, and the little I can understand is scaring the daylights outa me."

She didn't say anythin funny but she's laughing like what Somerset said she was: an angel.

Then suddenly she changes. Says, "Now look, you. Up there on that roof, those moments before you leapt, you were thinking hard and fast—I saw you thinking. You gotta think every time. I've gotten hurt when I've been sloppy or distracted. Think hard, and don't let any of them think for you. They'll get you killed."

She crushed her cigarette out in a dish and lit another.

"His nibs, Mr. Mack Sennett, master of all he surveys, he wanted to put a star on my door here. I wouldn't let him. I need to know every time I take a pratfall or dive off a cliff that I'm a human person in a human body that breaks same as anybody's. Watch people like Hank and Roscoe and Charlie when they seem so uncontrolled as they perform—and watch me. Watch us hard, cause we're thinking all the while that camera grinds. You're feeling chipper now, but you'll not feel so chipper the first time it goes wrong."

Grinds. Now I knew what that camera reminds me of. A coffee-grinder. Same kinda handle, and a similar box.

She looked at me hard before she spoke again. "Just… Go into this with your eyes open or it will break your heart. It'll break your heart anyway, but if you don't stay wide awake it'll break even the broken pieces."

"Miss Mabel?"

"Shoot."

"You're not *so* older than me, are you? I don't mean to disrespect."

"I've been in front of a camera damn-to-near every day since the beginning of 1910. I'm a hundred years older than you. Otherwise, I'm 19. Twenty in November."

If I keep at this will I be a hundred years older than Fred?

"Fifteen when you started?"

"I was earning my own living at thirteen."

"I've been a farmhand dawn to dusk since age nine."

"There's a new gal here, Haver, Phyllis Haver. Looks 22. Fifteen. Don't tell Mack. Now me, I didn't start on the stage or in the circus, like most around here. Learned in front of the camera and learned from the camera, like you'll have to."

"I read how you were raised in a convent."

"So I was. And I came from a big Southern plantation family—near Atlanta—and you should have seen my gown at our Southern belle balls! I was an orphan slaving in a Chicago sweatshop wishing I had kin. And my sisters and I mended nets in our Maine fishing town where my father and brothers drowned in that terrible, terrible storm. I tell reporters whatever pops into my noggin. They know it's malarkey but they don't care, just so's it's a good story."

She lets cigarette smoke curl out of her mouth slow and even.

"My mother had eight children. I watched three of us die before I was eleven. One of the pox, one of pneumonia, and one of 'general weakness,' saith the doctor. That's something I shall never tell reporters. And why am I telling you?" She gave me a hard look, just a sec, then, all friendly, "So ask about the commerce of Tunisia!"

"I'd hafta pretend to ask, if you get me, and I don't wanna."

"Good for you," says she. Goes to a steamer chest that's standin tall as us near the door, and as she opens the steamer she motions me to her. In the chest are stacked draws, and hangers for clothes, and rows of shoes. We're pickin amongst those when she kicks off hers, rolls off her stockings, flutters em like banners, watches em fall. Then, bright as bright, says Miss Mabel, "Let's compare toes!"

On the divan, in the quiet of night, I stretch out my legs and stare at my feet. I blow smoke on em and wiggle my toes—Miss Mabel liked mine better than hers and I liked hers better, though really there wasn't much difference. There's a fullness here, just me on the divan . . . a fullness.

Anyway, it was Miss Mabel's shoes that made the trouble—the trouble I had on my first for-real flicker jump. I'da been fine barefoot.

Never told her, naturally, she bein so good to me. And didn't she come to watch my first "shoot"?

I was tickled she did so, but Mr. Sennett was none too pleased. "Haven't you got scenes to shoot, Miss 19-Year-Old Director?"

"Thought I'd watch the Master first and learn oh-so-much and be oh-so-impressed."

My costume was not much more than a sweet cotton dress, billowy at the shoulders and all down the chest—which I liked, as it concealed my flatness—then thin at the waist and billowin out again to flutter pretty as I ran. Also, it hid my blade-rig good. Of course, I wore a pair of Miss Mabel's shoes, white, with dark laces and wedge heels and soles of leather.

Nobody told me the flicker's entire story, cept I was to hold this pillowcase full of paper money and run. Where I'd run was the excitement.

The Keystone's sheds were made any old way, as I've said, cheap lumber slapped together, one shed leanin toward another as they settled. I was to run across three flat rooftops, and the Kops were to chase, and Roscoe was to chase the Kops, me runnin deer-like and all-out while the Kops did their falls and antics behind me with Roscoe doin his stuff behind them—a camera on the ground to the side of the sheds would follow us all in one "take," as they'd say. The three sheds we was runnin over were a yard or more apart, and that would take some jumpin, and they weren't the same height, and that would take what it took, and then I reach an edge where there's nowhere left to run and I do my leap, dropping the pillow case as I go, comin down on Pasha who's costumed like a Dago vender, his cart full of bananas that had their stems clipped close. Roscoe clipped them carefully himself. Mr. Sennett stuck a separate camera on the ground behind Pasha's cart, so's to shoot the leap as I hurtled down without interruptin the biz with a new take.

"We gotta get this action the first time," says he, and it's cause the Kops followin me, they tumble off the roof, hopefully safely, landin in mud still thick from the rains and made muddier with buckets from the well. Mr. Sennett wanted it "the first time" cause if we had to do it again the Kops would have to change into fresh uniforms and "that would take forever."

To "top" these "gags," Roscoe would sail off the roof onto the banana-vender's cart. He was not pleased at this arrangement, going on about how the "bits" weren't enough "worked out," and how we ought to spend the day doin that.

"Nawp," says Mr. Sennett, meaning 'nope,' and he spits a tobacco wad brown as the mud. "Might could be more rain. Lost two days to this rain already, and with everybody on salary."

He was right about rain comin. I could smell it. But I'm too nervous to add my two cents.

Roscoe goes to the vender's cart, examines it, gives it some strong shakes, kinda arranges the bananas, makes sure he clipped all the stems, looks to the edge of the roof, looks to the cart, tells Pasha to make sure the cart stays just where it is.

"Ready as I'm gonna be," Roscoe says, with that little-boy smile, when just now he'd been grumpy. Movies change mood faster than you finger-snap.

"Catch," says Mr. Sennett , "don't look straight at the camera. Avert your face."

"In the air. Sure thing."

Miss Mabel laughed.

Mr. Sennett smiled. "Guess you'll do."

Miss Mabel says, "Someone get a ladder! Catch, go up there and make the run to the edge now, so you can time your jump."

"Who's directing this biz?" Mr. Sennett inquires.

"A great and noble man, that's who," grins Miss Mabel.

"Boys, do what she says." But he didn't have to say that. They were already leanin a ladder on the shed. I'm up it like a monkey, steppin on the roof, and right away I see trouble.

As we'd gathered for the work and the Boss explained the biz, I asked no one in particular why these sheds were so "damned" rickety (rememberin Miss Mabel's desire that females curse). Hank Mann, he says, "'Cuz no one knows week to week if we'll still be in business," and everybody laughs, Mr. Sennett the most, and he says, "Not quite time yet to build for permanent. Soon, maybe."

Well, I take a light run for practice down the roof to the edge and I feel under my feet how it ain't built even. They've covered it with tar-paper, which is still rain-wet, and there's puddles where the roof dips. Miss Mabel's leather soles, they slip. Runnin light like I am is alright. Runnin full out, like I will be, that's a whole different trick.

Course, I say nothin. Don't want to seem a shirker or, as Miss Mabel would say, a chickenshit. Still, Mr. Roscoe Arbuckle had his point.

Suddenly I'm weak as a kitten. Had to take some deep breaths, but sneaky-like, so they don't notice I'm takin deep breaths. Breathe into my stomach, not into my chest.

I'm down the ladder with my best carefree smile.

Sommie's there.

Says I, "You thought this up?"

"Enthusiastically. Something just a bit grand, so you'll impress. I've every faith."

As I'm walking away—cause Mr. Sennett yelled, "Positions!"—Sommie says to Miss Mabel, "Young she is, and crude, but she's the right sort."

What's he doin bein proud of me?!

So now the Kops and Roscoe and me are poised on a shed-roof to begin our run across the next three roofs. Me, I'm lookin hard at where the puddles are. That must be what Miss Mabel means by "thinkin."

No audience this day. Everybody else is workin. And we're workin. I'm workin. A job of work, as Daddy would say—my first off the farm. Takin our positions I'd asked Roscoe what happens after this biz. Kindly and patiently he explains to me, "You're Minta. She's dressed the same. Next scene is the Kops splashing around in the mud, greedy for the paper money that's all scattered, while Minta and me splash off through more mud and, all splattered-like, we catch a streetcar to get away. What happens before all this, I have no idea, but by tomorrow they'll figure it out." And he grins as only Mr. Roscoe Arbuckle grins, like he's grinnin with his whole big body. Under that smile he's not grumpy like he was, and he's not worried. I see he's concentrated on what comes next—on his job. I'm seein that and it's helpin me, and just then two fiddlers, a man and a gal—where they came from, I didn't see—start to fiddlin a ho-down and Mr. Sennett yells, "Grind that camera! Make with the funny business, kids. Action."

Off I go, a jump of just two feet'ish, to the next shed, careful of the puddle by its edge, and I'm runnin, holdin my sack, and it's like this:

There's no sky above me, no world around me, no buildings, no trees, I've got eyes for nothin but where my feet'll be in about three strides, and there's a thrillness in my legs and the fun of the dress billowin, and Kop commotion behind me of pratfalls and yells, and fiddlin in my ears, furiouser and furiouser, and I'm a deer leapin onto the next shed which is just about a yard of a leap but that shed's maybe a foot higher and its flat roof angled a little down a ways so I don't see the puddle I land on and my feets go out from under me in a swoop and the dress is over my head and thank the Lord for petticoats! I'm rollin forward with the fall cause I know those Kops are close behind and they ain't stoppin, and I'm losin paper dollars from my sack—and I'm havin this thought, fast as fast and clear as clear: it's good the sack spilled, the Kops'll make an antic of that—and I don't even know I'm up and runnin again until I am, and I'm thinkin, I'm thinkin, like she said to, lookin hard ahead, and the jump to the next roof was perfect and then… I kinda sledded. Really enjoyed it. Like a skid, those leather soles on that wet tarpaper could skid good, me balanced like on skates, and I'm off to the last roof gallopin toward that edge where I'm to make my leap and I'm aimin for the spot but my balance totters as I hit just the very edge of a puddle and the foot on that puddle wants to slide some other way—later they complimented how I did good biz with that totter, but I was shy of takin credit cause inside that totter was one slow instant where I thought I'd tumble off the edge of the roof onto my head—surprised me later to see it on the screen, cause my body did a kind of dance that looked out of control but in control too, and I righted me, kinda tiltin into my run, and hesitated not a jot at the roof-edge and I'm off in the air headin up into my sky—and rememberin to drop the pillow sack straight down like I'd been told.

Before the jump there's Willie and after the jump there's Willie, but in the air there's somethin that's my own as nothin was ever my own.

Then gravity remembers me and I sail on down.

Pasha caught me sweet as anythin. Not til after he gets me firm does he let his legs slide in the mud and fall, me atop him on my back, concentratin on holdin my legs pointed high up so's not to muddy my Mabel-shoes—got a laugh when they screened it, but wasn't intendin fun, just scared like crazy of muddyin those shoes in front of Miss Mabel.

I'm glad I'm facin up cause I got to see a rain of Kops a'flailin arms and comin down and heard their splashes and grunts and one "Oh shit" of pain, and then there's Roscoe in the air like a great balloon.

Looks like he's comin down on me and Pasha!

But no, he comes down on the cart, and I see why it was bananas, and why he'd clipped their stems himself. It was like he landed on a cushion, banana-meat squirting every which way and all over me, and the cart collapses under him, and he doesn't take a breath but that he grabs a glob of banana, stuffs it in his mouth, gulps it, grins straight at the camera, then he's up and splashin through mud toward me who will soon be Minta herself, when they do the next take, her on Pasha's stomach in the position I'm in, and then away those two will run.

"Cut!" yells Mr. Sennett. "Well done. Good fun."

The fiddlin stops and Miss Mabel's pullin me up by my hands to plant a big wet smacky smooch on my mouth—and I guess that's three Keystone gals I've kissed!

"Napoleon," says she, "we'll not worry about this young one."

"I think I broke my wrist," says one pained Kop. "Sorry, Mr. Sennett."

"Tend that man!" Sennett barks. "See he gets all he needs."

Wish I'd said something like, "Got another jump for me today, Boss?" But my heart was beating like as to break through my billows and it was all I could do not to cry for happiness.

I'll tell you, a body is a funny thing to walk around in. It needs this and that. Folks have opinions about it this way and that way, and so do you. You got to go here and there, depending on what the body you're inside of looks like and needs and desires. Meanwhile, you're you, and you're different from your body, but you're not either, cause it's you. Uh-oh. My mind's much too excited.

2

ABOUT A MONTH AFTER MY FIRST LEAP we had to be at the Keystone before dawn and it was all my fault.

Days before, "the boys," as Miss Mabel calls em, they came up with a biz that scared me plenty and I couldn't wait to do it: I was to hang off a car that's hangin off a cliff.

But they chickened, decidin it's too rough. They'll use dummies, they decided. The car'll go backwards over the cliff, hangin on wires that the camera won't pick up, and the villain-dummies'll fall to the beach far below, while the me-dummy's rigged so it's hangin from the windshield. They're figurin how to rescue my dummy while I'm wantin to tell the "fellers," as Miss Mabel calls em, that *they're* dummies—but it was Mr. Mack Sennett and Mr. Coy Watson, and you don't speak like that to them unless you're Miss Mabel Normand. Mr. Watson, he could rig some dandy biz—and Brick was there, too, chippin in. Me, I'm just a girl jumper with no say, cept I did say.

Interruptin, but with a smile, Mabel-style, I says, "Tell you what a dummy can't do. A dummy can't hang from the car, climb into the driver's seat, make like to drive the car straight up the cliff, while you 'fine fellows'"—that was Miss Mabel's phrase I stole—"are pullin it up by the wires, and there's a camera at the cliff's top shootin down, keepin the wires out of the shot, so it looks really like I'm drivin straight up the cliff and the camera sees me and the beach far below me. Then you get a close-shot of smilin me as the car drives up over the cliff-edge, safe and sound."

Well, if it had been just us, and not so much racket in the Ghost Building of everybody shootin flickers all round us—if it had been, like I say, just us, you coulda heard a pin drop.

Mr. Sennett takes off his tight-weaved straw skimmer hat, scratches his head, spits a brown wad five feet, looks at me, puts his skimmer back on his head, tugs it down tight.

"You'd do that?" says he.

I just grinned.

Mr. Coy Watson, he's a sharp, wiry, bright-eyed man, and he'd figured careful what piano wires could hold, and how many it took to hold what, and how to knot em so's they wouldn't snap. Tied every knot himself. Wouldn't let nobody else near his wires. Amazing, the biz he could finagle with piano wire.

He was a man folks listened to. Never said he could do what he couldn't do.

Mr. Sennett's looking at Mr. Coy Watson. Brick, he's shakin his head, shiftin his weight foot to foot.

Says Mr. Watson, "We could rig it, Boss. Weld handles all over the back and front seats, so's she's got plenty to grab on. Place em so's the camera won't pick em up. Two cameras. One on the jutting outcrop, there"—he's squattin down, running his finger in sawdust, drawin—"shooting like we would with the dummy. Second camera shoots down from the cliff as we haul up the car, getting the downward shot and the close shot in one take. That car, I've strengthened every weld on it that matters. I figure three sets of wires pulled by a winch on the heavy truck. Two sets'd hold her, but we'll use three. We could do it."

"Two cameras, hey?" says Mr. Sennett. "So it's one on the jut, there," he nudges the sawdust sketch with his shoe, "and one for the downward shot and the close shot?"

"Cept," says Brick, who I see hates all this, "we can't do the close shot that way. Willie"—Brick don't call me Catch—"she's doublin for a twelve year old. Does Willie look twelve to you?"

"Fair point," chimes in Mr. Watson.

"I," says I, "I keep my face tight scrunched, like this"—and I show em—"on the downshot. At the cliff top we stop, I leap out, she climbs in, keeps her expression crunched the same, *then* smiles big as you do the close shot. But Mr. Sennett, fair's fair—that's an extra ten bucks my way, seems to me."

"Make it twenty," says the skinflint. "Damnation, make it fifty. Cause when Mabel hears about this she's gonna kill me, and you getting fifty just might mollify her enough to but half kill me. Anyway, you thought of it— that's called *writing* in this game and I pay for it."

He steps back. Looks me up and down. "You've been paying attention to how we do, Miss Catch." He looks to Mr. Watson. "She's sharp as a tack."

Oh I wish Miss Mabel had been there.

"Suppose next you'll want to direct," Mr. Sennett says.

"Not me. Not ever. I's a satisfied girl."

"Then you're the first. Watson, we'll have to push back the shoot a couple'a days, to give you proper time—more damn money—but…" I'm no longer listenin.

I'm all tingly-nervy. It's dangerouser than anything they'd yet cooked up for me. Mr. Sennett, I saw he respected that. I never had no full-grown man show me that kind of respect.

So it's decided, and I'm lookin to find D'Varn so as to brag, but Brick, he pulls me aside, angry—hurt-angry. Says, "Why ain't you scared'a this? *I'm* scared of it, but not you. It ain't natural."

Daddy'd say those very words. "You ain't natural." Say it angry or exasperated or sad even, and I hated it. Now it's Brick. He sees I'm bristlin. Then my eyes betray me, tearin.

"What's wrong?" says he.

"Like me as I am, mister, or not at all."

And I huff off.

I was full as scared as Brick wanted me to be when I had time to think about it. Scared's OK, if you're scared only in your eyes, so long as your body's not scared. Tingly—your body needs to be tingly, but not scared.

Had to be at the Keystone fore dawn—me, D'Varn and Esther—so's to have all mornin at the Palisades to shoot in west-pointin sun, then all afternoon shootin the cliff shots in east-pointin sun. D'Varn, she had a part in the flicker. Es, she'd drive one'a the cars—Es and Miss Mabel bein not just the only Keystone females who could drive, but two of the only Keystone drivers period.

Naturally, I couldn't sleep the night before. I'm sittin and smokin and dozin and smokin more. Dozed smokin once—burned a pillow cover, but the smell woke me in time to snuff it. Kept the biz from my mind—once you know what you'll do you mustn't "think it to shreds" was Miss Mabel's counsel. And I was antsy about waking D'Varn. That woman don't like to open her eyes. When it came my time to wake her, she was a study—cursin, kickin at things and rantin how I was some kinda beastie, pretty to look at but in need of a muzzle. "Two muzzles! Your muzzle needs a muzzle."

"Yes, Ma'am," says I.

"Cigarette!" she barks.

I scramble like a coolie to find and light one and stick it tween her lips. She takes a furious puff, coughs, puffs, and coughs more. Rises from that bed like Venus on the half-shell, which now there's a print of, framed, on the bedroom wall, a present from her banker who's named Billy.

Says she, "Shoulda left ya on the street where I found ya."

"Watch them slurs, auntie, they ain't sophisticated."

"I'll sophisticate you, Miss Snotnose," and she aims a kick that I dodge slick as you please. "This is all your fault."

"I know," says me all proud. "Now give us a mornin kiss."

"It ain't mornin. It—is—not—morning. It's the goddamn middle of the night."

"Come on, you. Give a slut a kiss. You stay grouchy and it'll make you— how you say it?—'wrinkle prematurely.'"

Says she, "It's you that's the devil, not Charlie."

Suddenly she's kissin me like it's the last kiss of all. She steps back surprised, like she did sometimes. Our kisses were full of surprises.

"That's all you're good for," says she, soft and sulky. "Too damned good."

"You wait till I'm sophisticated someday, then just see."

"That'll never happen." And she's all love-eyes.

You love D'Varn like lovin a storm or a proud horse or a tiny bird or the lady in tights on the flying trapeze or that iris flower we'd seen be proud and alone in the rain, she was all of that to me. You could make a list long as your arm as to what she's like, and you could tell er, and she'd say, "Go fly a kite."

"What was you just thinkin?" says she. "What—were—you—think-ing."

"Your right grammar will come back once you're coffee'd up proper and full awake."

"Don't evade me."

"Was thinkin how even naked you move like you're wearin a great long cape—and it swirls as you move."

"Humph," she humphs, but pleased. "Don't imagine that buys you forgiveness for this wretched wakefulness at this miserable hour."

But she's got her pronunciation back and she paces up and down swingin her invisible cape, feelin it, bein the actress. Then she pouts.

"I don't wanna," says she.

"Don't you? With the good role they give you, Miss Actress?"

"Gotta fall off a motorcycle, thanks to you. Damn it, Willie, I'm not a comedienne."

"'Play it straight,' like Miss Mabel says—the biz'll do the funny for you."

"Look who knows so much." She tears up. "I'm afraid. Happy now, are you? I'm scared of that damned motorcycle. What if I hurt my face, what if I get a scar?"

"What if you break your neck?" was my contribution.

"Well, girlie," says she, "today you're gonna see some great acting. I'm going to act like I'm not scared."

"Don't you always?" says me.

She smiles just a little. "How come I can't stay pissed at you? I must be weak-minded."

"That must be why," says me.

She comes to me and cups my face and kisses me tired-like.

"Always you make me happy," I tell her, "just bein near you. You know you do."

"Now who's weak-minded?" Then she says, starin off like she does, "We count our 'always' in weeks, don't we? In days." Then she snaps her head toward me. "I intend to stay pissed at you today. It's a matter of principle."

See, D'Varn wasn't only her name, it was a tight garment she had to wriggle herself into and out of. D'Varn is what she'd set herself to be, and she was too stubborn to quit it, so every day she found her nerve and D'Varn'd herself up to a faretheewell.

Dressed and ready in the chilly dark, warm in our mouths from the coffee made special for us in Hotel Hollywood's kitchen, we waited on the wide front steps for the studio car, us and Es. Es looked rugged in her long fur-trapper's coat that hung open and swayed when she moved, and her floppy wide hat, and a revolver stuck in her belt. The cowboy kind, a .45, long-barreled.

Me, I'm wrapped warm in my bright blue shawl but my legs are goose-bump cold under my dress and my hair falls loose beneath a bonnet.

D'Varn's pacin and lightin the next cigarette off the glow of the last, scowlin under the pulled-down brim of a red velvety fedora.

As for Es, she importantly checks her pistol for the second time.

"Still got the same six bullets like the last time you checked?" snaps D'Varn, puffin away.

"Eight. It's a Special."

"I can think of at least eight people worth shooting this morning. You shoot them and our divine Willie can stab them. I call that a picnic. Christ, the company I keep."

"Anybody needs killing," says Esther, "it'll have to be Willie or me that kills them. You can't even step on a bug."

"In these shoes? Damn right. But you," she points her cigarette at me, "you'd step on a bug with your bare foot."

"Would and have," says me.

"You people!" says she. "I could throw up."

There's no one speakin on Hollywood Boulevard but us, no one smokin, and no one pretty. From the east there's the smooth chug-a-chug of an engine and we look and it's a fine little open-air motor-car with bright headlamps, Mr. Coy Watson at the wheel, a cigarette danglin from his lips.

He stops before us, flicks the cigarette into the street, tips his cap and says, "Ladies."

"Mr. Watson," says I.

"You," D'Varn means me, "sit in front. That way all I'll see of you is the back of your bonnet. And did I neglect to mention it's a *silly* bonnet?"

Me, I'm actin like ridin in a motor-car is proper and normal though I never had done so. I was plain thrilled. We'd been goin to the Keystone on the Big Red streetcar—we called em that cause they were big and red—and even when we shot a flicker near the Keystone down at Echo Park Lake we'd most often all pile into a Big Red, camera, Kops, prop-box, the whole crew, which thrilled the "civilians," as Mr. Sennett called everybody who did anything normal in life. Now here I am in this vehicle.

"Nice motor-car, Mr. Watson."

"Like it, Miss Catch? Brand new 1914 4-cylinder Studebaker. She'll reach 40 miles an hour, and hold it, even up a grade."

"How steep a grade?"

"Easy-steep, if you get me." He grinned.

He'd turned around in a neat half circle—called it a "U-turn"—and we're headin east.

I decided right away I enjoy motor-cars. The leather smelt fresh and that seat just kinda fit my frame, and the engine-purr, and the breeze, and the heavy oil smells, and the vibration that was smooth and dependable, well, it all made you feel important-like, specially bein the only car in sight, with its two big round electric lamps up front blazin through the dark.

D'Varn was bent on spoilin it. "What kind of a name is Coy, Coy?"

"Family name." He said it like that was all there was to it and no more askin, thank you kindly. "What kinda name's D'Varn?"

"A memorable name."

"Big day, Miss Catch," says he, brushin her off. "You got me earning my wage for sure this day."

He flashes me a frank smile. Mr. Coy Watson was proud of what he'd figured for my biz, proud it impressed Mr. Sennett and humbled Brick, who looked up to Mr. Watson, though they were about the same age. I think it was that Mr. Coy Watson had a wife, and a house full of kids, and walked and talked like he had a place of his own in this world, while Brick, well, did not.

"Coy?" says D'Varn, up to somethin. "What do you think of Brick directing this biz today, I wonder?"

"I think only of my job, Ma'am." Oh that *Ma'am* would needle her. "Brick'll do his job right regular."

I notice he too has a pistol. The handle of a revolver sticks out of his right pants pocket.

We're goin easy as you please on the hard-packed ground of Hollywood Boulevard, east from the hotel at Highland Avenue, and there's houses of the rich set back from the street behind curved driveways lined with palm-trees high as high, and all about there's orange groves and strawberry fields, and it's like we're a ball of oily and leathery smells rollin through heady fragrance risin off the ground and hangin from the branches. At Cahuenga there's a few small stores for sundries. Then there's Vine, a dirt road flanked by—by pepper trees, I think they're called; and down that road was the barn and grounds where Mr. Cecil B. DeMille shot *The Squaw Man* that we'd just seen in a theatre, and it was oh so many reels long and run over an hour—it was supposed to be serious but we laughed like it was a Keystone, it was that silly—cept for the ending when the Injun gal lost her half-breed kid to rich folks. That riled me, a child taken from its mother.

Now we drove on into the dark, past more fields and houses, through many fragrances, and the smell of dawn coming (dawn does have a smell, at least it does if you're me), us four people with two pistols and at least one knife in a motor-car, with a day ahead of us that was happenin cause'a somethin that popped outa my very own mind, me snuggled in my shawl and enjoyin the chill on my legs, certain-sure that we all four felt the fun of it, even she who'd sooner spit than admit it.

We stopped but once. Grumbles from the back seat as Mr. Watson points to our left. Night's lifted just enough to see what his sharp eyes seen to the side of his beams: a mama-possum lumberin toward the middle of the street, and on her back are four tiny possum babies, and one was all white and surely blind and I knew it would soon die. The mama-possum would know that, too, but she'd carry it and feed it best she could regardless.

Our back-seaters craned over the front seat to see.

"Wouldn't want to scare her," says Mr. Watson.

Says I, "Nobody with sense bothers a mama-possum."

"Know that, do you?"

"Fret her babies, she'll eat your hand off."

"Guess we're safe enough in the car."

He's grinnin.

We watched the possum family, the fur of that poor albino baby shiny white under Mr. Watson's headlamps. The mama shuffles back and forth slow-paced across the road.

D'Varn lights a cigarette and lets the match burn down before she blows it out. Says, "My mother had nothing in common with that possum."

It wasn't like D'Varn to say such. If there's one thing us Keystone movies had in common, it was bein mostly mum about our families and the past— the exception bein Mr. Sennett, who'd talk proud about his mother, and Miss Mabel, who'd smile sweet and lie her head off. Seemed only Mr. Coy Watson had a family to be proud of.

Driving through the Keystone gate as the sky took a little light, there was Mr. Walker, bright-eyed, grinnin and tippin his cap "right regular," as Mr. Watson would say. I never saw a person so satisfied as Mr. Walker with life just as it was, ceptin, again, Mr. Coy Watson—and, at the moment, me.

Oh, there was a grandness to this day. Lined up in the lot, shiny and ready, were several motor-cars and a flat-bed truck. Mr. Watson jumps out of his car without openin his door, rushes to my side, and grandly opens that door for me. Then he's off, without similar attentions to D'Varn and Esther. Esther smiles at D'Varn's scowl.

Groggy folks stir about, but Brick strides up not a bit groggy and waits while Es and D'Varn open their doors and step off the runnin-board. Brick plants himself, pushes his cap up with his forefinger like he does—that beat-up cloth cap with the stiff brim, a cap that once was maybe beige but now was the color of the earth, perched atop Brick's red hair.

He looks us up and down, like we was horses he was buyin. "Mornin, ladies."

D'Varn looks him up and down back. "Well I'll be go-to-hell—that's a director's look you threw us, mister. You come by that honestly or copy it?"

"Bit of both," Brick grins goofy, cause he can't help that, it's how he grins. Lights a cigarette.

"And that's a tailor-made you're smoking, sir," says D'Varn. "Not rolling your own on your big day?"

"Won't be time to pause for that, I figure."

"Lest your fingers tremble?" says she.

"Now you mention it, that would be embarrassing," and he grins more, and she's irked that he's not irked.

He turns to go, stops, like he's just remembered somethin. "And, uh, Miss D'Varn, Hank'll be driving you to Santa Monica in that kettle"—kettle is the side-car of the motorcycle—"so's you can get good'n'used to it."

"Is that an order from my director?"

"You betchya. Believe it or not, it's for your own good."

"You!" She's turned on me. "You're gonna pay."

"Got a cigarette?" I say.

She fishes one up.

"Got a light?"

She strikes a light and fires me up as she says, "I'm only being this nice so I won't feel guilty when you fall off that cliff."

I take a nice drag, time it like she would, then says I, "I love you."

"You are a pill."

Then I'm off, cause I got somethin to see.

It's a two-seater open "touring car," as they call it, and by now I know its every inch. I'd watched Mr. Watson blacksmith grab-handles on the insides of the doors and through the floorboards on the frame. He'd drilled through the cushions to fasten em on the seats. And on the back of the front seat he'd put three handles, at different angles. Like I'd seen Roscoe inspect that cart and clip off banana stems himself, I'd climbed all over that car every which way when Mr. Watson was done with his fastenin. I'd reach for this handle and that, from every angle, and tug with all my might. Mr. Watson, he got the idea of riggin a hoist with a winch so's the car stood straight off the ground, hangin by piano wires, and I'd climbed all over it as it hung. Didn't want no surprises when me and that machine was hangin off a cliff, and neither did he. He watched a while, then gave me two more handles—one on the dashboard (he didn't know, either, why they call it a "dashboard") and one on the steerin column behind the driver's wheel.

"That should do er," says he.

Hangin on that car I came up with one especially nifty piece of biz, which I intended to keep to myself and spring on em, but Mr. Watson seen.

"Sure you wanna do that, Miss Catch?"

"Any suggestions?" says me.

"Pray a wind don't gust up."

So now that car gets loaded with cameras and prop boxes and film canisters and Mr. Watson's gonna drive er. I see he's watchin to make sure the equipment don't mess in no way with my handles. I sure liked how he managed his work.

"Safe as houses, is it?" That was Sommie, bleary with drink.

He puffs his pipe, shakes his head, smiles weary.

I see in his eyes that he's worried for me. Touched my heart, it did. Then it hits me that D'Varn's not angry at me and not so scared for herself, she's terrified of what I'm up to. Gee.

"What?" says Sommie.

"I can do it, Sommie. Honest."

"My dear, you are a born chancer. The question is, can I bear to watch?"

"OK with me if you close your eyes."

"Dare say I could, but I shan't. How else to stand by you but to watch? One must stand by one's own."

"I preciate that," says I, curtsey to him.

Brick's voice of command rings out. "Willie! Get in costume! Double-quick!"

"Well, now, you," says Sommie. "Go to."

Esther tells me, "Being late is for prima donnas, Catch—and we've got one of those in the family already."

"Sorry, Es. Excited, I guess."

"Think today you're a big shot?"

"Excited, is all."

We had the dressing room to ourselves. Minta and D'Varn had changed and gone.

It was D'Varn's notion that I need a dresser and for Es to be that dresser. I'd kept insistin on my privacy and my screen, and Mr. Sennett let me get away with that, and, as per D'Varn's plan, I insisted on a dresser, too, sayin this farm girl had trouble figurin fancy clothing proper, even with a mirror. Mr. Sennett said fine, so long's I paid my dresser outa my wages. I paid a dollar a day for my "fittings" (that's a D'Varn word). Es didn't need my money but I paid her anyhow cause I told Mr. Sennett I would. Only needed a dresser twice or thrice a day, which didn't take much away from what-all else Big Es did at the Keystone.

How this dresser business come about was queer as queer.

One night it's the three of us in the sittin room, smokin and drinkin, with D'Varn goin on about this and that, with Es and me her audience, so to speak, and I see D'Varn's got somethin up her sleeve, and finally she springs it.

"Esther"—that was serious, when D'Varn called her Esther—"need you to do something for me."

"I'd do anything for you."

"Be Willie's dresser."

"Be which?"

"Her factotum. Valet. At the Keystone. She needs one. You realize that, right? Willie here, she jumps off buildings and smooches her twin sister—yeah, missy, I told Es the day you told me—and Willie pulls her little knife now and again—but she's susceptible to impulse and suggestion, if you get me."

"Am not," says me.

"Are too. And she"—

"What's this 'she' stuff. I'm right here."

—"*she* doesn't think about what *she'll* do till after *she's* done it. *She* needs a keeper. Or we'll lose her."

"And that," Es says, "would just break my heart, wouldn't it?"

"Break mine," says D'Varn. There hung a quiet moment while that sunk in. "Break my heart to lose either one of you."

"Until you're ready to lose us." That was Es.

Which caused more quiet.

After which D'Varn pressed on.

"You understand, Es, even if missy here doesn't or won't. Thinks she can get away with anything. Well," she turns on me, "you can't. You won't."

Es says, "Everything's changed since she's come. And I hate it."

"But you're in it," D'Varn says.

"Yes, I am."

So it was done and Es was my dresser and we never spoke of that conversation again, none of us, though I wanted dearly to ask Es how, if she hates me, why don't she act like it? Cause, ceptin for wisecracks, and sayin things to prick D'Varn, Esther doesn't hate me a bit.

So here was Es dressin me that chilly morning.

"You don't need a dresser anymore," says Es, quiet.

"I know."

"I know you know."

"You pullin out?"

"Nothing of the kind. I like doing it."

"I hoped you did."

"I do."

"I know you don't hate me."

"Never said I hated you. Kinda hate her."

"You don't really," says me.

"Kinda wish I did."

She rubs a big hand up'n'down my flank. Course, I like that. She'd taken to doin that. I liked that without thinkin about likin it.

She's smilin, glinty-eyed.

"Can't figure me at all, can you, Catch?"

"Not much."

"Neither can our D'Varn, though we won't tell her so." Her palm's up'n'down my thigh. "Know when I knew I might trust you, Snatch? When you pulled that knife on me."

Then she does something she ain't done. She starts to roll my tightie-rig panty, roll it fold over fold, down so's I got to press my thighs together.

"You mind?" says she.

"Kinda don't. Kinda do."

"I just want to see," says she.

"Then do so."

She rolled till my pantie-rig fell to my ankles. I'm shiverin.

She's lookin me up'n'down, smilin slow, then cups my face with her big hands. I thought maybe she'd kiss me again. I wouldn'ta minded. Instead she gave my face two little slaps, one to a cheek.

Drops her hands and looks at me more. Says, "You don't have body-hair anywhere, it's the damnedest thing."

"Jus fuzz."

"D'Varn never talks about how you've got a dick. Not to me, except when she told me. I'll bet not to you either."

"Nope. She don't."

"That's a cute dick, Willie. No hair, like a child's. Does she let you screw her?"

"No!"

"Do you want to?"

"*No.* And no again. I'm—not—a boy. Boy-feelins—never had em."

"I can't see you as a boy. You'd make a terrible boy. But that is a fascinating dick, seeing as you're girly. Does it ever get hard? Oh, look, it's doing that somewhat."

"I don't—I don't thrill much that way."

"Does she suck it?"

"Esther!"

"Does she?"

"No." (That was a lie.)

"I would. With *you* I would."

That made me flush all over—and I was all a'sweat already.

"D'Varn," says I, "says she hates suckin." (That wasn't a lie.) "That's for the so-called men, she says." (But she likes it with me sometimes.) "Can we stop talkin about it—please. I hate all the words for it, I don't know why I have it. I could tell the story of my whole life without ever mentionin it. Esther! Stop flippin it!"

She was flippin it with her thumb.

"It's cute," says she.

"Stop!"

She stopped.

Loud knocks on the wood wall! I jumped. Even Esther jumped.

"Will you dames get a move on in there!"

"We dames take our time, and you can lump it, buster." Then Esther's voice gets whispery. "Thanks for showing me. And—I like your dick."

"Thank you."

"On you, it's sorta girlish."

I swear, that's the nicest thing anybody ever said about me.

So now you see why Daddy hated me.

The sky was taking light as Es and I stepped outa the shed. Es adjusted herself, makin certain of her pistol, the Special, prominently stickin from her wide belt beside her shiny brass buckle. And she rolled up her pants and I saw there's a small gun handle stickin out her boot. She checked that, rolled down her pant leg, and off we went, attired proper and well-armed.

"Hey," says she, "you forgot your shawl. It'll be chilly by the sea."

"Wouldn't know. Never seen a sea."

"Never been to the beach? And you the only one of us who's lived all your life in Edendale?"

"The sea's a day's mule-ride west'a here. Hotel Hollywood's as far as I've got to, and not on a mule."

"The Big Red goes to the Venice pier."

"Well, I didn't know."

Went and got the shawl, then we quick-stepped into the commotion.

The Keystone's still buzzin about, readyin. Commotion, activity, all sorta mysterious-like cause it's never happened at this hour.

Brick's standin by the auto we're to ride.

"So, Mr. Brick," I greet him, "why you lookin at me so pained-like?"

"The other day, what I said about objecting to your biz—you didn't like that much."

"Didn't like it at all."

"It's just, Willie, you confuse me. And, well, don't expect me not to speak my mind."

"Don't you expect me to keep my trap shut when I object—you big lug," I smiled.

He smiled back. I swear, that goofy smile under those smart ruffian eyes, how could you help but like the guy?

He opens the door of the wide back seat and doffs his cap, usherin me in.

Folks load autos with stuff and argue serious and in fun about who rides with who, and Brick's off to supervise, and D'Varn's stuffed herself into the kettle side-car of the motorcycle and Hank Mann's on its seat holdin the handlebars and revvin up. I wave at her, she sticks her tongue out at me, I do the same back. Engines are goin, and it's all somehow louder in the liftin dark, and our engine starts up under me and I didn't even see when Esther cranked er and got in, and now Sommie, red-eyed, hatless, the only one on the lot bare-headed, gets in beside her in the front seat and slumps down with, "Dear me, an expedition."

Here comes Minta under a wide feathered hat and carryin a dummy that's her same size wearin the same outfit and hair. Minta's talkin to it.

"Minta, old girl," says she to Dummy, "we'll ride in the lead car with the Di-rector himself." And she gets in on the other side of the back seat sayin to Dummy, "You can sit on my lap, but no funny stuff like these lavender gals."

"I like your friend," says me.

"Sewed her up myself," says Minta, settlin into the seat. "Daddy was a locomotive man, we lived near the rail yard, and cross the street was a cathouse, the girls sitting in their windows with nekkid bosoms shining in the sun. They wore red and violet garments hemmed low to expose their busts, dresses my mother seamstressed and I helped her. I thought those gals were the prettiest."

"You got your dummy weighted right," says Brick, "so's it'll fall like it oughta?"

"Such a question, Minta!" says Minta to Dummy. "As though we don't know our business!"

"I didn't assign you to this car," Brick points out.

"Yet here I am, Mr. Di-rect-or. If you want Catch all to yourself then that's just too bad."

Brick blushed red as his hair and turned his attention elsewhere. "Sommie, you got a gun?"

"I am harmless, and intend to stay so."

Says Esther, "Brick, the way you've been bossing this morning, I figure you've bossed before."

"Some."

"Where?" says Minta.

"Here and there."

"The man doesn't wanna say what the man doesn't wanna say," says she.

I move over and Brick gets in beside me, barkin, "Lead em out, Big Es."

She starts up but Hank Mann zips by on that motorcycle as D'Varn in the kettle shouts at me, "I hate you today!"

The sky's takin more light, the city's shakin off the night, a one-horse milk wagon with its man dressed in white is leavin bottles of milk on porches beside slabs of butter wrapped in waxed paper, and Greenberg's Kosher Bakery wagon leaves loaves and rolls and bagels the same, and there's jinglings of rein-bells and the heavy purr'y vibratin of engines, and the clang of the Big Reds that pass one way and t'other on the tracks, and we're on Sunset Boulevard, called that cause it heads toward the sunset, all the way to the shore, they say, and we're passin that Famous Players-Lasky studio of Mr. DeMille's off Vine, and there's folks linin up outside a gate like they do at the Keystone to be hired if needed, rough types like us, and they hoot and holler when they see Big Esther drivin, cause most ain't seen a woman drive, and they're cat-callin at Brick'n'Sommie as to what kinda men let a woman drive em, and Es pulls her pistol outa her belt and waves it over her head, and Brick says, "Don't fire that thing!" as Es does so.

Time to ask, like I been dyin to, what our armaments is for.

"Edison's thugs," says Brick. "The Patents Trust." He explains how Mr. Thomas Alva Edison himself, who invented flickers, is "aligned," Brick says, with "powerful interests" back East who want to "keep monopoly," Brick says, and have all flicker-makin to themselves. The outfits out here—Keystone, Famous Players, Mr. Griffith's new bunch, and Mr. Ince out on that cowboy ranch—they come for the sun and cause The Patents Trust ain't bought the law hereabouts, we movies bought em first. We're safe enough on our lots cause we hire tough people and there's always guns around. "Send a crew to the outskirts," says Brick, "sometimes there's trouble. So we arm up. Anyway," he grins, "it's kinda fun."

"Minta," says Minta to Dummy, "I owe you an apology. I've not introduced you to our companions. Course, there's not much to say. Three here—Big Es, Sommie and Brick—no one knows where they come from and they ain't about to tell. And Catch has the name of Willie and no other name at all—showed up near-naked out of nowhere. But we're not all so mysterious at the Keystone. Fred Mace, he was a dentist. Hank Mann painted signs on the great buildings of Manhattan. My Roscoe, he's been on his own since age of 12, singing and clowning to earn his honest living. Mabel was a respectable artist's model, advertising Coca Cola no less, earning her own keep since age 13, right as rain. Me, I was up to Frisco, end-girl in the chorus—an end-girl needs her wits about her or that chorus line'll flop across the stage like a soggy strand of spaghetti. End-girl keeps them straight and turns them sharp. There's some here with histories, is all I'm saying, so don't let these shady folk give you a mistaken impression."

"Can I speak to her?" says me. Minta faces the dummy my way. "Sweetie," says me, "we're fixin to throw you off a cliff."

Minta huffs—"in character," so to speak—and turns the dummy from me.

We're west of Hollywood, in the country. Sunset ain't a boulevard here, it's a dirt road, twistin through country too hilly for farms, soft hills, a'plenty with flowers and small trees and, well, just country. We turn then on a road that curves southwest.

Brick's lightin his tailormades one off another.

"Mind if I try one?" says me.

"I'll give you one, sure, but, yeah, I mind."

"Well, pee on it, then."

"Come on, Willie, don't high-hat me. Here."

I take it and he strikes a wood match on his thumbnail and cups the flame and lights me.

"It's just, Willie, there's such a thing as the future."

I inhale contentedly.

"I'm saying," he says, "a woman who smokes, who will marry her?"

Almost ate my cigarette. Minta's laughin and Es whoops.

Says Brick, "Guess I better change the subject."

"Guess you better had," says Minta. "Passing those tailormades around might be a start. And I happen to be a married lady who smokes or a smoking lady who's married, take your pick."

"Willie." Brick's voice is hushed, so everybody's really listenin now.

"That's me," says me.

Gotta admit I liked that he liked me. I'm a greedy little thing.

"It's not comedies I want to make," he's sayin. "One day, and I don't think that day's so far off, I'll make flickers that stand with the working man."

"What about working women?" Esther says from behind the wheel.

"Sure," says he. "I'll be fair. I mean it. Fair to all. And the pay'll be split by everybody even. I mean it. I do."

Oh, brother. Sincere, that's Brick.

"Willie?" says he.

"Still here," says me.

"I know how it is, that lavender stuff, you and D'Varn."

Big Es, she squeezes that rubber bubble that honks the horn. We all jump. It's a loud horn.

"Sorry, folks," says she. "A pigeon on the road."

Brick's tryin to whisper now, cept he's gotta be heard above the engine. I suppose if a man's set on makin a fool of himself there's no stoppin him.

"It's just," he says, and stops. "It's just." Stops again. "It's you ain't been with a man yet. You marry up and be with a man, you'll be fine as anyone."

"Got some gum?" says me.

He flutters some, fishin in his pockets for a Juicy Fruit, sayin, "D'Varn's not a bad person. Just a slut."

Minta liked t'choke.

"Then so am I a slut," says me. "I said so just this mornin. Slut, slut, slut, that's me."

"No, don't say that! I didn't mean such. You're… you're…" Brick sputters out.

"Outa your league?" says Esther at the wheel.

Bless the man, he laughed. "It appears that way, don't it?"

So that's the ocean. I suppose sky is big, cause it's everywhere, but ocean feels bigger than big and deeper than sky is high, heavy too, and it writhes and writhes. Folks down there on the beach, tiny from here, they let it touch em, the ocean's touchin em. I won't, not ever, that huge writhin somethin, not ever gonna touch me.

I'm supposed to be gettin acquainted with this cliff. I've never seen such a cliff. It's ever such a long way down.

I feel eyes on me. Turn. It's Brick walkin toward me.

Stands beside me. Plants himself. Takes a breath. "Here's a Juicy Fruit." Hands me the stick of gum. I unwrap it, fold it into my mouth, flip the wrapper down the cliff, watch it shoot off on a sea-breeze.

"What's that?" I point to a fuzzy kind of wall stretchin across this ocean a mile or so off.

"Willie, that's a fogbank, don't you know? Creeps in at night, this time of year, creeps back out to sea in the morning. Sun'll burn it off soon."

"So the smell of the fog back on the farm—is ocean . . ."

Brick says soft, "I shoulda waited. In the car. I know I shoulda. Couldn't hold that stuff in and out it came. Sorry."

"Dunno what you want me to say." Then: "You saw the farm I come from."

"I saw it burn."

"I lit that fire. On purpose."

"You—did what?"

"Heard me right. That's what I think of families and settlin down and *any* of that."

"I declare. You—are quite a gal."

"I am quite, quite, quite a gal."

He took his soft cap off by its stiff brim, shook it out, put it back on his red head. Says, "I got a crew to boss." Turns, and a few steps on he says over his shoulder, "You're set on being someone I'll never understand—but if you're a good girl you can ride the camera-rig with me!"

Some minutes later and I'm still lookin over that ocean and down that cliff.

"They call this the Palisades." It was D'Varn.

"I call it goddamn high. I never been so high up, yet all I'm doin is standin on flat ground."

"Well, dearie, let's you and me go tell that to Brickie-boy. Let's us tell him that snookums here has come to her senses and she'll keep her hands off me and even quit smoking if the big strong man will only marry snookums and protect her night and day from all Palisades everywhere."

"Esther wasted no time tellin."

"Minta beat her to it."

A gust come up off that ocean, pulled at my bonnet and tugged at my hairpin hard enough to hurt. D'Varn's red velvety fedora blew straight up and we watched it sail down, down, down.

"That tears it!" she stamps her foot. "Look what you did! I wouldn't be standing here but for you!"

"*I* wouldn't be standin here but for *you*."

And instead of backin off the edge like we had any sense, we stood there more.

"I don't think I like that ocean, auntie—but I can't take my eyes off it."

"It does that to you," says she.

"Why, I wonder."

"Why would *why* matter?"

She hooks her arm in mine and backs us up a few steps.

"Willie," softly says she, "your knack for troublesome situations surprises even me."

Keystone cars and trucks are parked side to side on the grass, and all about them there's stuff like cameras and prop-boxes and a make-shift make-up table with a standin mirror beside, and a red-crossed first-aid box beside that, and film reels in cans piled atop each other near a black tent for re-loading the cameras, and all watched over by three Keystone *pistoleros*.

Keystoners hang about the cars, sittin, standin, kneelin, waitin. The newness of being here has wore off, we're itchin to work. I kind of edge to where Brick's in confab with Mr. Coy Watson.

"Coy, this biz today—I've been thinking—anyone ever done it before?"

"Not to my knowledge."

"Oh, man."

The two chuckle soft.

They see me overhearin.

I curtsey . . . and turn from them quick-like, to examine the little girl I'm doublin, who's not so very little. Twelve, thirteen maybe. Her name's Lottie and her mother is Mrs. LaRouche, who Lottie is terrified of. The girl sees we're dressed just alike, and our hair's just alike, though I'm half-a-head taller. I wink her. She looks quick at her mother. Brick's approached them. I've strolled a slight bit away—so's not to be obvious—but can see him talkin to Lottie and how Lottie looks at her mother and nods as her mother repeats back what Brick just said, though Brick's right there. "Dear, your scene's not till afternoon so let's don't get your costume mussed." Turns to the director. "Mr. Brick, I'll see to that, you bet."

Mrs. LaRouche, she dresses like a lady and calls everyone Mister or Miss and never stands more than two feet from poor Lottie, who isn't "poor Lottie" when the camera cranks. Then she'll smile to break your heart, or wink, or weep, anything they asked, until that noisy camera stops, when she'll freeze back into poor Lottie.

"Na'ow," says a raspy deep voice to Lottie, "ain't you a little thing worth kidnappin? I'll say so, I will. Pretty as a picture."

Lottie's eyes go wide as wide.

Raspy-voice is new with us, name of Wallace "Wally" Beery. Big, beefy, with a leer just kinda planted on his puss no matter what his mouth happens to be doin. It's in him deep, that leer, and it spreads from his eyes to his whole round fleshy face. Like he's warnin you about himself.

"Sir," says Mrs. LaRoche, "please do not speak to my daughter at this time."

"Well, na'ow, just bein friendly with the miss. So's she'll be comfy in our scene, me bein her kidnapper'n'all. Wouldn't want her to fear a stranger, would we? Cept as playactin."

"Be that as it may," and Mrs. LaRouche whisks Lottie off, while Lottie looks over her shoulder at raspy-voice with eyes that say "sorry."

He turns to me, his leer seems to gleam just like his eyes. "Now you're a little girl that's not a little girl."

"That means just what?" says me. My hands go a'sweat.

"Meanin you're interestin to kidnap, bein as how you're not"—he paused there just a sec— "a *little* girl."

And he laughs from his belly like he said somethin funny. I give him my evil eye, but that don't faze Mr. Wally Beery. His jokes, I see, are for him alone, and he likes it that way.

"Be seein ya," says Mr. Wally Beery, and off he strolls, slow, an easy rollin sort of stride, like he's got no care in this world.

Now Brick calls us all to heel and lays out the biz.

"We'll shoot the easiest first," says Brick. "That's you, Al, and you, D'Varn."

"Sugar, I'm never easy."

"Just so we're straight on this: Wally and Minta kidnapped the little rich girl, Lottie. D'Varn and Al are in pursuit—D'Varn's Lottie's big sister, Al is D'Varn's intended."

"That's a comedy in itself," huffs D'Varn.

Al St. John's nervy-skinny, thickly freckled, redder of hair than Brick, quick to take umbrage.

"Doll," says he, "remember your life is in my hands."

"Sure you can drive that kettle-bike?" says D'Varn.

"Dunno. Probably. We'll see." He winks a big scrunch of a wink and gets some snickers.

Brick says, "The camera-car will pace you, Al," and he points to where. "Al swerves the bike when D'Varn does her arm-biz, there," he points again. "D'Varn tumbles out of the kettle as Al tips the bike and goes over the handlebars."

"I'll go straight over forward, Boss, and roll," says Al. "Not to worry, I'll land in the shot."

"I pace the bike'n'kettle," says Esther. She'll drive the camera car. "Want me to swerve when he swerves, stop when he stops?"

"Would make for a helluva shot. Can you?"

"We'll see." She scrunch-winks like Al.

Brick says, "Coy, can that camera-platform handle the torque?"

"Glad you asked," says Mr. Coy Watson. People titter. "Yeah, it can."

"Doin that," says Hank Mann, "you want me on that platform, Brick? To hold the tripod steady on the swerve?"

"Good man," says Brick. "Let's get set."

I'm thinkin to wish D'Varn luck but Minta's there first.

"Miss D'Varn?" says she.

"Minta." Before a scene D'Varn has a particular face. Like a blank sheet of paper you could draw on. That's the face they'd put on billboards one day. The big smart eyes that give away nothing, the wide shapely mouth, and her expression that says, "I know a secret—yours."

"I've done this biz, sister," Minta's saying. "It's no piece of cake."

"Meaning what?"

"You're not a natural pratfaller, D'Varn—that's what I mean. If you let the swerve throw you out of the kettle, you won't be in control. Best to tumble with the swerve and dive out. There's a temptation to break your fall with your hand. Do that, you'll break your hand."

"Land on my shoulder and roll," says D'Varn, "and be sure to tuck my head?"

"That's the way!"

"I've been watching, Minta, but thanks." D'Varn arches her brows. "You're being awfully nice."

"Don't you think it. It's just that I could not bear, I positively could not bear, everyone feeling sorry for D'Varn after she's busted up her pretty self outa ignorance."

"I'll try to spare you that."

"Many thanks."

Minta couldn't help being generous, so long as she did it her way. I saw D'Varn's respect for that, and saw D'Varn meaning to learn it—not for doing it, for playing it. Once she could act it, maybe she'd also do it for real. But she'd have to get the act down first.

How you rig a camera-car is, you suspend a wood platform to stick out in front of your engine-hood. It's fastened on two wide thick planks of lumber bolted to the auto's frame on either side. The platform's got railings, hammered good, so's not to wobble. It looks sturdy till you're standin on it and movin fast and the wind's whistlin up your dress and your dress is billowin out.

We're ridin on grass beside the dirt road so's the shot won't be bouncy. Hank Mann's a'squat on his butt on the platform, heels braced against two posts that hold the railing, and he grips the legs of the tripod steady for when Es swerves and brakes. Me, I'm up there holdin what they call a reflector, which is just a white sheet nailed on a wood frame, and I hold it up at an angle to shine sun-glare on the shot.

I'm just tryin to be a good sport, "pitching in," as they say, like Hank Mann. Maybe I oughta be at the car with Mr. Watson checkin the piano wires, gettin more used to the cliff, lookin down so's the height won't shock me when I'm hangin there—"preparation," as Roscoe calls it. But I'm excited to be on the camera platform, mixin with Brick and D'Varn and Es and Hank, how everybody's eyes dart to each other, voice-tones shaded soft and edgy, that sense out of nowhere that somethin important is happenin.

Here comes the boy with the slate. It's just a wood-framed slate like we wrote on with chalk in grade-school, cept now what's chalked is the title of the flicker—"Napping and Kid'napping"—and the number of the scene. Brick cranks the camera at it, the kid steps away, and Brick nods to Al and D'Varn, says "Set?", and Al nods, and D'Varn nods, and Brick says "Set?" to Es, and Es says, "Everything's jake." Then Brick says the day's first "Action," steady as you please.

We start to rollin and it seems fast to me, and I'm holdin that reflector so's I got no hands free to steady myself on the rail, me tryin to wedge my butt against that rail for steadiness. Barefoot I could grip with my toes, but I'm wearing shoes for my scene, slippery and leather-soled—forgot to take them off.

D'Varn's doin biz in the kettle, waves her arms, pokes Al as if by mistake, and Al lifts his hands from the handlebars to poke her back, the bike swerves, Al grabs the handlebars like he's panicky, he straightens their ride, dust flyin behind them, and D'Varn does the biz where she waves her arms more and slaps Al in the head. Al jostles his head back and forth with wide-open eyes. Brick yells "Now!" and Al makes like he's passing out and swerves that handlebar, Es swerves the car the same, but I don't see what I most want to see, which is for Al to tumble headlong over the handlebars as D'Varn dares her first spill.

I didn't see cause Esther's swerve knocked me back on the rail, I'm tryin to hold that reflector steady, but the swerve's got me goin backwards as my leather-soled shoes slip forwards, and when Es hits the brake and skids a swerve, well, don't you know over backwards I go! A backwards flip over the rail—a 360, pratfallers call it— and oh I'm in the air in a kind of roll, now facin the ground that looks like it's comin up at me, and it's good I got agility cause somehow I come down on my shoulder instead of my nose.

The back wheel of that car stopped close enough to my foot so's I could point my toe and touch it. Two inches more skid, my left foot would be smack under that wheel, crushed useless.

My right arm's killin me—shoulder, too. Es and Brick are pickin me up real gingerly like, and everybody's sayin what people say when you make a bad accident.

I'm blurry and not hearin good. How I landed knocked out my breath and I'm gaspin, then tryin not to puke, but up it comes, up and out. My mouth's all stinky and I'm spittin out the stink.

Brick's first scene on this pic and my first accident as a movie.

Es wags her fingers in front of my face, asks me how many do I see.

I bit her longest finger.

Made them laugh.

But now Esther's finger's all bloody.

I'd bit my tongue! On the fall! And realizin it hurts like the dickens and it's bleedin a gusher. They're slapping dirt off my duds with Minta calling for wet rags to sop off grass-stains while Es says that don't matter, the camera won't pick up the stains, and all the while I'm green of stomach and just plain green, ashamed as hell of doin an amateur thing like pitchin in while in costume. I lean my head forward, spittin blood, careful not to get it on my dress. Camera would pick up blood.

Me, I'm far inside my clothing. Their doin's are fuzzy-like. I just want them all to go away.

They didn't.

D'Varn, she comes at Brick so's I thought she'd slug him.

"Trying to kill us both, mister?"

She's damnation-mad, and it was like a face had been stripped off her face to show a face underneath that's white and bright and ugly.

Brick, too, had a new face. A hard face. Not embarrassed or pained. No apology.

"Me," D'Varn's sayin, "I don't pratfall, so you order me up a kettle spill. Girlie here, you let her tip over. I'm ok, and she better be, or I'll dry-gulch you, count on it."

"I made a mistake." Brick's voice was tough and even. "Won't happen again. Now you back off me."

D'Varn kinda smiled with her damnation face.

Now she stoops to where I'm lain on a blanket on the ground.

I try to say "How'd you do?" My tongue made it "Howth thu thu?"

"How -- ?"

"Thu thu."

"—I do?"

"Yeth."

"Oh, baby," and she grabs and holds me, for real, like she never does front'a folks. "I did fine, sweetie. Not a scratch. Just achy, a little achy."

"Thorry Ah missth ith."

"Don't talk, Catch." That was Mr. Watson. "Take a slug of this and swirl it in your mouth. It'll sting. Then spit. Or swallow if you like."

I swallowed. That was fine. Es looks into my mouth. "Swelling will go down in no time." She looks up at Brick. "You're a lucky guy."

"Yeah," says he. "That's how I feel just now. Lucky."

My shoulder's throbbin but I'm keepin that to myself.

"Good news," says Es to me. "Your tongue will sting for days."

"Thanth."

"Shut up. Don't talk for a while."

"Canth anywayth."

"Shut up."

"Early lunch!" Brick hollers to all.

Laying on that blanket, I notice for the first time that it's pretty here. We're maybe a hundred yards from the cliff. The trees are large and they bend away from that ocean. The sun is warm, the breeze is cool, the air smells of water and salt and spring.

Brick says, "Hank?"

"Boss."

"She won't be able to eat. Take that motorcycle and find her a bottle of milk."

"You got it."

It *is* pretty here. I'm thinkin how good we work together, us movies. For some silly reason I'm in a good mood all of a sudden.

Brick won't turn his face to me. He strides off by himself.

"This'll take him down a peg," says D'Varn.

I'm thinkin not. He'll be better for it, I'm thinkin.

She and Es light cigarettes. Es sees I want one. "No cigs for you for a day or two. Don't wanna infect that tongue."

"Shith."

So now it's a picnic, peaceful as you please, us movies spread about here and there. Them guns stickin outa belts and pockets, now they're lookin to me like make-believe.

"On location," as they call it, they prepare for us each a box lunch—rather, there's a colored gal, Virginia, she makes em and tends em and hands em out. A sandwich, a pickle, a piece of fruit, each wrapped neat in wax paper—and if you want another piece of fruit, there's usually some citrus trees nearby and you just go pick one. Course all I have's my bottle of milk, which tastes to me a little flat, bein used to fresh-from-the-cow all my life. And there's tin cups, and folks ladle water from a barrel hooked to the side of the winch truck, where Mr. Coy Watson and his crew lunch together in the truck's shade.

Minta's over with Lottie and Mrs. What's-her-name, LaRouche, makin conversation, and I see from here that Mrs. LaRouche ain't pleased but Minta doesn't care. Sommie's over yonder in the shade with a book. D'Varn and Es gab under a tree near the cliff. Brick's off by himself at the stunt car, also with a book. Al St. John and that Wally Beery fella are eatin and sniggerin. Hank's takin a snooze, his hat over his eyes. Looks as close as Keystoners get to bein regular folk. Cept for the guns.

Well, if Brick ain't gonna look at me I'm gonna look at him. Off I go.

He's sittin on the grass with his elbow leanin on the running-board of the car that's to go over the cliff, and he pretends he's still readin, though here

I'm standin. I nudge him with the toe of my shoe. He looks at me like I just fell outa the sky.

"Whath'ya readin?"

"You shouldn't speak. It's Jack London. *Martin Eden*."

"So whish isth ith, Jack or Marthin?"

"I'm in no mood for you, Willie. Don't laugh at me."

"Justh a li'thle? Thith muth?" I held the tip of my forefinger near my thumb. "Thith muth?" I spread my fingers wider. "Tith?" Spread my fingers wider still.

"Alright. Sit down."

I do so.

"But give your tongue a rest."

I stick out my swollen ugly tongue at him.

"I'm serious. I been figuring. For some reason I'm stupider around you than I am around anybody, ever. I don't like being stupid. It's not your fault, I know that. But I don't like—*being stupid*. So I'm gonna steer clear'a you. I've made a resolution. So. There it is."

I'm hurt and it shows and that makes me mad.

"And you look so *damned* cute," he adds.

I'm less mad.

"You're wearing a milk moustache," he says.

He licks his forefinger and wipes the milk off my upper lip, slow.

I'm decidin to be less angry when he says, "But I mean what I said."

He slams his book shut like he's slammin a door. Strides off with his tough-guy walk.

I wanna run after him. But I don't.

Don't get me wrong, I don't want to kiss Brick, or the like of that, I don't think I do. Just, no grown man ever looked at me so bright-eyed and lovin. I guess I'm selfish but it was a sweetness too rare to turn from.

I picked up two sheets of paper Brick left on the running board. It's today's scenario, it tells what biz goes where. The typewriter pressed each word into the page, so's you could feel em on the blank side; I ran my fingers over the teeny bumps of letters. Found a stone, put the pages where he left em on the running board, and placed the stone upon em to hold em down.

Then, me, I mosey over to D'Varn'n'Es. My left arm's throbbin and I know that's not good, not with the biz I got, but it's like I'm pretendin it's someone else's arm and that my own arm'll come back to me when I need it.

Of a sudden I get what's goin on. I've been a Miss-Me-Not-Me, but not realizin. I'm in costume. Twelve-year-old girl. Was it the costume makin me sillier than I had to be? Cause play-actin will make you nutty, specially when you don't know you're doin it.

I sit down with D'Varn and Esther and it's like I'm invisible cause D'Varn is in her own personal spotlight, philosophizin, sayin, "We are a ruthless bunch, we movies. If we weren't ruthless to start with, the camera makes us so. Isn't one of us wouldn't do anything for that camera."

"Not me," says Esther.

"Then you're not really a movie."

"Am so."

"Are not."

"Am so!"

"Are not!"

They're slappin at each other and laughin.

"I see," D'Varn turns to me, "your talk with Brick went not so well, you little fool."

"Fool is right," says Esther. "Damned fool."

I felt better now.

D'Varn turns to Es and says, "Let me ask you, college girl. Brick reads a lot, and Sommie, too, and that sort of figures. But so does Mabel read. Should I read a book, you think?"

"They say it's never too late," says Es. "In your case, they're wrong."

"Humph," humphs D'Varn, and lies back and lays her head in Esther's lap. Her honey-colored hair drifts over Esther's blue overalls. Seems that me bein a fool is all the lecture I'll get. So I mosey'd off and left them to be pretty with each other.

As I near Sommie he says, suckin each word like a lozenge, "*The Psychopathology of Everyday Life!*" He waves the book at me. "By a Viennese physician. Crabby chap. Sit you down."

I did so.

"Mabel gave it me. We're neither of us keepers of books. I give her mine, she gives me hers. They eventually end up in Props. Feeling quite better?"

"Yesth an no."

"Your Brick"—

I tried to say "He's not anything of mine!" but it came out like Polish.

Sommie understood my Polish. "Oh, he's yours, my dear, yours for life—if you want him you've only to pluck him."

Of a sudden, like Paul of Tarsus on the road to Damascus, I see it all, I see that D'Varn is right, Esther's right, Sommie's right, so very right. I'm a blind snot of a fool. Did I get so afraid! Sommie's goin on and all I can be is afraid of stupid me not seein what I need to see.

But just can't I *like* him? Where's the harm?

Sommie's sayin, "…and I sense profound confusion in this Brick. There is, of course, his social outlook, admirable, perhaps, on its surface, but, really, my dear, to want what is fair midst an inherently unjust Nature, well—how shall I say?—it puts one in a terribly frail posture. Mark me, this man's bound for sorrows. Now you take Watson—sturdy chap, infuriatingly confident, but has his right to be. Does what he says he'll do, every time. Thinks things through, not deeply but thoroughly. Thoroughness, that's Mr. Coy Watson. There's the man Brick wants to be. But your Brick"—

"Sthop thaying thath!"

"You're correct to be upset. Too *complex*, Brick is, to be remotely like a Watson. Cares too much about too much. My belief is that if one is to be *complex* one needs a proper outlet. Drink, for instance. Or physics. Or to be like you and leap from yon high building into a barely adequate net."

"Ahm *complexth*?"

"I believe so."

"Shith."

Nothin for it but to make a resolution same as Brick's but opposite. Keep my distance.

Picked myself up and left Sommie flat without a word, the movie way, and strolled to the cliff edge. Sometimes Esther, just sittin on our divan, smokin a cig, she'd say softly to no one, "It's no use." For some reason I thought of that, feelin the breeze off that ocean.

"Well, na'ow, and how pretty you be, the little girl what ain't a little girl. Pretty as a picture, I say, you standin there all in white, and your dark shiny hair blown by sea-wind."

"M'ther Beery."

"Mister, is it! 'Wally' is good by me. Colleague to colleague, so to speak."

I turned to him. Somehow the way he holds himself, and the leer that's all of him, makes him even bigger than he is. I caught the notion—just-like-that—that this Wally Beery might push me off the cliff. I was scared of this person, and as soon as I knew it I hated myself for it.

But I met his eyes full on, you bet.

"Na'ow, it hurts a fellow's feelings, to be disliked for no reason—I see you dislike me, and I apologize right here for however I inspired dislike in one as pretty and—I'm searching here for me word—intricate! That's me word! Found it. Pretty and intricate as you. And a right chancer, too."

"Thankth," and I curtsey.

"Was I complimentin? Suppose as I was. And you thanked me. Well, na'ow, that's what I call an improved situation."

I'm lookin in his leerin eyes and what I see is: He's smart. Really, really smart.

"I seen you take that spill. Thought sure you'd break a bone, but you're as made of rubber you are. Supple, they call it. Guess I'm hoggin our conversation, as you can't speak right today. They say you started in jumpin off a building. Now ain't that some nerve! Any eye can see you've got some terrific nerve. Me, I started at the Essanay, up Chicago way. Cold town, Chicago. Can you imagine how I started in these flickers? Come up from the circus, and started at the Essanay playing a—you won't guess—a Swedish maid!" He laughed that laugh of his, a laugh all for himself. "Guess I'll leave you now to your contemplations."

As he walked slow away, he turned his head to say, "Imagine, you, a bloke beefy as me startin out in such a way. A Swedish maid. But did I get the laughs? Had em rollin, I did. Rollin."

Brick the Director Big Shot, he's got all'a us pow-wowin again, us in a circle and him in the center. He'll be talkin and turnin till he gets almost eye-to-eye with me, when he turns the other way till he's almost to me again, talkin bout how D'Varn and Al St. John are back on their bike'n'kettle, chasin Beery, Lottie and Minta in the stunt car. Fiddling with the grass, lookin at the clouds, admirin the trees, that's me. If Brick does look at me, I won't be lookin at him.

Then Brick's voice changed. Tense, sure, excited. He's figured new biz: The Beery-Lottie-Minta car nears the cliff, the camera-car is right beside it, both cars swerve and do "a one-eighty" in a skid so's they're facing where they came from, "and that, *that*," says Brick, "that is when the audience sees, for the first time, that we're comin to a cliff over the sea!"

"Sure ups the ante, Boss." That was Mr. Coy Watson himself.

Brick grinned. I was glad for the sap.

"Can you drive that swerve, Esther?"

"Try me."

Who says she won't do anything for the camera?

"Wally?" Brick needs his vote, too.

All eyes on the new guy.

He's been crouchin. Now he raises himself to his full bigness.

"Well, na'ow"—which is a tick I'm gettin sick of—"I am the best driver in this world, and the safest."

"That better not be brag," says Minta.

"I'm not one for bragging, Mrs. Arbuckle. Boastin, yes. Why, madam, I even boast of my boastin." And he gives that throaty chuckle that's all between him and him.

"Pardon *me!*" That's Mrs. What's-her-name, LaRouche. "We will not. My little Lottie will not participate."

Oh, boy. Everybody but her knows it's time for fun.

See, the drivers, they get a vote, cause if they say they can't do it there's no scene. But actors, actors work or go home. And stay home.

Brick stands quiet for a bit. Looks at her: "Then go home."

"I beg your pardon."

"If you'll not work, leave."

Little Lottie's eyes are, like they say, big as saucers.

"We'll drive you to the streetcar and give you your fare. Only—don't come back to the Keystone. Ever."

"You've not the authority," Mrs. LaRouche declares, "you've not the authority to ban us, sir."

Brick smiles. "See how Mr. Sennett treats someone who walks out on a shoot."

"You can't finish without us!"

"See this piece of paper. It's the biz for this day's work. Watch."

He tears it in two, crumples the lower half, lets it fly.

"Sommie, can you figure a new ending?"

"I'd be delighted."

"What," says Mrs., "about our fee?"

Brick smiles. "I'll double it myself if you can get one dime out of Mack Sennett after you leave this scene."

We're all enjoyin the daylights outa this. Then, of a sudden, I felt sorry for that woman. Nobody likes her—includin and especially her terrified child. And Mrs. LaRouche knows it. That's horrible.

Then I didn't feel sorry no more.

She says, primly, "Lottie will do it."

Says Brick, "Thought it was too dangerous?"

"I've reconsidered." Here it comes. Right on cue, Mrs. LaRouche says, "We shall want a larger fee."

"Do you?" It's D'Varn, her face quiverin angry, her cheeks ugly-white. "Here's a five spot. Take it." She holds it out. "Want more? Ten? Twenty? Either it's too dangerous for the kid or it's not. Money don't change that."

The fun's gone.

"Well, na'ow"—oh, brother—"there, there, everyone. Little miss," Beery says to Lottie, "you've my own promise, my sacred word, there's not a wit of danger. Think I'd risk my neck? For a flicker? There's no chance'a that. And when we're done I'll treat you and Mother to ice cones. Flavored ice, there's nothin more refreshin."

That woman don't know where to look.

"Mothers," D'Varn hisses.

"Let's get to work," says our director.

"Na'ow," says Beery to Brick, "fer an anarchist, you boss like a reg'lar capitalist."

Don't you know Brick blushed?

Their car-biz went alright but I can't tell you how. I didn't watch. Had my back to it the whole time. Not outa squeamishness—I believed Wally

Beery, and of course Esther too. I didn't watch cause it was time to mind my biz. I was all over that winch truck tuggin on this and that with my bum arm to see what the arm could take.

Mr. Coy Watson's laying out his piano wires and testin the winch motor. He seen what I was doin.

"Let me take a look," says he.

I hold out my arm. He feels real careful around the fingers, the wrist, the elbow, up to the shoulder, all round the shoulder.

He sees where I wince.

"I'm stronger than I look," says I.

"Yes. You're that. Good luck."

I'd best pee before my biz. Don't wanna let out a stream while I'm hangin off a cliff.

I hate peein on location.

I'm a very private pee'er.

On a street where there's houses but no stores, the director'll send a guy with a five-spot to knock on doors and find a home that'll let us come and go, chaperoned two by two, to the outhouse in the backyard. Stores, it depends. The newer ones have bathrooms. A grocery or bakery, they figure with us goin in'n'out we'll buy somethin and they're right, so they get five bucks and our business. Of course, bars love it—cause gals ain't normally allowed in bars. The deal is, with our gals in bars, we post a big guy like Pasha who stands with a baseball bat at the door of the "loo" (as Sommie calls it) so there's no funny business.

In a park, there's usually outhouses but this ain't a park we're at. There's fields and trees and some houses too far to walk to. The guys find some tree or big bush and do their business behind it. Gals are another story. Two find a concealed spot and one stands watch while the other makes.

I'm all about the biz now and in no mood for company.

So I trudge up an incline, down a path, up another, pick a stand of bushes. I'm hid good. Then, what with takin off my leather tightie that I made myself, nothin happens. But I gotta make now. I really do. It's that I'm tense and can't. So I'm patient, it starts to flow, then wouldn't you know?

"Well, na'ow."

I'm up from my pee-crouch in a flash and gettin my knife and, damn, I squirt on my shoes. My Miss Mabel shoes!

My heart's thumpin fast as a small bird's. I'm on one side of a stand of bushes and he's on t'other. We can't see each other but it feels like we can.

"Not to fear, m'dear. Saw you goin here alone-like, and I'm thinkin you need a guard."

He never sounds like he's tellin the truth. Always sounds like, whatever he says, he's meanin somethin else.

"Go on, na'ow, and I won't listen to you hiss. I'll plug my ears. There."

No way I can make now. I'm strugglin to pull on my tightie fast while my knife's in my hand, trying to be quick and not stick anything significant.

"We done yet?" says he.

We?!

I'm done and my blade-hand's tremblin. I'm frightened. Not cause he's big. There's that, but that's not it. It's that I feel my will to stick him. I know I want to.

But that didn't stop me.

I stepped out slow.

He hears me and turns to me. (So he really turned away. I'm confused.)

"Well, na'ow," says he—could'a killed him just for that—"lookee, lookee. You must think the worst of me, and me just bein helpful-like."

"Maybeth I do'th n maybeth I donth. Maybeth yeth, maybeth noth."

"Na'ow, that's just what I been thinkin toward you. Maybe you are and maybe you ain't."

That made my knife-hand stop tremblin and grip.

"An I wonder," says he, "just where you been keepin that blade. I'll have fun guessin on that, I will." Now his voice snaps like a whip. "Stow that thing or I'll take it from ya. Think I never fought no knife-wielder afore. You ain't gonna stick me."

"She doesn't have to. I'm gonna shoot you."

It was Brick, behind Beery, revolver at the ready. I'd been starin so hard at Beery I never seen or heared Brick come.

"If he don't, I surely will." That's Es behind Brick.

"If they miss, it'll be me." Mr. Watson.

"This," says Beery, "changes the business, it does. I was a'feared I'd have to wrestle this lass, she havin lost her head as she has." There's a big smile on his puss. He rubs his chin. Laughs. "Well," says he to me, "I see you're highly thought of hereabouts. I do see that."

"See this?" Esther gestures with her Special. "Don't lay in wait for her or anything like that. One of us'll getchya."

"That motion is seconded." That's Brick.

"And carried." Mr. Watson.

"Am I too late for the fun?" Minta's run up. In her long-fingered hand is a lady-like derringer. "Seen one then another of you march off gun-in-hand and I was sure there'd be a spot of fun."

"I seen him follow her and I followed him," Brick says.

"And I followed you." That's Watson.

"And I the same." That's Es.

"Oh, brother," says Beery, and he throws his head back laughin. A no-kiddin, deep-from-the-belly laugh. "Highly thought of, you are, Miss Catch, impressively so. Well, na'ow, just so's you folks know, I seen her go off alone and figgered she'd best not be."

I'm seein that he sees the fun of it all, this damned smart bastard. The fun these folks had drawin their guns and makin their threats, and the fun he was havin, proud of himself, like he didn't care which way it went cause everyone was havin fun.

I got no tolerance of bein afraid of any man, but Beery I feared.

We all stood starin at each other while Beery, he laughed more. Then, of a sudden, it was over. Folks lower their guns, Beery's still chucklin, and we walk off in a group, Beery as much in the group as any, and nobody spoke more but for what I said to Brick.

"Thanxth."

There's a snag.

The biz is like so: Wally Beery swerves the car so's it's maybe twenty feet from the cliff, facing away from the sea. Car stalls. Minta and Wally get frantic, Lottie tries to escape, Minta holds her back, Wally's fussin, tryin to pop the clutch. He pops it in reverse by mistake and the car lurches back-wards and speeds ass-end-first over the cliff.

On screen you'd see it with "inserts," as they call em, of Al St. John and

D'Varn chasin in the bike'n'kettle, plus a close shot of Wally's hand popping the car by mistake into reverse.

To shoot the car racin backwards the plan was to "undercrank," as they call it. Crank the camera slowly as the car drives slowly back to the edge of the cliff. Cut. Beery, Minta and Lottie get out. We replace Beery and Minta with their dummies. Attach the wires. I get in, playin Lottie. Mr. Coy Watson fastens his piano wires, then me and the car slip backwards over the cliff. All the action's shot slow, as I say, undercrankin. For the flicker, they'll run the projector at regular speed and what you see on the screen will be lots faster. That car'll roar toward the cliff and over the edge.

Good plan, right?

I see Mr. Coy Watson, Hank Mann, and Al St. John standin off to the side, watchin together, waitin, and I get a bad feelin. They know somethin Brick don't. And they ain't tellin. Not out of meanness. It's just the way here. Brick's a green director, green as spinach, and if he makes a mistake it's his to make.

Brick sees how they're lookin. He looks at them. Then he does a slow 180 and stops when he sees the sea.

Looks out to sea, looks up to the clouds, says, "Can't undercrank, can we? Wind's come up. We undercrank, on screen those waves in the background—they'll jump and hop like kittens. It'll look like a trick cause it is—we'll lose the thrill. Kills the gag. So - can't undercrank. Gotta do it for real."

Everybody waits for the director to fix this.

That Brick, he's not rattled. He's studyin to himself.

I see it now: This is a man of action. Has been, always. That's when he's comfortable. That's when he has no fears.

"Listen up," says he. "Wally, Minta, Lottie—cameras—highlight screeners—set up, just like we've said, plus an insert close-shot of Wally popping the clutch. We'll get that first. Then we'll do your biz in the car, like we said, but, when Lottie tries to escape, Minta will wallop Lottie on the head with her handbag and Lottie will sink outa sight between the seat and the dash. Then I command 'freeze,' and we cut."

They do so.

Brick then says, "Everybody out of the car. Mr. Watson, please set up Minta's dummy in the posture she just froze in. Beery, get over here and give me your hat and your jacket."

They do as told.

Brick-as-Wally gets in the car, revs it. Everybody is real quiet.

Brick says soft, "Camera and slate."

The cameraman starts to crankin, the kid comes out with the slate, stands there a sec, steps back. Brick says "Action" soft, then revs her. Tires spin on the grass, take traction, Brick pops the clutch and that car bolts backwards. Too fast. No way he stops.

It's like I'm already seein him plunge backwards over that cliff to his death when he swervy-skids and does somehow stop, not a foot from the edge, I swear.

Me, I've not taken in breath.

There's this moment nobody says anything.

Brick says, "Cut." Flat like that: Cut.

Then everybody's yellin, clappin, carryin on—even D'Varn.

Brick's *in* now. Now there's nobody here wouldn't do what-all this director asks, lickety-split.

I'm so proud of us. Wave-the-flag, strike-up-the-band proud! I'd rather be a movie than anything.

Mr. Coy Watson runs to Brick and shakes his hand. Hank, Al, Minta and, yes, Wally Beery, they crowd around pattin Brick on the back and all. He's got that goofy smile pasted on his puss like it'll stay there days.

Says grinnin Brick, "I'm a damn fool."

Says Mr. Coy Watson, "You surely are that."

Sommie gives me a peck-kiss on my forehead. His eyes don't know where to look.

"This is a perfectly unnerving day."

He trots off—Sommie trotting!—to where the cliff curves out a little to form a kind of knob that sticks out about ten feet long and four feet wide. Brick'll work the camera on that knob, right at the edge. As many folks as'll fit—D'Varn, Es, Minta, Wally, Sommie, Hank—crowd on that knob. Looks dangerous to me. Others lie on their bellies along the cliff, their heads over the edge to watch.

Here we go.

Mr. Coy Watson's tied his piano wires to the car and I've watched him knot em. He looks to me, smiles, nods.

The guys on the truck work the winch so the wires go taut. Mr. Watson heads back to the truck to work the winch himself.

Al St. John gets in the car and gives her just enough gas to drop the back wheels over the edge. Shuts the engine. Climbs out over the windshield.

Didn't know I was nervy till that back axle thunked against the cliff-edge as the car went over.

She's just hangin there, that car.

I climb on the hood. I step over the windshield. I duck out of sight behind the dash, where Lottie-dummy has slumped after Minta donked her.

I'm waitin there, lookin at the dummies.

I say to Minta-dummy, "Here's where we earn our money."

Winked at Wally-dummy. It winked back with a leer.

Not really—I'm just sayin, cause by now I'm agitated.

Brick calls out, "All set in there, Catch?"

Why'd that fool pick now to call me "Catch," first time ever he did?

I grabbed two of Mr. Watson's handles on the floorboard. I see he drilled through the board and welded them to metal. I gripped tight.

"Catch, I said you set good in there?"

"Seth."

"I'll call Action, we'll count to three—one, two, three--"

"I know howth thoo count!"

"—then she'll drop. So be set."

"Seth, goth'amnit!"

"Action. One. Two. Three!"

Didn't realize. I just didn't realize. Figured they'd kinda ease the car down, but no, that car dropped with a lurch and me—I just dropped! For one teeny sec it felt like fallin.

But I'm ok. I'm hangin from back seat handles, kickin at the air. It's me and the air now. The fun's begun.

But not for my shoulder. It's like there's two of me and one is in a lotta pain—a lot—and the other doesn't care cause it's really fun.

I look down. Not so much fun. Cliff feels like it's gettin higher by the second.

The car starts in to sway.

Didn't expect that. When it hung from the winch at the Keystone it hung straight.

Well—now it swayed.

Everything feels like it's takin forever and I feel a fear that I'm messin up the biz by takin my time. That was a good fear. It made me get to work.

A lurch! We drop some more.

And there's dirt and pebbles and head-size chunks of cliffside fallin at me.

Piano wires—they must be diggin into the edge.

We never figured on that.

That lurch, it was to make sure the dummies fall. I'd forgot that was the plan.

Minta-dummy went down—oh, far, far down—she seemed to take her sweet damn time to hit the rocks below.

I kick off my shoes and watch them fly, end over end.

Forgot I'd have to do that. Goodbye, Miss Mabel Shoes, my favorite pair.

Wouldn't you know Wally-dummy's snagged. He's not fallin.

The "boys" didn't think that out either, did they?

I'm hangin over nothin and that goddamn Wally-dummy's spoilin my biz.

But that's good, cause now I got somethin to do.

Ok, shoulder. I need a little mercy on this.

Wally-dummy's hangin, snagged, on the driver's side, and I'm hangin bout three feet away on the passenger side, and I let go with a kick, all my might, I kick that Wally with one leg and kick im with the other.

But he's still snagged.

What with my kicks that car plays its tricks and sways harder.

A rain of dirt, pebbles and rocks. Are there big rocks up there?

I'm mad now. That goddamn Wally's gonna get me killed.

Serves me right for wantin t'kill him.

Of a sudden, I don't care what happens. Not a bit. Not at all.

We're swayin anyway, so, knowin full well and what-the-hell, I push off from that car with both feet and rear up both legs and with both heels I kick Wally where he's snagged and over he goes.

Car's swayin somethin devilish.

So now's when my left shoulder shoots a pain all through me, head to toe, and I say, "No, you don't! You do not!"

So I do the surprise biz I'd worked out—though I hadn't planned it for swayin.

I time the sway, and I know where my handles are, all over this long car, and I let myself fall, just fall maybe three-four feet to where there's handles on the rumble seat, and I grab at one with my good arm and just hang.

For a sec it musta looked like I lost it, fallin for real.

That'll make the payin customers sit up straight.

Never doubted I could do it.

Rested my bad arm, just hung there from my good arm, watching the movies on the knob watch me. Everybody's watchin but Big Es. She's turned away.

That's when the gust hit. Well, course that's when a gust would hit. Even the goddamn wind wants a part in the flickers.

The gust is comin up from the sea, and the gust behind the first, and the gust behind that, as wind fills the car-seats and now that car's actin like a sail, swayin more and more, chunks of cliff-top are fallin, big as bibles, and those that hit the car burst into soil and pebbles.

I'm thinkin, Ok, Mr. Wind, here we go.

You wanna sway, we'll sway.

Don't you know that wind felt fine on my legs and blowin up my dress? Woo!

I turn so's my body faces the car, I grip handles with both hands. Then up I go handle over handle, climbin over the rumble seat, till I dig my bare toes into upholstery. I'm headin for the steering wheel and that motherless car's swayin.

The steering wheel presents a difficulty.

I gotta push off hard from the back seat—jumpin up, is really what it is—while I keep hold of a handle with my good arm—then reach for the steering wheel with my bad arm. Need my good arm keepin hold of a handle in case I miss the steering wheel with my bad arm. But if I don't miss the steering wheel, if I grab the steering wheel, then it's my bad arm that's grabbin it. Then I'll hafta put my whole weight on my bad arm for the time it takes to pull me up—that little time it takes my knees to clear the top of the front seat and bear my weight as my good arm grabs the wheel.

No way around it. For just a sec my bad arm's gotta bear me.

Biz-thinkin ain't like other thinkin. Happens in less than a blink. Has to, or there's no you no more.

I make my move and I'm seein red.

I didn't know that happened. Thought it was just a sayin. But it hurt so much the world went red.

But I'm hangin now from the steering wheel. With my good arm.

Occurs to me sudden-like that the wheel's not made for this and what if it breaks?

Know what? I laughed. I'm hangin from that wheel hurtin like the dickens and laughin.

My bad shoulder's a'pulsin as I slip me into the driver's seat.

Now I'm sittin, and feelin heavy, cause I'm pressed against the seat by that good old force of gravity. I'm sittin lookin straight up, it's a crazy feelin, but I can let my bad arm be. It's not lettin me be, but I can let it be, cause I'm ok now, if the car's ok.

I make like to drive the car.

Someone on the knob musta signaled Mr. Coy Watson cause the car starts slowly up, with more cliffside "rain," and I'm bent over the wheel eggin it on, and with the pull from the winch the car quits swayin so.

Then guess what?

Bump!

And fallin cliff-chunks burst on the windshield in front'a my face.

And again, bump! And the same.

And again. And a rock cracks the window right in front'a me.

Right in front'a my face!

Now I'm goddamned alarmed.

A heartbeat. Another. Still. Just a kinda spray of loose dirt and the pebbly sound it makes on the car.

What happened was—they tell me later—what with the swayin, them piano wires dug deep into that cliff. Gave the car a different angle going up than it had going down. Its frame bumped into the edge of the cliff. We was stuck, me and that car, hangin off a cliff.

Everything's just still. But we're not swayin. We're wedged against the cliff's edge.

Bump. Clatter of "rain."

Then we drop!

Not much, but it surprised hell outa me.

What happened was, Mr. Coy Watson's givin the wires some slack to get a run on that ledge and power me over, not usin just the winch to pull me but the whole truck. He's drivin the truck to pull me up.

And—they tell me later—Watson's terrified that with the added strain the wires might, just might, snap.

Well, they didn't have to tell me that later, I thought of that then and there.

Me, I'm figuring—faster than talk can say—that if we go down I wanna be on top of the car, not under it. I ain't thinkin of pain now, I'm way too crazy-scared for pain, I'm clamberin over that windshield and then I'm on the hood facin straight down—but, hey: I'm still "in the biz," as they say. I'm kneelin with my knees wedged against the windshield, and my hands reachin over the windshield onto the steering wheel, yankin on the steering wheel so's it looks like I'm tryin to pull that motherless, godless, thankless car up the cliff by my own strength—while, by the way, it feels like half the goddamn cliffside is rainin on my back. My hair's gonna be so filthy-dirty.

What happened then was—they tell me later—there's Brick's frantic yellin of "Can't move that truck again, she'll fall! Stop cameras! Throw her a rope!" Cept the cameramen—Brick on the knob, and the other guy on the edge shootin straight down—they're both so excited they keep crankin even though Brick himself yelled "Stop!" He yells but keeps crankin.

Lucky he kept crankin or he'd'a missed the best biz.

Watson doesn't hear Brick over the truck's motor so Watson guns the truck and WHACK, the car jumps forward and up, I fall down over that windshield, into the front seat, grabbin on a handle with the only arm that could, the good one, and I coulda gone clear on down but my agility took over and sorta bent me into the front seat.

The car clears the cliff-edge. Second camera is waitin on it. What does that camera see? Me in the driver's seat, holdin that wheel, grinnin.

Can't remember what happened just after. Next thing I knew, I'm lyin on the grass, flat on my back, lookin up at my sky, grinnin and grinnin. And hurtin and hurtin. But grinnin.

Then there's Mr. Coy Watson lookin down at me as though from the sky, his hat in his hands.

"Catch, I couldn't be sorrier. Some smart cookie I am. I shoulda figured those piano-wires for digging into the cliff—course they would, it's obvious, and I didn't see it. Stupid. I am sorry. If anything had happened to you, and you with that arm, I…"

"Mr. Coy Watson, sir—I'll hang from your piano wires anytime."

"You—you are a brave, game kid. Anything I can ever can do for you, you just ask."

"Same here, sir."

All in all, *Nappin N Kidnappin* was a pretty good flicker. But my biz—I was surprised how quick it played. Felt like I hung off that cliff half an hour. Nope. Maybe not even three minutes? And less on the screen, what with editin.

We gathered in the projector shed to watch. Sommie and me and D'Varn and Es sat in that order in the front row. D'Varn's passin a flask between us four, but I can't drink yet—my tongue's not so swollen anymore but still it stings horrible. The left arm's in a sling. "Nothing broke or torn, you must be made of rubber," Doc said, "but for a week don't give it any strain. And I mean not *any*, as in *none*. After that, massages and such should put you right."

D'Varn's too D'Varn to play comedy really, but she comes off game—that biz with Al St. John on the bike'n'kettle looked even better on screen than it had for real. Their spill came off perfect, cause they'd been slappin at each other just before and they hit the ground in arm's reach and Al Saint-John started in to slappin again while laying all crumpled and D'Varn returned fire.

"Good biz, kids," says Mr. Sennett.

D'Varn's eyes teared, she was so proud, but looked straight ahead so's not to show it.

That little Lottie, "the camera loves her," as they say. As for Beery, anything he's thinkin jumps straight at you, the camera reads his mind. And there's Minta, of course, who never makes a wrong move—stuff you don't even notice right there watchin her, but in shiny black and white it "plays," as they say.

When that car races backward at the cliff you can't tell it's Brick, you think he's Beery, and, brother, he stopped not a moment too soon—another foot and goodbye mister.

At my biz everybody's gaspin and eekin and "Oh my heavens!"—even though I'm sittin right there and they know nothin bad happened.

Kickin Wally Beery got a big laugh, specially from Wally Beery. And me on the hood tuggin the car up the cliff, that got a "topper"—a laugh bigger than the big laughs.

"A whopper of a topper," Mr. Sennett says, and Miss Mabel, she whoops!

The flicker ends with what they shot while I lay on the grass. The crew went down to the beach at the bottom of the cliff, where Wally and Minta kinda shake themselves off, cause nobody dies at the Keystone. Minta looks at the big guy and takes off after him, slappin and kickin im, he's tryin to fend her off, fallin backwards, and we're all yellin her on, that little thing bossin that big thing, til Wally runs into the surf and she runs after him and he takes to swimmin with her swimmin right behind. Then that "K" trademark fills the screen, abrupt as always, cause Keystone flickers never end, they just stop.

"Lights," says Mr. Sennett. He goes over to Brick. "Not bad, for a socialist."

"Anarcho-syndicalist, sir."

"At least you're not a suffragette."

"The room's full of em!" That's Miss Mabel. Gals hoot in agreement.

Mr. Sennett grins. "Suffragettes and reds makin me money. Ain't capitalism grand?"

He spits a wad four feet into a "cuspidor," I'm told it's called.

"So, Brick," says Mr. Sennett, "how'd you know when to stop, driving backwards at that cliff?"

Brick's eyes get bright. "I'm looking straight ahead at the crew and the first woman who did one'a these"—he scrunches shut his eyes and averts his face—"I hit the brakes."

Says Mr. Sennett, "All in a day's work, kids."

Strange, how it all came out. If we'd figured in advance that those piano wires would gouge that cliff-edge, we would never'a dared—yet that's what got our biggest laugh.

And what strikes me peculiar was how I'm sittin right there in the dailies-shed with everybody, and everybody knows I'm fine, but, on the screen, when it seems I might not make it, everybody sittin beside me gets scared witless. They know I made it. I'm right here. But, no sirree. To them, I'm up there, on the screen, and they're scared for me.

That night at our fuckeries D's careful of my injuries, touchin me like I'm made of glass, and I know I'm pleasin her, but—not all of her? It's like she's also watchin us as though seated on some hard chair across the room. When we're done, smokin and sippin, we're silent but not calm at all. I'm wonderin, and it seems she's wonderin.

"You've overshadowed me," D'Varn says. "I didn't expect that. I love you, but I don't like that."

HOTEL HOLLYWOOD

LOUISE BROOKS

In writing the history of a life I believe absolutely that the reader cannot understand the character and deeds of the subject unless he is given a basic understanding of that person's sexual loves and hates and conflicts. It is the only way the reader can make sense out of innumerable apparently senseless actions.

1

SOME DAYS AFTER, I'm pretty much better—and D'Varn seems to be over my "overshadowing." My arm came back. My tongue unswelled. I could smoke. So, smokin, I'm sittin on the white bed not exactly naked, sportin but a red satin pantie—a scanty thing among several that D'Varn selected special. She'll open the third draw down, daintily select one, hold it high and say, "Fetch!" I stand tippy-toe and pluck it cause I am, she says, "a good bitch." When it's just us, those special panties are all she likes for me to wear. Says she studies my "lines," meanin how I stand or sit or slouch and, as she would say, how I "recline." D'Varn favors that word.

"Recline, my dear," she purrs, "I have plans."

She's sittin at the dresser in somethin filmsy, occupied with her latest enthusiasm, which is to pluck her eyebrows into thin curved lines. D'Varn's eyes are big as Miss Mabel's but hazel'y green, and, with her eyebrows plucked and her wide lips painted, her face is all mouth and eyes—cept when she "profiles" and her lip-paint and plucked brows "accent" her fine chin and strong "proboscis," which now I know means nose. I learn lotsa words these days around D'Varn. When I told her Miss Mabel has a Thesaurus she got herself that same book.

Me, I'm reclinin and watchin her at her fixins and I'm happy, cause, when it's just us, I can watch her do whatever and be head-to-toe content. If I had my way I'd wear more than panties cause the fog's come in and brought a chill, but with D'Varn I have her way, not mine, and that's fine, cause I belong to D'Varn. For however long she'll have me. And it's ok, it really is, that she's not in the way of belonging to me. I know D'Varn. I know she can't belong to anyone cept to what she sees in that mirror, which ain't quite her, so she don't even belong to herself—I guess.

She's workin her face there, pluckin while tryin this and that expression, which she can do forever, practicin her actin. She'll say, "My expressions shall have as many—gradations—as many gradations as yours one day." Then: "Brick," says she, sudden-like, speakin without lookin at me, watchin her face change in the mirror as she talks, "Brick, he's not show-people. He shouldn't be amongst us. Oh, he's a right guy—irritates the snot outa me, but he's a right guy. But what's not right is him being amongst us. His heart's in that anarcho-syndical falderal, 'the workers,' 'the people'—well, we're not them. We're show-people. We want to make them laugh or cry, he wants to make them better. And us, too, he wants to make us better. Well, *I won't have it.* I've got no use for it. Any-hoo, he hates rich people and I mean to be rich." A moment, then: "Missy Willie, care to contribute to this conversation?"

"Nope."

"That fellow takes you too seriously. And you take him too casually."

"I've learned that," says me.

"And?"

"We kinda made a pact to steer clear of each other."

"If it's a pact, and you're steering clear *together,* that's not really steering clear. That's like there's a string tied between you."

"Auntie D'Varn?"

"Yes, dear."

"Shut up."

But she won't. Says, "The poor sap can't help but be obvious. That's a male prerogative—you know what a prerogative is, right?" Did too know; learned just the other day. "Men can afford to be obvious. A gal's got to be obvious and not, at the same time. Wears a body thin, always having to be two things at once."

"I know some about that," says me.

"And it makes you wonderful," says she.

Says me, "Why's Esther awfully low lately?"

"The Honorable Arabella Esther Heinz has had the weeps off and on since *you* did your biz at the cliff, the poor thing."

Didn't want to know more and let that drop.

D'Varn, of a sudden, stands and walks three steps tippy-toe with all her height. I thrill, watchin her long body do a kind of whirl on one foot, dance-like. Then she toe-steps back to the dresser-stool that revolves as she sits she turns on the stool this way and that way. "I want to dress up."

"It's midnight," I'm shocked, "Where you goin?"

"You dress up, too."

"Where we goin?"

"Out walking. Let's get pretty for the fog."

We dressed as for a big do, selectin this and that, "Oh, that's not right," tryin on somethin else and somethin else.

"Well, na-ow." That's Miss D.

"Not you, too," says me.

"Well, na-ow," but like a cat's meow. "Poor old Beery. Four pistols he had pointed at him?"

"Four. And he's not poor anybody. He liked it."

"This hat or this?" asks she.

"That," I pointed. "I like you in feathers."

"We'll both wear feathers. And lace gloves. And shawls, for the chill. Pointy shoes, and our colors will match."

We're selectin and posin and gettin all excited with wantin what we'll do after our walk, our wantin is in the air like a fog in the room, and there's the fun of waitin on our wantin so it seeps all over us.

"Sommie," says she as we dress, "Sommie is really very clever. Asked him yesterday, 'If little Lottie's mommy-bitch called Brick's bluff and walked out on us, could you *really* write Lottie out of the story?' 'Nothing simpler,' says he"—and D'Varn is doin Sommie, but not real well—"'however, it required that your bike'n'kettle take another, more difficult spill—to top the first. You spill, the getaway car disappears into the distance. Title card: Five Years Later. A one-reeler becomes a two-reeler. Second reel, Miss Willie"—of a sudden, in her voice: "There's four that never call you 'Catch.' Sommie, me, Esther and Brick."

"Brick did the other day," says me. "He's called me Catch since the Palisades."

"Humph. So, Sommie says, 'Second reel, Miss Willie plays the girl as, oh, seventeen years of age. You and St. John have searched for her all this time, tireless, faithful. You finally spot her, by chance, she and her captors. They're rich on the kidnap fee, and you're poor from paying it. But they've kept Miss Willie anyway, for some reason I've yet to concoct. You spot her, I say, by chance, she and her captors. You call the Kops, chase ensues, and we perform precisely the same finish, over the cliff, et cetera. You're reunited with Miss Willie. Happy ending. Now I think of it, it's quite the better story. A shame that obnoxious woman capitulated.' And I'm more than a little annoyed with how, to Sommie, you're Miss Willie and I'm plain D'Varn. Course I say so. Sommie, he says, 'She is Miss Willie and you are D'Varn. Exactly correct.' 'You're such a snoot,' says I. 'Also exactly correct.' But isn't he really clever? I'll hire Sommie someday, see if I don't. And that day is well on its way. If I give him a big paycheck he'll call me Miss D'Varn, he will."

Says me, "He won't."

She looks at me, looks at the mirror, pulls me over to look at us both in the mirror. "I think we are perfection now." From imitating, she still had some Sommie in her voice. "Come, my beauty, the fog awaits. It's lonely and it needs us."

How I feel bout Hotel Hollywood is that twixt our rooms and the street there's passages and drapery, fancy fixtures, and the doors to so many rooms, then a great bronze-bannistered stairway for us to "descend," saith D'Varn, into the lobby with its shiny mahogany front desk and its fireplace and plush chairs and coffee-tables and lamps and cuspidors and ashtrays and potted plants, then the long porch with its pillars and wide front steps—to me it's the *Arabian Nights* right up to its turreted towers, built just for us, to stand twixt our private rooms and the wide mixed-up world.

Thrills me every time to walk from our rooms to the street or from the street to our rooms. So I know D'Varn's wrong to say I'm gettin spoiled. I can't be spoiled. I know that about me.

The clerk behind the desk, his eyes go wide. He says, like it's a question, "Ladies?"

Says D'Varn, doing Sommie, "We fancy a stroll. If we've not returned by dawn, dispatch patrols."

He shakes his head and rings his bell. A sleepy bellboy, maybe twelve years old, his uniform crumpled from sleeping, he kinda stumbles in so's to open the front doors for us.

"Hold out your cap," D'Varn commands.

He doffs his cap and holds it out. She puts in a silver dollar.

"Go back to sleep," says she smiling.

He smiles like you can't believe. She just gave him two day's pay.

Out we step.

That fog. Thick, it was. We walked down the wide steps of Hotel Hollywood and fog parted in swirls for us, lit bright by the hotel's lights. Scents of ocean, and of fresh strawberries across the way, citrus groves all round, roses, night-blooming jasmine—that fog wore perfume! We lit our Egyptian gold-tips, fog-wisps glowed at our flames, and, oh, those soft flower-aromas and our leafy smoke, and how fine she looked to me and how fine I looked to her—I had no more to ask of this world which gave me so much just for steppin out a door.

"So how much money you make now?" That question wouldn't have been romantical to anyone but D'Varn.

"After the biz off the cliff I've been raised. Fifty a week, plus the leaps, plus when I make up biz 'to further a story,' which is different, they tell me, from biz that's just biz. Furthering a story is *writing*. Comes out to eighty dollars, give or take. What's a body to do with that kind of money?"

"Purchase shoes at the best cobbler's," she says happily, "hats at the fanciest millinery, stockings at the finest hosiery."

Makin more for doin fun than doin hard work makes no sense to me. For a farm girl this is quite a discovery, to learn that the great wide world is, above all, silly.

"And," says she, "you could pay for our rooms now, couldn't you? Then we wouldn't need anybody."

I felt so much like a bright light the fog shoulda glowed all around us.

"Can and will," says I. Oh my, oh my. "Uh—does that mean no more Billy the Banker?"

"I have uses for Billy the Banker. But this'll make him nervous, and I need him nervous."

"Why?" says me.

"You'll see."

We're fancy-footed in high heels and the fog takes each step and throws out each sharp click so's it sorta echoes.

Heavy clops of a horse. From a cloud of fog steps a tall animal with a sleepy cop atop.

"Ladies!" says he, like he's saying, "Unicorns!"

D'Varn, she curtseys and I follow suit.

"You're movies, am I right?"

Again we curtsy. He shakes his head, smiles sorta, clops into the cloud, and wearily over his shoulder he parts with, "Womenfolk smokin in public. Coulda ticketed ya. Fined ya. Arrested ya…"

Further from the hotel the fog darkened but for gaslights glowin and flickerin. I'll miss the gaslights. There's talk of electric streetlights. I'm against em. But progress is progress, they say, and tall power-poles line the boulevard at intervals, wire linkin each to each. Makes Hotel Hollywood bright, so I suppose it's alright.

Me and D'Varn, holdin hands, walkin slow.

"We could be anywhere in the world," says D'Varn.

"Anywhere there's gaslights," says me.

"You." She tugs my hand sharp. "We're two beauties alone in the night and anything could happen."

"That's why I wear this!" and I dropped her hand and pulled my blade.

In these duds, puttin the blade back is harder than getting it out. I'd made a rig that fit lower on my leg so's I had to dip to get to it, like a dance-step, but I'd got swift with practice.

"I didn't mean that kind of anything, Willie, I meant anything wonderful."

I'm hiking my dress to put back my blade and D'Varn says, "Good biz. Shows lots of leg. I'm going to—*incorporate* that—in *my* flicker."

"Give a kiss here and make it snappy," says me.

Don't ask me why but we kissed like we were cryin. It just came over us. A burstin feelin.

Then, of a sudden, she's with the biz again: "That French-Canadian gal at the Keystone, who plays the violin and won't call it a fiddle and won't play anything hillbilly—what's her name?"

"Vivian," says me.

"Vivian! I wish she was walking behind us in the fog playing a lovely melody. I can almost hear it. Hear it?" Almost did, cept it was a sad music of D'Varn always wantin somethin that's not there. "One day I'll hire Vivian to walk behind us in the fog and play a waltz. You'll see!"

"So you've hired Sommie and you've hired a fiddle player. Anybody else?"

"Oh, I have a list."

"I'll bet you do."

"I do! And I'll hire you."

"You won't either," says me. "You're my queen, I am your loyal subject, but you ain't my idea of a boss."

"Sassy strumpet. Kiss."

All those aromas of flowers afloat in the fog and the taste of D'Varn's mouth.

"Look at all we get for free," says she. Very un-D'Varn.

Says the voice of Esther, "Not one thing's for free in the wicked city."

Esther just sorta appeared. Decked out in her finest, those enormous titties pushed up so's they practically spill out her gown. Plus a hat that's a platform for flowers. Her left hand holds a pair of high heels by their heels. Her right arm hangs loose from her shoulder like it doesn't belong to her, and in that right hand is her Special.

"Walkin," she starts to say, and can't quite get the rest out, drunk as she is, and she starts again, "walkin barefoot quiet in a fog and all I see is—bitches."

"Miss Esther," says I, "why you holdin that gun?"

"I like to."

She says nothing more, but kinda drifts off, stepping deeper into the cloud. We walked on.

"Think she's still with us?" says D'Varn. Louder D'Varn says, "She's welcome to walk with us. She should know that." Softer: "Poor thing, now she's got the two of us."

"Got us how?"

"You know how. She learned on the cliff that she'd caught double trouble. To employ your vernacular: Ain't happy about it."

Pulled my shawl tighter round my shoulders.

We'd stepped into a darker, thicker cloud. There was barely a glow from one gaslight. D'Varn lit a cigarette and waved the lit match in a circle til it burned out.

"Listen," she said. No footsteps, no clip-clops, no engines. "That's pretty. I think the fog appreciates us."

"Till I saw ocean I had no notion our fog smelled of it. Wonder if Fred's seen a beach yet."

"Is Fred like you?" asks D'Varn.

"I didn't know what I'd be like on my own, so I don't know what Fred's like on her own."

That made for a quietness as we're walkin toward a bright patch in the fog, oh, about two blocks off.

"D'Varn?"

"Missy?"

"When's your birthday?"

"Don't know."

"How can you not know?"

"I picked 1895 for the year. Makes me 19, which is probably about right. Haven't decided on the day, so as yet I may be 18. It's not very important, is it? Somebody has a birthday and sometimes I'll say, 'Today's my birthday too!' That's how I celebrate. I've meant to pick a particular day. If you must know, I'm kind of afraid to." She made her voice brighter: "Maybe Christmas?"

"Maybe Halloween."

"You!"

"I know! I know D'Varn's birthday!"

"Don't tell me," says she.

"Cause?"

"Cause if you tell me I'll believe it, and what if I hate it? I believe every goddamn thing you say, is the trouble. You didn't know that, did you? So OK, Miss Smarty Willie, what's my birthday?"

"The 4th of July."

"Oh my!"

And D'Varn starts to cry. Like she's altogether-of-a-sudden another person. Then she realizes she's cryin and she acts it a little bit. Then: "That's perfect. You, you. My Willie. From now on and for keeps, the 4th of July. That'll be in the newspapers someday. Someday it'll be on my gravestone."

She turns away from me. I hear her take a deep breath. She turns back to me. Grips me strong in a hug and I feel her tears on my face.

"Willie!"

"Auntie?"

"I have a birthday!"

Some bakery nearby was startin in with the scent of Heaven sweetenin the fog. Also a waft of stink, burning silver nitrate film, from Mr. DeMille's studio a bit to the south in the dark.

"Here we are," says D'Varn, flickin her cigarette into the mist. "Take a gander at that."

I'd been ganderin as we walked.

Bathed in brightness was a billboard big as sin. Bigger than three flicker-screens, and a good bit taller. One humongous face. A dark-haired head big as a house, her long hair kinda stringy like it's wet and flowing behind her like it's drippin, bare shoulders like she's naked, and she's lookin up toward something above and she's all eerie of expression. Her head's so big, if she had a body to fit it she'd be tall as four-five-six power-poles and wearin not a stitch.

The lettering's near as tall as D'Varn: *WHO IS THIS WOMAN?!* And, smaller: *4 Reels.* Smaller still: *A Mutual Masterpicture—Shown Soon at Leading Theaters.*

"Gee." That's me.

"Isn't it beautiful?" says D'Varn

"You're prettier."

"Of course I am. I mean the billboard."

I thought it was what Sommie might call a "monstrosity," but kept my trap shut. D'Varn was in raptures as the fog's mists floated about shinin from the billboard's glary lights.

"I'll see to it," says D'Varn, "that my first billboard is right here, in honor of this evening when you gave me my birthday. You'll see my face on billboards so large! And you'll know that somewhere in that *enormous* head there's thoughts of you."

"I'll be thrilled to be so important in your *past.*"

"Willie, did you ever dream of a fairy-place where anything could happen to anyone?"

"Anything's kinda big, D'Varn."

She takes my hands. "Hold hands with me as we step prettily into the kingdom of Anything." But right then she goes: "I don't want to give you up, Willie, I want to stay just here. Always believe that."

I got trembly, which she saw, and she said: "Let's go home. Cause—you know."

It's like a song's refrain, how we'd do.

She'd say, "Let's go home, Willie. Cause—you know."

I'd say, "I know."

"When we're home, I'll make you very happy."

"I'm happy now," I say.

"I'll make you happier."

2

D'VARN'S BIRTHDAY-PROUD NOW, set to charmin herself into how the Fourth of July *truly* is the day of her birth. If D'Varn's what to go by, actresses are good at charmin themselves into the belief of anything they want. It's like she says bout the malarkey she feeds Billy Her Banker: "I do not lie, I *perform*."

So she'll say, "Willie, there's somethin I've learned about you. You have the gift of sight. You looked into my soul and you knew—you knew—that my soul came into this world July the Fourth. That's real as limburger cheese."

She ain't lyin, ain't funnin. She's performed herself into an honest-to-Betsy, real as cheese, July Fourth birthday.

Says all her life she'll have me to thank for her birthday—says this whispy-like, with that way she has of puttin you in her past though you're sittin right beside her and her hand's warm on your thigh—those long fine fingers squeeze ever so slightly, her pointy filed nails dig in just a little, and she stares away, not even lookin at me, and says, breathy, "Willie—you're so beautiful."

I feel beautiful cause'a her, but am I?

I ask.

Says she, "How you stand, how you move, even how you sit still—how your catty body folds when you sleep—it's like—I don't know what it's like."

"I don't recognize her that you're speakin of."

"I *know*. Me too. Mabel says the same, looks at herself on screen, says, 'Who is that person, I wonder.'"

Says she, "Your face—how a cat always watches, never just looks but *watches*." Then, quick as you finger-snap: "My face when we're loving—tell me."

"I can't. I'd feel silly. I just . . . love you."

"Listen to us," says she, "talking sappy. We're impossible."

"Your new favorite word, impossible."

"Well, we are."

We're a'snuggle on the divan, her hand on my thigh, my hand on her hand, and while we speak not once do we look at each other, but each looks out into the night-dim room as though we're lookin far across a great distance. Somethin is movin in that distance and it's us. And that *us* comes closer and closer. When it gets real close we'll start in on each other with terrific hunger.

I'm not for talkin dirty but I'll pucker up and try, cause, aside from bein movies, what we liked best, and did most, folks call dirty.

Me, seems I've been chasin after my body from the start, tryin to keep up with it—how it looks, what it wants, what it does. Since I was little my body's always schemin to get me into some kinda trouble. But it ain't my fault how it looks, what it wants, what it can do. The Lord made it. So fault me if you like, but fault Him too, and good luck with that.

At the Keystone I learned this body of mine is good for stuff other than chores and mischief. It's got agility that's good for flickers and it's deep down good for dirty.

I feel lucky cause I am, and never luckier than when I woke that first mornin beside D'Varn on that big white soft bed, fairy-tale soft. On Daddy's farm we slept on hay-mattresses that crackled as you settled into em. Hay, straw, you changed the inners when it got too flat so's to again be bulky and crackly. Roll over and a strand of straw might poke you. D'Varn's bed was like you slept upon a cloud to wake somewhere high over the world.

That first morning, lucky as I felt, I felt just as stupid and embarrassed. I was naked. Never woke naked before.

Would she still like me?

What-all we'd done in the night was all over my body like it was still happenin in some echoin way.

I'm awake and she's awake. We don't speak, don't move.

I don't know what to do.

"Go to the bathroom," says she.

I was glad of that cause I had to pee but was too nervy to stir.

When I got back she went—left me alone in that bed wonderin.

She comes back, twistin a cigarette into an ivory holder, stands there lightin up like she don't even know she's naked.

I look at her and it's my eyes gobblin her up. She likes me lookin at her. She pulls back the sheet and looks at me. That soft sheet movin slow down my body, and her eyes on me all over.

She puffs her cigarette. Between puffs her lips move in little ways, like she's talkin without sayin. Finally: "You have hardly no bodily hair at all."

"Fuzz," says me.

"A creature is what you are. Smoothest of the fair." Then, how a child might, with words like bubbles poppin: "I'm thirsty!"

Gets us each a glass of water, poured from the porcelain pitcher. Hands me mine.

"Don't sit up. Lie on your side."

I did so. Propped my head with a thick pillow.

I sipped my glass. The tastes of last night, musty in my mouth, washed with water clear as clear.

I drink mine and she drinks hers and she takes our glasses and puts them on the vanity. Gets on the bed sittin with her knees tucked under her.

"You didn't tell me if you liked it last night?" says she.

My voice was tiny: "Didn't you know?"

"Will you stay with me here?"

"Stay?"

"Stay with me here and be mine. Belong to me. I'm nowhere near done with you."

"I'll stay. I'll stay and stay."

"But I'm the queen. What I say goes."

"I'm not much good at bein bossed."

"I won't boss you. I will rule you."

Slow-like, she stretches herself out beside me and mounts me full length with her entire weight. Her mouth finds my mouth and in goes her tongue with a hunger that gets more hungry as she kisses me and I'm wonderin if I'm doing it right and then I stop wonderin about anything. She's pressing that bone—"pubic," she'll call it, or "public," I'd get confused tween the two— she presses that bone onto my left thigh, pumps that with so much push and whap it hurts me and hurts bad and I love the hurt so, that hard pu-bone whappin me and her titties mushin me and she's holdin me so hard and we're breathin so hard, and she's moanin, and me's moanin, and when she's done and all sweaty and limp upon me I feel like everythin in me is dyin happy.

She rolls off me.

How a kitty says meow I say, "Why?"

"Why?!" She coughs, but it's a laugh. "Why what?"

"Why—why does *that*—feel so fine? It felt so fine."

"Bright eyes," as she lights another cig, "you can know what's what without knowing what's why."

Newness followed after newness.

She right away goes and buys a drawer-full of tight bright silk panties for me to "lounge" in. I know it's cause she prefers not to see my thing, which sets fine by me. I'm lyin on that white plush rug, propped on pillows, and she's sprawled on the sofa, wearin nothin, smokin, one long leg crooked at the knee, t'other leg spread wide with a high-arched foot restin on my thigh, and it's like her "kitty," as she calls it, stares straight at me while we just pass the time of day.

"There is," says she, "a rule of life the world over and it is, I believe, the basis of civilization." She pauses. "Actually, I heard this from Sommie. He didn't say 'rule,' he said 'law.'" Sommie'ish voice: "That law reads thusly: Beauty may do as it pleases. Beauty makes its own rules."

"Gee, auntie. That's deep."

"Do you mock me?"

"Somebody gotta."

The foot that's on my thigh gives a kick.

Says she, "I'd asked Sommie could he figure out Mabel Ethelreid Normand, since I can't figure her at all. So that's what he answered and I liked it."

"What's to figure about Miss Mabel? She's wonderful."

"But not as pretty as me. Don't forget to add that."

"No one's pretty as you."

"As for Mabel Normand—the woman is a loon."

"But that's her job."

"I mean a 24-carat loon. One week, she's got two ex-boxers teaching her their trade—and she stays at it till she thinks she can punch like a man. Another week, she charms an aviator into teaching her to fly. Flew solo after four lessons. You do know, don't you, that she's got no contract with Sennett? Refuses to sign anything—yet she's the star! First thing she did out here in the great West, she learned from cowboys how to bust broncs. Can you believe? And all the while she's studying French when she's not riding bareback or throwing firecrackers."

"Don't forget her geography," says me. "And her reading."

"That Vienna doctor with the nasty mind," says she. "Mabel told me. And her lavender motor car. She must know the meaning of 'lavender.'"

"I don't."

"Means us, sweetie. Dykes, lesbos, muffhounds. I have a theory: Mabel Normand is a virgin. I don't think she and Mack have ever done it."

"Well, men and women aren't supposed to til they're married. Maybe"—

"Eat me," says she.

"Pardon?"

She puts her hand on her kitty.

Those first times I was all nervy. See, by now the whole time we're talkin we're all over each other with our eyes. We know we're gonna do somethin, that's why we're hangin about like we are, but we don't know what or when, and while she talks she'll idly run her hands here and there over her body, and me the same, and we're watchin each other's hands on our bodies, so now it's "Eat me" with her hands on her kitty and in an itsy-bitsy voice I say, "I'm afraid."

"It don't bite. *Doesn't* bite."

"I'm afraid I don't do it right."

She tells me again, like she has before, to take my time and not to just be lappin at it but pretend my tongue's a finger.

Then my mind goes that'a way on its own. I'm on my knees leanin against the sofa and doin her kitty with my mouth while her long legs hang over my shoulders and she's lovin it and I'm lovin it but also I'm *thinking*! Thinking, like my mind can't shut up. Thinkin about pigs, cows, horses, dragonflies, dogs, cats, I've seem em do it all my life and never seen em do this. Dogs and cats'll do it on themselves, not each other. But when D'Varn "eats" my rump, I have seen that. At the circus. One elephant just casually lifted its trunk and pressed that trunk deep, deep into the rump-hole of the elephant in front of it while folks are screamin and laughin and mommies and daddies are turning their kids' heads away and puttin hands over their kids' eyes, but I struggle free of Daddy's grip and jump away—musta been maybe ten—and see that long trunk come out of that rump with its tip curled round a bunch of fresh hay. Cross my heart and spit, I seen that. While the elephant-wranglers went nuts tryin to get them elephants out of sight.

"Take your time," D'Varn says low from far away, and I take my time, not thinkin anythin now, until she's ridin wave after wave of "Oh, oh, oh," she's pumpin into my face and my face feels like it's part of her, how I could feel all over my body what I was doin to her and I felt it through the skin of my face, not just my tongue, pushin my face into her terrific wetness, and, at the same time, of a sudden, I wanted to laugh about the elephant.

She pulls me by the hair up on top of her, my face and hair's all wet with herself, and she licks my face with lotsa small purry kisses, sippin her own taste.

I slide off the sofa and she does too and we're on the floor kinda entan-gled, and—this would make good biz for a flicker, but of course you can't— she reaches for cigarettes and matches and water-glass all at the same time while she tries to keep as much of her skin rubbin on as much of me as she can, and she's raisin herself up with stuff in her hands and she totters and the water spills all over me and we're laughin and that water felt shocking lovely.

She lights a cigarette and gives it to me, lights one for herself, yawns like a cat—tobacco and D'Varn-taste enjoy each other in my mouth—and she finishes her long stretch of a yawn, puffs the cig, gets a quizzical look.

"No, really, that Mabel," says she. "I'd bet money she's a virgin."

I thought of it as a kind of song and our voices were sing'y when we said it.

"I'll make you happy," she'd say.

"I am happy," says me.

"I'll make you happier," says she.

I'd say I was happy but I also wasn't. I was something too ferocious to call happy. She made me feel lonely and scared and beautiful and beautiful'est, all at once. Lonely cause sometimes I'd say "I love you" and she'd just look at me, eyes full of love, but wouldn't say the words though she knew I wanted her to.

I loved doing anythin she wanted but that scared me, too—like it made me bigger and littler at the same time. I loved her but sometimes wondered if I liked her. I wouldn't of jumped off that roof, that first time, if she hadn't been there, all of them lookin up at me, but *she* was lookin up at me and *she* was wantin to be proud of me and off I went. I'd never seen anyone so beautiful, yet she thought me—strange me—a beauty. And I didn't know what my face does until I saw her face change as she started learnin me.

Her face had been—how can I put it?—abrupt. Click, one expression. Click, another. Like she's sayin to herself, being an actress, "Now I'll show this, now I'll show that." Learnin me, it was like she learned about expressions in between the "clicks," if you get me. But she tried to learn my walk and couldn't. I glide. She sashays.

I made D'Varn happy. I knew that.

So one night we were on pillows on the white rug, a flowery breeze soft through the window, damp and sweet, those scents and our smells, and I turned away from her to reach for cigarettes, and she said, "Stay just like that, precious." I did so, and felt her face on my bum, and got all choked up with sweetness as she pressed her face into my crack, lickin, tonguin, on and on, but peaceful-like, calm, like I'm lyin on my side in a kind of dream, smokin, layin the cigarette on the end of the glass table, reachin for the brandy snifter, sippin, all the while she's doin what she's doin, and I watch my smoke curl up and fade into the air while she's down there on my rump with her lush tongue.

I almost didn't know when she stopped, cause it had gone on and on in such a kind of way that it's still goin on. But she put her hot hand on my hip and turned me over to her and smiled into my eyes. She kissed me so I could taste me. I sucked on her tongue. Musty, it was, flavored earthy, not even a little bit dirty.

She lights up and I light up again. We lie on our backs watchin our smoke.

Says she, "I go lost with you," and blows smoke across my nipples. "We're impossible."

"Impossible" is not so bad a word for love, but I'm pretty young and don't know much.

How we'd throw pillows anywhere on the rug, pillow-fightin some as we did so, then throw ourselves on the pillows, grabbin at each other all over, slurpin and lickin and pullin and pickin—hittin too, slap, sting, pinch, slap, slurp, suck, archin ourselves, on our backs, on our bellies, on all fours, the different smells of our different parts, satisfyin that sweet ache of the nipples, then we slow down and breathe together and light cigarettes and sip brandy, and once, lyin that way, our wildness tired but wild still, and D'Varn says, "Softly, softly, gently, gently, closer and closer, always and never there."

You never knew what D'Varn would say.

Then she's atop my face and I'm mouthin her kitty with my eyes wide open lookin up at her belly's curve and her breasts floatin and bouncin, her honey-colored hair backlit and haloed round her head, she leans forward pressin down on my mouth so's she'll almost break my neck and I see her throat move with her hisses, her moans, moanin my name like it's hurtin her.

One night, we're lyin on the floor all a'tangle on each other, tired out with lovin, and it strikes at me and I speak it: "The Bible says we'll go to Hell."

"If this is how you get there, how bad can it be?" Then says she, "The Lord put secret places all over us."

"Never before heard you refer to the Lord."

"Hold out your hand."

I did so. She licks on my palm, in between my fingers, sucks on one, bites on another, tickles with the tip of her tongue, my nipples are blazin, my hips are pumpin, and off we go till we're too tired to go on, we're dozy, and she says, like she can't give it up, "Pick a spot on me."

The crook behind her knee. She's a big strong gal. Things got dangerous, let me tell you.

So we've picked our spots, we're done, we're sweaty, hair stringy and tangled and damp.

Back to cigarettes and brandy. And brushin each other's hair. "Ouch," with the knots, ouch, ouch, ouch.

"D'Varn?"

"Baby?"

"Sometimes it scares me so, what we do."

"If you're not a little scared, you're not doing it right."

One night, sort of early for us, I'm in the black silk panties and she's in nothin and we're ogling each other and she's got a queer look and I'm wonderin what's what.

It's like she's tryin to figure somethin. She lights a cigarette and points with the cigarette.

"Did you notice that?" says she.

"That" is a wax-papered cube of lard that looks damned out of place on our glass coffee table amid the swan ashtrays, white and black, the gold-tipped Egyptians in their holder, and the wee wood matches in their wee vase.

"Know what that is?" says she.

"Course. Cube'a lard." Doesn't she know I can smell it?

"We're going to need it."

"You gonna cook me?"

"I've a friend," says she, "three friends, my wands. They think you're beautiful, too, like—*as*—I do."

I will absolutely not give her the satisfaction of askin what she's talkin bout.

She goes to the bedroom and I hear her open the closet with its mirror doors and she comes back with a carved wood box that I ain't seen before. Pale brown wood, tight of grain, delicate lookin, polished shiny.

She lays the box down so that, when she opens it, the top is between me and what's in it.

"These are my wands," says she. "I'll unwrap them from their pretty scarves, one by one."

She lays them out on a white pillow, one by one, and I can't believe what I'm seein.

She unwraps a large silk hanky she calls a scarf.

"Ivory," says she, laying out the first.

Unwraps a purple silk hanky.

"Obsidian," the second.

Unwraps a black silk hanky.

"Crystal," the third.

Each was long and thick and looked like a man's thing. A big man's big thing.

The ivory was white, but like it was washed in tea. The obsidian, black. The crystal was clear. I was frightened.

"What do you think, Willie?"

"I can't think a damned thing."

But I was thinkin, actually, of the craftsmanship, and what sort of a world this was that had people makin such things and puttin such care into the makin.

"Lie on your belly now."

I did not move.

"Your queen says: Now."

I did not move.

"You need brandy. I'll bring it to you."

She did so.

I couldn't take my eyes off them things.

This woman, who never once mentioned *my* thing, she's got these things settin in the dark of the closet all the while.

Most often avoided *my* thing like it wasn't there—which suited me perfectly—but she has these things in the dark of the closet.

She hands me the brandy. I gulped that tart burn'y liquid and gulped again.

"Go on now, you," says she. "Lie on your belly."

I did not want to. But I did so.

"Pick one," says she.

"One'a *them*?"

"Pick."

"Crystal's the scariest."

"Crystal, then."

I hear the crackle of wax paper unwrapping.

She greased my crack with the lard and then it was oh-my-god.

A lotta oh-my-god.

Crystal is cold and hurts and just at first I was too scared to like it til of a sudden I couldn't get enough of it. She's sayin how beautiful I am, she's moanin it, and I'm so scared and so crazily weepy-happy. When she finally pulled it outa me I missed it bein in me, my hurtin hole could feel *missing* the way you miss—well, whatever it is you most miss.

I felt wounded, but wounded in some kind of good way.

I was cryin, softly cryin. I turned from her, curled up in a ball, cried, she asked why, I did not answer, I just cried like cryin was all of me. When that stopped, I felt clean. Said so.

"You feel clean?" says she.

"I do."

Turned to her. Her gorgeous face was sweetness itself, sweetness and worry, and so tired.

D'Varn says soft, "I don't understand. Did I do wrong?"

"No. No, no, no, no, no."

We slept holding each other.

I was happier than anything.

I wake sometime later with that happiness all over me. D'Varn, she's deep asleep. I'm sittin, kinda rockin back and forth, to and fro, eyes clinging to her beauty in this dimness, memorizin, wanting never to forget, and I never have. Then I looked inside me at what I had to look at.

The last time I'd seen "hard ons," as they call em, was in dreams. Mine'll get hard sometimes but I don't look at it. I see em, the hard-ons, as they was in this over-and-over dream.

Same dream. This dream. I'm six or seven maybe. Daddy, he'd bought me an outfit. "Time ya dressed like a boy." Spent some money on it too, as was not like Daddy. Knickers, shoes, suspenders, the works. Overalls for farm work. Sayin, "Mother's as allowed you dresses two-three years too long. Alright for little uns, lotsa folks does that, once upon a time me too, Ah was little once, but y'all are now a boy, doin boy-chores, Ah expect boy-work of ya, and y'gonna have the look like what ya are."

"I ain't," says me.

"Let's us see."

I expected the beatin. He kinda outdid himself but in the dream I expected that too and when a beatin goes on long enough it gets kinda dreamy itself and you forget to hurt.

Beatin's over, I'm kinda drunk with it, that's how you get after a bad one, and I thought he was done. He was not done.

"Now here's the rule Ah'm making fuh this here contest, son, this contest that Ah'm gonna win. Ah ain't takin that dress off ya, ain't rippin it off ya, Ah am beatin ya t'within a inch a your life til YOU take it off ya. Then we gonna BURN. Burn all your girl'y things. Gonna make Mother and sister WATCH. Gonna make my POINT."

That beating re-commenced. All he got for it was more "Ain't." All I got for that was more beatin.

Mother and Fred were scared like you can only be in dreams.

Daddy, he suddenly went all cold. "Ah'm goin out and diggin mahself a hole."

It had come on dark.

Mother brought me to her bed—hers was different than Daddy's—Fred come too, all three in the bed, and not a word.

We heard him dig, then he made a fire by the hole and we saw its glow.

We were "powerful scared," as Mother would say.

We heard men out back now with Daddy, laughin-like, I don't remember words, and Daddy, he comes in, picks me up, throws me over his shoulder, Mother says at him, with a voice so fear-trembly, "I'll kill you in your sleep, I'll kill you in your sleep," and I'm held over his shoulder by his great strength wishin she'd not said that, he'll beat her for it sure.

He lowers me into the hole. It's round'ish, and just about my size. I'm facin the fire, and it's high, and it's bright. And suddenly I'm a'circled with the shadows of grown men. And what I see in the firelight are their things. Their things hangin out their pants. And two were straight and hard and the others were long'ish bent.

One by one and all together they peed down on me.

And did other things with their things that splattered down at me.

Then I wake.

Cept, come a certain morning, I woke from that dream and told Fred. She busts out cryin. Scary cryin. I hug her. She whispers, "It's not, Wil. Not a dream. Daddy went off with those men. You were passed out in the hole. Mother pulled you out. Mother lifted that dress off you, I got water and soap, we scrubbed you clean, and it was like you didn't feel or see or anything—you were not asleep, you were not awake, we were so scared for you. I threw the dress in the hole and buried it, filled in the hole. Mother, she got out a dress outa our drawers, all clean and pressed, and put it on you, and took you to your bed, she'n'me, and she went and got the shotgun, and extra shells, and she'n'me sat either side'a your bed, and waited, and waited, and you slept deep, and Daddy come home, he was quiet, he stood in the doorway of our room holding a lantern up, saw us three, said only, 'It's over.' Never made a peep about your ways again. Just hated you is all."

I'm feelin everythin and nothin.

"Wasn't a dream?"

"Wasn't a dream. You woke next day cryin, thinkin it was the worst night-mare ever. Mother told me, 'Let her think so.'"

"Not a dream, Fred?"

"Gonna be ok today, you?" says she.

I waited quietly. Chored quietly. Till afternoon. Mother was nappin. Daddy too, his afternoon nap. Fred darned in the front room. I didn't worry about my sister. I knew she'd be fine.

I loosed my longish hair. Put on my sister's favorite thing to wear—the neck-to-foot white nightdress she'd always say she wished she had the nerve to wear all day—it buttoned up the middle—I grabbed that beige coat of hers with the slim waist and fur collar. Folded the coat proper. Shook out my hair more—cause I felt pretty. Stepped into the kitchen, which faced out the back. Poured oil from the table lamp, a splatter here, a splatter there, struck a match, lit those curtains, watched em catch, and stepped out the back door barefoot.

Took two long strides, planted my feet wide, my back's to the house and I'm likin the flame-throbs hot on my behind.

My fire had caught good, cracklin loud. I held the folded coat to my chest. Through my mouth I took a breath—tasted wood-smoke on my tongue. Then I ran. I can really run.

FAMOUS PLAYERS

AGNES DEMILLE

The sagebrush in the rain, the eucalyptus in the rain—
you see, spring was such a marvelous thing there.
The grass would be tangled with the lupin, the poppies …
all of it just blooming wild in the gutter, in the open
fields, between your school-house and the next house—
flowers everywhere—I cannot tell you!—
gather them up by the armful!

CHARLIE CHAPLIN

There were times I'd build sets without any idea
of what I was to do with them. 'Where do you
want this staircase?' they'd ask. 'On the left,' I'd say.
Why, God knows. You place yourself in a labyrinth
and try to find a way out.

LILLIAN GISH

We were constantly alert for mannerisms, gestures,
facial expressions that we could use . . .The city smelled
like a vast orange grove—and the abundance of roses…

1

HURT AGAIN. The other arm. And the knee, the left. Now it's me with a cane!

Not my fault this time. A simple piece of biz, Hank Mann and me, and we're not even foreground, just "background mayhem" to be tripped upon by Chester Walrus and Big Mack Swain—I'm to zig and Hank's to zag while we knock furniture over and the point is to fall on our marks and get tripped upon, like I say, but just as we're nearin our zig-zag spot there's this little kid right on it, and, so's we don't trample the kid, we slam into each other, POW!—we hit hard and landed twisted on a pile of junk. Mr. Coy Watson comes out of nowhere, sayin he's sorry-very-sorry, and he picks up the kid— the toddler's one of his, he's got maybe seven kids. Well, as Mr. Sennett says, "It's all in a day's work." Just sprains and sore weakness, nothin important, but here I am on a workday sittin on a park bench in the sun.

You hear a lot of "we're behind schedule" around the Keystone. So when Mr. Sennett goes nervy on us to "make up the time" he'll send a crew on a Big Red trolley to shoot a "park picture," as we call em, usually at nearby Echo Park Lake. In a park picture it's as Sommie says, "Various people become enamored of various people to whom they are not wed." At the Keystone the worst thing for a marriage is a walk in the park—or, really, to leave the house in any way, shape, or form.

I'm on a shaded bench on a paved path that slopes to Echo Park Lake, but the bench is on a curve and doesn't face the lake. I can look over its back and see a crew at work: Devil Charlie, Chester Walrus, and herself, D'Varn, a co-star at last. Also the Vivian who's an actress (not the Viv who's a fiddle-player). Charlie's directin as well as actin, and of course there's a camera-grinder, also a props man who "schleps" a big wooden props-box for just-in-case, and it's got film canisters and a first-aid kit and box-lunches and what-all. They're fixin to shoot, talkin, pointin this way and that, mimickin—

rehearsin. They're across the lake and look to be about two inches high from where I sit. And all the while this big bright Los Angeles goes back and forth in autos, wagons, and Big Reds that couldn't care less.

I came separate, on my own. I'm to myself today, wearin my lavender-suede Mabel-shoes and a hat to match, delicately-shaded gloves and stockings, a locket round my neck (with nothin in it), and the thinnest and flowingest summer dress—plus a dainty purse, plus my new cane, a substantial one, from the props building. Legs crossed, showin lots of ankle, but the Edendale police know us, so I'm not likely to get shooed off as a suspicious unsavory woman—though folks strollin by stop conversin as they pass and pretend not to notice a gal alone lookin as I look.

Across the lake from me, tall D'Varn struts in a dark, tight'ish suit, sportin one of her rogue'ish wide-brimmed hats, and she's gesturin to Chester who's seated on a bench. A camera's set up on both, then on him, then on her, then on him gettin up, then closer on the two of em smoochin like crazy, which is funny in itself, even from across the lake, cause Chester's so much shorter than she. They smooch some more. What's all that smoochin about? Is it even allowed? Camera's grindin on and on, Charlie's laughin while Vivian's cringin and hidin her eyes but laughin too. Finally D'Varn lets Chester go and they're all laughin. Next set-up's on Charlie, huggin a tree, kissin that tree, then tippin his hat at that tree.

Passers-by have stopped to watch.

Charlie's takin off his baggy pants!

But he's wearin normal pants underneath. Bows to his spectators.

Then Charlie hands his tramp-coat and derby to the props man, who puts them in the wood box and takes out a proper jacket and straw skimmer-hat for Charlie. The crew, includin D'Varn, head off to the Big Red trolley stop. Charlie starts a walk around the lake. He'll pass near me if he goes far enough.

And so he does. Points his cane at me.

"Miss Catch! Just the person."

I raise a gloved hand in a small wave. My hello's in my smile.

He stops before me, gives me his quick little bow and tips his skimmer, same as he done with that tree. I touch my hat-brim.

"Might you accompany me for a coffee—and a slice of pie?" He sees my surprise. "I know just the place. A short walk. In fact, it's why I prefer Echo

Park, though the park by the zoo offers more variety."

"Happy to, sir." I rise on my stout cane. "Thanks for askin."

"That's a cane for London fogs and the beating of ruffians."

"We're the ruffians around here, mister."

"So we are," he smiles, "so we are."

I take his arm and we match steps, cept with my slight limp. He imitates the limp, so we're limpin together, then he's back to walkin regular. D'Varn's taught me to let the man do the work of pickin the conversation, so I'm mum.

"May I sound you out a bit," says he. "I know you're special friends, of course—but just a bit—about Miss D'Varn?" I make to disapprove but he rushes on. "Because I am in the process of finishing my second and *last* picture with her—*not* that she isn't quite good—she's quite good!—so are you, as a matter of fact—but"—he looks at me hard. "I shot the *last* scene of *this* picture first, in order to know where we were going this time round. Mack loved my idea, called it 'poetic justice.' I'm in a folding-chair in a cheap picture-theater, front row, and Vivian's on my left, and D'Varn's on my right, and let's just say they are being very nice to me. Unbeknownst, their two hulking husbands come from behind and, picking me up bodily, heave me through the film-screen. The end, yes? Any little story could get to that ending. But what *she* does, your friend, asserting her stamp, she takes over the *beginning* of this little picture by playing neither like a girlfriend nor a straying wife but—and I noticed you watching—she played a prostitute! And I went with it, because"—

"She's very beautiful," says me.

"She is! But that's not why. I don't know why. Now will Mack go with it, that's the thing? Because—I don't see how—the censors . . . It's *lewd*. That is a fact. *Not* what I wish to do. *I* directed and yet—I fell in, I fell in with her, with her *atmosphere*. Never again. And don't you know the first picture we did was worse? Worst I've done yet."

"She loved it," says me.

"I'm sure she did." He liked telling me this next part, in spite of himself, cause he did the poses as we walked and people stared and laughed.

"My character is an artist, a painter, D'Varn is his model, she poses on a pedestal, clad only in a wrapped sheet, standing so!" He stands so. "Beside her in the shot, just a little in the background, D'Varn's placed a statue of a naked woman who looks much like D'Varn, and is posed somewhat like her, standing *so.*" Again he stands so. "D'Varn's idea, mind you. Next, in the shot, left to right, but further in the background, she places *another* naked-lady statue. Then, as we view left to right, comes me, my head bobbing more or less around—forgive me—the crotches of those two statues. Not actually, but it's a flat screen of course, so *actually,* since that's what one *sees?* Which your friend knew very well, didn't she? And I, alas, did not realize. When viewed, our performances have nothing to do with anything but *highlighting* the nude statues! Once you look at it that way it has its own hilarity, I suppose, but is it comedy? I told Mack, I bet him, *The Face On The Barroom Floor* will never play, it won't pass the censors, *and* it's not comedy. I stood against its release. So what did Mack say? That if they censor it in Boston it shall make all the more money in New York. And, to top it all, that awful ending . . . you saw it? Pure frustration. I could have screamed when they screened it, watching myself be a goo-goo man chalking circles on the floor! But I didn't know what else to do and one must reach THE END somehow."

"What I wanna know," says me, "is why you cast my friend a second time?"

"Mack dared me to. After all, what could go wrong in a park picture? She's cunning, is what."

"I wanna know somethin else, why you never cast me?"

He says nothin. Like he didn't hear.

We're at the corner of Sunset and Echo Park boulevards. Busy and noisy. Big Reds on Sunset goin both ways, clangin together, autos and trucks honkin, wagons, one-horse cabs, and a delivery truck, a flatbed parked practically on the sidewalk, and on that truck is a long sign, and it says *EVERY BOTTLE STERLIZED* in big letters that dwarf the smaller *Coca Cola.*

"Well, now, answer me, Mr. Devil Charlie—why not me?"

He's ignorin that we're about to cross a busy street. Steps off the curb and stops. I do likewise, who gives a hoot? Cars honk.

"We're similar in height," says he. "You're slim, as am I. And—agile as am I. You can do nearly anything I can do."

"Miss Mabel's got agility."

"Not like ours. If I cast you, then where's the contrast? Comedy must have contrast—big-little, fat-slim, tall-grouchy, pretty-ugly."

"Well what's your contrast with Miss Mabel? You're 'similar' in size, both dark."

"Isn't it obvious? I'd expect you to know. Mabel—is a good person."

Two teamsters luggin wooden crates of bottles off the truck slow down traffic across the street, vehicles honk at them on that side and us on this side, and we scramble past em, Charlie tipping his hat, me touching my fingertips to my bonnet's rim, the teamsters carry their boxes through glass-paned swingin doors under a sign that reads MEDLIN'S EATERY—GRUB'N'SUDS.

"Ah, here we are," says Charlie.

A chalk-board in the window reads:

SPECIALS TODAY

Creamed Chipped Beef—5 cts

Fried Oysters—20 cts

Liver And Onions—15 cts

Corned Beef And Cabbage—15cts

Oxtail Stew—10cts

Tripe—5cts

Pork'n'Beans—10 cts

Coffee And Pie—one thin dime

Pig's Feet FREE With 5 ct Beer—As Many As Ya Dare!!!

Pig's feet?

There were booths, it wasn't a bar but a restaurant, so I'm allowed. Sawdust on the floor and scents bitter'ish and sweet from hops, pies, oysters and onions, and that friendly aroma of warm beer. Charlie's takin pleasure watchin me be fascinated by placards framed under glass, each with a saying like WHY NOT?—and EVERY-THING WORKS IF YOU LET IT—and TIME'S EVAPORATING—and WHY IS MY LIFE?—and IF YOU DO IT ALL TODAY/ TOMORROW WILL BE BORING. Also, in a place of honor behind the counter, flanked on each end by mirrors: PHILOSOPHY GETS YOU PIGFEET.

Charlie's expects a comment and I satisfy that with, "You just never know in Edendale."

There's a fellow alone in the booth nearest the door. I swear the look on his face is sad enough to curdle the cream in his coffee.

Charlie tips his hat as he guides me to one of the swivel stools along-side a long counter, then he sits himself beside me. Behind the counter, in a starched apron, is a big'ish fellow, bearded, eyes sad and kind, but he brightens as he sees us and hails out, "Mr. Chaplin!"

Charlie, who rarely is loud, hails back, "Mr. Medlin!"

And both laugh. Which is also rare for Charlie.

They shake hands sort of formally across the counter.

Mr. Medlin ganders at me appreciatively and says, "Why, look what you've escorted into my humble establishment."

You know I don't mind bein on display. I flash my eyes and smile my "Anything" smile, and poor old Mr. Medlin is a little taken aback.

To Mr. Medlin I extend my gloved hand. "Willie's the name, but they call me Catch."

He takes my hand and bows. "James Medlin, proprietor."

"Your sayings interest me, sir."

"Their purpose: to instigate conversation! Or thought. Odd how rarely the two go together, don't you think? Or do you think?"

"Mr. Medlin," says Charlie, "we'll be having coffee and pie, and, no doubt, some thought."

"Apple or cream, Mr. Chaplin."

"Cream, if you please, Mr. Medlin."

Like they're performin a vaudeville act, but without punchlines.

Medlin's coffee was rich and perfect, and the cream pie was dreamy. (Cream pies we throw at the Keystone are of a lather you can't actually eat.)

I nodded at a military photograph framed on the wall, in which a younger Mr. Medlin was prominent.

"Cuba, '98," says Mr. Medlin. "Regular Army—no Rough Rider show-offing. We had a sergeant who sparked my passion for philosophy. He'd say, 'My philosophy is'—and then it would be how deep to dig a latrine or something about shining buttons. Now, those Spanish soldiers, Miss Catch, weren't wild about being in a war but some were ornery enough, and one afternoon when we're getting shot at from three sides I decided, 'This is philosophically inadequate! If I live I shall further investigate philosophy and decline to re-enlist.' Therefore—free pigfeet! Buy a five-cent beer or present a gem of a philosophic sentence and your award shall be a priceless pigfoot."

Charlie starts in but Mr. Medlin stops him with, "Schopenhauer! I gave your Schopenhauer not only an hour but an hour and a half. Smug and gloomy, Mr. Chaplin. I won't have it. No pigfoot for Schopenhauer. Excuse me, please."

Down the counter he serves a cop a beer and declines payment as, wielding a scraper, he expertly sweeps the foam off the tall schooner. Then he turns to that solitary sad fella and tells him, "Yes, I said Shopenhauer is precisely a fuddy-duddy! Any objections, buster?" The man pays Mr. Medlin the tribute of an almost-smile.

He's back with us and Charlie's eager. "Mr. Medlin, how about this: You can hear the trolley's bell under water! Roscoe and I played a scene on the lake in which our boat sank, and us with it. The first thing we remarked as our heads bobbed up was that we'd heard the bells! An experience rife with philosophic implications, I would say."

"A pig's foot worth, Mr. Chaplin. Miss Catch, do you like my pie?"

"I could float away with delight, Mr. Medlin. Understand, I don't have any philosophy at all, but I won't disappoint, cause I have a friend who has plenty."

"*That* man, Somerset!" Charlie says. "I can't help thinking of him as some sort of butler—and not even a butler—an actor playing a butler."

"Don't you rag on my Sommie," says me.

"I suppose he reminds me of—me, in a way—another Cockney gutter-runt trying to work up some class."

"Miss Catch," says Mr. Medlin, "your philosophy, if you please?"

"Like I say, it ain't mine, it's Sommie's. But here goes: The relative—and the absolute—exist in the same—continuum."

A spoonful of delicious cream pie and a sip of rich coffee while Mr. Medlin considers.

On the counter, in arm's reach, rests a massive jar of disgusting pig's feet submerged in some awful-lookin fluid. Mr. Medlin ladles one of them pig's feet out and places it on a saucer.

"Now that statement would presume," says he, and thinks a bit—"that statement would presume a continuum *larger* than either the relative or the absolute. Which would in turn imply that this continuum might just be large enough to contain what-all we've never heard of yet, neither relative nor absolute, and what could that be? Strange and wondrous, Miss Catch, strange and wondrous." He slides the saucer across the counter to me. "I don't mean to be forward but allow me to ask, is this your first foot-of-pig?"

I ate the dang thing. I don't intend to be philosophy-smart again lest I have to eat another.

2

MISS MABEL ATTENDS BOXING MATCHES any chance she gets, so I guess she knows what she's talkin about when she says Hank Mann walks like a boxer—also Mr. Sennett says Hank's the toughest guy on the lot. Hank does walk different, on the balls of his feet, a slight spring to his stride, arms at his sides slightly raised, hands curled lightly fist-like and game for any biz you got. Now he's walkin toward me, costumed as a Kop.

It's a bustlin normal day at the Keystone, commotion in the Ghost Building, collidin scents and sounds and yells, sudden surges of this fiddle or that mouth-organ from different directions, and if you're waitin to be "on background" and you're a guy, you're likely at the never-ending dice game of costumed and not-costumed gents under the Ghost Building, and, if you're a gal, you're likely at the north corner sittin around a table playin cards and crackin wise. Me, I mostly like to watch whatever strikes me. I'm floozy-dressed for a café scene, waitin to get shoved off a bandstand, land on a table, roll off it, and have folks trip on me. But Hank-the-Kop interrupts that intention.

"The Skipper wants you," says he.

"I'm due up," says me.

"Not if the Skipper wants you."

We're out the Ghost Building and I start for Mr. Sennett's office but Hank says, "Nope."

Instead, Kop and Floozy are out the gate crossing Alessandro as a Big Red clangs by and passengers gawk us, then we enter the "expansion," the even bigger lot across the street that's got a really tall Ghost Building with two-story split-level sets, so new it's not fully there yet. There's paint-smell, noise of saws and hammers, sawdust scent, the street-traffic's louder here for some reason, and then a rank whiff that I've smelt before. I'm wary. Whiff gets stronger. We're at the foot of a stair onto a second-level set. Up the stairs.

We stand in front of a door and Hank knocks.

"Skipper?" he calls.

"That you, Hank?" Mr. Sennett calls back.

"We're here."

"Come in on three. One," and a camera behind that wall starts to grind. "Two," and another camera grinds. Oh, brother. "Three."

Hank twists the doorknob, pushes the door open, and with his hand on the small of my back he kinda glides me in ahead.

Mr. Sennett's behind a desk and he's not alone. Now, our Mr. Sennett is a big fellow, six feet or more, and built solid, but the lion that sits on the desk—a big, male, maned lion, sitting kingly—Mr. Lion makes Mr. Sennett look boy-size. And I get the impression Mr. Lion don't like the all-of-a-sudden racket of the cameras. First a growl, then a roar.

I got chills all over, including my privates, and even Mr. Sennett reared back a bit.

"Howdy, Catch." Then he beckons by crookin a forefinger. "Closer. Make sure you're in the shot."

"Happy to oblige. Who's your friend?"

"Not so sure he is a friend."

Mr. Lion tolerates us so far.

"I'm gonna blab at you," says Mr. Sennett, "and you're gonna do some biz."

"Really?" says me.

"Anything you want," says he.

I'm not taking my eyes off Mr. Lion as I "inhabit" my floozy get-up.

Hank's still a step behind me.

I talk back at Hank without turning my head, my eyes and smiles fixed on that beast. "Hank, take my arm like you're pushing me forward."

"If you say so."

"Go slow. Anytime."

We're nearin that critter as I point my voice but not my face at Mr. Sennett. "Skipper, talk like I'm supposed to be payin attention to you."

He does so, sayin any old thing.

Practically face to face with Mr. Lion's *enormous* head I'm talkin nonsense-bla-bla straight at that beast, ignorin Mr. Sennett, and the lion's lookin straight into me, and I'm bla-bla-bla-bla-bla and Mr. Sennett's tryin to get a word in edgewise, leanin further across the desk, which maybe ain't a good idea cause, as Mr. Sennett moves, Mr. Lion twitches. My bla-blas go louder and jollier. Mr. Lion ain't sittin anymore; he's on his all-four-paws, and he kind of angles himself, his tail shoots straight up, and out his ass-area there powerfully spurts a stinky spray straight at the camera crew that's to my right—and those ninnies yell! Well, Mr. Lion, he don't appreciate that. Swirls his great maned head in that crew's direction, his big body sorta swirls in behind his head, and, oh, Mr. Lion leaps—not at the crew, precisely, but past them. A shotgun goes off! Rips a wide hole in the Ghost Building's canvas wall as Mr. Lion pounds-pounds-pounds out the set's door and down the stairs I just come up, and we, all of us, scared stiff and still, vibrate from our feet to our hair-tips with the pound-pound-pound of Mr. Lion's beastly-big paws.

You'll have to get somebody else to tell you what happened next cause I have no idea, except nobody got et and that lion was corralled alive.

I'm still vibratin when I say, without proper reverence, "Mr. Sennett, what the Sam Hill were you thinkin?!"

At which we in his "office" go helpless with hysterical laughter right then and for the foreseeable future, whenever any of us brought it up.

Mr. Sennett never did answer my question. He didn't even say, "We live our art."

Says he meekly, "It was gonna be a promo reel."

The stench of lion-spray stayed in my nostrils all that day. They had to junk the wood and canvas that got wet cause there was no gettin out the stink but to burn that stuff to ash. Those who got sprayed had to leave for wherever they bathed.

3

WE'D GOT US A NEW DELIGHT, D (as I sometimes call her now), Esther and me: silk robes of bright colors out'a China! Pricey, true, but this very silly world salaries me like crazy so I have three such robes, we each do, and mine's ice blue, forest green, and crimson red. D's are golden and silver and, God help us, pink. Esther's are snow-white, cream-white, and pitch black. Wondrous robes, a'flash with embroidered dragons that all but glow. China silk up and down your body. The word is *exquisite* (a D'Varn word.)

Here's an oddness. Separately, D'Varn and Esther each have asked how I can sit and sip and smoke on this white divan for hours alone and not be bored? Answer is, I don't understand *bored*. I understand what they're sayin, but I don't know how to imagine it. I've been restless, sure, but bored never. I try to explain that I sit and sip and smoke and watch what there is to watch, like the smoke hoverin, or the changin light outside—listen to what there is to listen to, hotel noises, street sounds, wind when there's wind—and see where my mind goes, almost like watchin a flicker.

But D—she don't do anything like that. So what's she doin lately on the big white bed with the door closed, not goin out, not spendin time with me or Es, but in a room alone, very much not the D'Varn we know and love and endure. Also, I hear her speaking sentences softly careful-like, but too quiet for me to make out and I'm reluctant to stoop to snoopin, until it came to me to rush things—not snoopin, just throwin open that bedroom door and bargin in.

She's smirkin. "Wondered how long it would take you."

"You are holdin a book."

"Memorizing it! *If I have sinned, let my beauty answer for my sin.* Sweetie, *SHE* is me."

"She?" says me.

D holds up the book and in three big letters the cover says **She**.

Says D, "In the language of savages Her name means *She Who Must Be Obeyed.*"

"That's you all over."

"I want to tell Esther in my own way, so don't you tell her."

"You jokin? Tellin her as quick as I can run down the hall."

She Who Must Be Obeyed screams her protest as I fail to obey and, barefoot, my ice-blue shiny dragon-robe swirlin all over my nudity, I long-stride-run down the hall passin potted plants lit by gaslamps on the wall, to bang on Esther's door.

Es opens, wreathed in sweet-smellin smoke and wearin her cream-white dragon robe. (D was in the pink, is why I didn't mention it. How does a body wear pink?)

Says I, "You need to see somethin."

So Ice-Blue and Cream stride to see what's what, glowin with dragons.

D'Varn's on the big white bed, no book in sight.

I say, "Might as well take that book out from wherever you hid it, cause I'll tear this room apart to find it, you know I will."

Reaches under the covers and there's the book.

"Flutter my girlish heart!" flutters Esther.

"Why didn't anybody tell me about *reading*?" bawls D, mightily offended.

"Some of us tried."

"You didn't tell me it was *fun*. How could you leave out that it's *fun*."

Says me, "Do I really have to look at your hideous pink a minute longer?"

She strikes a pose as she casts off her robe. *"The brightness of my being shall burn thee up, perchance destroy thee."*

"I have no doubt," says Esther. "Really? H. Rider Haggard? You rise up out of ignorance for H. Rider Haggard?"

"Not ready to tell all about it. But *sit, so, and tell me, for in truth I am inclined to praises—tell me, am I not beautiful?*"

"Even likeable sometimes," says Esther.

"As yet thou hast no cause to fear me. If thou hast cause, thou shall not fear for long, for I shall slay thee. Therefore, let thy heart be light. Now, to thee I doubt not that this thing is a great mystery, therefore I will not overcome thee with it now."

"Who'd give you that book?" says me.

"That would be telling," says she.

4

TWO ELECTRIC FANS BLOWIN at each other from shelves on facing walls. They hum their one note hard and click-click-click as they rotate side to side, slow, but even so the old dressing-shed is stuffy, hot, stinky. A proper dressing building's goin up, built for permanent, with bathrooms, even showers. This shed'll get torn down and no one will miss it.

We've got it to ourselves at this end of our working day. D'Varn's creamin off make-up and I'm waitin on her. She's wiped half the cream off, but stops now to stare into the long mirror which runs the length of this table. Lights a cigarette. Speaks to the mirror.

"Struchio camelus."

"Struchio who?" says me.

"Not a who, a what. I learned ever so much today, and I'm ever so happy about it. Struchio camelus—that's science for ostrich. Do you even know what an ostrich is?"

"Sticks her head in the sand?"

"They don't. Not ever. That 'popular misconception' is utter nonsense. I learned that today."

"Auntie?" says me.

"Do you actually have an aunt anywhere?"

"Supposedly. In Tennessee."

"While Willie, known amongst us as Catch, leapt and romped with the likes of Normand and Arbuckle, do you want to know what I was doing as D'Varn-who's-gonna-be-a-star?"

"Can't wait to hear."

"I co-starred in a half-reel 'educational'—with ostriches. In point of fact, they, the ostriches, were the stars. I am the tall pretty gal pointlessly strolling about an ostrich farm so our worthy ticket-buyers can gawk at struchio camelus. Did you know there are two ostrich farms in our general vicinity? Did you know ostriches have the largest eyes of any land animal? I'm so angry I could spit."

"Ladies don't, may I remind thee."

"Oh, you. You! Goddamned huge mean-beaked fucking birds. The male of the species can be nine feet tall. The hens—hens, mind you!—are seven or eight feet. Scared the piss out of me to be near them. The title of my own little 'vehicle' is *Our Largest Birds,* and there I am amongst them, with my scientist guide who's a foot shorter than me. Get the joke? I am one of our largest birds. Just a well-dressed ostrich, me."

"Must be my fault," says me.

"Everything is. They're long-necked, like me. Long-legged, like me. Willie—why don't these people respect me? They wouldn't put me in *Our Largest Birds* if they respected me at all."

"I'm not so sure of that," says me. "Charlie's afraid of you."

"Goddamn him—and you—and everyone. I'll show you people."

"You will. I ain't just sayin that. I know you will."

"I know I will. I know that. You wait, goddamnit, you'll see. Sennett'll be bragging, 'She got her start with me!' Unless—unless—unless I am mistaken about—everything."

At this worst possible moment in comes Miss Mabel Normand with all flags flyin.

"Hello, you gals!"

"Mabel," says D, "did you know—do you realize?—an ostrich can run at speeds up to forty miles an hour?"

"Do tell," says Miss Mabel. "Miss D'Varn, tonight Catch comes with me. I'll drive her home when we're done. Arch your eyebrows all you want."

Oh, D'Varn was archin.

"That's a good look," says Miss Mabel. "Check it in your mirror. Use it."

"I have," says D. "I always do."

Mabel says, "Have I stepped in doggie-doo? Catch, I need you to watch our dailies. I need your eyes on some biz cause I want you in on the topper."

She looks to D'Varn, troubled-like. "You're invited, too. Really."

"No thank you, really."

Miss Mabel sees and points to D's by-now-well-worn copy of *She*—it was laying on D's handbag. Miss Mabel asks D, "Can I borrow that when you're done?"

"I'll never be done with that book, Mabel. *To She shall they go, and her vengeance shall be worthy of her greatness.*"

Miss Mabel looks hard at D and says, "It's not what we see in the mirror, D'Varn. It's what the camera sees in us."

"Well said," says D, with a respectful nod.

Mabel nods back the same, then waves at me to follow as she swoops out.

"She'll be with you in a sec!" D yells after her. Reaches for my hand and I take it and she holds mine hard and I hold back hard.

D'Varn says fierce, "Don't leave me."

"But I gotta, cause"—

"I don't mean now. I mean: Don't leave me."

"D?"

"Don't leave me to be with *her.*"

"Wha?" says me. "Miss Mabel? You crazy?"

"She drives a lavender car. Maybe she likes you—like that."

Speechless, me.

"Willie, I couldn't stand it. Especially not now. Don't leave to be with her."

"Oh, auntie, don't you know you've got me for as long as you want me, any way you want me?"

She let go my hand. Smiled tired. "Go on, you."

I went on.

A FEW DAYS LATER, on a Keystone break for lunch, I see D'Varn sittin alone, costumed as a rich gal, high button shoes, all sortsa layers and frills, the look of money, alone on the top step of The Porch.

When you see a Keystone and someone's steppin up or down a porch of a nice family home, it's always the same porch, vine-covered—the porch of what usedta be the farmhouse here. There's D'Varn, fancy white lace gloves folded neatly near. Beside her gloves, on a wicker stool, one wide-brimmed feathered hat. She shapes her nails with a pocket file—doin so, she watches her hands like there's nothin else in this world. Cept she's holdin her mouth tight and her lips quiver.

Glares me to a stop with, "Get lost, you."

A breeze ripples the muslin that covers the Ghost Building so's its soft flapping eases off the noises of Keystone busyness.

"Been crying, my queen?" says me.

"Certainly not."

"Liar."

"Big shot. You do foreground biz with the likes of Mabel Normand, while me, I'm all fussed up for—background. Just two weeks ago I was a co-star. What did I do wrong?"

"Upstaged the stars, maybe? But don't tell me you're cryin on that, I won't believe it. Somethin about you and Banker Bill?"

"Not like you think." Her face scrunched. "Not *as* you think? Sommie's lessons. Grammar and el'o'kyou'shun. I pay. He didn't want me to, but I got my way, no surprise there. You know what was hard for me? Prob'*ab*'ly. Probably. All my days I've said prob'aly. Prob'*ab*'ly. I'll prob'ab'ly go insane, what do you bet?"

"*That* wouldn't make you cry," says me.

"You're a silly damn puppy that wags its tail at any silly damn thing—and doesn't know or care there's such a thing as *tomorrow* in this world."

"Did you just call me a dog?"

"I likened you to a puppy. That's different."

"I like bein a puppy."

"I know you do. Irritates the snot outa me. Now *me*—I'm *this close* to my dream—I'm manipulating—for all I'm worth. *For all I'm worth.* I'll tell you about it—but not just yet. *So close.*"

"Sounds like a good thing," says me.

"Shows how much you know. Scary—to dream so hard—to be *so close*—ohhhhh—piss-yourself scary—and then you come walking along, pretty-pretty, and you don't seem to need a blessed thing. I need—a lot—an awful lot."

"I need you," says me.

"You don't, Willie. Don't you know?"

"You're wrong," says me.

"I hope I'm not," says she.

Her eyes, my eyes. Heartbeats.

Of a sudden she's boarded another train of thought. "You'd be amazed, amazed at what a man will brag about in bed, a man who thinks he's so important—specially—*es*'pecially—when this important man believes his gal loves him *sooooooooo* much."

"You give him that impression, do you?"

"Artistically."

"So he tells you what?"

"Tells me enough to hang him if I don't get my way. But I will get my way. I'm nearly there. Now leave me alone. Got to think. I *was* thinking, until you showed up."

"And thinking makes you cry?" says I.

"I happen to be alarmed at what I think of, alright? Now scoot, scram, vamoose, I mean it—but kiss first, if you must. Kiss my hand."

She holds out her hand and I curtsy and take it and kiss.

"All better now, my queen?" says me. "Mother used to say that a life without sadness is like a meal without salt."

"Screw your mother."

I stick out my tongue and make a rude noise.

"Don't you dare cheer me up," says she. Quick like a lizard her tongue scoots out and back. "Scram."

Just then this schoolmarm sorta gal, who follows after Mr. Sennett with notebook and pencil in hand—I never remember her name—she's runnin toward us in that waddlin way of women too ladylike to flat-out run.

"D'Varn, the Skipper says for you to change to floozy clothes. Café biz background. Not too cheap a floozy, he says, so you wear a decent hat."

"Piss on him and shit on you."

"Ten minutes!" says the schoolmarm gal.

I go with D to help her change and the whole time she's steamin fierce and teary.

"Piss on it, shit on it. A floozy with a decent hat. It'll be the same set as always, a piano joint where people dance and eat and spirits are served. A gal who'd go alone, who owns a decent hat, she's not loose, but she'd like to be—a shop girl daring herself into some fun—or a grifter pretending to seem like such a girl, while her beau lurks somewhere with a blackjack, and they're a pair looking to roll a sailor"—she adjusts her posture and expression to what she's sayin.

"How do I look?" says she.

"You're completely beautiful," says me.

"Why *now*? Why wasn't I completely beautiful before? When I looked like a lady?"

"You always are completely beautiful, D. I just said it now, is all."

I got called to my biz as she headed to hers.

Then it's some later and I'm waitin on D'Varn at the gate and here she comes, still in her floozy'd get-up.

"Done for the day, my queen?" says me.

"Mabel's queen of the movies, don't you read *Photoplay*? She's queen and doesn't give a hoot for it, not a hoot—the greatest comedienne in probably forever and she does not *care*. I could strangle the life out of her. *I'm* gonna be queen of the movies, and even you don't yet know it."

"Don't be telling me what I do and don't know," says me.

D'Varn did her floozy act all the Big Red trolley ride back. Wardrobe fumigant stank on her. On the trolley she smoked to shock those worthy ticket-buyers and maybe get us arrested. (Course I had to light a cig too, to keep her company.) She showed not only lots of ankle but some leg. (Course I had to also.) She stared darkly at respectable gals who scowled and squirmed but couldn't meet her eyes. When guys leered at her, she made a shocking gesture toward them. Of course the conductor and driver, both uniformed up, didn't care a damn and enjoyed the show—we Keystone gals ride this line all the time and wink the conductors when they pinch our rears.

At our stop D bounded off the trolley and walked ahead of me with long forceful strides that I didn't try to match, up the wide steps of Hotel Hollywood, through the lobby to the stares of all, with D radiatin I-don't-know-what, as though if she could shrivel us all to ash she would. Way down the hall to our door before me, went inside, locked it! Even though she knows I have a key. I unlocked it, but slow. Opened the door slow too.

She does not speak. Nor dare I.

Her floozy costume's on the living room floor.

She's in our bedroom, doin poses for the vanity's mirror. Expressions of somebody ugly inside. I turn to go but no, "Keep your ass right here," says she.

I do so.

Nude in high heels she stands, arms at her side, all the way haughty, and don't I love it? Even now, when she's bad-dangerous, don't I love it?

But I do not love how she builds a laugh, quiet-to-loud, and all the way mean, till that laugh cracks into cryin, how you cry when you don't want to but have to.

Then she goes quiet. Smiles.

Circles me, studyin me. I study her. She studies back.

"Get my book from my purse," says she.

I do so.

She tells me, "Open to the folded page, read what I've circled."

"You're supposed not to mark up books."

"Do as you're told."

I read: "*It was She herself. She was clothed, as I had seen her when she unveiled, in the kirtle of clinging white*—kirtle, D?"

"Sommie says it's a kind of petticoat ladies wear over their other petticoats."

"And he'd know how?" says me.

"Read," says she.

"—*kirtle of clinging white, cut low upon her bosom, and bound in at the waist with the barbaric double-headed snake*—snake!—*and, as before, her rippling black hair fell*"—

D'Varn finishes, "*in heavy masses down her back.* I'll need a terrifically expensive wig. Read."

"*But her face was what caught my eye, and held me as in a vice, not this time by the force of its beauty, but by the power of fascinated terror. The beauty was still there, indeed, but agony, the blind passion, and the awful vindictiveness displayed upon those quivering features, and in the tortured look of the upturned eyes, were such as surpassed my powers of description.*"

"Now, you—watch me—not looking at me, watch me in the mirror. Read it again, and look at me in the mirror at the same time—you can do that much, can't you?"

I did do it, sorta. Her face settled into its most beautiful "musculature," then moved to the description like to music, until her expression was something I beheld with, not terror, like it says, but, like it also says, fascination.

"My face did like the writing?" says she.

"I'm afraid so," says me.

"Afraid of what? It's *acting.* I'm an *actress.* Light me a cigarette."

I do so.

She fetches her gold dragon robe, sorta slings herself into it. It hangs open in front. She sits on the bed. Spreads her long legs, with her feet pointed inward. Her honey-haired kitty sorta glows for me. D sees my interest and shuts up shop, swings one leg over another to cross them firmly.

"Know who I look like in that floozy costume? Know who I played way at the back of the set where the camera could barely see? And on the Red Car? Do you—know?"

"How could I?" says me.

"How could you!" She coughed a laugh. "I looked like my mother. That's who *you* thought was fairest of them all, 'completely beautiful,' did you say?"

"I didn't know."

"I know you didn't—and that makes it worse."

"How?" asks scared me.

"Just does. No reprieve here on this."

"You're always"—

"Completely beautiful"—

"Completely beautiful to *me*, D'Varn. I just said it then, is all. I always think it."

"You just said it then, is all. And you can't see how that makes it worse, fuckin freak that you are. You *are* a freak, you know that, dontchya? A freak, a freak, a freak. You insulted me. Bad, real bad. It's worse that you didn't mean to."

She's lightin one cigarette off another.

"Billy Banker can't make me feel like a tramp, cause he's ten times the tramp I am. But you—you think I'm nothing inside, a beautiful tramp is all. Surprised I can act."

"D—I don't think you *are* anything, anything but D'Varn, wonderful'est"…

"Stuff it. Shut your mouth."

"No. I love you."

I'm standin square in front of her now.

Her hand, it comes up so fast and WHAP on my face and my head snaps back.

I taste blood.

"If you wanna hit me, auntie, hit me, if it makes you feel any better."

"I love you, honeybum." It's not her honest voice. "I love you, honeybum, I just want you to do this one thing. It's not so bad."

She takes a breath. "That's what Mamma would say. Do this one thing, one thing, one thing. 'You're my little money-pot, with your pretty honeybum.' she'd say. By thirteen I was used to it. Not—before thirteen. Not before. Took a goddam while to get used to 'one thing,' 'one thing,' 'just this one thing.' 'Just this one thing with this nice man, we've got to make our way and you're my money-pot with your pretty honeybum.'"

Esther's knock at the door.

"Get it," D snaps.

I do so and see Big Esther and I bust into tears and scamper to the bathroom.

Now D'Varn's screamin awfully, cryin, throwin things, and Esther's wranglin her. I hear hard slaps, peek out, Esther's hittin her, hard, and again, and D'Varn's got this pitiable thankfulness shinin out of her eyes as Esther's hittin her.

It got quiet. Only throaty, chesty sobs.

I hear Esther. "Come on out, Willie."

Out I come.

D'Varn's on the rug, huddled, makin those sounds.

Esther, her face set hard, sits me on the divan.

"She gets this way," Es says. "First time since you've come along. You've been good for her."

"She has NOT!" D'Varn's up again, her face so pained. "You look at me, you. You think you're so special all you gotta do is eat my ass and it all goes away. You think you're so wonderful for me to touch that it all goes away, everything, everything before, all goes away, fucking cunt. Then comes today and you say *she* is so beautiful, 'completely,' you say."

"Ok, now, D." That's Es. "Listen up to me."

"Don't have to, don't want to."

"You shall."

"Or you'll beat me up some more?"

"If that's what you need. I'll do anything you need."

"I know what you'll say."

"Maybe you do, maybe you don't. You're making something Willie's fault when you know it's not. You are cruel, we three know that—and *we* know, you and I, you need your cruelty. But Willie? Willie is the purest person we know and that is true and you understand that and I understand that."

D, all snarl, "Is—that—so?"

"You fall apart," Esther says. "You just do. It happens sometimes."

"Not to you."

"I fell so apart such a long time ago, I'm just pieces of what I used to be. You, you're pieces of what you're going to be."

"Big Esther!" says D. "Knows so goddamn much! Knows so goddamn much about me!"

Then D'Varn is all of someone else, some sort of old. Oldness shines from her eyes, twists pain around her mouth, sayin to Esther, "I am so sorry—*she's*—seen me like this. I wanted this never to happen—around *her*. Why did she say—what she said?"

"Doesn't matter," Esther says. "You know how things get when you dress like Mamma."

"Why do I—do that?"

"Maybe because you loved her. You were her good daughter."

"Loved my mother?"

"I'll take Willie with me tonight," says Es.

D'Varn almost smiles. "Can't trust me, can we?"

"Not a whit," says Es. "Got what you *need* here? Got enough?"

"Enough," says D. "More than enough."

"And brandy?"

"I always have brandy."

"Alright, then. You come with me, Willie." To D'Varn: "Got your pipe?"

"Somewhere. Just go."

"Sure you have it? Should I go get you one of mine?"

"Go."

A weakness had come upon me. Esther had to help me walk down the hall to her door.

Inside, piles of books, this way and that, wherever there's room. As for Esther's bed, it's unmade and none too clean? Brandy and wine and ash stains on bedsheets. Esther likes it "pungent," is her word.

Sits me down on her horseshoe divan. Bouncier cushions than ours.

She gets me brandy, lights her cigarillo, puts it tween my lips. Makes me dizzy. I hand it back and say, "We're not enough for her, are we?"

"Not nearly," says Es. "But you knew that."

"I liked it better when I knew without knowin."

Freak. Daddy's word for me, in D'Varn's mouth, which had been all over me.

We light cigarettes. With her cig hangin from her lips, Esther unbuttons her buttons and unclasps her clasps and steps out of her clothes, turns for me to undo her bra, I do so, and there she is in bloomers and stockings and wedge shoes and her tremendous breasts, aureoles big as silver dollars. She lights a new cigarette off the one she had in her mouth that's just half-smoked. Shakes out her thick long auburn hair.

I, by the by, wear my crimson dragon robe this whole time. She bends to pull out the bow and spread my robe some. I like that she did that. We sit near to near, on her divan.

"By the time I found her," Esther tells me, "D'Varn had run away from her Mamma, taken the name D'Varn, whoring in a sleek Manhattan cathouse. Not a tragic figure of any kind. She was born into whoring, it was a way of life, she had no notion of another. In a birdcage that day, hanging from the ceiling, if you can believe it, dressed in lace that opened at all her parts, and she didn't have to pose she just had to *be*—be D'Varn. Quite a moneymaker. She looked like a kid and not like a kid—you two have that in common, though she can't look like a kid anymore. What I was doing there, I was with a gaggle of suffragette medical do-gooders making check-ups on females less fortunate who'd been led down the path of ruin. I took one look at that girl in that birdcage—my dear God, she glowed—and so smart, such smart eyes—one look, and I had to have her. Told myself it was to save her and make her free, but I wanted—to have her—own her. Broke ranks with my do-gooders and—bought her. She cost a fortune. I told myself a lot of Hungarian goulash as to my noble intentions et cetera. Nobility my big ass. The Greeks would say Aphrodite possessed me and I had no choice but to obey and live out my fate. It did feel that way. Try this one on: *To stand in the center of love, and slowly turn round, to behold its vast expanse, far as eye can see, with no attempt to make sense of any of it, nor to excuse any of it, nor to justify any of it, nor to praise nor to damn any of it, but to behold it only, to behold it from a place you make your own, a place of slightly lit stillness.*"

"Gee," says me.

"That's a quote from an ancient Greek. Ask me which ancient Greek."

"Which ancient Greek?"

"This ancient Greek. Me."

And all of her starts in to sob. "And now I'm losing her, we're losing her."

I open my arms and she comes to me.

I rock her some and get scared with her, we comfort ourselves with ciga-rettes and more brandy while, big as she is, she stays sorta reclinin on me. Like it's the most normal thing, because it is, I ease down to her pussy and do her with my mouth.

Then I recline one direction, she the other, legs entwined, and we're lookin at each other.

"You," says she. "What goes on with you this minute?"

"You're dryin on my face."

D'VARN'S OUT DOIN SOMETHIN I'd probably disapprove of if I knew what it was. Cigarette twixt my lips I'm pawin through the closet lookin for somethin to wear for D'Varn's "entrance," as it always is, *if* she comes home, cause all I got on so far are red nail-varnish and panties—but of a sudden I come across Fred's coat. Oh, oh, oh, once we thought this poor coat was so wonderful—and so it *was*! Just-like-that. For us.

D's key rattled hard in the lock and rattled me. She slams the door open, slams it shut behind her, sees me, "Don't say *a goddamn word*."

Sails her hat across the room, kicks off her shoes, tears away her coat, rips herself disrobed, makes for the bathroom, slams that door too. Bathwater's runnin. Which means she's cryin.

Two cigarettes later out she comes, not even dry. I feel her shiny nakedness in my chest.

Drippin, she takes a seated posture on our divan, removes the cigarette from my mouth. Inhales it deep. She's thinkin like fury.

"Big day tomorrow," says she. "Big goddamn day."

"It's Sunday," says me.

"You're gonna come with me, you're gonna keep your mouth shut, you're not gonna ask questions. And wear your knife-rig."

"Always, when we go out."

Soft she says, "Your brandy, please." I hand it on, she gulps it down.

Now she's up and throwin pillows on the rug like she wants to kill the pillows. Throws herself down on em just as hard. On her stomach. "For Christ's sake fuck me."

"Which—which wand?"

"Your tongue, you little cunt."

Clearly her shiny butt needed hard slaps first, which D appreciated with a rush of tears. Then I tongued as her sobs eased.

COMES MORNING AND IT'S SUNDAY. D'Varn's up early by her own will! Lookin like a statue, so still, nude, straight-backed but leaning forward, lookin, peerin, not-at-but-into the mirror.

"Calm," says she. She looks to me. "Do you see calm?"

"I suppose."

"A calm, graceful expression?"

"I suppose."

"Not too familiar, not too distant?"

"You could say so."

Looks in the mirror. "I need this face all day. It's-all-the-same-to-me, I-cannot-be-annoyed, I-understand-everything-and-oh-I-don't-care. Wear your suit today, the one you don't like anymore. And the small dark fedora. *No questions.* No comments, either. We cannot look defenseless."

"When do you ever look defenseless?"

"This is business. When I take out a cigarette, light it before anyone else can. With this."

Fishes in a drawer and fetches out a fancy new-fangled lighter. Tosses it to me. Looks to be real silver. Has weight.

"Time to dress," says she. "Esther will fetch us in an hour, and drive us to Famous Players."

"We could walk," says me.

"We arrive in a car, we depart in a car. We decline all invitations, if there are any." Softer. "There better be."

Esther's new touring vehicle, classy, long, shiny-gray, *two* back seats, plush, scents of leather, oil, road dust and orange blossom, orange blossom, almost like the air weighs heavier there's such orange blossom.

Then just a little ways down Vine . . . axe-men choppin at the wide grove across from Famous Players. Four-horse teams pullin up stumps. Fellows whappin branches off trunks and sawing the rough cuts smooth; others chop trunks into logs. Slain trees lyin leafy, full of fruit, their fragrances pourin forth. That sharp smell of fresh-cut live wood. Lemon also in the air.

We've stopped for a two-horse buckboard stacked with logs.

"This *is* Sunday, ain't it?" says me. "Even Mr. Mack Sennett don't work on Sundays."

"He sings in a papist choir right about now," Esther says.

"Ain't it against the law in this town, this sort of Sabbath-day work?"

"Apparently not anymore."

My right hand's in D'Varn's lap, she's holding it with both of hers, and through our summer-thin gloves I feel her heat. She squeezes hard.

"We're ok, D," Es says. "We won't be late."

Esther guides her big car slowly around some workers, then pauses again for two little girls barefoot in cotton dresses walkin holdin hands singin dee-dah-dee-dah trills. Then Es turns left on Selma, and takes the first right into the north gate of Famous Players. D'Varn nods at the gate-keeper who doffs his cap. She tells Esther, "Park right by the barn." A big paint-peeling red barn. So this studio, too, rose up from a used-to-be farm.

D'Varn's by the car dressed like the proper'ist lady cept her exquisitely gloved hand places a cigarette twixt her lips. She waits. Gives me a dirty look.

"Oh," says me. I fish in my purse for that lighter, flip it open, snap the button down and up shoots a flame right at her cigarette tip. She has on that face that she practiced. Says, "Let's go, girls. *Be not affrighted.*"

I was wantin to go into the barn but she led away from it. Everything looks so in-its-place here. New buildings, nothin slapdash about them. Nothin any-old-way about anythin. Even where pieces of sets lay piled up against a building it looks somehow orderly. There were folks around but compared to the Keystone these people seem to walk on tip-toe. Two ghost-buildings, one much bigger than the other and way bigger than ours. We stopped at a long wide brick wall with no windows, a very wide two-door door, a smaller door near that, and a high peaked roof.

By the way, I'm dressed in a dark blue two-piece suit, jacket and skirt, and the skirt's tighter than is decent and I'm way high-heeled so I gotta step mincie. My hat's a big white bell with brim upturned on the left and down-turned on the right. There's fru-fru pinned on it by D herself. White gloves, of course, and a collared shirt open at the neck, no less, open for two buttons down, to reveal a silver pendant. I feel out of place, but not so much so as the gent approaching us, nor his "entourage" (an Esther word).

"Behold," says D, "Mr. Ulysses Tiberius, and company."

"My lords and my ladies, all hail the perfection of D'Varn!" says this Mr. Ulysses Tiberius.

"Uly," says D, "you smell like a whorehouse."

"My dear D'Varn, gentlemen have been scented since before the Caesars."

He swings a lacquered walking stick that has a silver top, plenty fancy for show and heavy enough to do some damage. Jeweled rings on his thick naked fingers, black-black Homberg hat gleamin of money, bow tie, gemmed stick-pin in his collar. Lavender suit! Never seen the like. Cloth so fine it seemed to float on him. Patent leather shoes gleamin, but very small feet for such a big bear of a guy.

And just behind him, a gal who'd come up to Esther's or D'Varn's shoulder but she carries herself tall in that get-up—loose-fitting blouse (more fine cloth, kinda colorless), tucked into loose-fitting pants of the same fabric. Flat cloth shoes, like moccasins. Tar-black hair, sapphire eyes, and I know I've seen her sometime.

Plus "factotums" (a Sommie word).

Mrs. Sarbossian! Dwarf-lady Wardrobe boss at the Keystone—whom, come to think of it, I ain't seen around lately—bonneted, bright-eyed and scowlin. Various men you knew were movies because they walked like they belong here, white shirts buttoned to the collar, ties, casual jackets of this or that style, cloth slouch hats. Two mugs straight out of a Griffith gangster two-reeler, dark turtlenecks, dark hats, all swagger. Those two kept their eyes glued to this Ulysses.

He introduces D'Varn to Sapphire-eyes. She's called Violet and I remember where I've seen her. Of a sudden a suited gent runs up and hands this Ulysses a folded page of paper. He opens it.

"Silence!" he commands. "DeMille would consult with me. Actually," his tone to D'Varn is confidential though all can hear, "he wants to see my star. But he'll not, till he sees you *first* on the screen. Which is when we sign contracts. So! M'lords and m'ladies! To your tasks! D'Varn, the ever-knowing Mrs. Sarbossian shall enrobe you. Your friends shall come with me?"

"Esther stays," D says hard.

"As you wish, all and always as you wish."

I know by how Es holds her handbag that it's heavy with her eight-shot Special. And I know she wears a little pistol somewhere about her person.

"I anticipate DeMille!" Sticks out his hand and one of his people runs up with a prettily wrapped package, places it on Ulysses' palm, where it balances like a tray. "Herein, his gift." Then, *"Allons-y!* Get you to your tasks!" Sudden movement into the brick building, with little Sarbossian leadin or draggin D'Varn by the hand. D kept her face, though. Ulysses called after them, "Tell the musicians not to wait for me! Tell them, *Play!"*

The thugs stayed.

So I'm "entourage" now, me on his right, Violet on his left, headed for a flight of some dozen steps and up into the giant ghost-building, with thugs in tow.

"You," he addresses me, "are you not Willie? The leaper?" Before I can answer, "Of course you are! I 'vish-ualize,' I 'vish-ualize' a fantastic entrance for you in our *She."*

"Swell," says me. "What's this one do?" I nodded at that Violet.

"Violet! Ah! Circus all her life this one, born to it—The Great Cadenzas! Marvelous family. I'm her uncle."

"He is not," says Violet.

We're up the steps.

Ulysses calls out, "Sire!"

He's hailin a sturdy-lookin fellow, shiny riding boots, tight'ish pants tucked into the boots, a holster that sports a small revolver, a flannel shirt open at the collar, wire-rim glasses, slightly bald, eyes like two small dark storms.

"My liege, for you!" Uly hands him the package. "A most fanciful hashish, Cecil. Tunisian."

"Thanks." Like a bark. And a person appears as though that's just what she was waitin for and Mr. Cecil B. DeMille drops it into her cupped hands without lookin at her.

"Uly," and Mr. DeMille puts his arm around this Ulysses guy who's twice his size, leadin him off, while we all follow, "this picture, this picture— *The Call Of The North!* It's a journey of death, a man compelled to walk hundreds of miles across barren freezing snowy plains, no food, no gun, armed only with love. But what do I need most?"

Ulysses takes a thoughtful pose and says, "Snow?"

This ghost-building is empty of sets. Down one whole side, end to end, are different levels of wood platforms connected with chutes and covered with what I know by now is sail-canvas, and piled on the canvas are uneven mounds of packed soil. On a wide ramp at the far end, a company of workers roll a line of wheel-barrels loaded with white stuff up from street-level. Shovelers scoop the white stuff from the wheel-barrels onto those dirt mounds on the platforms, then the barrel guys turn round for another load.

Mr. DeMille reaches into his pocket and comes up with a handful of the white stuff. "It's called asbestos. It films like snow, but brighter. We're going to have a storm like nothing yet filmed. The first blizzard in Los Angeles! The first indoor blizzard anywhere! See those airplane propellers," and he points to several mounted propellers in front of which are mounds and mounds of the asbestos white stuff. "I fly my own aeroplane, don't you know? As I speak, we're building the DeMille Aerodrome near the tar-pits. Those are my propellers and my propellers are my storm."

His propellers are about a hundred feet down this ghost-building from us, but they're not directed at the dirt packed platforms. They're pointed at us.

"Camera!" DeMille calls out. A camera-crew between the two propellers starts grinding.

"Lights!" From above we're splashed with bright lights. Electric lights in a ghost-building!

"Hit it!"

A blast of wind knocks our hats clear off our heads, the flakes are everywhere, in our clothes, in our mouths, in our eyes, up our noses, I hate this man. Couldn't have been more than thirty seconds but damn.

"Cut! Ha! Now—fetch their things!"

Factotums go about finding hats and what-all, while we scrape and slap the stuff from our hair and off our clothes, spit it out, nose-pick it out.

Violet whisper-hisses, "He's such a nasty a little boy."

Mr. DeMille don't bother to so much as to rub his precious asbestos out of his thinning hair.

Yells into the shadows. "You got that, right?"

"Got it fine, Mr. DeMille," the shadows call back.

"I want that footage developed right away and taken to my home at I-don't-care-what time of day or night. I emphasize: *I don't care what time of day or night.*" He remembers Ulysses' existence.

Uly isn't scrapin or swattin the asbestos from "his person," as Sommie would say. He's pickin at each flake on his hat, which he places upon his head firmly as Mr. DeMille says at him,

"Uly, I've had an Episcopal priest on the payroll two weeks, praying for snow. Would have preferred a Baptist, they're fervent, but no luck. I asked one, and he objected, he said, 'It's *June* in California. Thou shalt not tempt the Lord Thy God!' But are all things possible to the Almighty or not?'"

Ulysses says, "Cecil, your prayer *has* been answered—with asbestos!"

"That's what I like about you, Uly, you're never at a loss." Turns to the cameramen. "Gents! Mr. Tiberius will deposit a reel with you in, what, two, three hours?" Uly nods. "I want to screen it first thing tomorrow, 7am sharp."

The crew responded with eager smiles. I had the feelin that if you respond any other way you don't work long at Famous-Players.

Such music! Ulysses calls them a "string quartet" and they make a sound like clouds changin shape in the sky, and changin color, and risin and dippin. D'Varn's nowhere about. There's no furniture in this brick building, just a few chairs. Staircases here and there go straight up the walls about twenty feet to walkways that run all around the building. About six feet below that high ceiling, rafters stretch across the space from one end to the other. Lotsa pulleys and ropes like some sorta clipper-ship, lotsa wires, all havin to do with large lights in box-like contraptions hung from rafters, plus guys up there, very agile, doin this and that energetically.

Ulysses Tiberius stands with none other than D'Varn's now-moustachioed Billy Banker, who's straight and proper in his stiff too-much-starch banker-clothing topped by a small bouncy banker-derby. Billy Banker is tryin not to look so foolishly at Violet while he pretends to listen to Uly. "Dear boy, it's French picture-people who know lighting. Gaumont—the studio, Gaumont—you know it, of course?—you don't?—Gaumont has had such set-ups almost from the start. A decade ahead of America in everything but—verve!"

"You're not American?" Billy queries.

"I should say not."

"Gosh."

How is a big-kid sort of person, like this Billy, some big-shot banker? D'Varn says it's cause he's gonna inherit his old man's bank.

Violet is lookin right through him. I swear it's like she could *walk* through him if she felt like it, he's so not-there to her.

Billy dares speak to her. "I understand it was you, Miss, who wrote our *She* photoplay?"

"Miss did precisely so," says Uly.

Violet doesn't flick a facial muscle.

All the lights go out, all the lights go on, out again, on again, then some are on and some aren't—and it's like a passageway of light goes from a door at the far end of the hall, pools of light about three feet apart that end a yard or so from us. I spotted Esther across the building from me, on the other side of the light-path, standin by herself. The string musicians play on in the dark, but they've changed from that music of clouds to something low, swaying and maybe a little angry.

Ulysses, like a ring-master, calls out, "My lords and my ladies, in the Tales of the Thousand And One Nights we are told that love rends all veils!" The light-circles brighten and there's D'Varn in the farthest one. I hear a camera start to grind a little behind us. "See as we illumine Ayesha's lovely form with an unearthly splendor!"

Smoke! But it don't smell like smoke. I don't know this smell. It blends with the building's smell of new bricks. And it's not smoke, it's mist. Some gents hold mirrors so as to reflect lights beaming from the rafters into the mist. They move about, angle their mirrors this way and that, the light moves and the mist moves and it's quite somethin.

D'Varn's steppin slowly and sometimes turns as she steps, arms stretched and bent in tender-slow gestures and—it's not a gown—I don't know what it is—a sort of crown that's almost a helmet made of what look like pearls that fit so's to frame her big eyes and . . . D is happy in a way I've never seen, and you wouldn't guess unless you know her, she's happy way down deep . . . what she's wearin can't be diamonds, must be cut glass, but wee and bead-like, strung on a kind of netting that don't even pretend to be a blouse or a dress but the whole of it fits sweet, head to toe, and you see everything of her body but not really, cause the beads gleam so, and that garment don't start to be dress-like till it sorta billows below the hips, where it's pearls to the knees and her legs emerge naked as she steps, and she drags behind a long "train" hanging from her shoulders . . .

Ulysses says to Violet, "Ustane, is she not like the full moon rising in her beauty?"

Violet poses and says, "Oh Bil'lali, very like . . . so like." Then drops the pose. "Life is just one disguise after another."

I know where that kind of talk gets you pigfeet.

For those hours Esther kept to herself in the shadows watchin, just watchin. I felt her, but there was no goin near her. Somethin about the little I could see of her through patches of bright light and stark dark, just how she held herself, made me know not to go to her until she moved slightly. Then I stepped just a little toward her. She saw and faced me and I came near.

"Hi, Esther."

"I thought about shooting her—just the way she was when she stepped into the light so happy—shooting her so that nothing else would ever have to happen to her. So she could die happy. Look at her." We stare as she poses and moves for the camera in that get-up.

Esther says, "She looks . . . untouchable."

I thought of that when we got back to our rooms and D put a finger to her lips and softly went, "Shhhhh. Not a word." She'd said almost the same to Billy Banker as soon as she noticed him before: "Don't distract me, William. Not a word."

Now she pulls sheets off our bed, saying, "That music . . . I still seem to hear it," and drapes a sheet over the mirror on the vanity, turns her hand-mirrors face down, tucks sheets around the mirrored closet doors. Asks, "Did you shake hands with Violet-Ustane?"

"I did not, D."

"She's *strong.* Strong like Brick or Hank. Charlie's strong too, much stronger than you'd expect, him being so slight. Ustane. Bil'lali. Says Uly, 'We shall address one another with *She*-names only, Ayesha.' Ayeshaaaaaaaa . . . I am Ayeshaaaaaaaaa . . . And did you see . . . ?" She stretches into an akimbo posture.

For the Ustane screen-test Violet wore patches of furs that left little to guess about. All she did was, easy as you please, her left leg rises till it's straight out in front of her, then up and up till it's straight up in the air, while she stands on her right leg still as still. From there she twists herself from contortion to contortion that I never imagined a person could manage. Ulysses said several times, as though he liked to say it, "a contortionist by trade."

Me . . . I saw what Esther saw when Esther first saw me.

"Auntie," says me, now we're at Hotel Hollywood, "do you remember Violet from before?"

"What before? Never saw her before in my life."

"When that Pathé Lehrman set the lions at us? Everybody scared out of their wits, not believin it as it happened—one of the extras, a gal, wet herself and collapsed. Sommie tried to help her. She damn near bit him. Violet."

"Naw. I bet not."

"One question?" says me.

"About her?"

"No."

"Ok then."

"Why Esther and her Special? Why make sure about my knife?"

"Nothing bad was going to happen but Uly had to feel matched. Had to feel it in the air. He's actually kind of nervy of you two. Willie—don't take this the wrong way . . . I don't want to be touched tonight. When I put on that . . . garment . . . when I moved in it, I felt such waves of—I don't know what—I felt . . ." She stares off like I'm not there.

Then, without mirrors to cue her, she did just about the same faces Ulysses asked for in her close-up tests, as he'd say, "Flirty, Ayesha . . . resigned . . . horrified at ugliness . . . horrified by something morally horrible . . . disgusted—ha! . . . differently disgusted . . . *understanding* . . . come now, Ayesha, *understanding,* convince me you understand me, ah, very good . . . smile . . . a different smile . . . again, differently . . . FURY! . . . dignity . . ." Hadn't I seen it all before, and more, me reclined on our wide white bed, she on the swivel stool, intent with her mirror, lost in her own face, "doin" me, "doin" Esther, "doin" people she'd point out in the park or on the set? That face was always meant for everyone and here today she'd revealed it all to everyone. I felt so small. She smokes cigarettes, sips brandy, walks around and around—nothin on, of course—runnin her hands over her body as she steps. I thought it was somehow important for me to watch, but couldn't help dozin off some. I'd startle awake, light a cigarette, sip a brandy, watch, doze. Woke to see her huddled in a corner like a solemn little girl.

The phone! I'm a groggy "What time is it?" and she's "Seven-thirty!"
Oh, she's so excited, in pain with excitement.
Sheets are off the mirrors. She's wide-awake and drunk.
Picks up the phone, drops the phone, drags it by the receiver to me on the bed, places it so's we both can hear.
"Are you there, Ayesha? What's wrong? Can you hear?"
"Just fine, Uly, Bil'lali, baby."
"DeMille has seen your footage, he is thrilled, and—contract's signed! Famous Players-Lasky distributes. Ayesha Pictures will in effect belong to them, they get a bigger chunk than we'd like, but they are to finance— THREE PICTURES! We'll make fortunes, you do know! Three! *She— Dragonelle—Lady Godiva.* Uh, your Banker, William, as you wish, is *out.* He will be destroyed. He won't get one dime back. We ace those who threw in with him, and thus we ace William's reputation as well and ask me no questions so I'll tell you no lies. Did you ever doubt me?"
"I'm doubting you now, Uly, you gorgeous sly bastard. Let it all be true, at least for today."
"Words to live by," says Mr. Ulysses Tiberias.

ESTHER

SAPPHO
All colors tangled together

SARA TEASDALE
You who have waked me cannot give me sleep.

EVERYTHING'S CHANGED and everything's stayed the same.

Is that supposed to happen at the same time?

We're in our nighties, me and D, and she's been all-out nervy since Famous Players a few days past. I sit upon our white divan, and I'm fetchin as can be, but she's distracted with a gold-tipped cigarette in a long silver holder that she waves through the air as she paces and swirls, sayin, "They can't shoot our picture until it's *designed*, Uly says—'none of your slapdash,' Uly says—'all shall be á la Gaumont!, no Keystone falderal,' Uly says. Willie," and she lays her silver cigarette holder in the black swan ashtray, lights another cig and sticks it in my mouth, lights still another for herself while her cig in that ashtray is still lit, and she's sayin, "Willie, they're going to make drawings or paintings of every scene, every shot, and make every costume, all before the first set-up. They'll want me at all hours for fittings, and if I don't love a costume I'm to rip it up! Uly says I've got to love what's on my body. And—we'll have rehearsals, Uly says we must rehearse. And, as we proceed, Violet—whose actual name, according to Ulysses, is Veronica—I'll call her *Ronnie*—she'll 'flesh out' our scenario and they'll figure up a budget that includes every last thing."

"What's a budget, D?"

"An—accounting—sort of. For the slam-bang stuff we must 'coordinate' with Famous Players, 'a tight schedule,' Uly says, and there's ever so many people to hire. It's complicated, really complicated, and I didn't expect that, and I want to understand it, all of it."

"Ronnie, huh?" says me.

"Hush," says she. "*Pay no need to what I seem, seeing as thou canst not know what I am.*"

She lights herself another cigarette though she's got one burnin in the white swan ashtray and another in the black swan ashtray, then she starts in to whirlin her arms in slow arcs through all our many-cigarettes' smoke, like it's those mists she's pranced through, but it's smoke, see, and I start in to coughin, and she's coughin, and now I'm cough-laughin, it annoys her to be laughed at, and I'm up slammin the window open while she's slappin at me as I go about stubbin down butts.

She's started in to slappin crazy now and I do somethin I don't often—grab her by the shoulders and spin her so's she lands on her ass hard on the divan. D'Varn looks up at me with, well, a certain expression. Sometimes she likes bein thrown around hard.

So . . . after we've engaged in fuckery, we're entwined on the floor with our brandies . . .

"You can close that window now," says she, with that wily smirk of hers. "I feel a chill."

I did so.

We re-entwined.

"Ulysses," she says, like it's a sentence all by itself.

"Does he have a real name?" says me.

"He doesn't have a real anything," says she, "but what he knows, he *knows.*"

She tells me Uly doesn't want her at loose ends. He says to her, 'Loosey-goosey's no good for you.' Wants D to keep busy at the Keystone and not think of anything "until he tells me what to think. Which I let him think he can. *Such is the tale, my love, and now is the hour at hand that shall set a crown upon it.*"

D'Varn's asleep on the rug—passed-out's more like it. I lay a blanket on her and lift her head gently to work a pillow under it. ("Every gesture is important," says Miss Mabel.)

Whispers I to the dark, "He hasn't got a real anything." Boy-howdy!—which is what Mother'd say when surprised, which she almost never was.

I'm not a *real* girl, I know that. Not a real boy neither. We stunt for real but our stories ain't. Gotta be about half the people on these picture-lots don't go by real names. That Mr. DeMille fella, he pays real money to a real scrubbed-clean boy who follows Mr. DeMille around with a real folding chair, and Mr. DeMille'll just sit, without sayin or lookin, and don't he expect that chair to be right there under him when he sits? He does and it is, I seen it—but does that feel real to you? Cause it don't to me. My feelings is real—to me, anyhow. Anyway they're all I got to go by.

Violet . . . well . . . *that* didn't take long for D'Varn to arrange. (Not "Veronica," by the way, much less "Ronnie." Violet is Violet.) D's started fittings for the *She* picture in the nighttime, plus nighttime rehearsals at Uly's half-finished Ayesha Pictures lot at Gower and Hollywood—schedule's uneven, this night or that. Things aren't yet "in place," Uly says, for D to leave the Keystone, but maybe by the Fourth. On such nights of fittings and rehearsals, well, sometimes D'Varn comes home, sometimes she don't.

Doesn't make excuses anyway, I'll say that for her.

That's when I got "next to myself," as they say, and finally felt bad for Esther.

See, when D'Varn would go off with Billy Her Banker I'd get murderous and concentrate on castratin, cause that comes with bein a farmhand and I'm deft at it. Different, though, when D'Varn would chuck my chin and tell me she was off to "visit" with Esther. She'd be just down the hall for the night and I wasn't murderous at all. Esther had first right, I'd taken that from her, and Esther stayed anyway. Sure, such nights I'd be lonely, but lonely is a thing you can work with. Sit, smoke, sip, let the mind wander. There's somethin sweet to that.

After all, D was with me most nights. Esther decided to take her hits. That's called bein tough. So now I had to be tough too.

That, or "throw in my cards," as they say. Which I wasn't about to do.

It was like some real serious game of spin-the-bottle. And it wasn't always D that did the spinnin. Came a night of D'Varn and me at our dirties and an awful BAMMING shook the door.

Lickety-split she extracts that obsidian wand from my posterior. The smell shies me up. She dips the wand into the ice bucket with our champagne, while BAMMING goes on louder.

I turn over on my pillows, fish round my ankle for my silk panty—yellow, it was.

BAMMING bams on as D'Varn rises sorta unsteady, unlocks the door, opens it wide, naked as Eve, and there stands Big Esther wearin not a stitch, a brandy bottle in one hand, a *long* rubbery wand in t'other, and on her head a wide-brimmed hat of flowers'n'feathers.

Her eyes are red with weepin, thick lips curled with sneerin.

Gives D'Varn a full stare. Then me.

"Jesus Christ, Esther!" says D'Varn.

Esther says, "I'm sicka the botha ya." Esther's big rubbery bamming wand, it looked so like a man's thing—she waves it in her hand, it bends from side to side. She clenches it like she's fixin to bat us.

D'Varn whisper-shouts, "You'll wake the whole floor!"

For all that it could get us arrested, them two standin naked in the hallway was quite a sight. D'Varn tall and svelte and every part shaped sweet. Esther tall and big, muscle'y in a womanly way, shiny auburn hair near long as a cape. She shoves past D'Varn and there she is, feet wide apart, towerin over me. I hear D'Varn come in and lock the door but I can't take my eyes off our Esther.

Thick shiny auburn hair glowed around her kitty. *Huge* titties, *huge* thighs. Her belly hung in shiny folds—shiny, I say, cause her skin gleams that white they call "alabaster," so pretty, and there's so much. Her titties, her whole big body, made me kinda melt.

She tough-laughs a single "Ha!" and her alabaster ripples all over.

While atop her enormity sat that flowery feathery hat.

Raises her bottle to her lips, chug-a-lugs.

"Brandy," says she. "Have some."

She pours a little on me.

I ran my hands where it splashed upon my body and licked my fingers.

"Damn you," says she. "Damn you, I like you. Probably love you. Shit."

She kneels forward then plops backward on a pillow next to me. Lays her cock-wand on a pillow all its own. Sails that hat to the sofa and shakes out her beauteous hair.

D'Varn sits a bit away from Es and me. We three, we're sittin in a triangle on the floor, lookin from one to the other.

"What now, ladies?" says D.

Esther gives her no attention, eyes all on me.

"You've never come to the end of your rope, have you?" says she. "You don't even know what that is. Take off those ugly panties. Yellow, on your skin, really?"

I did so. Without lookin at my thing. But I felt it free in air.

"That was a good one, D," says Es, "commanding that I be Willie's dresser. You knew what would happen."

"I knew no such thing."

"You knew and you knew." Es stretches out one big leg—that, for all its bigness, is shaped perfect—and she presses the flat of her foot on my thigh. "Of all the lonelinesses," says she, "the worst is angry loneliness. That's me. But poor you," she says to me, "you're doomed and don't know it yet. I'm doomed, too, but I know it. Not D, here. No doom's big enough to knock over our D."

I went for a cigarette. They watched me light up, then they lit up too. Esther passed around her brandy. Not a word did we say. The candles burned down some. What with lightin cigarettes and passin the bottle we three edged closer together. Not in any S-E-X kinda way. D'Varn told me people did that, three together, but that wasn't in the air and anyhow I'd never.

Lightin cigarettes, sippin, not knowin what to say, there in the half-dark, just bein with each other in this way, three—friends, I'd put it— gettin good-and-drunker, quietly, together.

"A disappointment, is what," says D. "Here are we, in a situation the very stuff of smut, and we're quiet as a painting."

"What would you know about paintings, pray?" says Es.

"You took me, remember. Back east. You took me on a train to see paintings."

"I do remember."

"A hall full of paintings," says D, "paintings of gals doing what we're doing right now, except for the cigarettes"—

"And the cocks," says Esther. She pats her long rubbery cock, then reaches to lay one thumb on my thing, just one thumb, just momentarily, presses on my thing. Without my wantin to, my thing stretched some and got harder.

"Yes," D'Varn says, "except the cocks. Odalisques! They were called odalisques. And one was so too smoking, and you"—she nods to Esther—"you said *that* was disapproved of in the press, an odalisque with a cigarette. They'd be naked, but not all naked, thin garments on big girls—big like Esther, Willie. Sitting around, pillows and all. Bright colors. God knows I'd seen gals lolling about with not much on, but these painting-women, they seemed contented and calm. That puzzled me, I wondered, 'Where in the world?' Esther, you had college words for it all. What did you think, you could get me conversational so I might go home and meet the family?"

"I'd *love* for you to meet my family, D'Varn, it would serve you right."

"How young?" I zip in. "How young were you then, D?"

Esther's eyes teared up. She said, "Think I'll call it a night." So sayin, Es stretched out on the floor. "Blow out the candles, Queenie."

D'Varn did so. Esther went just-like-that to sleep, deep.

The room is dark but not near pitch, and, I swear, I guess our three bodies caught what light there was cause we naked ones so-slightly glowed. And then there's my match and D's—yellow glows—and our cigarettes, orange'y glows.

"How young were you, auntie, at the odalisques?"

"What's it matter?" says D. "Your age, more or less. Less, actually. But she didn't lay with me till another year. I wondered why—after all, everybody else had done. By then I figured: Born in a cathouse, live in a cathouse, die in a cathouse. Esther—poor thing, those first months of me living with Esther, in my own private luxurious room she'd just look at me and long for me. I didn't get it, at first. I was hers, she'd bought me, for *thousands,* she could do what she wanted—what was I going to do instead, walk the streets? Leave her luxuriously 'appointed' townhouse, with its servants and its chef? Then I got wise. She wanted me to want to, not have to. One night—oh, it was maybe a year, really, I guess less, it doesn't matter—I tip-toed into her room, scooted into her bed. She mothered me, sistered me, fucked me. Taught me really it could be wonderful. Saved me. But don't think I don't resent! Because I do resent. She wants me to be—a good person—just because she's the best person in the world, and she is, doesn't mean I have to be. Good ain't good enough for me."

"You said *ain't,* auntie."

"Sometimes it suits."

Soon, right there on the floor, she's snorin prettily. Esther breathes soft and deep. Not me.

And that's why God invented cigarettes and brandy.

2

SO ESTHER TOOK TO COMIN BY sometimes by surprise. For instance, one night she's at the door with a sheet draped about her, braided flowers round her forehead like a crown, a sash about her waist and her long cock in that sash.

Steps in. D closes and locks the door. Esther strikes a pose: "Who am I?"

"The silver dollar's Lady Liberty!" says me.

"Pretty fair. Yet . . . I am not she. Bottle!"

We're where we belong, D'Varn and me, sprawled prettily and near-nakedly before the divan on our rug and pillows. Es towers over us to brandish her cock like a sword: "I command thee!"

"I obey thee!" says me.

I hand her the bottle, she chug-a-lugs.

"You are royalty?" offers D.

"Never," says Es.

"Hint?" says me.

"I am military."

"In a sheet?" says D. "Julius Caesar!"

"Thank God. I'd begun to fear that the blind and willful ignorance hobbling our nation would overwhelm, once again, my girlish devotion to culture. D'Varn, you've redeemed literacy in the name of whores everywhere."

"Stop talking college."

"How would *you* know Julius Caesar, ignorant wench?"

"Saw the play! Got kidnapped into it by Mable, who was wanting a sober evening of highfalutin bullshit and *not* wanting to be alone, because she can't stand that, so she grabbed me, her guest of last resort. It's a damned long play."

Big Es lets the sheet drop. Naked Esther deserves a statue of her. Two statues.

She stretched out twixt D'Varn and me on her belly, placing her great cock, as she always did, on a pillow by its lonesome.

"This little one," says she, meaning me, "can't take her eyes off my ass."

"Why would I?" says me.

Huge, muscled, molded, satiny white.

"I," says Esther, "attended Vassar. You strumpets ever hear of it? College for rich girls. We put on plays. Shakespeare—even tarts like you have heard of Shakespeare. Girls play the boys. With my size, I'd be Julius Caesar, Macbeth. Not Hamlet, he's too willowy. Appeared in *Hamlet*, though—two roles, Ghost and Gravedigger. You don't even know what I'm talking about. Girls were always getting crushes on each other and being so goddamned coy about it, and we'd have dances, and half of us would dress like men, bunch our hair into derbies or top hats or stuff it down our backs under white shirts, full suit-collar-and-tie, dike-like. We girl-boys posed for Kodaks, chocolate cigarettes stuck between our lips as we'd slouch like toughs with an arm around our favored frail. I really *wanted* education, that's what a damn fool I was. Studied. Put a value on my mind.

"Every semester I'd go nuts over some shiny-eyed girl—not coy about it either. Would have been kicked out, but rich girls, *really* rich girls, don't get kicked out on 'morals'—academia loves a bribe. They tried lecturing decency into me, as though they knew anything about it. Learn a lot of crap they'll never let you *do* anything with, write crush-letters to wispy cunts, graduate, get married, have children for your servants to raise while you get used to being useless—*that* was the plan!" She slugged down brandy. Then: "I'm afraid of myself. You afraid of yourself, Miss D? You should be."

"I'm not scared'a myself," blurts me.

"Not scared of herself," Es says to D, "and first thing she did was pull her knife on me, just cause I kissed the thing."

"Willie," says D, "has a right to be scared."

"She sure does," Es agrees. "Willie-girl, how long do you think you'll get away with being you?"

I look from one to the other and each looks back hard. Says me, "How long? The rest of this night, for sure. And probably tomorra. That's as far ahead as I go."

I take a big brandy swig. Pass the bottle round. Light a cigarette and pass it to Es. Light another and pass it to D. Then I light one for me.

"The secret of life," Esther says. "We collegiate pussies waxed rhapsodic about the secret of life. *Beauty is truth, truth beauty. In Xanadu did Kubla Khan* decree one fancy cathouse. Here's one for you—real deep: Study mythology and you shall see there is no *male* god of sex, except perhaps Pan, who's a beast—and no *male* god of love, but for those obscenely pudgy Cupids."

Then up Esther rises and declaims: *"Everlasting Aphrodite! You! You of the shining mind!"* She sinks back down. "My over-enthusiastic translation of Sappho. Not so bad either, *shining mind.*"

Esther's eyes tear and her face scrunches to swallow back a sob, at which D'Varn slaps Esther a whack on her wondrous ass.

"Stop that, Esther, goddamnit. Just quit. The secret of life is right here in this room. Can't you admit we're having the time of our lives? We get away with murder at the Keystone and we get away with murder at this hotel, and hereabouts we can get away with damn near anything, because the circus has come to town to stay. You want deep? That's deep. I'll wear the world on my finger like a ring—you'll see!"

"D'Varn, you've gotten almost to where you can speak English, congratulations. At the Keystone you are but one of Mack Sennett's 'smick-smack beauties,' to employ his own expression, and that's all you are—and that's all you'll be in *She.*"

"At the Famous Players, Miss stuck-up Esther, you saw what I'll be in *She*—and you can't handle it!"

Then of a sudden D'Varn's *at* Esther, a fistful of shiny auburn hair in each hand, pullin her hair hard and kissin her full on, and Esther's kissin back, which never have they done in front of me, till Esther pushes D away by the breasts and D's squealin about how that hurt.

"Esther," says D, "you should come see my costumes. Watch a fitting! See the drawings of what we're going to do—and the paintings!—paintings of *me* being *She*!"

"I do not consort with demons," our Esther says, "nor mix with goblin-men."

I laugh. "*That's* why Violet peed at the sight of lions! Doesn't it say in your books, Esther, that a demon can't help but pee in the presence of a lion?"

"Why, yes," says Es, "it probably does say, somewhere or other."

D's a'blushin. "I'll throw *you* back in the street, Miss Catch."

"Hey," says me, "who pays for this room now?"

"Good for you!" Esther claps. "Nor should I consort with a cunt that lets a demon feed upon her—but I'm a fool to the end, aren't I, D'Varn?"

Three angels walked on our three graves.

"This evening is a failure," D decides. "Can't we just gossip? If you sluts don't give out with some good gossip you can both go sleep down the hall."

Gossip did look like a good way out of scary-talk, but I got sparked by "you can *both* go sleep down the hall." My inners got plenty active at that moment toward Esther. And it showed. Sleep down the hall? I swear on the Bible I didn't think of that *up at the front of my mind* till right then. But there it was now, in my damned shining mind. I'm wantin to go sleep down the hall. I been wantin to since that other night, but in a hidin-from-myself way, not up at the front of my mind.

They pretend not to notice my thing's response as they fall to dishin snide—how Miss Mabel, bless her heart, orders her maid every night to sleep in her same room on a cot by her bed, the poor thing—and Devil Charlie don't socialize with nobody but walks the streets all night alone *playin a violin!*—and D saw Kodaks of Wally Beery's tiny wife Gloria with a *belt* around her neck *buckled* at the *throat*—and Chester Walrus and Devil Charlie have bet money that Mr. Sennett is a fairy, which is why he'll never marry Miss Mabel, who D is certain is a virgin, and Esther ponders how maybe Mr. Sennett is the sort of fairy that don't know he is one "like half the goddamned men that ever were," but Sommie—who everyone says is one— is *not*, which got Esther and D'Varn on the subject of *men*, a word they say like how you crush a cigarette butt.

By now we're drunker than shit, of course.

D wags a finger at Es. "Didn't you ever, ever dream about boys?"

"Not once."

"Not ever?"

"Not ever."

D darts her stare at me. "Willie?"

"Nope."

"What about your Mr. Brick?"

"He ain't my anything. Gets on my nerves, sure—but I don't feel— squishy with him."

D'Varn glowers. "You two—you two got no ambition. If you got—if you *have*—ambition, men are unavoidable."

"That's men all over," says Es. "Unavoidable as hell. I hate every last one of them."

"That sounds exhaustin, Miss Esther," says me.

"I don't hate you, anyway, Catch. Strange, prettiest you. Hate myself, if that counts."

How a person can hate their own self is somethin I'm not about to ask. Asked instead, "Esther, why do you hate men?"

"They are *in the way*. That's why. No matter what you want to do, there's some goddamned man in your way. It's hateful."

"Not," says D'Varn, "if you're the rider and he's the horse."

"Sommie's awful nice," I say.

"Sommie," D'Varn says, "is not really a man, no more than you are. We don't mean him and we sure don't mean you. You don't smell man'ish ever."

"Let's see if I can explain, little thing," says Esther. "Men are just like— *men*. Just the swellest creatures ever."

D says, "They're swell, you bet."

"Peachy," says Es.

"And important!" says D.

"Oh, by God, they are important! Don't let them forget for a second *how* important."

"Gentlemen," trills D.

"Gentle, right."

"And bright, so bright!" sparks D.

"They know all about women," Esther says. "Just ask them."

"Brick," says me, "he thinks if I was with a man I wouldn't want to be with you anymore."

"That chump," says Es. "He looks straight at you, Willie, and does not see you."

"Or"—says D'Varn, and starts to laugh—"maybe he does!"

"Maybe!" Es delights. "I'll bet he *does*!"

D'Varn and Es get to laughin to beat the band while I'm just confused.

D'Varn says, "If he does see, he doesn't know he sees."

"Too true," Es opines.

"The life I come from," says me, "they're dead certain that such as we are Hell-fire bound—but at the Keystone folks don't seem to mind."

"Well," Esther says, "first off—they don't really know what you are. As for us, that's a little different. In show business—vaudeville or opera or the legit or the ballet or the circus and burly-que—we can carry on as we please so long as everybody pretends it's a secret. Everybody knows, and gives it a wink, and pretends not to know. That's the way in high society, too."

Says D'Varn, "The wink is how they say I'm-in-on-it, I'm-no-fool. If it gets so they can't pretend, you watch out! They get mean. They're thankful for a lie, if it's the lie they want to hear."

"Aren't we all," says Esther.

"Don't you start," says D. "Life's easy: Figure out what you want, figure out how to get it."

"Me," says me, "I got what I want."

They both look at me like I am a hopeless fool past savin.

"You," is all D'Varn answers. "You, you. Brush my hair, you. Rise up off your pretty tush and get us brushes and bring another bottle back."

I do so.

Soon we're all three brushin each other's hair in a tight nude'y circle on the floor, brushin, drinkin, smokin, riddin ourselves of any unwelcome sobriety, brushin, drinkin, brushin, pretty as you please, gettin kinda lost in it. I'm brushin honey-colored locks, D's brushin auburn, Es is brushin dark, all of us kinda caped with our hair, shiny honey, shiny auburn, shiny dark, night-bloomin jasmine waftin through the window perfumin us all.

"Mermaids," whispers Esther. "Valkyries. Valkyrie mermaids."

"Val-kees?" says me. "What's val-kees?"

"Takes too long to explain."

"I just have to *not* know what you're talkin about sometimes, is that it?"

"It surely is."

D'Varn—surprise, surprise—grinned wide like she never does, bright as a bell, showin her gums. "This right here is a pretty good Hell."

3

JUST THE NEXT NIGHT, D'Varn's asleep in her beauty by candlelight on our white bed.

I'm sittin on her swivel stool, lookin at her, then swivelin at the closet mirror to see me full length, then swivelin toward the vanity to see me head and torso. Plus the vanity's got two side-mirrors that'll move back and forth and I kinda play with em, movin em back and forth.

Never had much to do with mirrors. Mother allowed none. Fred was my mirror. Mother taught us to fix each other proper for church and schoolin. I'd get it right on Fred, she'd get it right on me. It was regular groomin, spit-curls and pins and how your hair hung, how your garment set. Never saw make-up till the Keystone. Still hardly don't, cept amongst us movies.

It only seems strange now, no mirror at the farm. Daddy shaved and fussed with his bow-tie by feel. I can't see him carin enough about mirrors to want one or not want one. It was Mother didn't want them, and if I asked why she'd say, "Why—is a crooked letter."

Now here am I with all these mirrors. The three of D'Varn's vanity, and, like she does, I angle the two side-mirrors so's to see my behind-self in the full length closet-door mirror behind me, plus on the vanity by the powder puffs lie D'Varn's heavy'ish silver-framed hand-mirrors. Sometimes she's got one in each hand so's she can mirror every inch of her.

Mother said I'd have to think to get through this world. I feel a complete failure at that project, but anyway at D's vanity I'm lookin at me and thinkin. I light a cigarette, take a drag, watch the smoke, stand up of a sudden and let my nighty fall to my ankles, crush the cig I just lit into a black swan ashtray, light another—in D'Varn's mirrors it's all done twice and three and more times.

Sit back on her swiveler, swiv this way, that way, and stare—at me—starin at me starin.

I'm pretty enough. Real pretty, dependin. I've chanced into good lighting, strong shine from our drawin room, candle almost out in here, nice shadows, who wouldn't look pretty in this light?

First time we seen a flicker, me and Fred, I got stomach-fearful. We snuck off with a nickel apiece to see wonderment, but, alone, just us and strangers, it shook me that there could even be such a thing, another whole world runnin alongside ours, lookin like ours but all grey, black and shiny white, which we could see but not touch or smell or talk to, and see people talkin in it but we can't hear, and we watch hard and of a sudden there's this whole other view with no warnin. So I got to where I'd accept, ok, there's this whole other world and it wants us to watch it, and we want to, and we pay to. But there's a strangeness. Seein flicker after flicker we get so we forget that, but that don't mean the strangeness ain't always there.

And here I've jumped inside that whole world that's runnin alongside a real world.

I *am* really very pretty.

I see me from behind in the full-length mirror on the closet door.

Very pretty, and if I stand, like so, there's my "perfect" tush and long legs and long dark shiny hair. Lookin at me from behind, you can't tell. I taper at the waist nice.

Now I turn some. There's my thing and my flat chest.

All in all, there's somethin here in these mirrors, and what's here in these mirrors is a question I have never asked—

What am I?

I spent the next day makin my living, about which nothin is usual, as Mr. Sennett's always remindin us how we're some of the first movies ever in this world. Now again I'm sittin, sippin, smokin at her vanity. D's "visiting" our Esther. I am this minute a little loaded. Electricity's down at Hotel Hollywood, as happens some. Took this oil lamp from under the bathroom sink, lit it on D's vanity. Coal oil. The lamp's in the mirrors along with me. Electric light is steady, it don't move, and its shine is kinda white, while a coal oil lamp burns yellow'ish and pulsing-like. I turn up the wick and this bedroom glows. Turn the wick down, down, down, it's all shadows—mirrors darken but for a small flame in each—while straight above the lamp, on the ceiling, is a little bright orange circle. Turn the wick up, the circle widens, turn it up some more, you've got your glowin room.

That's what I've been doin with the question "What am I?" Flarin it up and down.

No way around it, "What am I?" is—as they say around here—deep.

"I can be deep as them, goddamnit," says I to I and I and I and I.

Can't burn down a question like you can a farmhouse. There's no goin around it or steppin over. It's like some kinda gate you just gotta go through—can't get where you're goin otherwise.

Esther can saunter in here when she's of a mind and Queenie D visits Big Es when she damn well will. What am I, nailed down? Hoodoo'spelled? It's a free country! I'll strut there, wearin very little, cause that's how they do. I mean to qualify, in black silk pantie, a pearl'ish see-through half-slip, and a camisole top negligée thing—"transparent bodice," is what. Silver ankle bracelets.

Rouge and such? Naw.

She in the mirrors is not Miss Me-not-me. She is me like I like to be.

My lantern, as I walk, swings my shadow up and down the hall.

Listen at Esther's door. Don't hear a thing. Hit a good knock. Another.

"Willie?" Esther whispers.

"I'm lonely," says me.

Door opens. "Don't be. Have a brandy."

She's lookin kinda silly in a frilly nightie. Sometimes, I must say, our Esther overdoes a look.

"We are smoking hashish," says she, "and you can't have any."

"Didn't ask, did I? And why can't I?"

"Because I don't like the idea, is why."

D'Varn speaks from the shadows, "Our smoke'll get her sauced anyway."

I turn down the lantern. In dimness I see . . . when I was here that one time before I couldn't notice anything really, I was too upset, but now I see that Esther's rooms are bigger. Her divan's longer than ours and horseshoe-curved, in the corner. Deeper rugs. I follow Es into a large bedroom lit by candles. Hangin from wall-hooks and pegs are hats, guns, a Kodak case. Esther takes my lantern, hands me a snifter.

Big damn bed, with a canopy, fancy-frilly, where D'Varn's naked and bunched up, huggin her knees and smokin a small pipe. Es climbs on the bed—it's maybe three feet off the floor!—and pats the spread as a way to say come on up, but I stand lookin.

I know they see my figure through my bodice, with silver ankle bracelets a'glintin.

"Pretty as a fresh bruise," says D, smilin down on me.

"What am I?" says me.

Nothin from them.

The bed's high enough up, with them lookin down.

"I'm not a man," says me. "So—what am I?"

Their hashish smells sweet. D passes Esther their pipe.

Says Es, "Come up here. Let's examine the merchandise."

"Up, up, up," says D.

"I did not come for fuckery."

"Not offering any," Esther says. "Get up here with the big girls."

I climb up and there we are. D'Varn reaches out one long-fingered hand and, smilin a lazy kinda smile, touches me here and there, but not like S-E-X.

Esther's sayin, "How did you *know*, D, about our Willie? At the first?"

"A glow off her. The way she looked at me. I didn't think twice about it."

"That's painful to hear, dear."

"Then don't ask, dear."

Esther has her hand under my bodice. Then on a thigh. "It's all," says she, "so strangely smooth. Makes me want to break things."

Now ever so quietly I am startin in to cry—and I'm not feelin weepy, is the mystery. Tears. Not cry-for-happy either. Just . . . tears. Which they ignore.

"Esther," says D, "her nipples. They're crazy, her little nipples. Sensitive as a two little clits."

They inhale their hashish deep and I'm smellin it deep.

"So, tell me," says Esther, "how do you get off?"

"Off?" says me.

"How do you come?"

"Esther?"

"Achieve orgasm—a most unladylike thing to do, but how do you?"

"What are you askin?"

"How has D'Varn pleasured you? Where does she pleasure you best?"

"All over," says me. "All over me she pleasures me. Ever'where. *You* know that, auntie," I turn to D, "you *do* me to make me moan, do me all over? Is that what Esther's askin?"

Says D, "I listen to your body. I learned how from this one," nods at Es.

"Painful," Esther says.

"What, Esther, I was going keep myself only for you, stay with you forever?"

"Something just like that, yes."

"When did you know I wouldn't be like that?"

"From the start," says Es.

Them angels were back, walkin on our graves.

Says Esther, "Miss Will—that's how you come, all over and anywhere?"

"*Come* is stupid," says me. "I don't come, I—*go*."

"Now that you mention it…" Esther sorta smiles.

Those two look at each other and smile, I don't know why.

Says Esther, "Do you know people in Poland can't talk about their toes?"

"Esther?" says me.

"Can't talk about their toes. Poles have no word for toes. They use the word for fingers, but fingers are not toes. That fascinating item is in Dr. Sigmund Freud's *Psychopathology of Everyday Life,* recently published in English but available in German about ten years ago. I read German, of course. Oh, I too read Mabel's books—before she even heard of them. Don't misunderstand me, Mabel is impressive to have latched onto Freud, but—Sommie calls us ruffians and we are, present company especially, so be impressed or shocked, as you like, but—I also read Freud in French, but you mustn't tell Mabel, she tries so hard with French. I read Freud in different languages because different languages understand differently. Where Dr. Freud has deciphered you, Miss Wil, is his theory—well, actually, it's an hypothesis"—

"*Will* you get on with it," says D, "and stop showing off!"

"Freud has a concept called 'polymorphous perverse.' That's you, Willie."

"Where's my knife?" says me. "Sounds like I need my knife."

"What you need," says Esther, "is to listen."

When she tells me what she tells me, it's *me.* "Complete sexual satisfaction" possible just about anywhere on my body.

"Like as though every part of my body is just as alive?" I ask.

"Like as though," says Es, "indubitably. The nasty doctor says we all have that ability as tots but lose it as we get older, but *you* somehow neglected to lose it."

"Poly-more-fuz," says me. "That's a name for what I am?"

"A *scientific* name," says Es, "for *some* of what you are."

"Polly's more fuss," says D, "more fuss than she's worth this evening."

"Scien-*tific*," says me. "Hot'diggity."

Esther laughs, "I shall start calling you Polly!"

"Don'tchya dare!"

"Oh, yeah, little thing, who'll stop me? Polly, my little Polly Anna, Polly Pervy, Pervy Polly!"

Says D, "You two stop flirting before I throw up!"

"You, you pert troublemaker," Es opines at me, "are a polymorphous perverse personage who somehow occupies a strangely feminine body with masculine attributes."

"What about what D'Varn said, lesbian?"

"Who knows?!" says Esther. "I surely do not."

"On the other hand," D'Varn nudges in, "if you're somehow *not* a girl, and have to be called a *boy,* then you're normal cause you like girls."

"Normal she is clearly not," Esther says.

Maybe it was the hashish, or maybe it was somethin else, like how some candles had gone out and dimmed the room, but D'Varn snuggled into Esther's lap and curled up, then I guess I nodded off some, but woke enough to reach for cigarettes on the phone stand, lit one off the stub of an almost-melted candle, and saw Es wide awake, sittin up, D'Varn's head in her lap with eyes closed and breathin even, and Esther looks over to me, smiles slightly, and goes to whisperin, *"Beware! Beware! Her flashing eyes, her floating hair—weave a circle round her thrice . . ."*

4

ESTHER HAD HOPED D'Varn would be different than she is, but Esther also knew better. I don't need for D'Varn to be different. Sure, she's been at her "fittings" two days. Called in ill at the Keystone. Hasn't called here. But if D'Varn was nicer, where would I be? It ain't her "nice" that I love. Wants to wear the world as a ring on her finger. What a thing to need.

I do think that Esther, sometime in her past, kind of decided to be sad for keeps. It suits her. I can't see a jolly Esther. It's her sadness made Esther kiss me before D'Varn could, and Esther's mouth tasted of red wine.

I . . . am gonna . . . bring a bottle . . . of red wine . . . to Esther.

I choose a get-up that's got "contrasts" (D's word—and Charlie's). Darks and lights. See-through scarves mostly, bright white silk tighties underneath. Ankle-bracelets, cause I'd noticed Esther liked that. High heels. No hat.

Ain't I a caution?

All the while not-not-not thinkin that I'm doin a big thing. How each thing you do changes the next thing, and the next, and the next . . . all the way down the hall.

I knock soft. Nothin. Then her doorknob twists and her door opens. Esther's in a velvet'y robe, deep red. She pulls it tight around her.

"Good," she says. "You've come."

I said nothin.

She says, "You're fifteen? Sixteen?"

"Goin on seventeen," says me.

"And now you have two lovers."

I hand her the bottle.

"Come in," says she. "Cigarettes, over there." Points to a deep-brown carved stand. I pick a smoke from an open engraved silvery box and matches from a smaller box just like it. Light up. She's uncorked the wine. Pours the red, which is really sorta purple, into two small tumblers. We sipped.

With mouths tasting of those sips we kissed, slow, a kiss that had nothin to prove.

She rose up to turn on a wall-lamp to show me a drawing—in a frame—a drawing of a woman who looked some like Esther—and a woman who looked lots like D'Varn—and the Esther in the drawing half-sits up in bed, her nightgown pulled down some, showin an upper swell of breast, and the D'Varn lays upon her with an arm around her and her head on her shoulder and chest, eyes closed, yet it was not a restful atmosphere.

"You draw that?" says me.

"I'm pleased you think I'm a genius, but no. And, if you care, it is the original. Drawn in 1862 by Dante Gabriel Rossetti for the cover of his sister Christina's slim book, *The Goblin Market And Other Poems.* You sit still—I shall recite."

Very still I sit on that huge horseshoe-shaped divan.

"I'm a little nervous, Catch. I've sort of planned this."

"Knew I'd show up?"

"Couldn't know. Could only want."

I sat. She took the wineglass from my hand and crossed my legs at the ankles, just so. Lit me a cig, put it to my lips, then starts in to sayin, *"Dear you should not stay so late . . . Should not loiter in the glen . . . In the haunts of goblin men . . . Did you miss me? . . . Come and kiss me . . . Hug me, kiss me, suck my juices . . . Eat me, drink me, love me . . . make much of me . . . Look at me, I'm trembling . . . She clung about her sister . . . Kissed and kissed and kissed her . . ."*

You'da thought she'd take charge, but she didn't. I pulled the bow that tied her robe and parted the folds.

Us two was utterly different. Nothin like. The *sweetness* of us, far as far from what had been.

Brandy. The drink burned slow inside, our cigarettes burned slow, and if the whole world was burnin I wouldn't care to know, and if told all I'd say is, "Gotta burn sometime, why must I mind?"—then I'd be back to doin with Esther.

"Catch, D'Varn's as good as gone."

"Esther—at this moment—I don't care."

"You will. I will. As though the moon is never to rise again, we'll never see that moon again."

"She wants us to be like this," says me, "that's what I think."

"So she won't feel guilty ditching us," says she.

"Esther, I don't wanna hide from her about us."

"She knows and knows."

"Still and all, when we're out front with it, she'll be mad."

"Operatically so." Then: "Catch—if I left town, would you come with me?"

"Don't wanna say a yes, don't wanna say a no—I like my job, a lot."

"Fair enough." Then Esther says, "I've piggy-backed on D'Varn's ambitions because I only wanted her. Then you gave me something else to want, back there on the Palisades—and a lesson in how alone I am, really. Now here you've come, and here I pray you'll stay. I could build a house for us up the hill. Buy you an auto, teach you to drive. You could go to the lot when you pleased."

Says me, "You really could, couldn't you? My. What would you do?"

"I was, I am, a good doctor, and I could be a better one."

She rises, steps to the bedroom, comes back with a black leather satchel, says, "Here's my doctor's bag, and there's another in the boot of my Oldsmobile." Unfastens latches and draws from her satchel an instrument I've seen in illustrateds. She screws its two prongs into my ears. They're on little hoses that connect to a wider hose that connects to a bell-like thingamajig.

"My stethoscope," says she.

Places the bell over my left breast. Says, "Listen to your heartbeat, darling."

I listened to mine, then I listened to hers.

GRIFFITH

KARL BROWN
*. . . the news seeped out that the great
D.W. Griffith was moving his entire company
to Hollywood . . . not more than
a hundred steps from our front door.*

D.W. GRIFFITH
Every foot of film is precious.

NED COBB, AKA NATE SHAW
*The boll weevil come in this country after
I was grown . . . Yes, all God's dangers ain't
a white man. When the boll weevil
starts in your cotton . . .*

1

THIS OR THAT TIME during my day's work my rump might yaowl for want of somethin fuckin it which kinda hypnotizes me from deep inside—and Es and D move wands so differently! Or my nipples take to burnin on their own. Well, you can't be feelin such stuff and leap off anything higher than a curb. You gotta be all the way inside a fall and wide awake so's your agility takes over. Let's just say one day S-E-X messed with my agility and I hurt my left arm again.

Anyway it's a really pretty day and my arm hangs in this sling, good for nothin but to hold a parasol that's yellow and embroidered with roses of red. My shoes are tannish, soft leather, low heel, pointy toe. I'm properly bonneted and gloved, a pale green long-sleeved blouse of softest cotton with cuffs embroidered sweet, a blouse to ripple some with a breeze, and a full leaf-green skirt that sways nice with my stride. Oh, and white tight transparent stockings embroidered around my ankles, a little risqué but acceptably so in Edendale.

Moseyin restless about the Keystone thinkin maybe I could be in somebody's background.

Sommie caught my eye where he sat outside the prop shed on a rocker, reading. Waved me over.

"Hurt again, are we?"

"It's nothin."

"It's always nothing."

"So how are the relatives of the absolutes? Fussin like everybody else's relatives?"

"I daresay they are. Tea?"

He'd set a bedstead table beside the rocker, with his teapot and two cups, as was his habit.

I've learned to sit like a lady if I choose to, ankles crossed and knees bent just so. A Me-Not-Me posture that goes with the parasol.

We tea'd. (One holds a cup with pinky pointed.)

"Life is headlong here," says Sommie. "An English day pauses for breath by means of tea." He sips. "To subjugate the Orient that I might indulge my cup of tea is, admittedly, a bit much—but I do so enjoy my tea."

"What's the book?" says me.

"Bless me, how polite! Where is our feral girl?"

"Left her in a mirror at Hotel Hollywood," says me.

"The book happens, like the tea, to be from India. Rabindranath Tagore."

"And that's a what?"

"That is a name. He is a contemplative poet. May I read aloud?"

"As you'd say, have a go."

He's flippin pages. "Ah: *Fool, try to carry thyself upon thy own shoulders! Oh, beggar, to come to beg at thy own door!* Like it?"

"No."

"And why not?"

"He's got no business sayin that to me, is why."

"Point taken. Another. *Evidently the only way to find the path is to set fire to my own life.*"

"That's in a book!" says me.

"This very one," says he.

"That's what I done."

"Set fire to what exactly?"

"Our farmhouse."

"Seriously?"

"It was very serious."

"Did anyone—my word!—die?"

"No, but I can't take the credit. They got out on their own."

"Did you want them to die?"

"No!"

"What did you want?"

"Wanted everything to change. And it sure did."

"Your friends here—they don't know their lives could possibly be *changed* in this fashion?"

"They do not."

"Hmmm." Then, "This Rabindranath fellow—first wog to win a Nobel

Prize. There's even talk of knighting the chap. Sir Rabindranath. And so, the world. Fancy a walk? A *long* walk?"

"D'Varn's gonna have some scenes later today, I sorta promised to gawk."

"I'm bound to say she's a treat to watch."

Hold on. Sommie never leaves the Keystone but for a shoot.

"Changed my mind, Mr. Somerset."

"The easiest and hardest thing to change."

"They don't need you here today?"

"Do they ever?"

"Don't you talk that way, you write the best biz, everybody knows it."

"Concocting risk-rampant silliness seems to have become my specialty," cept he said spesh-ee-al-ity. "But our scenarios are not proper writing. They require no style, and are, if anything, the obverse of thought."

"If it ain't writin, what is it?"

"No one knows, not as yet. We don't yet really know how to do what we're doing, do we?"

"Too deep for me. Where we walkin to?"

"Somewhat west, to have a look-see. That man Griffith has come to town."

You can't be a movie and not know that name.

"Let's us go then," says me.

Sommie rises, puts the book on the table by the teapot, and pauses to still his rockin chair.

So we're walkin. The sun is warm, the sky clear, the breeze light, and I wondered if, anywhere on Miss Mabel's globe of this Earth, was there another city scented by such flowers, so many flowers, on hillsides, lawns, planted fields, raw fields, and trees that give of oranges and of lemons, also magnolias, also night-bloomers. Fred would point to this one and to that one and say their particular names like she'd win a prize for knowin.

We just walked, quietly, enjoyin the newness that was Sommie and Willie out for a stroll, he in a faded tweed suit and round his neck a cashmere scarf of gray, though it's a warm'ish day.

"How come, Sommie, you never wear a hat?"

"Must one?"

"Every man I know does, cept you."

"Still—must one?"

"Guess not. Now you ask me somethin, if you like."

"I'll ask a favor. Please, no more hanging off cliffs."

"Can't promise."

"It was awful. When you lost your grip."

"Didn't lose it. Planned it."

"Heavens, child. Why?"

"Good biz! Once I thought of it, couldn't weasel out on myself."

"You didn't consider how we'd feel?"

"Kinda counted on it. And, hey, you! Who came up with the biz of cars hangin over cliffs?"

"I began this thread of conversation in an attempt to apologize for that very thing."

We turned onto a road plowed level that had several houses on each side, and there's this lady steppin down her porch step.

"Sommie, look at that big lady wearin that small hat."

"We mustn't stare—nor giggle."

She gave *us* the look instead, hatless him and colorful me, as we passed.

Got up my nerve to ask, "Sommie, how old are you?"

"I was born old. I hope to die young."

"I asked if you lived in the prop shed, you said you don't think of it that way. So, what way?"

"I am on a voyage. My quarters are in steerage."

"My sister called our best game 'voyages.' We'd get ourselves lost then make our way back."

"Good game. We of the Keystone are voyagers perhaps, but we're not expected back—excepting the formidable Mr. Watson, all on our lot show every sign of having left something well worth the leaving. I wonder at the people who stay. I wonder how they bear it."

"They go to the flickers."

"Yes, they do, don't they?"

We walked through a lemon grove, lemon-scent heavy in the air. Sommie led, now and then lifting from his jacket pocket a compass the size of a silver dollar. We kept to paths up hills and down, then happened on a larger street and what do you know? Clang'a'clang'clang! Fire-wagon bells! There it came, firemen holdin on for dear life, their horses pullin hard and gallopin pretty.

Says Sommie, "I read that our fine city shall purchase trucks for firefighters."

"I'll miss these wagons."

"You'll have good opportunity to miss them. They'll likely vanish. That report, summarizing our area's glories, purports that at present motor vehicles in Los Angeles County number in the thousands. If memory serves—and mine generally does, if I may say—California numbers 55 counties, of which Los Angeles County is first in the value of crops, first in fruit and dairy, first in lemon trees, second in orange and olive trees, second in poultry, and our—if I may say 'our'—principle articles of export are fruits, vegetables, wine, brandy, wool"—

"Sommie!"

"Can't stop once I've started—where was I?—wool, honey, canned goods, sugar, olives, wheat, corn, barley, petroleum, cotton. Notice what's missing? We are missing. Sennett, Selig, DeMille, Ince, now Griffith—not a word about us. Seems they're not proud of us. A town is always pleased at the arrival of a circus—and relieved when it departs, circus people being circus people. But our circus has come to town to stay."

"Did you get that from D'Varn or did she get it from you?"

"Admittedly, admittedly, I've enlarged another's metaphor. Credit where credit is rightly due et cetera."

"You're sayin the powers that be are prouder of their pigs and chickens than of us?"

"Quite."

"No wonder you don't wear a hat."

"Pardon?"

"What with what-all's stuffed in your noggin, a hat'd just pop right off."

He stopped walkin. Says, "Hold on a tick."

From his jacket pocket he fished a pack of ready-mades.

"Ain't seen that brand," says me.

"Richmondbern. British."

He came up with a wooden matchstick but was at a loss for where to strike it.

"Give it here," says me.

He did so.

Lit it on my fingernail. Fired up his weed.

"Brick taught me that," says me.

"Ah, Brick."

"No cracks," says me.

"Cigarette?" says he?

"Thanks, naw." As we walk on I tell him, "Gals get away with that around the Keystone—those cops know us—but here, in broad daylight . . ."

"And you wonder they're not proud of us? It's known far and wide that our profession, for some reason, involves constant, if haphazard, fuckery by all concerned"—he arched his brows at me—"excepting myself, I'm relieved to say."

"You don't do it?"

I coulda bit my tongue.

"I seem somehow to have been spared the impulse. Sweating bodies bumping upon one another, resulting eventually in the often unwelcome duplication of their persons in the form of a yowling wad of flesh in continuous need of indelicate ministrations. A futile business— the poor little bugger, after all, will one day be one of us. Seems not much of a goal. As for attraction to one of my own gender, which is apparently your preference, I see no difference in emotional impracticality, this gender or that. Not that I feel above it all—simply beside it all. Honestly—I like to think I've an able mind, but that cannot be so if the fundamental urge of my species is, to me, an inexplicable ritual. Fortunately others feel differently, or there'd be no one with whom to converse."

"You'd talk anyway," says me, "to a cat or to a tree."

"No doubt. You know, you're awfully nice."

"Maybe I'm not," says me, "but you and me get along."

"Yes, we do. In any case—the relative and the absolute exist in the same continuum, and I am proof of that in my person, as are we all."

"I like to hear you talk," says me.

"I exist, then, for you, as a disembodied accent."

"Can't get enough."

"Child, you are easily pleased."

"Not me. Oh, look!"

A bright red-breasted bird on a fencepost. Of a sudden it's on the wing.

"I do know your secret," Sommie says.

Sudden blush and sweat on my part.

"You are clever at hiding your mind. I don't feel anything said to you is wasted."

"Gee," says me.

That was when a mighty shadow moved upon the grass and we look up we see an eagle, and such an eagle.

"Oh my!" says I.

"Indeed," says he.

Didn't that eagle swoop low and rise high, and higher, and higher, to the tallest palm tree on the highest ridge?

"That, my dear, never happens in London. Nor will a cougar quietly and carefully appear. Nor deer. Nor raccoons, skunks, coy'otes. Not in London, Boston, or New York. Hungry?"

Consulting his compass, he steered us to a populated corner complete with a newsstand and vendors of hotdogs, ices, and pop. It's hard to hold a parasol and eat a hot dog so's the sauerkraut and mustard don't drip on your nice things, but I did so.

At the newsstand, three newsboys, "newsies"—one maybe nine, the others eleven or twelve—they're slouching about with caps atilt, smokin cigarettes and crackin wise, awaitin afternoon editions. Tough little numbers. I liked them, but they saddened Sommie.

"A grain of sand in an oyster, under proper conditions, may become a pearl. That may be your D'Varn. But when a pearl becomes a grain of sand . . ."

"You're just thinkin all the time, ain't you, Sommie?"

"And you're not?"

Now we finish up our pop and watch a cop direct traffic from high up on a wooden stage-like platform in the center of the intersection. He did it good. Sharp gestures. Miss Mabel'd like that. She should do it in a flicker, I'm thinkin, just when a two-seater auto with a lady drivin turns sharp around the cop's platform and a hatless blond gal in the passenger seat tosses that cop a shiny red apple—took him off-guard, but he caught it, laughed and waved to them gals.

"That spiffy vehicle," says Sommie, "was a four-cylinder Cadillac, model 1912, as evidenced by its exaggerated running boards and all-brass trim."

"Never know what you'll know next, Sommie. Bet them gals are movies."

Watching the cop on his high platform with his white-gloved smart gestures, and the whistle that hangs from his neck and is most-times in his mouth blowin high and shrill, we're crossin the street and my eyes are on him and then in front of me I see *her* right away, but she's lookin straight at me and not seein me. Can she really not? That's not possible. *Can* that be possible? I see her—different, not a farm girl no more for sure—but I see her. Of a sudden, near us now, she sees me.

"Willamina, that is NOT you!"

"Federica, sister—is too!"

And we're just standin there.

"*Ladies,*" Sommie says, "traffic has stopped, horns honk, the officer whistles, all is distraught."

Fred and me couldn't budge.

Sommie's tryin to budge us. "*Please* recognize this is not a Keystone," and so sayin he stands between us, clasps a firm hand to my arm and hers—with "I beg you excuse this liberty" to Fred.

When Fred's on the curb and sees the extent of the confusion that we didn't mean to cause, she lets out with that ripplin crazy laughin I've missed so—sorta half laugh, half war-whoop.

Now she cuts off that laughter like flickin a switch and her eyes are hard on me.

"Fred, can we buy you a hot dog?"

"I was crossin here for just that reason."

I pinch a paper dollar from my purse and give it to Sommie.

"Would you, Sommie? With the fixin's?"

"After I'm introduced. I am not your butler, dear girl."

"Oh, jeez. Federica, this is—Mr. Somerset, my good friend. Mr. Somerset, this is my twin sister, Frederica."

"Such a near resemblance," says he.

"Miss Frederica Adair," says she.

"Miss Adair," Sommie bows slightly, "enchanted."

"Enchanted!" Fred says. "Well, then, sir, likewise," and she curtsies smart.

"Excuse me, then, whilst I happily fetch your victuals."

As he turns and goes, Fred says whisperin, "He talks funny."

"He's British."

"From across the seas! Mother'd love that. Willie out walkin with a *foreign* gentleman. I swear."

"Sommie—we call him Sommie—he's a good friend."

"Willie with a friend. Who's this 'we'?"

"All'a us at the Keystone."

"The Keystone, is it? What'sa matter with your arm? Nice parasol."

"Hurt the arm doin—we call it 'biz'—the falls, the jumps, how at the Keystone you're always knockin about."

"That *was* you, then—the car hangin off the cliff."

"If you recognized me, why didn't you come see me when you knew where I was?"

"Reasons, is why," says Fred.

While we're talkin I'm sizin up Fred and I know she's doin the same on me. No make-up, of course. Long brown dress, tight-waisted, with a belt, very respectable. Her top is long-sleeved with flurry white cuffs. Grey-white gloves, nice. Brown button-up shoes with a low heel. Hair bunned up under a proper hat with a small feather, hat's pinned kinda sideways to the bun. No long filed nails like me. Hands set for simple, needful tasks. Fred, all business, out in the world. Heavier than before. Fuller.

"Willie, those ankle stockings! And you're—painted."

"Ever so little today! We need rouge and creams and special pencils and such, like they have on the stage, to—*accentuate!*—accentuate our features—for the—you know, the camera."

"Well," says she, "you're sure dressed not like anybody, my Willie."

"But pretty, right?"

"Pretty and fine."

But Fred's eyes didn't agree with her mouth.

Sommie, at that moment, brought us our victuals, saying, "Ladies, have yourselves a catch-up, don't mind me, I'll purchase a *Photoplay* and amuse myself."

I'm nervy so I pull a pack of ready-mades outa my purse and Fred says, "Don't you dare! *You* maybe can afford the ticket, I cannot."

"*You* wouldn't be smokin it," says me as I take out a wooden match, light it on my fingernail, and let sister-mine and all the world know what kind of a damn I don't give. And that cop, he's too busy with the traffic to care.

Says Fred, "You don't ask about Mother and Daddy?"

"Come with us, Fred! We're on a voyage, like me and you used to, we'll talk about every"—

"I have a job to get to, sister-mine. I can't go off just strollin about on a weekday like some people. Lunch is done and I gotta catch that Big Red and clock back in. And—our voyages—we were children then. We stopped bein children on a certain day when a farmhouse burned."

"Let's play grown-up then. I'm at Hotel Hollywood. Just give my name, the desk'll connect you. Just 'Willie' though. It's the only name they know."

"You—live in a hotel?"

"Lotsa movies do. Even Mr. Sennett. How will I find you?"

"Oh, no," says she. "You can't yet. Let's meet Sunday. Somewhere."

"Echo Park," says me.

"The arched bridge," says she. "Sunday. After church."

"Fred, we can eat off the venders and walk around the lake, maybe even row a canoe. It'll be fun. Grown-up fun, if that's what we've become."

Fred says, "And don't you dress so fine, cause I can't match it. *And bring me back my coat.*"

She chokes up. Of a sudden, hugs me hard. I hug back hard.

Fred turns away first. Walks fast and don't look back.

I watch where she waits for the trolley. She don't look at me.

Sommie's come beside me. Just says, "Families…" His voice trails. "Come."

He crooked his arm and I lay my gloved hand in the crook. We stepped forth.

"So I wonder," says I, "is once enough, do you think?"

"I don't follow."

"Burnin up your life—how your poet-fella said. Is once enough?"

"I certainly hope so. Handkerchief?"

Didn't know I was cryin. Took his handkerchief with sniffles and a thank you.

"She's lovely, your sister. Not as you are, not to drive boys *and* girls to distraction, but jolly lovely all the same."

"I'm a real enchantress, I am."

"Are we beginning to realize?"

I'm learnin about life, that what can seem *your whole life* can later seem like only some kinda dream. But oh, oh, oh, oh—I did not mean, I never did mean, to leave *her*.

There it was, on the south side of where Hollywood Boulevard stops goin west by north and cuts straight west. The Griffith lot had a fence—the same sorta ragtag, slapped together, taller-than-man-high fence like at the Keystone, cept it fenced a plot might be four-five-six times bigger than ours. In front, a crew of Dago shovelers dug up ground as for a sewer line.

We coulda taken the Allesandro Big Red trolley right in front of Mr. Sennett's, changed where Alessandro goes under Sunset, hopped the Holly-wood Big Red, and got off practically right here—for a nickel and a transfer, it woulda took maybe twenty-five minutes, but Sommie fancied us a walk that had got me Fred again.

"Sommie, please could you unknot my sling?"

The knot was at the back of my neck.

"Is that wise?"

"Won't have them thinkin I'm a gimp."

He did so.

I stretched out my left arm gingerly. Shoulder felt just a little stiff.

"Let's find us the gate," says me.

But Sommie just stands, so I just stand, figurin it's his outing and his move.

A Big Red passed, a few autos, a two-horse wagon fulla lumber—couldn't see the boards, but knew by the scent of fresh-sawed.

"I do hope they'll excuse our presumption," says Sommie, "intruding upon them."

"We're Keystoners, we do as we please."

"Is that what we do?"

He adjusts his gray cashmere scarf and straightens his posture. Taps his top shirt button, adjusts his starched collar. Pulls on his bow tie. "Let's, then," says he.

We walked west beside Griffith's fence, on the south side of Hollywood Boulevard, till we come upon a flight of stairs that climbed seven steps to a gate. Hollywood Boulevard, see, was graded level, and the ground here on either side was higher than the street by, well, seven steps.

Up we go. The gate wasn't locked and there was no Mr. Walker-type supervisin.

As we'd walked along the fence, what we heard on t'other side sounded familiar: hammerin, sawin, folks callin out this and that. Now we saw.

A patch of weed-covered land stretched far, with hasty-built shacks and buildings here and there, like at the Keystone, but more of em, and people all over carryin stuff, sawin, hammerin. A big ghost-building, bigger than the Keystone's. But like at the Keystone, and Mr. DeMille's, this lot usedta be somethin normal, probably another farm, and there was one house off by itself that looked like folks still lived there. Also, a troop of cavalry of the Confederacy, their horses tied to posts, the boys in gray smokin and sittin around and throwin dice, waitin. I knew what I was looking at cause Daddy had a picture-book of what he called The War of the Rebellion and Mother called the War Between the States—paintings of battles. Daddy's only book besides his Bible.

So that wasn't too un-normal, for a movie, but there was nothin normal about a kinda tent outpost, a ways down the fence, with cook-fires and tables and benches and colored folk, lots of colored folk, surprisin cause I'd never seen their kind hereabouts cept in ones and twos, and then hardly ever. Had to be close on fifty-sixty anyway, maybe a hundred.

I was curious to go near the colored's camp, just because. But Sommie says, "That architecture—anti-Bellum," pointing off to a street of fancy houses with a courthouse to boot, where folks in old-timey costumes gathered amongst one-horse carts or carriages and two-horse wagons.

Sommie looked toward the cavalry. "The gray, the gray." Then at the colored's camp. "And they."

"Sommie, we gonna just stand here?"

"Sorry?"

I was about to repeat myself when up comes this fella. "You two are movies, I can tell."

The fella's about my age, wears a slouch hat, chews a toothpick—reminded me of a younger Mr. Coy Watson, a boy with an able way about him. Sandy hair, crooked smile, gray eyes that look straight at you.

Sommie gives him a look. "You can tell, you say? How, pray?"

"You've got the stamp, is all. I'm right, ain't I?"

"We work with Mr. Sennett," Sommie says.

"Toldja. I'm Karl Brown. That's Karl-with-a-K."

He stuck out his hand and Sommie shook it, then me. Strong fella.

"I'm called Somerset. This is Willie."

Karl-with-a-K is lookin at me and he likes what he sees.

"So you're at the Keystone. How'd you get to be a movie?" says he at me.

"Just showed up. Then jumped off a roof. You?"

"Just showed up, like you. Live right across the street. Crossed to here first day they come, asked for a job straight-up, and they gave me one. Just like that. Same day."

"Fancy that," says Sommie.

"Ain't that the way?" says me.

"I work with the camera!" Karl-with-a-K says.

"Young man, what drama is Mr. Griffith filming, if I may ask?"

Karl-with-a-K crooks his head at the Confederates and grins. "It may have somethin to do with the Civil War—but don't call it that around here. Boss insists it's The Rebellion, but he *insists*. Gotta go, or Mr. Bitzer will gimmie what for. Nice t'meet you folks," Karl says to me.

Seems Griffith's movies come and go like Sennett's, but they're polite about it.

"Sommie, it don't look like anyone's about to throw us out."

He makes an effort toward brightening up, not very successfully.

"Yes," says he. "Quite."

He starts off, but not toward the big Southern street set. Instead, we stroll past various doins toward that old normal house. Behind it, and in front of an open carpenter's shed new-built, in what I guessed had been a garden, there stood a row of cannon. A fella's workin on one and we're watchin and he likes that.

"Now don't they look real?" He knocks on a cannon's barrel. "Made'a wood, with slim steel pipe running through. Watch this."

He lights a fuse, the cannon kicks, belchin fire and smoke.

We jump, he laughs, says, "That's what the Boss calls 'darb.'"

"Darb?" says Sommie.

"When somethin's fine, he says it's *darb*."

"Impressive artillery," says Sommie.

"Thank ya."

The guy goes back to work and we move on.

"Interesting," says Sommie, "that lad before, knowing we are movies."

"How'd you become a movie, Sommie?"

"Beginning to think I was born one—had only to wait for the bloody gadget to be invented. You, too."

Sommie's bolted where he is, caught by his mind, so I let him go at it and I drift off, moseyin toward the colored folk like I'm just strollin about, but I see those in their encampment nearest my direction notice me, none too happy about me either.

So here I am, close, meanin no harm, but still—an intrusion, I know it, can't help it, just got to go toward what I never saw before, all them colored folk with their tents, and the smell of fresh-washed clothing hangin brightly on lines strung twixt posts, and cook-pot smells of coffee and corn-bread and a pot of beans'n'rice which smells like Mother's, and closer I'm seein their chairs and tables are made of any-old-wood nailed any-old-way, movie-makeshift like at the Keystone, and I'm seein the colored are all kinda colors, browns, beiges, caramel, even gray'ish, and tans, and some real light tans, and some deep but *deep* brown that I could hardly believe, and some with skin shinin like it's polished, and I'm thinkin my color ain't flat white but cream-like with reddish tinge and Esther's is shiny-smooth white, and D's an ivory the camera loves, Sommie's sickly pale, Brick's reddish all over, Miss Mabel's cream like me, Hank Mann's olive, Devil Charlie too, he is very olive…

I'm all in my own mind that way, and these folk look away or look through me, and I feel terrible at my rudeness and set to go when a small round woman, hard sad eyes, she stares at me starin, steps out bold, says, "You gawkin like you are, them's yo manahs?"

"Rude, I know, rude, and I'm sorry—I just never seen."

"Nevah seen d'lak?"

"I swear. I'm from the Keystone. Off'n the lot, I don't feel right anymore, I feel like normal folk got it wrong, which can't be the case, but it's my feelin. And here *you* are."

"You a funny gurl."

"I guess."

"We nevah heard'a yall, neveh heard'a he'ah. Dey freighted us in on d'rails, fahv cars all t'ourselves, et'n'slept in em. Couldna find nuf'a us in dis Los Ang'les. Dey's colored he'ah, some, but Mistah Boss sez dey ain't raht, ain't got *d'look*. An Mistah Boss, I know he won't want you closer t'us dan you is, which is too close a'ready. Got no use f'trouble, we'uns he'ah. Best you git."

"Sorry again."

Could feel them watching me go back to Sommie.

"Sommie, did I do wrong?"

Before he answers, a sudden unmistakable sound from this town that's not a town.

"My word!" says Sommie. "Spares no expense. That man's put a church bell in that spire. For a soundless flicker."

As the bell tolls, folks mostly in costume head toward the set that's long as a block and a half of street. Confederate soldiers, gals dressed lady-like, kids dressed up and kids urchin-like, guys in top hats, and the darkest of the colored, mostly barefoot, children too, but some of the women lighter-skinned and dressed nicer and in shoes. Carts and wagons in motion, horses obedient. We follow along.

Sommie's sayin, "The chap's a jolly chancer. All these people! Why, the population of a town! And that's only the cast. How many carpenters, costumers, wranglers—the expense of it!"

And me, "Look at those buildings! Can't hardly believe it's a set."

"He means to convince," Sommie says.

We're near to where *he* is. I knew the man's picture, but I'da knowed who he was by how he handled himself—and what he wore, his jacket, tie, pants and shoes are perfection for a Sunday, topped by a un-Sunday wide white hat, one side-brim curved up high and cocky-like.

The workin folk are going about their business payin no attention to him, gettin this and that just so, the extras and cavalry takin their places up and down the fake town, groups of em, each group bossed by men with megaphones, settin them up just so—"As though they're posing for a painter," Sommie said— while several costumed folk gather about the important man, hangin on his every word, until he raises one long arm and wiggles his fingers and calls out, "Cigarette!"

Three or four fellas nearest him go to offerin him cigarettes and he selects one and somebody lights it for him.

"Many thanks." His voice kinda rolls around as though it's got its own echo built in.

We edge closer. He's talkin to his actors with that echo'y voice.

Me and Sommie take to whisperin.

"I like that hat," says me. "You oughta try one'a them, Sommie."

"I've neither the chin nor nose for it."

"He does have a large nose. But he's shorter than Mr. Sennett."

"Quite."

"Slighter."

"Much."

"Younger, I reckon. By how much, you figure?"

"In point of fact, they are exactly the same age."

"Naw, Mr. Sennett's hair's gone silver-gray."

"Nevertheless, that is Mr. Sennett's claim."

"Ramrod straight, this Griffith fella."

"Soldierly."

"Got a cigarette, Sommie, please?"

"I don't see Griffith's actresses smoking."

He gives me a cig and a match. I light up, and light his. "Now what-all's he doin?"

Mr. Griffith takes off his hat, takes off his coat, holds them out to no one in particular, and two of his people rush up to take em.

Of a sudden he's boxing! Weavin, bobbin, duckin, jabbin.

"Frankie Lee!" says the great man. "Let's have us a spar."

"Don't wanna dog out on you, Mr. Griffith," says a nearby Confederate, "but my wrist is sprained from yesterday."

"Hell's bells," says the great man, and boxes on, dances forward, dances back, jab, jab, jab, uppercut, bob, weave.

"Fisticuffs," says Sommie. "Apparently fond of 'decking' the recalcitrant. Our paragon's a ruffian, like the rest of us."

"You ain't no ruffian."

"I? A stowaway by profession. Rough enough."

Mr. Griffith is at his antics, and this must happen all the time cause his people take it as normal. Carpenters carpenter, folks movin stuff move their stuff, and his actors watch or talk amongst themselves while he goes at it.

Then he's not boxin, just kinda swayin, wavin his long arms, sorta chantin, "Seeeeeeee this garment that I wear? It was knitted by fingers of the dead. The long and yellow fingers of the dead…"

No one's particularly worried by that either.

"I require a pretty gell. Miss Geesh, Miss Geesh, a swirl, Miss Geesh!"

Lillian Gish—she's had her back to us, or I'da noticed. He whisks her around dancin as he tra-la-la's a waltz in a strong true voice. She's smilin like to die.

"Actin like a Keystoner in the Ghost Building! Look at im!"

"But no one else is," Sommie says.

And, just as sudden, Griffith's all business. Calls out, "Billy!"

"Right away, Mr. Griffith."

That's said by a round'ish small dark'ish man, and with him, carryin a tripod and camera, is Karl-with-a-K.

Mr. Griffith gestures for his hat and coat, puts them on, straightens his garments, picks up a large megaphone from where it's set on the ground, and holds onto it while talkin soft and intense to his Billy person, then gives a couple'a folks quiet instructions, they run off, and Mr. Griffith sits himself down in a paint-chipped kitchen chair.

Suddenly he's standin. "Flicker! Who said that? Who said 'flicker' in my hearing!"

Whoever it was ain't got the nerve to own up.

Mr. Griffith glares around with bright blue eyes, speakin like a preacher: "The flicker is a low thing! We make no flickers here'ah! We create a motion picture play'ah! Like no other!"

Now he's lookin straight at us.

"You two there—please." His arm makes like to sweep us to his presence. "I noticed you, of course. Welcome."

"Thank you," says Sommie.

"Our young colleague Mr. Brown tells me you're from Mack's lot."

"Yes, sir," says me.

"Make a lot of ruckus, do you?"

"We try, mister."

"Please give my friend Mack my compliments."

"We shall," says Sommie.

"And what do you do, sir?"

"The composition of scenarios, sir."

"Myself, nothing's written. It's all up here," and the great man taps his temple. "On a page t'would stiffen and go stale." His eyes drill me. "And you, with your pretty parasol?"

"Mister, I jump off buildings and the like."

"Do you? Hmmmm. How high the buildings?"

"High as Mr. Sennett wants."

"Hmmmm."

Looks me up and down. And, just like that, with another sorta wave, we're dismissed with a "Yes, yes." It was rude, but the way he did it felt natural.

The two people who ran off, they run back to him and he grabs the megaphone and booms, "Places! Places!" Softer to his Billy, "Fade innnnnnn," and Billy starts to grindin, and Mr. Griffith sweeps the megaphone up to his mouth and clarions out, "AC'shee'on! AC'shee'on!"

In seconds it was just like watchin real folks on some real street and the Confederate cavalry come ridin in, pretty grand, and everybody's cheerin, includin the colored, and Sommie says, low, "I believe I've seen enough."

"Me, also," says me. "There's something unnervin about that fella."

We left by a wide gate on the western edge of the lot and strolled north a ways to an east-west path sportin the sign "Franklin Avenue," which was high hopes to my eye, since Franklin's avenue was but a dirt lane, narrow, lined by trees sportin red berries and feathery green leaves.

Sommie says, "Lofty chap, for a ruffian, Griffith."

"Did you like him?"

"Not a bit."

"Me neither."

"Mabel and Mr. Sennett worked with him, do you know? Back east, at the Biograph. Our Mabel drove him mad, apparently, judges him to be 'sappy.' He gave Sennett his start, Griffith did. Assigned Sennett all Biograph comedies. Sennett cast Mabel for his star. Without which, my dear, we would not be here—so we, too, owe Mr. Griffith."

"And jus think, I woke this mornin free of debt."

"Yes, Mabel says of Griffith, 'A sappy shit,' unquote. It's a wonder she can say such things and yet *be* delicate, for delicate she is, even when calling out, 'Watch me make Mack chew his hat.'"

"Like when she sat on his lap and peed?" says me.

"Very like."

Walking west there's this big house, elaborate as all get-out, with wide grounds.

"Sommie?" says me.

"My dear?" says he.

"What the fuck is that?"

"Child!"

"Sorry," says me.

"That is, and they are, peacocks."

If a man gets called a peacock you know what that means—Mr. Griffith, come to think, is one. I didn't know peacocks was real, with blazin tail all a'furl. Plump rump, long neck, shifty eyes.

"Sommie, can it fly?"

"For moments only."

"I'll be damned."

"I certainly hope not."

We strolled beyond the peacocks. Sommie says sudden-like, "Interesting! So interesting. Griffith's antic behavior. And he uses no scenario! Ah, the relative and"—

I joined in, "the absolute exist in the same continuum."

"We are a Greek chorus," says he.

"I won't ask," says me.

"I suppose they were movies, too, in their day, doing what had not been done."

"I still won't ask."

A startling racket from behind turned us round to see horsemen break through a stand of trees onto the Franklin Avenue, hooves raisin dust and poundin thunder, ridin hell-for-leather straight at us—horsemen like I never seen, a ghostly cavalry of white-robed riders. Their capes billowed out cloud-like at the gallop and they had no faces—gray masks of loose cloth, slits for eyes. A'top their heads, long white cones pointed to the sky. Layered in robes like A'rabs they were, and robed were their horses, fearsome and bright, tremble'y grand.

Of a sudden Sommie's clutchin my bum shoulder, pain shoots through my arm, and with his lips a'brush my ear he hisses, "Here the powers of evil are exalted."

"What?" comes outa me as he kinda slides down my back. I fear he'll rip my dress as he sinks. He's moanin, "Too clean, too clean, all wrong." He's on the ground, puking out his insides.

The riders are upon us, rearin up and around, laughin, showin off, seems they don't notice Sommie, only me and my parasol—which is torn through and yanked from me by a reared hoof that I just barely duck.

"Whoa, now, whoa!" says the rider. "Sorry, Miss!"

I'm standin between them and Sommie. I'm scared cause he is. I bend toward him, as a dodge, then come up quick with my right hand full of knife.

"Say!" That's their captain—I take him for that cause only he sports a red cross painted on his white vest. "Where'd that sticker come from, girlie?"

Horses are huffin and whinnyin, settlin down from their gallop, riders steadyin them, riders that ain't got faces.

Now they gather round in half a circle, more than a dozen.

I'm shiftin, pointin my blade at this one then that one.

"You put that away," says one. What with their masks, I couldn't tell which. "We don't mean no harm."

"News to me," says me.

"We're stars of a picture," says one.

"The deuce we are," says another.

"It's called *The Clansmen* ain't it?"

Sommie's behind me, moanin into the earth.

"What's eating him?" says one.

Frustratin, not to know who's speakin.

"That's his business," I say. "What's yours?"

"We kill niggers."

"What for?"

"Cause they're niggers."

Says the captain, "Wait up, boys, she's one'a Sennett's girls, I seen her on their lot—the one I tolja about, jumps off buildings and stuff." That rider pulled his mask down. A cowboy who worked the Keystone sometimes, I didn't know his name.

"What's got you ridin down innocent folk?" says me.

That got em talkin all at once, cause they're rider-proud, how they're testin out if their costumes can "act"—"Mr. Griffith says our costumes do our acting." They ride to see how robes "move and hang," and can they ride hard in them? Can they see good through the slits? They ride around and around, then make their report, then the tailors alter the costumes till they're right.

Sommie rises slowly.

"Shall I tell you something, my dear fellows? I don't care a row of beans."

"If he don't, I don't," says me.

"They're just fixed on not liking us," says one.

"Let's go, boys." That's their captain.

They turn their steeds, spur them, and leave us dusty.

I'm sorry for my busted roses-on-yellow parasol.

"I'm covered in sick," says Sommie, wipin himself with his gray cashmere scarf.

He wipes best he can and lets that scarf float to the ground.

"Jolly pointless, now. Like me. Shall we walk back?"

"You pick the way."

"You don't mind my stink? You must."

"A born farmhand. Stink don't faze me."

Sommie says soft, singsong, "*Take your lover in the ring.*"

"Sommie?"

"*I don't care.*"

"Sommie?"

"*It's a gold ring.*

I don't care.

It's a silver ring.

I don't care."

With that, we take to walkin back.

"You're a proper handful," says he, "with that knife. Thank you for my defense."

"I guess they meant no harm."

He gives me a look I ain't seen in him before.

Walking, we spoke no more for some time. Kept to fields and hills, Sommie takin us out of our way to avoid proper streets, gettin us lost, findin the way again. We passed where we seen the eagle. Aromas of the lemon grove comforted.

He said, slow and soft, "Darkie children used to chant that, dancing in a circle. One chants, *Take your lover in the ring*, then all say, *I don't care.* Then another, *It's a gold ring.* And all, *I don't care.* Then *It's a silver ring*, and again *I don't care.*"

"Sommie, how would an Englisher know that?"

"How, indeed."

That was it and that was all.

2

ECHO PARK, WAITIN ON FRED. Nervous somehow. Church is out. Sunday folk, dressed church-proud, here for to stroll, lickin on ices, crushed and flavored and cupped, this fine Spring Sabbath. Here and there a baby carriage, a uniformed maid pushin the four-wheeler as Ma'mah and Pa'pah walk beside—not what *we* do with a baby carriage in this park, no sir, it's our Keystone-bound duty to contrive that such carriages take their splashes into Echo Park Lake whilst Kops flop over each other to save a prop doll.

One time Mr. Sennett got word the city was drainin this lake to clean pipes. He up and got Miss Mabel's crew down here fast as fast, no scenario, no nothin, made it up on the spot as the lake drained and they antic'd in waist-deep mud. *A Muddy Romance* resulted. Saw it not long before my arrival at the Keystone. Saw it with Fred.

I'm wonderin if she'll even show. Nervous, like I said. When we met up by accident she seemed not to approve of me, didn't she? I want like the dickens to light a cigarette, but I'd get ticketed sure, these church-folk'd see to it. And it would piss off Fred.

Got her coat beside me on the bench, all Chinee-cleaned and folded nice in butcher-paper tied with string.

Wonder if what I'm wearin'll be ok with her? I'm clothed plain as I can manage, since we don't shop plain, and why should we? So, a simple sweet full dress, light blue, wide waist-belt, fluffy pink-with-white lace top, blue gloves slightly darker than the dress, a properly small shiny-brown leather handbag, and a modest—*I* think it's modest—Sunday'ish bonnet, and I curled my hair real nice, maybe too nice? Maybe my outfit isn't all that plain after all but I did my best, I believe I did.

There's Fred. Other side'a the lake. I know by her walk, a no-nonsense walk. Twins, we are. She just knowin I'd sit on a bench near the arched bridge and wait and me just knowin she'd walk round the lake till she reached me, and us both knowin I wouldn't rise from my bench and run to her soon's I saw her but she'd get all the way to the bench and sit. And if we met this way again, we wouldn't need to say a word to agree to do it the opposite.

Now I am sinnin of a Sunday cause I'm judgin my sister. I guess I've got used to prettiness cause there ain't no young gal at the Keystone who ain't pretty some way or other, and—well, do not mistake me, my sister is right pretty, better than pretty, but her clothes are all wrong, her hair's wrong, she looks, well, frumpy—and dutiful, under that sun-bonnet. Dutiful Fred was and I suppose is, but frumpy never. White gloves. Not much of a handbag. Dressed for proper and plain.

Now she sees me. Marches right up to me, looks down, I look up, she glances at the butcher-paper packet. "That my coat?"

"Fresh-cleaned and pressed."

"Good thing, too—stealin my coat. I dunno, Willie." Then she smiles, but really, like she didn't do the other day. I smile. She sits on t'other side of the packet and says, "On the streetcar t'other day I saw a lady carryin groceries in two fishnet shopping bags—like Mother used to. Made me so homesick."

"How is Mother, Fred?"

Instead of answerin, she looks me up and down, says, "I'm not at all certain about the fancy on you, sister-mine. That's some fine cloth. And that hair. And face-rouge? Of a Sunday?"

"I'm a movie now, Fred. It's just our way."

"Well—I'm not at all certain, is all. But I do admire the shoes."

"Miss Mabel gave me them, my first paid day."

"Miss Mabel?"

"Miss Mabel Normand."

"You *know* her?"

"How could I not? We work together."

"The very idea," Fred says.

"Why would that make you cross with me? Sister-mine, wipe that scowl off your face!"

"I'm supposed t'just sit here while you know Mabel Normand. The same Mabel Normand on the covers of the illustrateds. Well—I'm not at all certain."

What we did then was just sit there. Two swans on the lake, white as white, but with red beady eyes, they sailed straight for our bench. They watched us and we watched them.

Says Fred, "They could be us, those swans. In a—*transmigrated*—a transmigrated life."

"Sister-mine! What's that mean, you and that big word?"

"Some say that after you die you come back as some other kind of life, such as a swan. Call that transmigration. So they could be us, these two swans—rather we could be them, after we die."

"I couldn't be a swan no matter what."

"It's just an example, Willamina. And you asked."

"Let's walk," says me.

"Let's," says she.

We're walkin, not arm in arm, as was often our way, but with Fred holdin her coat-packet to her chest.

Says she, "I left you t'other day wonderin what happened to Willie's eyebrows."

"We pluck em, to set em as we like."

"Ya'll are a fast bunch."

"Daddy said so, didn't he," says me, "that movies are a fast bunch. I can't deny it—and can't deny I like it. I'm suited to it."

"I never did imagine, Willie, how we'd be later, when full grown. Never occurred to me. Now suddenly, very suddenly, here we are grown." Then: "Do you see—*do* you see—that folks notice you? As they pass they notice. I'm not sure what they see."

"They see a movie," says me. "A right pretty movie."

"I'll give you that, sure," Fred says. "When do you have time to fix your hair so? Braid it or bun it is all an honest workin gal can manage."

"It's part of the job, Frederica. If I'm doublin for someone, my hair's gotta be like theirs, and I've had to learn how to do that, and it involves a lot." She's lookin at me like I suppose I looked at folks my first days at the

Keystone. "Doublin is—say Minta—Minta Durfee her screen name, Mrs. Arbuckle her real name—she's an actress, a comedienne, but say in a flicker she's gotta run on a rooftop and jump down into mud? Our Minta ain't jumpin off no rooftops. You can either do what I do or you can't, ain't no in-between. So they'll shoot her runnin but shoot *me* jumpin and landin in the mud, then they'll stop the camera, I'll get up, Minta will lie in the mud, and they'll continue shootin. Cause our clothes and hair are just alike, and cause when you double you're careful not to let that camera get a full-on look of your face, cause'a that in the theatre *you* don't notice it's not Minta jumping cause the scene goes by too quick."

"Look at you," says my sister. "A movie. I'm startin in to believe it."

"Oh, I'm havin t'learn so much so fast, Fred."

"Learn what, for instance?"

"For instance, when we make up, careful with the rouge, not too much—red films as black. And careful of the shenanigans—it's not unheard of that, for a joke or to revenge a slight, there's mustard in your make-up and you got no time to wash, gotta do your biz regardless, face burnin."

"You love it, don't you, Willie? You do, I can see that."

"I do. I do love it, Frederica. Like I was born for it. It's the only thing in this world that makes sense to me."

Says Fred, "I knew it was you hangin off that cliff, for sure. How you moved, the way you kicked, I went, out loud, 'Oh my dear Lord, that's my sister.' Lucky I wasn't with Billy."

"Who's Billy?"

"Let's have an ice," says she.

"Let's," says me.

We're havin our chipped ices—Mexican ices, they call em, cause it's Mexicans that sell em. The syrup flavors were orange and lemon and we both picked lemon. We're standin near the water watchin people in canoes and paddle boats on the bright sparkly lake, and flowers that float on leaves in the water, lickin on our ices very careful so's not to get a stain. A considerable hawk circled calmly on the hill just west.

"Lookin at that hawk?" says she.

"I am."

"Minds me of that aeroplane that circled above our burnin home. Our home burned down, did I tell you, Wil? Musta happened just after you lit out, I figure. Some coincidence."

"You know it wasn't. And I didn't think you'd mind."

"Didn't. At first."

"Think of you every day, Fred. And Mother and Daddy. I'm still a farmhand."

"No, you are not. Remove your gloves, Wil."

I did so. And she did so.

"I figured," says she. "Look't your hands." Takes mine in hers, feels of my palms and of the pads of my fingers. "Gone soft. Not underneath. Feels hard and strong underneath, but the skin to the touch now is as soft as the rest of you. Mine, too. Farmhand, you? I trolleyed past that hotel of yours. Willie's gone and got herself some class—of a kind."

"And Willie ain't apologizin for it, not one damn bit."

"Language!"

"Sorry."

We'd done with our ices. I take her wax wrapper that held her chipped ice, and I step off a little to cast hers and mine into a wire-mesh trash-barrel. My outfit wants to sway a little more than sister approves of, I see that.

"Willie, I didn't hate you for burning down our home. You knew I'd get out."

"True."

"But you left me flat, Willie. I hated you for that. Bitterly, I did."

"And I stole your coat."

"Don't you smile at me when I just told you I hated you. I hated hatin you."

"Let's us go sit in the shade, Frederica."

We found a shade-tree on a soft slope, the bustling-of-a-Sunday lake spread out before us. Wonder if passers-by would still think us twins. Maybe Fred's wonderin the same.

"Fred—you *hated* me? I find that hard to believe."

"Believe I was aggravated so as to pull out all your hair, I swear. No, Willie—I always love you and I also hated you. *You left me flat.*"

There was no gettin around that.

"I thought you'd thank me," I told her.

"That," says she, "is a fantastic notion."

"I can't be sorry, sister-mine. I'd be lyin."

"I can see that. Yeah, if you said 'sorry' I'd get aggravated for sure." Then: "Got to tell you. You don't deserve to know, in a way, but you also do. Losin the farm, God punished Daddy bad."

"That was me, not God."

"Was too God. Bad rains in February, after the fire, remember?"

"I've reason to remember well."

"Them rains flooded out what was left of our place. Swept everythin away. Fire or no fire, God did not desire Daddy's farm to stand. And Willie, if not for your fire, that Los Angeles River flood mighta swept us away too. How do you like that?"

"You mean I saved his life?"

"All our lives, I reckon. Might be. Maybe we'd'a made it, but—waters risin in the night, no warnin…" She let it drift.

"Sommie's gonna love that," says me.

"It was fate itself, to lose that farm," says she. "That's when I forgave you—sorta."

"Well, don't be too quick to. It was not God, not fate neither. *Me*, sister, and it was fun."

"I'll bet it was, for you."

"You didn't have fun when that Keystone fire-wagon showed? Oh, I was watchin, I heard that laugh of yours. They made that picture, too, did you see it?"

"A asylum," says she.

"Asylum? That's what Mr. Sennett calls the Keystone now and again."

"Daddy—put Mother—in a asylum. Hollydale, it's called. Little town of Hondo, not too far southeast, but not easy to get to—Erickson Avenue, Hondo, I memorized that. He'd arranged it days before the fire, Daddy, just waitin on the right time. Was gonna take her away from us."

"Take her away?"

"Come dark, after your fire, we were hungry. Our neighbors never liked us or Daddy, but, good Christian people, they fed us and gave us blankets for bedrolls and a tent, also a lantern. Pitch dark, I wake and that lantern's bobbin off, Daddy holdin it, plus a shovel. He had a secret place, it seems. Buried money there, and where he got that money I know not. It musta come with he and Mother from Tennessee"—she said the word as our parents did, *Tenn'essee*. Mother's from Missoura. Daddy, *Tenn'essee*.

"He comes back before first light, says, 'I'm takin yer mother to a *in*sane 'sylum, it's called Hollydale, it's in Hondo, some southeast'a here, and it's on a street called Erickson, if y've a mind to visitin.' Then he plants a twenty dollar gold piece in my hand. 'There's that,' he says. 'I'm done wid y'all.'"

I just listened. Tried to imagine Fred just sittin there as he led Mother away. I'd'a stove in his head with the nearest rock fore I'd let him do that. But I got no right to an opinion, do I? Cause I run off and left opinion-rights behind me.

"Have you visited her?" says me.

"It's a long trip, Willie."

"So you ain't."

"It's a long trip, there's figurin to do. I got complications." Then: "You're thinkin you'd'a stopped him. I'm sure you would'a. Then what? That's what I asked myself. It was too much for me, sister-mine. All of it. Too much, and I ain't ashamed t'admit it."

Sommie says families are snake-pits. Hate to believe it's me, me and Daddy, that's the snakes.

Look't these nice families, I guess they're nice, strollin around Echo Park Lake, picnickin under shade-trees, showin off their fineries of a Sunday. I wish I believed a one of them, that they are as tidy as they seem, but I do not. Why do they like our Keystones so much, tell me that?

"Let's walk, Wil," says Fred.

I say, "Don't forget your coat."

She's right, the way I look does get some attention. And then I see somebody really gettin attention. Damn. That's Lottie LaRouche, little Lottie, scared'a Mommy no more it seems, little Lottie that I hung off that cliff to double. Rouged up, sashayin, eyebrows, lipstick, the works, arm in arm with a handsome youth in his mid-twenties, I'd say, and she no more than twelve-thirteen, lookin seventeen at least. And maybe slightly heavier in the wrong place? She sees me, pretends not to, doesn't want me spoilin her game and why would I? Then she throws me a glance with a general smile that's for the whole world.

Lottie and me—two movies.

"What are you thinkin so hard on?" says Fred.

"You ready to talk about this Billy you got and why he couldn't know your sister is a movie."

"It's not that he couldn't know it. It's that he couldn't know it *then*. Toldja, I got complications. Billy's big on family, family this and family that, and if I go, 'Oh my God that's my movie sister!' he'd'a taken me right to the Keystone to see you, invited you to live with us"—

"Hold on right there!"

"I will not hold on—he woulda invited you to live with us, and I was not ready to consider anythin of the kind, and you well know why. I had to scout it out first, think it through. I've told Billy you'd run off from Daddy's violence before the fire."

"You married!"

"That's comin."

"So you're not?"

"It's *comin*. When he's saved enough to buy our rings and things."

"What does Mr. Aint-saved-enough-Billy think you're up to today?"

"Visitin Mother's grave. Often of a Sunday I tell him I must go alone to visit Mother's grave until we're wed proper."

"Mother's grave. Daddy puts her in a insane asylum and you kill her. What a family."

"You burned her home down around her ears, Miss What-a-family. Jeez, Wil. When we—Billy'n'me—*are* married, I'll have to buy a tombstone and set it somewhere myself. Didn't think'a that till just now."

"*That's* not a problem, sister-mine. That's what we call 'great biz.' I know folks can help with that, and they'd do it too, I'm not kiddin. This is somethin, actually. Bet Sommie can make a scenario of it. We can get you your tombstone, it'll *really* get planted in a *real* graveyard, and no one will be the wiser. *And* we'll make a Keystone of it! And I'll get paid extra for comin up with the idea. Which I'll split with you, cause there'd be no idea without you. What should be the inscription?"

"Well, I don't know," says she. "You're serious?"

"Hell, yes."

"Don't swear! But if you can—Willie, that would be wonderful. See, I had to tell my Bill she's dead, our Mother, cause if he knew insanity ran in our family he flat wouldn't marry me. He just would not, I know him."

Now I hate him. She sees it in my face, says, "Not your way, I know. But he's my man and I mean to keep him."

"You sure you're gonna?"

"He dotes on me, Willie. I'm sure of him. And let me say I don't care whether you like him or not—just so long as you pretend to."

"And how did you meet this wonderful person?"

"You had somethin to do with it. Remember that oil-rigger rentin the spare room?"

"I could pick him out of a line-up, maybe."

"He was somethin-or-other Boyd, or Boyd somethin-or-other. Night of the fire, he comes with Mr. Billy Brown, a rigger he'd met at work that very day. They was gonna ask us to a dance!"

"Daddy woulda shot em.

"Billy woulda shot first," says she.

"And?"

"Well, they see our situation and Renter Boyd is screamin and yellin bout his stuff, his stuff, but Mr. Billy Brown calms him down, tips his hat to me, and off they go. Very next day, Mr. Billy Brown comes back, checkin to see I'm alright."

"Why wouldn't you be alright, you with a twenty dollar gold piece?"

"I was not alright. I was confused. No one in the world givin a high hoot about me. But here comes Billy Brown. Not about to abandon a damsel in distress, is Mr. Billy Brown, and—it's a long story, but Mr. Billy Brown and I live in sin in snug rooms downtown."

"Live in sin?"

"Sin. Willie, sin is pleasin—once you get used to it."

"Like to screw, do ya, sister?"

"Language!"

But she bursts all over laughin that zany laugh that's only hers. And I laugh with her. We laugh till we're tired. We're twins alright—just like me, she was out from under Daddy's roof and into bed with a stranger.

"Fred, what kinda respectable landlord allows you two to live in sin?"

She pulls a ring from her purse. "I wear this and often I quote Scripture."

Well, it's a fault of mine, I know, but I refuse to be outdone by my twin, so I just have to say, "I'm livin in all kindsa sin, sister dear." And I tell her about D'Varn and about Esther.

"Dang, Willie. I thought you'd be shocked at *me*"—

"I am."

"Well, I'm all-over shocked at you. But nobody knows—but nobody knows *about* you but those two, I hope, I hope?"

"Nope. Nobody."

"So you're safe."

"In a manner of speakin."

A few heartbeats passed.

After which Fred said, "My twin—you make pretty fair money, don't you?"

I blushed hot and red.

"Well, yeah—I do. I do the risky biz. Want a gal to run through fire and jump off a four-story building—I'm that gal, I'll be doin that next week. And Miss Mabel Normand, she thinks I could do actin. I'm of several minds on that one."

"You'd *act*? In the flickers? My dear Lord."

"We're startin in to calling them motion picture plays.'"

"You ain't yet told me—how much cash money do you make?"

"Well, I make up biz and at the Keystone they call that writin."

"Stop stallin on me. How much?"

"It's uneven, dependin on the danger and if I come up with some good biz."

"Willie-sister, I will start in to hair-pullin if you don't answer me straight."

"Eighty dollars a week, some weeks. Fifty, a slow week. Week of the cliff-hangin, got me more than one hundred."

The expression on Fred's face—I never saw that expression before, nor imagined there was such an expression.

"I've got a good honest job, Willie. Work behind the counter at an important downtown store that sells all kinda stuff. Tony folk attend that store and what we sell is pricey. Silk stockings at two dollars! Hats at ten!

Work ten-hour days, six days a week. It's a good honest job and it pays good for our kind. Twelve dollars for a six-day week, can you imagine? Fourteen if I become counter-manager, and I will. As good as it gets, for our kind. More'n Daddy ever totaled weekly, farmin hard. And now you're of the kind that buys what I get paid to sell. I saw it all over you at that intersection, lookin like a loose woman with your fancies."

"I *am* a loose woman. So are *you*."

"I don't *feel* loose, Willamina."

"I *do*. It suits me."

"I don't know, Willie. I'm not at all certain."

"I'll give you anything you need, I'll"—

"That's not what I'm sayin and you know it. Mother didn't raise no lazy daughters who couldn't account for themselves. I'm accountin for myself good, if unconventional, not Sunday-good but honest and—I just don't know, Willie."

So now we're walkin without talkin, without even lookin one to the other.

"Willie, do you—I mean, knowin these grand people and these excitements, and makin all that money—do you think now you're better than me?"

"I don't think it and I don't even know what it could mean and them's the most surprisin words you ever spoke to me."

"Let's sit again," says she.

We got two bags of peanuts from a Wop vender and found a shaded bench that faced Alessandro, where trolleys pass loudly.

"Fred, remember when we'd ride to school, both of us, on that gray donkey?"

"Ol' Pete. He liked us."

"And we wore one-piece dresses, and went with bare feet, and Miss Hennessey would kiss us on the lips sometimes when we were very good."

"And they're like these here folks, they didn't never figure you out."

"Nobody does, then or now, cept Esther and D'Varn."

"Willie, member those white jasmine blossoms that grew right up the side'a the house, and there were lavender, mint, marigolds, verbena, roses, geraniums, all round us, and I'd say their names at night to lullaby us both to sleep?"

"I remember. Very well."

"And member how, after milkin, Mother'd have us set the wooden churn near the stove, to sour the fresh milk. And we'd decide by a coin-flip which'a us would plunge that churn's blade up n down, and little lumps of butter'd form, and we'd separate butter from milk, and the butter'd go into the wooden mold that was round and had flowers carved on it that showed up on the butter?"

"I remember, Frederica. I remember washdays. We build a fire under that big black wash- pot in the yard, fill it with water from the well—back and forth with those heavy pails"—

"That scrub-board, that lye soap. Scrub out the stains, boil the wash in the iron pot, then the rinse-tub"—

"Wring it out, hang it all to dry—we *worked,* Willie, together, and—how could it all change, just-like-that? That's what I cannot understand, that's where I lose my certainty, deep down."

"I'm a movie, sister-mine. First thing I learned of us movies is that, for us, things tend to happen just-like-that or not at all. Just-like-that is every day for me."

"I hate it," says she. "I won't have it in the life I want. I flat won't."

"Tell me this, anyway: Still carry your blade on your thigh?"

"I do." Fred patted her thigh. "That blade gives me the feel of past days."

"It was your notion."

"It was, wasn't it? I'd forgotten that."

"And Mr. Billy Brown says what?"

"Oh he's all for protecting ourselves 'by all means necessary,' says he. He's grand about it. Loves a firearm, any firearm. Says he'll teach me to shoot, but hasn't yet." Then: "Willie, you make *so much* money, I don't even know how to think about it."

"Oh, Fred! Fred, Fred, Fred! Damn the money, I don't care about it, you *know* I don't."

"Don't let my Billy hear 'Fred.' He's proud to call me Frederica. Says it's a fancy name, a lady's name, and it does him good to say it. So just let him be so."

"What else is Mr. Billy Brown proud of, dare I ask?"

"Don't be that way. It's just… I feel so bad about this, but it's just… Billy can't find out about you-know-what. Can't find out you're not—what you look like. Can't find out ever."

"Fred*erica*! You ashamed of me now?"

"Never. You know I'm not. But I do love Billy, I guess I do, and he's a man's man, and, sweetie, if he knew about you really, he just might up and shoot you. I don't mean cause he's mean. But he's a man and he does before he thinks. It's okay bein a movie and doin movie things, I believe that would fly with him, but besides that Billy's got to think you're, you know, normal."

"Does he think you are?"

"I'm more normal by the day. I'll make it there, I swear."

Heartbeats.

"Oh, Willie, Willie. We were a family. With all our faults, a family. No more, not ever more."

She reached to my face and stroked my cheek. I took her hand to kiss it, I kissed it, I slowly let go her hand.

"Daddy hated me, Fred."

"He couldn't help that," says she.

"You think?" says me.

"There wasn't much *to* Daddy."

"Well," says me. "Never thought of it like that."

Then I saw that glint in her. That somethin in her eyes. She's crazier than I am, I know this, I've always known it. I saw the glint brighten and just then, for no reason, that ripplin zany laughter, with the war-whoop and all, and she's on her feet and swings around and pulls me up from the bench by my two hands and we whirl that way in circles for moments as of old, and she cries *WILLIE!* and kisses me full smack on the mouth with a loud wet kiss—then prims herself, smooths her garments lady-like, says, "I could do with another hot dog."

We're done with our hot dogs and pop, I've got a mustard stain on my dress, and we're waiting on Fred's trolley.

"Wil - what did you love about our farm?"

Leave it to Fred to ask about love. I took her hand and led her under a shade-tree and we sat down, two grown ladies on the grass, sixteen years old, sure, but sometimes you grow up fast in this world. I felt so much older and so much younger than my Fred.

"Well, Wil—what? Tell me."

"You. Us. Mother."

"I know that, but—loved what we did, how we did, love the *farm*? Cause I miss it like the dickens, Willie. I miss havin chickens and our own eggs, a cow and our own milk and butter, the garden—the garden was Mother's, she was magical with it, you got to remember that, and I've her gift—that garden, Willie, the vegetables and flowers, the varmints Mother was always in a struggle with, even when she went silent she gardened, she cooked, did you love the kitchen-smells, was it *so* easy to leave?"

"Frederica—it was all I knew, wasn't it? All I thought I'd ever know. I ain't smart as you but I was never stupid or silly, I knew I was sorta safe there, and that I would not be safe elsewhere, if you see my meanin. I had—a pride in my work, I did. Even Daddy knew I worked good. But he *hated* me, all the time, every day. I'd'a realized sooner or later my nightmare really did happen, those men, their things, peeing on me, and that's not all some'a them did, they hand-pumped their thing, and—I passed out. Don't put blame on your head for tellin me it was no dream, but, when I knew, I didn't take a thought, I just *did*, is all, did what I knew to do, and I'd do it again, there'd be no stoppin me, love wasn't enough to stop me. You can be normal, maybe, but not me. I had to leave that farm so bad I made sure it wasn't there to come back to."

"I loved it more than I knew, Willie. I loved you best about it, but I loved the *farm* also. Farmin life." And with that, and solemn-faced, and holding her butcher-paper-wrapped coat to her chest, she rose and stepped toward the trolley station. A Big Red was comin and clangin.

"What'll you tell your Billy about the coat?"

"Somethin. Anythin. I'll figure it on the trolley."

"I'll see you again soon?"

"Course you will. I'll call your hotel. I'll figure when."

"You figure a lot, do ya?"

"A lotta lot." Then: "You take care'a yourself, Willie-sister."

"Always have, always will."

"I have, too, and I'm tired of it. I want to be taken care of."

"I hope you get whatever you want, you know that."

"I do know that," she says.

The trolley came, she got on, a gentleman gave her his seat. As the trolley clanged off she gazed at me out the window and I gazed at her.

THE FOURTH

CHARLIE CHAPLIN
What do you want a meaning for?
Life is a desire not a meaning.

H.D.
. . . she, shameless and radiant . . .

STEPHEN FOSTER
Rained all night the day I left
The weather it was dry
Sun so hot I froze to death . . .
Shut my eyes to hold my breath . . .
Susanna, don't you cry

1

TIK-TOK. A minute past midnight and into Saturday the Fourth. Fred hasn't called. I wonder if ever she will.

Now a minute-twenty, twenty-one, twenty-two into D'Varn's birthday. She ain't here. Last Monday, Ayesha Pictures started shootin *She*. Ain't seen her since the day before that, cept she snuck up sometime or other and took all her pretty things from the closet and the drawers, but left her two silver hand-mirrors and ivory-handled hair brushes, varied shades of lip-gloss, rouge, that white powder she likes, all for me . . . which is generous, if you're her.

A knock. Esther's knock.

I open. Look her up and down. "We match," says me.

Full length silvery silk nightgowns to the ankles.

She holds folded blue towels that look brand-new and—

"It's the towels, not me," says she, as I'm about to ask since when did she perfume her "person."

Cept I wouldn'ta asked, cause as she comes in I see she's shaky, how she kinda drops herself onto the divan. "Light me a cigarette, Catch. Please."

I do so.

"God does not exist," says she, "but He punishes all the same."

"Esther?"

"I cannot help my desires."

Oh, my. I pour us brandies.

"Willie, you must promise you'll forgive me. And never tell D."

"Promise made," says me. "Forgive you of what?"

"I—have a need. Have had. But never, not ever . . ."

"I'm here, sweetie."

"You don't want to know?"

"Who you talkin to? I jump off"—

"—buildings for a living, yes. This isn't clean like that. This is . . ." She smiled so tired. "One step this-a-way from crazy."

"Esther?"

She stands up. Let's her gown drop. Stands me up. I do likewise. She tucks the towels under my arm. Perfumed towels, strong perfume.

"*Come away, oh human child*"—she touches my face—"*to the waters and the wild*"—leads me by my free hand—"*with a faery hand in hand*"—pulls me into the bathroom, sits me on the tub-rim, revolves me round so my feet are in the tub. "*For the world's more full . . . of weeping . . than you can understand.*" She gets in the tub, kneels before me, presses my feet together side by side, kneels into me so her boobs fill my lap, which hardens me. Her long loose heavy shiny auburn hair's everywhere. She presses her face to my chest as I hold her, tight, tight, tighter, and I feel her peeing upon my feet.

Warm. Smelt like my own. She's done and sobbin. "Don't hate me, Willie, don't hate me."

I'm givin little kisses wherever my mouth finds her, shoulder, hair, eyelids, cheek.

"Sweet Esther, Big Esther, you been holdin this in all this time for years and years? And it's nothin really, kinda sweet, really, cause it's you." She takes to weepin like to die, holdin me like to kill. It hurt! A lot! Could barely breathe.

When she lets up I'm cryin too, just kind of catchin what-all made her cry.

Now she runs my each foot under the "Cold" faucet, then with perfume-towels dries em so gently and careful I feel like an apostle.

2

I SUPPOSE IT'S *my* beautiful big soft white bed now, as I'm the one payin—mine as much as it ever was anyone's. And on *my* pillows, wrapped in *my* sweet sheets, all the way under *my* fluffy covers, lies my sweet big Esther, sleepin snug as Jonah in the whale. That woman's gone somewhere far. Best to let her sleep. I leave a note and go.

Pointy-toed soft-leather shoe with a slight heel, buttoned to below-the-ankle. Silk stockings. A ten-dollar lavender skirt with lots of sway. Belt's got a sideways 8 buckle. My second-best lavender gloves, with my third-best in my purse beside the pearl-handle double-barrel derringer gifted from Esther. A frilly this-and-that fifteen-dollar rose blouse, a sheer white neck-scarf, my parasol's red-white-and-blue, and I'm topped with a yellow flair of a bonnet. I sashay down the wide stairway into Hotel Hollywood's lobby, lean on the front desk and tip the man a silver half-dollar to call for a motor-car cab. The bellhop kid, whose tick is to all-the-time fuss with the chin-strap of his cap, I curtsey him as he bows to me and he gets a silver half-dollar tip so's I can see him smile as I exit the hotel to await my ride.

The motor-proud cabbie steps from his vehicle and touches the brim of his hat as he opens the door and gets an eye-full of ankle and shin as I climb the running-board into that new auto.

I guess I ain't heart-broke.

Two bits for the ride and a silver half-dollar tip as cabbie opens the door and again hat-doffs me at Keystone's gate.

Says he, "I know'd you were a movie."

"You bet," says me. "Happy Fourth!"

The huge Keystone front-gate double-doors are opened wide and festooned. Red-white-and-blue streamers, colored helium balloons that strain at their strings, Keystone posters—*Mabel! Charlie! MABEL'S STRANGE PREDICAMENT!*—several-sized USA flags, a Confederate flag, and, "What's that flag, Mr. Walker?"

"Mr. Sennett's from Canada," he smiles, with his gray handle-bar moustache, respectfully touching his cap's visor. I go tippy-toe to kiss-press my red lip-rouge onto his cheek. "Don't wipe that off, Mr. Walker, and you'll get some more, you'll see."

"Oh, Miss Catch."

Gunshots! With whoops and hollers. Says he, "Expect they'll be shooting well into evening."

The air was wonderful with scents—cook-fire smoke, campfire coffee, barbequed meats, roasted corn, popped corn, beans-and-rice, fried potato slices—hotdogs, of course, with boiled sauerkraut—spigoted barrels of frothy beer and iced cider and towers of small tin pails for to drink from, and flavored ices, honeyed rice-balls, fried bananas, fried ochre, fried green tomatoes, it's all like a long word of old from the Bible: cornucopia!—spread upon tables wherever, with lotsa utensils, jars of water, piles of linen napkins—plus EVERYONE is here, and strangers too . . . everyone cept Esther and D'Varn. And just like on a workday there's music from all directions, an accordion and Jew's harp thataway, fiddles here, mouth-organ there, and strings of Chinese firecrackers pop-pop-pop-poppin.

A tawny-haired barefoot tot, girl-child of the Watson clan, but whether daughter-cousin-neighbor I've no idea—she goes about bumpin into folks cause her concentration's on the ground.

"Miz Catch!" Looks up after we bump. "Look!"

She grins and holds up a small'ish net-sack full of variously-sized spent cartridges.

"I'm collectin em," says she.

"Got a derringer shell in there?" says me.

"Nope, I don't think."

"Let's fix that."

I take her by the hand to the edge of the doin's, point my derringer high north-by-east where there seem to be no dwellings, hopin for the best. "We gotta whoop first, girl." We whoop. I shoot and shoot again. The girl-child squeals joyful. I unlatch the barrel, the spent shell falls onto my palm, they're hot, I blow on em, then drop em in her little sack and she couldn't be more pleased as we hear, shrill and urgent, "Ellie!" She jumps. "Thanks, Miz Catch."

"You're welcome, Miss Ellie."

Up runs Watson Junior, age nine'ish, kid-size cowboy hat, play-holster with cap-pistol, breathless-eager. "Ellie, we need you! Miz Catch, come watch us, we're makin a flicker!"

We're walkin, Junior's talkin. "See *there*, Miz Catch, the fence where it's by the apple tree, I climb the fence there on my way to school and short-cut cross the lot, and Ellie and the other littler ones, they crawl under the fence *there*, where a tree root's busted it, but Mr. Sennett's bought the next patch over, so he's to be taking this old fence down and he'll build, Father says, a taller new fence round *that* lot where they'll build-for-permanent and we'll halfta go roundabout to school."

"Is that so?" says me.

"Every word!"

By the back fence there's Mr. Coy Watson, jacket-less in a shiny-black bell derby, bright bow tie, and brighter white starched shirt-cuffs-and-collar, brass cufflinks flashin. Beside him, bonneted-for-a-Sunday, though it's Saturday, sturdy Mrs. Watson holds her latest swaddled babe. They're amidst a passel of kids, Junior's size and smaller, plus Minta Durfee Arbuckle, with her rich red hair piled in a tower of coils pinned with little flags and ribbons, and she's instructin a girl-child, also a redhead, who stands about eye-height with Junior, Minta sayin, "Ginger, here's how you be a damsel." Minta flutters her eyes. Ginger does so. Minta tips her face down while lookin up and smilin and flutterin. Ginger does so. "That's all you need, kid."

Assorted activities center around what looks to be a motion picture camera, cept it's just the right height for a Watson-looking lad a head shorter than Junior. This littler Watson, he's got his jockey-cap turned backwards cameraman-style. And the camera, well—mounted on a tripod is a black box with a crank-handle on the side and a brass tube stickin out the front. The lad swivels the box on the tripod and cranks the handle. It sounds real!

"How d'you like it, Catch?" says Mr. Coy Watson.

"What makes the sound?"

"In the box," he grins, "playing-cards tacked to a spool that runs em over a nail."

Minta's beside me and says, "I'm told it's D'Varn's birthday."

"So they say," says me.

"I'm told to expect big things," says she.

"I see we're in for some high kickin," says me, and I gesture at her very-high-heeled shoes and net stockings that set off a red dance-hall dress like in Western illustrateds. Then I ask, "Minta, is that a pendant?"

"Roscoe says it's the littlest pistol ever, and it's loaded, but Roscoe says don't shoot it, lest it blow up."

It hangs from a silver chain twixt her titties if you can find em. She's almost flat as me.

"Everybody!" yells Mr. Coy Watson, directin our attention at the youthful director. That boy says, in as deep a voice as he can manage, "Let's make it move, kids!"

Camera cranks as Injuns threaten Damsel and little Ellie, Junior's Cowboy to the rescue, a chase, a fight, Damsel's oh so grateful, kisses Cowboy's cheek to prove it, The End, and all applaud.

Then Junior asks, all eager, "Did I hit him right, Father?"

"Good fake, Junior!" says his Daddy.

And the Injun asks, "Did I fall good, Miz Catch?"

"Didn't hurt yourself, didja?"

"Naw!" He grins.

"Then, boy," says me, "you fell good."

And here's comin Devil Charlie with three little Charlies in tow wearin three little derbies, sportin three little moustaches, wieldin three little canes.

Devil Charlie looks to Minta, "I've finally found myself, and myself and myself and myself," then bubbly-giggles, beams the eyes, and does a skip.

Me, I can't stay still like a good girl, so I go, "Hey, camera-kid! Wanna shoot another reel?"

"Do I!"

"Aim er here and keep up!"

He's crankin and I'm callin, "Charlie! Chase me!"

I make like the wind is blowin my parasol so's I can barely hold on as Charlie waddle-runs and three little Charlies waddle behind im best they can—so it's like the wind that's caught my parasol bumps me against a ladder leanin on a shed and lifts me clumsily but quickly rung by rung to the roof and Charlie's at the bottom of the ladder and Mrs. Watson's screamin "You little Charlies stay off'a that ladder!" and Charlie's on the roof comin at me doin that thing where he goes forward sideways hoppin on one foot, a'tilt, and seems about to fall and about to fall and about to fall, and I do the same on my other foot so's we're facin each other hoppin as though we're about to fall, right to the roof's edge, where I jump straight up—twist in the air as I let my parasol fly—and come down straight so's I grab the roof-edge with both hands to break the fall, kick off twistin, and land almost lady-like with a dip in my knees—and look up to see Charlie's speared my hat with his cane and he does a Charlie-dance, playin with the hat, and lets it soar off, as Mrs. Watson says, in no uncertain terms, "Oh, that's just terrific! Now we'll have an afternoon of kids breaking their bones trying to do the same! Junior get some mattresses from Props! *Some* folks should know *better.*"

And I'm, "Sorry, sorry, sorry—shoulda thought—bye, bye, bye," as Charlie's comin down the ladder, and me and Charlie and Minta kinda slink away, not lookin back, but I hear Mr. Coy Watson say, "I got a cold vat of peach ice cream here waiting to be dished if you kids want!"

"Peach ice cream! Peach ice cream!" high voices pipe.

Minta, very curious. "Miz Catch, what about your parasol and hat?"

"I ain't going back there, honey," says me.

Says Minta, "You'll spend this day shamelessly, girlishly hatless?"

"Alert the press!" says me.

"Gotta find my Roscoe lest he drinks too much too soon." She winks me, smartly does a dancer's spin, and strides on through the bustlin fair, and each stride exposes her left thigh.

Well, I ruined my second-best lightest-lavender gloves with my roof-rim biz. I peel off one, peel off the other and toss both over my shoulder. Fish my third-best out from my purse. Refresh my lip rouge, and, as I do so, up dances Soft-Shoe, as I call him, cause he's as likely to soft-shoe as walk, and he's bobbin a sign on a stick that reads

Tips his hat, and, with hat in hand, points me the way.

To the great world they are Mack Sennett's Bathing Beauties but on the lot we call em the Daughters of Destiny. Destinies, for short. They come in all shapes and sizes, tend to be enthusiastic, and every Destiny fills her bathing outfit to a T.

It's the old Ghost Building, lookin little compared to the new one. Sail-canvas walls and top are peeled back across the front. Destinies are every-where, some in soaked swim suits and some not soaked—some on staircases that stand all by themselves, even a curled stairway with bannisters—two sit in a tub full of bubbles. And there's plenty of tubs!—loaded with chipped ice and Coca Cola bottles, bottled beer, bottle-openers hangin on twine from tub faucets and nozzles, two bits for a Coke or a beer (outrageous!), but it's served by a Destiny, and two bits more get you kissed.

Hangin above it all, the width of the Ghost Building, a gold-yellow banner snaps in the breeze and its red lettering reads

Mabel Normand's PANAMA CANAL Pool !!!
Guess When It Will Open !!! Could Be Any Day Now !!!
Four Bits A Ticket !!!
WINNERS Split HALF—And HALF goes for The Sisters Of Charity !!!

Don't know as the Sisters could approve of Destinies in beach-garb capped with white-white long-winged Sister-headwear, but quarters are flyin for sure as those gals clang those coins into tin pails guarded impressively by Pasha and several Kops, baseball bats at the ready.

"Pasha!" says me. "Happy Fourth!"

"Miss Catch."

"Destiny, I'll take four."

I flipped her a silver dollar.

"Name's Suzie," says she. Hands me four tickets. "Write your dates, sign your name."

I pick a pencil from her jar and scrawl dates on my tickets as they pop in my mind, "July 5," "August 5," "July 15," "August 15," signing each "Catch."

Hand tickets and coins to this Suzie, she tosses my coins in a large tin pail where they land with satisfyin clanks.

Watchin me do so are Minta and Roscoe, and, she bein so slight, slimmest waist on the lot, Minta looks very wee beside her hubby's enormity.

Next to Roscoe and Minta stands a Minta-size Coca Cola full-color advertising poster that's got 14-year-old Mabel Normand grinnin in a sailor suit and proud to hold her soda.

"Frenchies!" bellows Roscoe, "damned pointless frog Frenchies! Twenty-one years they tried to dig that canal in Panama and got nowhere. We buys it for ten cents on the dollar—thanks to Teddy Roosevelt, here's to him!"—Roscoe swings his beer-pail up, splashin Minta some, swigs and continues—"Frenchies couldn't do it in twenty-one years and here we done it in ten, it'll open any day now as they finish, they ain't sure just when, and they're expecting one thousand cargo ships to pass through the first year! I don't believe there's one thousand cargo ships in this whole wide world, but they're expecting them. We did it!"

"Who is this *we,* Roscoe?" It's Brick, spiffy as all get-out—look at that spankin new Panama hat and everythin starched head to foot, from new shiny shoes to his five-dollar tie and ten-dollar tie-pin, I'll be damned. He's wedged a long-barrel Colt .45 in his belt.

"This 'we' is the U.S. of A," says Roscoe.

"Ok," says Brick, "if by 'we' you mean five thousand working American fellas with shovels, dropping from malaria left and right, and getting not much for their labor but their own sweat."

"Aw, Brick." Roscoe can smile like an angel. "Today's not for socialism. Today's for, It's good we're all here in America together! So if you keep it up, I will sit on you. And I weigh three hundred pounds."

"Well, Roscoe, I'm all for a fella who's willing to sit down for his beliefs." Brick pulls out a sealed whiskey flask from his inside jacket pocket and breaks the seal. "Here's to ya!" Takes a swig. Hands the flask to Roscoe, who swigs and laughs, "Brick, I never before seen you take a drink."

"I save all my drinking for the Fourth," says Brick.

Minta's sayin, "Husband, you're enough of a handful on beer, don't get whiskey-looped."

In fact, exceptin this holiday, Mr. Sennett strictly bans spirits of all description from his lot—cept for Miss Mabel's apricot brandy.

Minta goes to tippy toes, which makes for a sight in that slit dance-hall gown and black-knit stockings, and what she whispers in his ear makes Roscoe laugh so's to drop his beer-pail, scoop her up, and walk off with her just-like-that, Keystone-style.

"Brick!" a high'ish voice calls out from behind me just before a blond Destiny actually throws herself at him. He catches her in flight without a flinch, and, though for just a moment he's off balance with the new load, he recovers nice.

"Hi, Dora."

"Hi, baby."

"Miss Catch, this here is Miss Dora."

"The famous Catch!" says Miss Dora.

"Hey there, Miss Dora," says me.

She tears her attention from me to give Brick a big tongue'y kiss.

"I," says I, "could use a kiss myself."

They're more than surprised, but I whirl away without a word and step up to the table where Destinies offer Sisters of Charity Benefit kisses for two bits. A Destiny laughs as I flip her a silver dollar—my purse is gettin lots lighter. She grins wide sayin, "Girlie, you asked for it." Four kisses, each better than the last. We finished with laughter.

I turned around into the cold stare of Mr. Mack Sennett. He was maybe thirty feet across the Ghost Building, but he's taller than almost anyone and could see straight at me as people passed between us and he's in an Uncle Sam get-up, red-white-and-blue, tall top hat and all, and he's taken off his hat so's he can stare the better, and sharply he nods to-and-fro sayin a silent *Nooooooo,* and I freeze, and I give a weak salute, nod to mean I-get-it, and he salutes me back as though to say, *No more nonsense this day,* and oh boy do I resolve to stay pert and pretty and behave.

He's got his point cause there's all kinda folk here ain't Keystone, ain't movies, just worthy-ticket-buyer civilians of the neighborhood—plus movies, of course, from Famous Players and Griffith's and Ince's, what-all, I guess there ain't as many movies in a single town anywhere in the world cept here, and a passel of them'll visit our Fourth, passin through and coppin free booze'n'eats or stayin till the fireworks, and I suppose the way my skirt sways, and me loose-haired and bonnet-less, well, you know, I suppose I'm scandalous enough as is.

"*I met a lady in the meads . . . Her hair was long her foot was light . . .*"

"Hi, Sommie."

"This is a day of days," says he.

"The Fourth always is."

"Nay, *this* is a day of days. On the other side of the world"—

"LUDLOW COLORADO goddamnit I told you before!" Brick's bellowin at Dora, who's determined, it looks from here, to stand her ground.

"Well, you don't hafta yell!"

"To get it through your head it seems I do. I shoulda been there."

"Well go there then!"

"It's too late." And Brick's voice cracks and he tears up and Sommie and me go to just kind of help in a helpless fashion.

"My dear man," Sommie says, and offers a handkerchief, which Brick turns down.

Brick pulls out his own. "Two months, two weeks, and one day past. April 20th. You don't know what I'm talking about do you? I guess a thing can't be forgotten when nobody knows in the first place. I guess Colorado's a far piece from here. National Guardsmen, they ambushed the striker's camp. Men, women, kids, shot em up. They admit 24 dead. I got a letter told of more. I shoulda been there. I'm—good in—that kinda tight—spot—I'm . . ." He goes quiet.

"He does this," Dora says. "Anyway, I gotta go tinkle. Keep him company for me, will you, Catch, so I can find him easy."

Brick says to her, "Aren't you supposed to be working these tables?"

"You're my job full-time today. Anyway, me-in-this-swimsuit does a job of work all by itself," and off she goes with an over-the-shoulder, "I'll wet it down some to cling more, baby."

I swear, in a carnival like this, things personal and secret can be out in the open yet perfectly private as everyone bustles for food and to gawk, talk, drink, shoot guns, and light firecrackers as a stiff breeze flaps the Ghost Building's sheets-for-walls and snaps that big yellow Panama Canal Pool banner just above where we're standin on an edge of the stage.

Brick takes out his flask and swigs. I can tell by the smell his whiskey ain't cheap.

Holds the flask out to Sommie and me but we decline.

"It's war," says Brick. "War on the working man."

"War all over, I fear," says Sommie, "and sooner rather than later."

"What'chu talkin bout?" slurs Brick.

"On the other side of the world," says Sommie, "this very day—and we have this by telegraph which excited our city's *Times* to issue an Extra—there has occurred the funeral of one Archduke Franz Ferdinand and his lovely wife Sophie, assassinated recently . . ."

"Sophie's a pretty name," says me. "I've always thought so."

"Yes, Willie, true enough. I think our Brick may have an inkling of what this means."

"Yeah," Brick says. "I do."

"From your gloomy pusses," says me, "I'd rather not know."

"No reason you need to, child. And that is, as our Brick may agree, a horribly sad fact."

"Yeah," says grim Brick. "Horribly sad."

"Not anymore!" pipes Dora, "*I'm* here. Come on, you lug."

Brick wraps an arm around her waist, says to Sommie, "Gonna fight for king and country, Mr. Somerset?"

"I should say not. My single purpose is to be harmless."

Brick looks at me, tightens his hold on Dora, and—smilin goofy but also a little crazy—he says, "I am not who *you* think I am."

"What a coincidence," says me, "I'm not either who *you* think I am."

"I *am*!" Dora says to Brick, "I'm exactly what you think I am, whooo! WHOO! Let's go!"

They do so.

"I'd say," says Sommie, "she has 'set her cap' on or towards him, however that usage goes."

"Whoo," says me.

"Excuse me, whoo?" It's Esther! With her shinin auburn hair flowin free all off her shoulders and down her back and down her front onto her cleavage, and her deep blue dress is tied tight with a white and red sash at the waist so's her dress presses against those breasts so's they're outlined perfect, and from her waist the dress spreads out over those hips and buttocks (as she swirls for me, girlishly un-Esther)—and that dress widely falls to her ankles where she's wearin cowboy boots spit-shined, and a pistol stuffed into each if I know my Esther, cept her dress covers the boot-tops.

I guess we just looked at each other for some moments, freshly happy, cause I don't recall Sommie wanderin off, only how pretty was this Big Esther and how pretty I felt in her gaze. I took her hand and we walked down Ghost Building's steps like we was a shiny bubble floatin on the Keystone's frothy Fourth.

We strolled without aim or care through this commotion of a picnic, till Esther raises her right arm and points high: "A daylight moon! I love that. Waxing gibbous."

"If you please?" says me.

"The moon waxes gibbous a few days and nights and then is full, then—wanes gibbous—till it's halved—then wanes crescent till it disappears—stays disappeared a while, then waxes crescent, is half again, waxes gibbous happily till once more it's full, and . . . on and on!"

"You're kinda 'gibbous happily' today, hey?"

"It's a dangerous thing to say, but, yes, very. I feel—forgiven."

"For what?"

"Who really knows?" Esther says. "But that's my feeling."

Oh, I see a bear, a collared and standin-up *bear*, and I hear me say, "At-least-it's-not-a-lion," while I realize this same bear is wearin what's left of my yellow bonnet and Miss Mabel holds this bear by its wrist just above the paw, and now this bear and she take to dancin, they're dancin, circle this way, circle that way, and it is a goddamn bear, circlin with Miss Mabel, as our Kops make way for them through the people, and there are children about—children!—in case this goddamn bear wants a snack, I guess, and the music's from a Wop's accordion, and Miss Mabel says at me, "My-Bear wouldn't hurt a soul, he's circus all the way! Wanna take a twirl, Catch?"

"Is that a dare?" says me.

"Naw," says she.

"Then I'll pass," which she gets a great kick out of, laughin her laugh.

"But come meet My-Bear, both of you—that's his name, My-Bear."

Concentratin very hard on My-Bear, just behind Miss Mabel, are two hunky gentlemen each holdin one end of a big heavy-lookin net.

"Go on," Miss Mabel sly-eyes us, "stroke his arm!"

I pull off my left glove, stroke the beast's forearm lightly—thick smooth fur!—and glove my hand again. But Esther, she half-rips off her right glove, grips My-Bear above its claw, then her long pretty fingers stroke My-Bear's arm from its shoulder down. Pulls her hand back slow.

"Got my eye on you two for some biz," says Miss Mabel, "but no shop-talk on the holiday. Say, I met My-Bear at the Biograph when we made two pictures with the same plot: The boys love me, but I love My-Bear!" She goes tippy-toe to look into My-Bear's eyes and kiss its cheek. "Then My-Bear was half this size, but oh our cast got really scared! Not," she says to My-Bear, "like these special friends here." She pats the back of a paw and My-Bear goes to all fours and she gets on his back and adjusts what she doesn't know is my busted yellow bonnet. (Miss Mabel, by the by, was as hatless as us.) She says, "They had some dumb name for him but I called him *my bear* so much that he won't answer to anything else so they're stuck with it." With that Miss Mabel rides on My-Bear's back, headed that-a-way, net-bearers in tow, while clownin Kops wrangle kids so's they don't get et.

Says me, "She's got her eye on us, huh?"

Esther says, "Mabel never speaks idly of work."

We moseyed about. The sun was at a slant. The heat lifted a little.

No one had any idea what would happen next.

Ulysses timed it perfect. See, you enter Keystone's gate west-to-east, and Ulysses knew just when sunlight would slant just right so's to bounce every which way if, as they say, you knows how.

Took Esther and I by surprise. We hadn't exactly forgot that this bein D'Varn's first July 4th birthday she'd arrive with all flags flyin and aglow with go-to-Hell. Still we hadn't either been waitin on her. We walked with a newness between us that was too good to smudge.

What with all the cook-smells and table-spreads, that day was one long meal eaten little by little as folk meandered between confabs and "attractions" rehearsed or unrehearsed. Ulysses' production caught us pullin off what gloves we still had and tyin each other's bibs as we're about to eat roasted corn-on-the-cob rolled in salted butter, yum. There came a swellin of commotion from the gate, but there'd been commotion off and on in most directions all day so we didn't pay heed until the bugles blew. A lotta bugles.

"It's gotta be them," says me.

"Fanfare for Ayesha!" says Es. "Are we in a rush to see?"

"I'm for stayin put," says me.

It was a good spot. Line-of-sight toward the gate but apart from the jostlin, where we could watch while munchin roasted corn.

Such gunfire as you'd think was from a battle—many nearest the gate shootin off into the air—where do those bullets go anyhow?—and then we begin to see—three lines of a dozen or so *big* women harnessed to thick rope, and the gals wear clingy pearly satiny robes slit up the sides to mid-thigh, and on their backs hang oval mirrors hung by a bright brass chain arrangement, and on every third step they dip from the waist down a bit, all the same angle, and don't that sunlight blast up to what's on that wagon—and some wagon!—three axels long!—and above its middle axel is a platform, round, that revolves by way of a crank worked by a big hairy person, and on that platform is herself, D'Varn, like no D'Varn I ever saw—fitted out with—

"Esther, what'ya call that thing she's holdin?"

"A trident."

She's holdin a trident that's taller than she is, and it keeps her steady, cause what she's wearin has gotta be too heavy, even too dangerous, for her to move. It's like somebody smashed mirrors and somehow fitted the broken pieces on this fantastic robe that hangs down her front and back, and when the rope-pullin-gals dip on every third step sun-rays hit D'Varn's mirrored robe and flash straight back into your eyes, you gotta look away and your eyes don't stop flashin before the next dip—and under that robe, which has no sides, D's all but naked, nuthin but tight lace on skin, cept her waist-to-pussy area's covered, there's also glitter-stuff on her flesh all up and down her, even her face, and on her head a many-jeweled tiara and her face . . .

"Esther, she looks"—

"Relaxed"—

"Relaxed, yeah! I never seen"—

"Nor have I"—

"I mean, all that gear, but"—

"Relaxed"—

"Like she's really"—

"Ayesha"—

"And seriously so—"

Behind her on the wagon there's two tiered rows of tall slim gals in white satin pants-and-blouses bearin sabers with which they salute on the third dip and their blades flash with sun—and in front of her, on a raised oval platform that's not as high and doesn't revolve, an all-but-naked glitter-skinned Violet worships this Ayesha by way of oozin into one convoluted body-knot after another that you wouldn't believe any human person could.

"In Pasadena," Esther says, "they call this a float."

Behind whatever this is called come four pairs of horse-women in white uniforms and brimmed hats cocked to the side, with each pair holdin a banner between them from poles fastened to their saddles, banners that read in lettering gold-on-red, *AYESHA IS SHE!—HAPPY BIRTHDAY, D'VARN!—HAPPY BIRTHDAY, AMERICA!—from IMPRESARIO ULYSSES!*

And behind them the buglers who, by the way, have not quit to this very day in my ears, play a ditty that blares especially on the haulers' dip.

And behind them, eight big drums in four-behind-four formation keepin the troupe in step.

What with how the food tables and such were set up, we were standin on what this day was kinda the Main Street of the Keystone. There was shiny sparkly blindin D'Varn, and it seemed like everyone in town was at the Keystone what with how many followed her and all close together, with that Dora on Brick's shoulders screamin and laughin, and Minta on Roscoe's shoulders beside them the same, and Uncle Sam Sennett taller than anyone—but people didn't crowd *him*, sorta parted the ways for him, and he's approached by none other than Ulysses, who's in a shiny purple suit, fingers full of rings, an impressive cane, a Stetson atop his head, and the float's near us now as Mr. Sennett calls out, friendly-like, "Well, here you finally are, Ulysses the Unmentionable!"

"Sennett, old friend, you were right! California! Los Angeles! A chancer's Paradise!"

And Ulysses starts in to singin full-voiced, and Mr. Sennett joins in full-voiced, and they're singin in some very pretty foreign tongue, and off they go singin their way by stunned us, as D'Varn's float comes close enough to touch while she stares over and past us, Ayesha to the bone.

And for just a moment I get this big swell of feelin that didn't come with words but, if it had, those words would say there's the first person off the farm who liked me as I am and if she hadn't I might'a never been a movie, and yes I've cried and cried for her but you know what? She's worth it. She can do what she wants, it's all right with me—that's my loyalty.

Then the float is past us and she revolves to face us and this time looks straight at us.

Then those horse-gals pass and oh my the buglers practically right in our ears till I hear a yell that can only be Miss Mabel's cut through it all, "Stam'pede! Stam'pede!"

Pigs, of course, don't exactly stampede, but a dozen or so large porkies free of their sty head fast as they may in our direction, and, well, you wanna avoid bein in front of that, so folks're busy avoidin, as the popcorn vender pushes his wonderfully-popcorn-smellin cart while lookin behind himself— so you want to avoid the cart too—and Miss Mabel, atop the popcorn cart, scoops out the kernels as they pop and throws em over her shoulder, movin quick cause fresh-popped corn is hot, and of course her popcorn is what's interested and directed these here pigs. As pigs came on we retreated to behind the tables—you don't want a two hundred pound pig to step on your foot with those sharp hooves—and we're tossin cobs at the pigs, greasin up our hands and splatterin our nice dresses, and there's yells between us and Miss Mabel as we encourage her stampede, which had now reached that gal-cavalry behind D'Varn's float, and those horse-women—circus, certainly— knew their trade and, droppin their banner, they deftly spurred their horses past by-standers and through that big hole in the fence, out to the adjoinin field, while that enormous hairy person, wearin I see a full-length rubber apron, scooped up D'Varn like it was nothin, and with her in his arms he jumps off the float like *that* was nothin, and then I couldn't see them no more. The buglers, of course, took off runnin and absent their blares the place seemed quietier even for the laughin and the shoutin. Somewhere I couldn't see, a proper band started up a brassy ditty. Keystone Kops herded the pigs with their nightsticks and seemed to enjoy it, makin up biz for the passing partiers, and Uncle Sam Sennett's walkin now with tough, savvy Hank Mann, also in Kop gear.

"Anybody hurt?" says Sennett.

"Not so far, Boss," says Hank.

"Well, we live our art," says Sennett.

"We live *in* our art, my good fellow," Miss Mabel says from behind them where I couldn't see. "And we can't get out!"

She steps in between the men, matching steps, and they walk on talkin.

"Would you believe once I taught a pig to wink?" says I to Esther. "Drove my sister crazy that she couldn't."

"Maybe it wasn't she who couldn't, maybe it was her pig. Look," her smile went away, "our D'Varn will search us out very soon, and I'd rather not—not today. So I shall leave you a little and wander up yonder hill to keep company with that daylight moon as it sets."

"You're comin back?" says me.

"Oh, yes. This is just something I'm bound to do sometimes. You'll get used to it."

"Gonna cry?"

"Not today."

And then I'm alone in the bustle.

I moseyed toward the brassy music.

A hoodlum-looking fella in expensive clothes and a beret, he steps right at me. Oh, it's the gent they call Pathé who hightailed it outa the Keystone my first day.

"Who let you in?" I say.

"Gate's wide open, and ain't you a rising star?" Cept he said *stah.* "Got me a nice little studio now over near Gower, double your pay."

"So's you can sic lions on me again? Nobody works for you who ain't broke, and I ain't broke." As he was about to further his pitch I grabbed his necktie—and blew my nose on it. "What duh hell?" says he, as I stroll on toward a goodly crowd gathered in front of a modest stage hammered together for only today, standin a yard off the ground, with a sailcloth the width of the stage stretched behind some musicians, and lettered on the sailcloth in red-white-blue paint there's **Presenting *THE RAGTIME CHOMPERS* starring *THE GREAT BERT WILLIAMS,*** includin a life-size poster of a colored man in formal clothes plus top hat and white gloves. The band is brass and banjos, with one clarinet and one washtub bass. They played like they knew what they were doin, noisy bouncy music, and I recognized them as guys from around the lot, carpenters, background actors, but here they were, and an upright piano played as usual by that library-lookin gal, and all of them in blackface, plus black hands and necks, and white circles around their eyes. As their tune kinda skids to a close, everybody playin crazy at once, the lead horn-man calls out, "Now! Yassuh! Ladies and gentlemen! Dat RE-nowned, dat IN-comparable EN-tertainer, duh GREAT BERT WILLIAMS!" And in blackface, light on his feet as all get out, dressed like the poster, from behind the banner soft-shoes none other than the scariest fellow on the lot, as far as I'm concerned.

"Well na'ow, well na'ow, pleased as punch t'see ya'll! Strike up duh band!"

That big beefy leerin son-of-a-gun Wally Beery can dance his dance, I'll say that for him. Can sing too, sort of, singin *Syn-co-pay-shun—rules dah nay-shun—ya can't get away from it! Naw!*

It caus-ez—ag-it-tay-shun—ya can't get away from it! Naw!
Even big shot pol-it-tishins schmoozin wid duh Rag musicians!
Ya can't get away from it a'tall!"

I feel a tug on my arm, turn around, and it's herself, D'Varn.

Just like that.

"Happy birthday," says me.

"Where's my present?" says she.

I reach for her right hand with mine, bring her palm to my lips, give it a lick, then a soft kiss.

"And many happy returns," I say as I let go her hand.

I hoped it didn't show that my legs were trembly. I hope it didn't show that of a sudden I wished it would rain. I didn't want her to see Esther in my heart, but I also did want that.

"Where's our Esther?" says she.

"Takin a private walk," says me.

"Weepy?" says she.

"Not today," says me.

"You know she'd give me anything, anything—except—not one dime to finance a motion picture. Esther has many-so-many dimes but 'I shall not mix with goblin-men,' she'd say. Anyway. I am"—she strikes a pose—"*worn thin with the tossing of my form.*"

"Feels like you've been gone—a while, D'Varn."

"Does, doesn't it. You're looking somewhat wild, Wil, what with that hair and the mess on your dress. We at Ayesha Pictures are making a wonderful photoplay!"

"Knew you would."

"Willie, our dailies are incredible. Our parade here, wait'll you see it for real on the screen."

"We'll be first in line, D'Varn, you know that."

"I do know that." She takes a breath. "Tell Esther hello for me?"

And with that she turned and I finally noticed somethin besides her eyes, namely, what she wore, cause she'd changed of course. A red kerchief on her head tied below her chin. A blousy shapeless vanilla-white linen shirt, long-sleeved, cuffs rolled at the wrists. A pair of men's blue Levis. Red, white, and blue. And simple sandals. I watched her go.

Now me—I'm dyin for a cigarette and rememberin Mr. Sennett's command that this day Keystone gals are not allowed to smoke around civilians, which of course there are plenty of. Also, smack in front of me rather suddenly is Destiny Dora, gone from bathin suit to circus tutu tights that interest and amaze those very civilians.

Destiny Dora says, "Have you seen my Brick?"

"Nope."

"If you do, tell im I'm lookin for im, dear!"

And off she went.

The old Props shed, where Sommie still lived, was off the beaten track of the festivities. The Keystone was growin away from it, so to speak. I went to its shady side, which is its rear side this time of day, to smoke and sit. The sun's well aslant. Wondered where Esther was and when she'd be back and if. Sat with my back to the wall and my knees up. Took off my shoes, which was a great relief. Looks like my stockings'll go the way of my gloves. And who's that? Why, it's Billy Banker, D's "mark" that Ulysses "ruined" with "finances" somehow, and Billy B. don't look so good—like he's been wearin that suit for as long as he hasn't shaved. No hat. Where his suit-jacket opens I see a pistol in a shoulder-holster. Gives me a look as he passes by—smiles, if you could call it that.

D'Varn, in her red-white-and-blue, comes after him with an air of sneakin about—shoots me a grimace, goes the way Billy went. I watch and wonder.

A second cigarette.

Sommie's digs are just the other side of the wall where I'm sittin. He's separated out his own space by linin up a few bureaus and flats. I knock lightly on the rear door of his "suite"—hear nuthin—door's not locked. All is tidy, stuffy and dim in Sommie's sanctum. Daylight seeps in through spaces twixt these walls of any-old-way planks-slapped-together. I set my pretty shoes by Sommie's bed, for a joke. Its sheet and cover are crisp and tight, no bumps or wrinkles. A desk with papers stacked neat upon a typewriter, a fountain pen on top, plus a inkwell and a kerosene lamp. A small wood-stove shines stubby and proud as its pipe-chimney rises through a hole in the roof.

Carryin only my purse, I'm makin my way lightly past the mirrors and statues and vases and beds stacked upon beds, tables upon tables, chairs upon chairs, different styles piled atop each other, rugs rolled, hat racks of utensils, hat racks of hats, and uh oh—voices. I duck down.

Billy Banker's voice, "I'm going to kill myself. So you've got to."

"You are not," D'Varn says.

"I promise, so you've got to, then I'll kill myself."

"I'll do it—if you really promise to kill yourself."

"I did promise, I really promise."

"How?" Then: "Is that thing loaded?" I hear clickings. "Okay—and now you can holster it back." I guess he does. "You won't kill yourself, you're too much of a turd."

"You are—unspeakable."

"Hey, I didn't bring the matter up, Billy. Promise to kill yourself?"

"Yes!"

"In that case, I shall take you in hand."

Sounds. And I guess he's on a rocker, it's creakin. She's sayin sweetie things, but sarcastic-like. Then it's all slurpin and breathin till he sorta groans, and I just had to stand up straight and see and look, cause maybe she wasn't doin such. Maybe this was just a "hand-job," as she calls it.

She was gobblin his thing. I threw up. Right there in front of them.

She pulls away, he moans "No" as his thing spurts toward the ceilin, spurts again, spurts once more, a yard into the air his goo arcs each time and falls back upon him, and he's blubberin, she's laughin, I puke on my stockinged feet holdin my head out so's not to hit my dress.

"You—both—deserve this!" That's what D'Varn has to say she as she laughs and flees away.

He stumbles after but he'll never catch her.

Now they're gone and I gotta clean this mess.

It wasn't hard to manage that in Props. I found me a pail and two deep pots. Hauled water from the pump out back. Tore sheets for rags. Scrubbed up our human stuffs from the floor and rocker, kind of trembly-shaky the whole time but the-doin-of-somethin helped. Scrubbed with hand-soap as I could find no other. Left it to Time to dull the odors. Peeled off my ruined stockings, stuffed socks and rags and all in the pail and in pots and took em out back. Then looked for Sommie's beverages, found rye whiskey, thanks be to the Lord, filled a cup, downed it, lit a cig, sat me down in the dimness of Props, and that's where Brick found me.

Drunk enough, it seems, not to notice the stinks.

"Dora's looking for you, mister."

"I been looking for *you.*"

That long-barrel cowboy-style Colt .45 that's hooked in his belt, his right-hand fingers tap-tap-tap on the handle and he smiles his goofy smile but somethin's happened to it, like somethin's got inside it. He took off his skimmer, threw it anywhere. Looked at me so hard. Came closer sayin, "Now what I'm gonna do—it's gonna seem like somethin it's not—it's gonna seem like a bad thing, but it's a good thing, and I gotta—for us. For our future."

He was on me so quick, strong with fury, stinkin of Scotch, sort of bangin his head against mine tryin to kiss me, and I'm pinned, can't get to my knife, and his revolver's pressin painful on my hip bone, and he's yankin up my dress and I struggle but he's so strong and bigger by a hundred pounds at least and—ker-plunk! He's dead weight. All-of-a-sudden, still as still. But breathin. Out cold. It was then, only then, that I start in *really* shakin, trembly, fearful, furious. Now he's off me—someone's pulled him off me.

Sommie's standin there with an expression on his face I ain't never seen, holdin a blackjack.

He rolls Brick over. Takes the Colt from Brick's belt. Pats him down. Relieves Brick of a jackknife. Unloads the Colt. Pockets the bullets.

Says to me, "Collect yourself for a bit. I'll make tea."

Off he goes with his quiet step.

"Got a hairbrush, Sommie?" I call at him.

So . . . I'm brushin my hair as we sit to tea at a prop-table by the soft light of his lamp. Brick's out cold still.

"Can I see that thing?" says me.

Sommie hands me his blackjack.

"Made it myself," his eyes gleam.

Really good leather, old, filled with—

"Whataya fill it with?"

"Lead."

The handle's a good fit. Not long and not hard, it kinda grips back when you grip it.

Says he, "No self-respecting seaman ventures ashore without his blackjack."

"You?"

"For years. Youthful years."

"You did this stitchin?"

"As I said."

"First rate, Sommie."

"Thank you. A vital skill for that calling."

I handed it back to him.

"Sommie, it happened so fast—no time to think. I still can't. Hey—*thank you*."

"I am pleased to have been of service, dear Willie."

Brick was comin to. Sommie, relaxed as relaxed can be, placed his blackjack by his tea.

While Brick waked I wanted to kick his face but I was suddenly so very tired. Also, barefoot.

Brick was realizin himself. Looked at me, looked away, looked again at me.

"You"—I'm hatin almost too much to get the words out—"you two-faced bastard. You piss-ant walkin piece'a garbage."

Brick tries to rise, winces, puts a hand to the back of his head and his hand returns bloody. Looks at Sommie. "Didn't you say you wanted to be harmless?"

"Harmless, not helpless."

"I suppose I should thank you," Brick says. "I suppose I did wrong."

Sommie says to him, "In future—see you keep your distance—from my friend."

"That's just it. Kept my distance. I can't. Not in my head." Brick's sittin on the floor, huggin his knees. "Willie—what I just did was—desperate, is all—I meant no harm"—

"Don't make me laugh, trash. Do not fuckin make me laugh."

"I swear, I'm just sure, if you just would, if you—then we'd be"—he started into sobbin, and, sobbin, spoke. "I've kept my distance goddamnit. What good's that done? I feel what I feel, what am I gonna do? Goddamnit to hell, I'm not a bad person, and I know you liked me, you like me, I just don't know why it can't—I don't why we don't—I'd do the right thing, I mean, that's what I want, the right thing, I just . . ."

If you'd'a told me I was gonna do what I did next, I'd'a called you crazy.

"Alright, then" I said as I stood.

"You'll do it?" says Brick.

"*Hell* no—I'll do *this*!"

And I picked up my dress all the way and held the hem in my teeth and dug my thumbs into my tightie straps and pushed my tightie down from my crotch to mid-way on my thigh and there it was—hairless and "girl'ish"— my "cute" dick.

Sommie goes, "Ha!"

Brick lets out a sound nobody can spell.

I squirmed back into my rig, spat out my hem, my dress fell back in place.

Brick, on the floor, his head twixt his knees now, went on with that sound. Puked right there between his knees.

As Brick rises up Sommie reaches for his blackjack, but no need. Brick, his face so pained, starts into screamin, twistin his head to and fro. No words. Screams. Then strides off, long strides, pushin stuff out'a his way, crashin into stuff, screamin, all the way through Props to the front door that he crashes open and slams.

I sat back down. Sommie patted, then held, my hand.

We stroll slow, Sommie and me, toward the festivities. I wanted nothin on my feet and nothin in my hands. Left behind shoes and purse at his digs.

"I feel like *everybody* saw me," says I to Sommie.

"I can understand how you might."

"What do you think will happen?"

"No idea. A man like Brick—mortified beyond expression, he seemed to me."

"And what about you? You and your blackjack!"

"Surprised, are you, at the discrepancies in my behavior? Do you think I could have knocked about the world so long without being something of a tough—in, I hope, a dignified fashion?"

"But"—I stopped myself.

"Griffith's riders. My response to Griffith's riders."

"Sorry," says me.

"Not at all. They seemed to arise out of nowhere from a distant time and suddenly I was but a boy once more. You see, dear child, as you are not *quite* a woman, I am not *quite* an Englishman. Oh, the relative and the absolute do exist in the same"—

I joined him on "continuum."

"So Sommie," says me, "what do you think of Willie-Catch now?"

Before he could say, we come upon Devil-Charlie dolled up in sporty duds, with a bright tight-weave straw skimmer atop his curly head—he's dodgin cream pies ably aimed by Roscoe, to the delight of many. Roscoe's cowboy'd up in a ten-gallon hat—the champ pie-thrower of the Keystone is Roscoe Arbuckle, throws with either hand and aims "uncannily," as they say—but Charlie, nimbler than anyone, dodges prettily, it's throw and dodge and throw and dodge till Charlie lifts his skimmer high above his head, thrusts forth his face with a smile for all the world, presentin his puss for a flung pie, everybody cheers, Roscoe lets fly—and angry-walkin Violet steps right into it, the pie catchin the whole left side of her head. I hadn't laughs in me, but everyone else did. There she is, long legs in satiny pants the color of her name, lookin smart no matter what, and, as Uly catches up to her, she's sayin, "I *hate* this place, I *hate* these people, that *goddamn* D'Varn!"

Ulysses is pickin gobs of pie from her neck and her ear, patterin away, "Tisk-tisk," as he whisks her off with, "Fear not, for they too shall be visited by the Destroyer of all earthly pleasures, the Annihilator of men, Allah be praised, God is great" and she's, "Shut up, you lunatic."

Sommie looks at me and I finally see his eyes are grey—gleamin grey— it's gotta be the way he's lookin at me, cause I never noticed Sommie's eyes this way. Says, "I shall tell you something amidst all this noisy frolic and then we shall never speak of it again, but I *must* tell you, because, to answer your question, you just did the bravest thing I have ever seen, and, in so doing, you gave my coward's heart a shot of courage that probably is short-lived. I am not an Englishman. Am but a Georgia lad, and trash at that. Youngest of a brood. My father and brothers woke me in the night to join them finally at what they did in darkness. I was eleven."

I'm starin very very hard and tryin very very hard to listen to Sommie midst all this commotion and I *am* listening but I wish he wouldn't speak, and I wish this because of his eyes, but he's sayin, "Taken into the wood and fitted with someone's snot-stained hood. It stank. They and their kind stood about a Negro youth bound and gagged. I was told to 'watch close' as Father sliced his organ off. Oh, that boy's scream."

Now I've grabbed Sommie's hand and our hands are squeezing tight and hurtful and he's sayin, "I was told to help light a fire and I complied. They removed the gag and hanged the Negro above the fire. He bled to death as much as choked and burned. And he was loud till he was not."

People are jostlin us cause it's no good to stand still in what's become a thoroughfare and they jostle us and we're stock still hand in hand and eye to eye. "Father cut the rope. Still alive, though barely, the Negro fell into fire. Father cast the boy's penis on the flames. Urinated upon them, they all did. Tried to make me do so but I could not. It would not come." Can't help but see over his shoulder that poster of Mr. Bert Williams and our own blackface Rag musicians still pounding their happy-noisy sounds that Sommie's voice rises from and dips under like somebody drownin as he's sayin, "The stenches seemed to seep under my hood and when I tried to take it off Father pressed it down on me and pushed it into my mouth. Kicked me about. Left me. When I woke I walked. Didn't realize I was leaving, just that I must walk, and I walked and I walked. One might say I walked so far that I became an Englishman. Mabel's Viennese doctor would make much-of-a-something at how I've had no, shall we say, *impulses* since—but his much-of-a-something, erudite as may be, would mean nothing, nothing, bloody nothing."

There's loudness all around us but we are still as still. I know angels visited our graves right then. Knowin where we each will lie, Sommei's grave far from mine but bound, angels visited our graves right then.

Then Sommie sees something behind me, turns me around, and here comes Esther, oh, I was ever so glad, I run to her, throw my arms around her, and it's squeeze-and-be-squeezed.

Sommie says, "I'll take my leave, if you don't object," and, with a slight bow, turns away.

I ask Esther, "Can we just be quiet for a time?"

Without a word we walked out the main gate to her new open-air three-seater auto. We lit cigarettes and she unlocked a compartment underneath the dash, brought out a flask and two tumblers. These were maybe the most satisfying brandy-sips of my entire life.

"Go home?" says she, "or stay for fireworks?"

"Fireworks, please," says me.

"Are you alright, Wil?"

"Just stay close and I will be. Tell you later."

The sun's set and dusk feels cool'ish all over.

Back through the gate I notice kids ain't runnin loose but stick close to parents and they're the kids of our people, not many civilians left. Folks seem in general drunker. There's two marvelous bonfires castin marvelous shadows. Keystone gals smoke and no one's tellin em not to. Music here and there, laughter here and there, occasional gunfire, firecrackers pop-pop-poppin. Folks are lightin sparklers and if they're far enough away you see the sparklers move but can't make out the folks.

A roman candle fires into the air! Then another! Both go zig-zag'y and people yell and duck as those balls of light veer at em. Firearms are discharged to a faretheewell, and then it's calm a bit with people waitin. Roman candles again goin every which way and it's like they're bein set off *at* us all and somebody says, "It's Mabel, ya think?" and another says, "Could be."

Pop-pop-poppin, and it's fun now cause it's darker, guns firin just to see the muzzle-flare.

A Kop runs our way yellin, "Everybody! Everybody! Listen to me! I'm not foolin! There's a feller shot hisself over there"—points behind him—"shot hisself through his own head."

One among those many shots—Billy B. keepin his promise? And then I think NOT SOMMIE and I tug at Esther and we go toward the gaggle but I hear Pasha's voice, "Nobody I know," so I stop, very relieved.

That became an unrehearsed "attraction" for a little while, though it didn't interfere with fireworks goin off and harmonicas playin and such, and now we're keepin to ourselves, Esther and me, watchin especially the wonderful bonfires as people step in and out of firelight, glowin-then-not, wonderful shadows movin all about, all sizes, shapes, dancin to this or that melody. As Esther and me beam at each other for no special reason the night is startled with "WHOOOOOOO-EEEEEEEE!" loud as a railroad whistle. "Whoooooooooeeeee! Everybody! Everybody!"

Dora! Carryin a torch, no less. She's run up to the top a prop staircase-to-nowhere wavin her torch, and after her, giggly-drunk, tipsy-walkin, is none other than Brick.

Oh my God.

"Everybody! Everybody! Got something to tell ya! Something special! This fella, this beautiful fella, look at him, this pretty fella—wants me to MARRY him! On his KNEES he asked me! And I'm gonna! And every one of you is a witness! I ain't lettin him outa my sight till we're hitched, so just watch out, floozies, he is MINE."

Hatless and giggly-drunk Brick says, "We consummated."

And Dora's all "WHOOOOOOOOOO! WEEEEEEEEE!"

And the crowd joins in with its various whoooos and weeeeees.

Esther says sees I'm shakin and shakin. "Baby, what?"

"It's not what I thought she was gonna say, Esther. Tell you later."

And right then the fireworks flew up proper and for real, red, white, and blue, people shoutin, "Happy birthday USA! Happy birthday USA!"—some folks laugh, some cry, huggin, smoochin, since, as you know, fireworks have a tendency to affect the people they illuminate.

Esther says, "Willie—don't think for a minute I'm not going to kiss you now."

"In front of God and everybody?"

I sure wasn't *not* gonna kiss her and our kiss was sweet-as-sweet out there in front of God.

I accepted her tongue into my mouth with all of me thrillin in front of God.

MISS MABEL

MINTA DURFEE ARBUCKLE

People used to tell Mabel Normand how beautiful she was and she'd just look up with those beautiful eyes and say, "Well, I didn't have anything to do with it, but if I ever amount to anything I'll take a little credit."

MABEL NORMAND

Afraid? Of doing stunts? Who said anything about being afraid? I'm usually in too big a hurry to be scared, but I absolutely know I am going to be killed. When I come through alive, I am so surprised that I feel quite sure it isn't myself at all, and want to be introduced to the woman that's hanging around in my clothes.

GERALDINE CHAPLIN

Comedy is the situation of nightmare.

COME MONDAY I'M LOOKIN over Los Angeles downtown, an umpteen-story building, the topmost floor, a fire-escape, a twenty-rung ladder, and me on that ladder on that fire-escape. It's not that I'm *not* scared, it's that I'm so thrilled. Certainly I'm the only person in this wide and wicked world doin this very thing at this very moment. Back and forth, back and forth, on this ladder a'swingin—they want me to scream, for the biz, but I can't scream for laughin, umpteen stories above the street with its autos and trollies and crowds and nothin cept Mr. Coy Watson's piano wires twixt me and eternity—while me, I think-sorta-without-words, What title-card shall our Sommie write about such a laughin gal?

From the rooftop Mr. Watson shouts, "Still ok on that ladder, Catch?"

"Fine and dandy, Mr. Watson."

"Give us a couple'a minutes, we'll shoot it from another angle."

"I got nowhere else to be."

And lookee there, across the way, on a side wall maybe fifty feet up from the street: laborers in overalls on a scaffold, two with long-handled brushes slappin down glue; two rollin billboard sheets over the glue; another with a plank on a stick pressin down the sheets—and as they work D'Varn's revealed, bright as bright and wide as wide, the gleaming savage queen of *She* lording it over this Los Angeles . . . and here's me, a little weepy on my ladder now, the only girl in the world doin such a thing this afternoon.

D'VARN LIKED SKIMPY–ESTHER, BILLOWY. My silken niceties—all billowy now. Makes movin feel kinda floaty. And when Esther lifts a billowy somethin off me, naked feels *so* naked.

I've kept my own place, that was mine and D'Varn's. I like havin to walk the hall to Esther and I like that Esther walks the hall to me. I like how we're not together every night but I know where she is—in her room—and she knows the same of me. She talks again about buildin us a home. I asked, "Why don't you buy this hotel?" She said she just might.

3

MISS MABEL HAD SOMMIE WRITE US A SCENARIO, so's she could jump with me. She instructed him to "mix it with fire." Went like this. Across Alessandro from the Keystone, on the corner of Effie, at the base of a hill so steep it hardly slants, Mr. Sennett fenced off a few acres to build still another Ghost Building and two "fronts," which are fake buildings, a four story and a two story, that look real from the front but have a depth of only fifteen feet a floor. Those fronts are braced from behind with long, thick poles sunk a yard into the ground. There's curtains on the windows and furniture in some rooms, plus a proper switch-back staircase with a bannister in a hall-like setting for indoor biz, and there's long rickety ladders for workmen and actors to climb to each floor and biz at the windows and upon the roof.

For our biz, the roof's covered with metal sheeting and on top of the sheeting they've spread all kinds of stuff that burns good when soaked with kerosene. At first the stink made me sneeze.

We're on the roof, Miss Mabel and me. Behind us, on ladders, guys with hoses stand ready to douse the fire after the shot. Below them are Keystone's very own fire wagons, two real ones, with Keystoners mannin the pumps. The idea was metal sheeting'll keep the whole place from goin up and that Mabel and me'll be off the roof before the fire gets to us or the sheeting burns my bare feet or both. In the "rooms" they got smoke pots at each window and guys behind them fannin out the smoke. Beneath us Keystone firemen hold a big round net.

The biz is, smoke billows from the windows—flames rise high on the roof and race toward us—but just before we're "engulfed" we jump four stories and hope for the best.

That's the simple part—the thrill, not the topper.

The topper is the gag.

That's the dangerous part.

Mr. Coy Watson says a real fireman's net isn't a net, it's canvas fastened to a "circular" frame, and it's got just enough "give" so's a person lands soft but don't bounce out. Our Keystone net is more like a trampoline. We're gonna bounce. The idea is to bounce straight up, if we can—which we can *if* we land right. We bounce, hit the net again, bounce again, hit it again, with Keystone firemen bizzin the whole time, movin our net this way and that till we stop bouncin—then it's ashes, ashes, all fall down.

I'm the frail in a cotton house dress, barefoot. Miss Mabel, she's "The Fire Woman"—that's the flicker's "working" title—helmet and all, her uniform a dark blouse, jacket, dark skirt, and big boots. She's savin my life cause the fire-*men* are scaredy-cat Kops in fire-suits and they won't climb the four-story ladder. We get to the edge of the roof, I don't wanna jump, the flames are right behind us—if our flames behave like planned—and she takes my hand, yanks me, and over we go, to bounce the best and funniest we can.

They'll shoot other scenes after they shoot that big one, given that the front don't burn down and Miss Mabel's still in one piece. Me, I can break— they could work in me breakin.

We're in place up there and they've got our smoke goin. It stinks too. They'll start the roof afire when Miss Mabel yells her "Action!" She's directin this number. Miss Mabel, she's soakin wet, cause, this bein the Keystone, when she's dashin up the ladder some fireman loses control of his hose and douses her so's she almost loses her grip. But that's not been shot yet, like I said.

"It's nice up here, ain't it, Miss Mabel?"

We could see down into the Keystone lot across the street. South and east, we see all the way downtown.

"Let's us pack a basket, you and me," says she, "and picnic up here. But for now - Catch, I wanna *see* the jump, get me? Legs up high, high enough to show our worthy ticket buyers a flash of your dear thighs." Then, to the crew, "Look alive down there!" She had a big voice when she wanted. "Grind that camera, Brickface."

Brick calls up that he's grindin. He's assistant director. Which of course makes me sick.

"Second camera?" calls Mabel.

"Grindin er, Mabel," that guy says. Brick'll shoot the leap whole and

Camera Two shoots closer on the bounces.

Mabel looks me in the eye as she calls, "Action!"

Them flames start up, comin at us faster than we figured.

"Oh boy!" That's Miss Mabel grinnin.

Now I'm bein the frail that don't wanna jump and she's "The Fire Woman" pullin me toward the edge. Fire's lickin toward my cotton dress, oh boy.

She grips my hand like a man.

That fire's heat is somethin.

Last sec possible, she yanks my hand and off we fly, my legs kickin up and out so high to show lotsa thigh as breezy air's kissin me way up my crack as Miss Mabel's hand holds mine and my eyes fill with sky.

In less than two blinks we hit that net just so, legs high, backs flat, and up we go.

Musta bounced two stories, maybe three, no kiddin, we're fallin now, and that ain't actin, holdin hands tight, flyin like we're one person with one mind and the same feel for the fall, then another bounce, harder to control, not so straight, so's we land not on the net but on two Keystoners holdin it, all of us in a tumble and tangle of WHAP onto the ground.

"Keep em grindin!" yells Miss Mabel. "Kiss er, quick," says she to the Kop nearest me.

He does so.

"Catch, wipe his slobbery kiss off your pure lips."

I wipe.

"Slug im."

I slug.

He makes like to conk out.

Mabel's yellin "Hoses!" Cause, this bein the Keystone, if there's hoses anywhere near they gotta aim em at us and drench us thoroughly—The End.

"Cut!"

Teary-laughin, she rubs water outa her eyes and looks around. "Anybody break anything?"

"I broke wind." That's the Kop I slugged.

Everybody's laughin and whoopin now with "Wasn't that a thing to do!" and "Day'um! I mean day'um!" and "Any man thinks he's tougher'n these two's got another think comin!"

Miss Mabel, she looks deep into me with tear-bright big dark eyes and kisses my lips with a wet sister-kiss.

I sat beside Sommie when we watched the rushes and it's excitin to see my dress catch fire at its hem just as I leapt. The fall put it out. Everyone in the projector shack, even Mr. Sennett and the Devil, hooted and clapped.

But it was two days later we watched the rushes. That day we jumped, Miss Mabel wanted to shoot her ladder biz before the sun moved much, so's the shadows'd match. On tighter shots we use "reflectors" to handle shadows—white bed-sheets nailed to wood frames. They reflect and spread light like butter on bread. But reflectors don't work with a bigger shot like the four-story ladder, so Miss Mabel had Costume make two Fire Lady uniforms and got me two identical off-the-rack cotton dresses so's we could change quick behind the other building-front, outa sight of the guys.

I swear, I didn't think nothin of us changin clothes together till it was too late to think.

Back of the two-story front our change was waitin, hung on wall-hooks. She turns her back to me, starts in disrobin; I turn my back to her, pull my wet dress over my head—not till it falls at my feet does my situation present itself to me.

I got my back to her in nothin but my tighties. If I turn, she'll see the bulge that's in em, not to mention my flatness.

Of a sudden she comes up behind me, rubbin a towel all over my hair, sayin, "I can bunch my mop under the helmet but we gotta get yours dry."

I'm hopin she don't notice my legs go tremble'y. Thing is, I'm scared but I'm likin this, really likin this, being this way with Miss Mabel. Not in the S-E-X kinda way, just that it feels frank and friendly. She rubs my head hard for a bit. "There you go," she says, "Brush it out."

The dry housedress is in my reach on a hook on the wall. I scoot it over my head, wriggle in.

"Stay put, you" says she, "don't turn round. You're not the only modest gal at the Fun Factory."

"Yes'm, Miss Mabel."

Seems she noticed nothin unusual. Me, I'm just brushin. Says she, "I get carried away by the dare when we shoot, but on the inside I'm modest, really, do you know?"

"I think I do, Miss Mabel."

"Why don't you ever call me just plain Mabel?"

"Cause I call you Miss Mabel, is why. And there's nothin plain about you."

"Why, thank you, Catch. Much obliged. Hey—I'm thinking we need you to act more. There's a good actress inside you, I really just know it."

"I really don't," says me. "I like what I do fine."

"No ambition?" says Mabel.

"Not a lick."

"Since I can remember, I wanted a career—not that I'm sure *this* is a career. I thought I'd be an artist, an illustrator. The family didn't like that. 'Think you're better than us?' they'd say. 'Not better,' I'd answer, 'just different.' That did not go down well."

"What'd they say to 'different'?"

"It doesn't bear repeating. Catch, you can turn around now."

I turned round into her bright smile.

"What do your people think of you actin, Miss Mabel—if I can ask?"

"They like the money I send home. Your family?"

"Ain't got one anymore."

"Sorry. I guess," she says. "I guess I don't have a family anymore either, really."

"I like it like that," says me, and I hear myself say it, and I do.

She brings her face close and whispers in my ear, "I like it too." Then, "I enjoy working with you. You're not afraid of anything."

"You neither."

"Cept when we are, right?"

4

HERE'S THIS PRETTY DAY. Here's the thrill, quiet in me still, about what Miss Mabel and me done. Here's Keystoners eating outa lunch pails and picnic baskets, also foodstuffs wrapped in waxed paper sold by Mex and Dago street venders outside the gate, and a hotdog cart of course. Keystoner shooting-crews and players, actors costumed this way and that, with that picnic feel a lunch hour has here. And here's more Keystoners, whose lunch is later, workin like ants nailin up new buildings "for permanent," or diggin in the ground layin pipe, or climbin poles to string wire. And here's me dressed for usual, like a decent gal, workday dress, shoes, bonnet, purse, schooled by now to skip lunch cause I don't know what I'll be called to do next and you can't do what I do on a full stomach.

Now here's Brick walkin a way that'll cross my way, and at first we pretend not to see each other, like we have since the Fourth, but apparently he won't pretend this time.

"Hello, Miss Catch."

I'm findin out I never felt hate before.

"Hello, Brickface."

"Only Mabel calls me that," says he.

"Let's see your ring," says me.

Holds out his left hand. I don't say anything. Withdraws his hand.

"How's married life, Brickface?"

"She doesn't seem to be the type but Dora really is a good cook."

I don't know whether to laugh or spit. He's sayin, as though he's a normal person, "*Tillie's* got everybody working hard. They say it'll cost fifty large. Fifty thousand dollars for a flicker. That's not right. Immoral. But they say it's gonna run six reels. They say there's never been a six reel flicker comedy in the whole world. First ever featured-picture comedy."

I can't make out this human bein no more, so it's just as well that Chester Walrus runs up, costumed like a cook, chef's hat and apron, and he yelps, happy as happy, "They're working!"

Everyone on the lot knows what he'd mean by "they"—flush toilets at the Keystone!

"A set for gals, a set for guys, in two sheds," says he. "Folks are lining up. Come see!"

"When I have to," says me.

"Hank Mann and myself, we rigged us a Model T generator outa sight—rigged it to a toilet seat in the guys'. Don't you know the first one we hot-seated was Chaplin?"

He imitates Charlie hot-seated. "That Charlie! Not one stitch of humor-sense about himself. Went into a fury. *That* was big fun."

And off Chester goes, fairly hoppin with happiness, sayin as he's goin, "Donchya worry, Catch, we'll not hot-seat the ladies'. But Mabel might!"

"This place'll sure stink less," says I to Brick. He don't say nuthin, walks off.

A fire bell's clangin lunch hour's end as movies go streamin by the dozens into the old Ghost Building, attired all kinda ways. It's a pretty sight, to my eyes. How in the world did the Lord see fit to give work like this to rabble like us?

Breeze picks up. The Ghost Building's canvas goes from ripplin to slappin. Sounds like big hands clappin. Riggers shimmy up ropes and race up ladders, workin the canvas to suit the breeze like sailors. And, like how your home smells a certain way that you like, there's that stew of scents you smell only here—sawdust, sweat, fumigant, smoke of pipes, cigarettes and cigars, plus perfumes, boiled coffee, wood smoke from the fire-pit, and what-all that steams off everyone's breath from mints to gum to chaw to gin. And I never get over how we got us a whole city in here—bar, café, hotel rooms and halls and lobby, staircases, jail cells, kitchens, bedrooms plain and fancy, train depot, except they're all in a mixed-up arrangement and each with just enough fixins to make a camera believe they're really here.

Tillie's Punctured Romance is shootin in the café—but not just yet. There's a row on, two tall people and a short person havin at it—grandstandin, cause everybody's watchin and grinnin.

The two tall people, they're Mr. Sennett and Marie Dressler herself—a big sloppy gal with a rubbery face that fairly changes any way she wants it to. I sorta know what "Broadway" is, but not really, cept it's where Marie Dressler is a big star pullin down *ten thousand dollars* for two month's work with us. And is she funny? She's a hoot. You wanna laugh just lookin at her—and she likes that. Says she, "Big and ugly is my bread and butter."

The short person in the middle is Charlie Devil, wearin not his usual. He sports no derby and his pants almost fit. On his curly head sits a straw skimmer, on his face a pencil moustache. A sash for his belt, a fancy'ish jacket that's seen better days, a bow tie, and a gentleman's cane.

"Damn the boy, Rivets"—that's Miss Dressler who calls Mr. Sennett *Rivets*—"for a week, mind you, for a week, Charlie's worn the same greasy collar with the same bit of dried egg stuck to it. Delightful boy—he's a delightful boy—but I will not play another scene until he ups and changes that filthy collar!"

Minta's beside me, of a sudden, fishin a cigarette from a pocket in her dress. A passin Kop strikes a match and lights her cig almost without stoppin. Hisses she, "Charlie is one grubby fella. I've seen him break off from eating to scratch his nostril with his fork."

Mr. Sennett's sputterin, "Now Marie, Marie"—it ain't doin him good. He turns to his Gal Friday, she of the library spectacles. "Get Charlie a clean collar."

Charlie heaves a big sigh, like it's a piece of biz. "I shall fetch one of my own. That way, Mack, it will fit."

Devil Charlie, quite the big-shot now, gets to "Mack" the boss.

Now he's off, without a nod, while Marie throws him another, "He *is* a delightful boy."

Charlie hunches his shoulders like she threw a stone at his back. Biz.

"That Miz Dressler broke Roscoe's heart," Minta's tellin me. "He wanted like hell to be in the first ever feature-length comedy, but no, Marie says only one fat person to a picture and she's the fatty in this picture."

Fiddles, mouth-organs and harmoniums start in all at once on different tunes for their different scenes while *Tillie* folk mill about waitin on Charlie's collar.

But here's Chester Walrus wavin a magazine and commandin attention.

"They're after us! They're after us, Boss!" Waves that magazine like he's swattin flies.

"Who would they be, Chester?"

"Says here in *Motion Picture News*. 'Censorship Reported Everywhere!' New York, Illinois, Ohio, New Jersey, Pennsylvania, Massachusetts, politicians yowling to make laws of censorship aimed straight at us like double-barrel shotguns, is what."

Marie Dressler grins. "Rivets, they aim to make you scallywags behave. They'll do it, too."

"Nawp," says Mr. Sennett, and spits a brown wad six feet, I swear, straight into a spit-bowl, then draws himself up to his full height to speechify. "I've given this some thought and here's how it works, kids. This censorship kerfuffle, it's good news. Tells us we're popular. Those goody-goodies fear us and are correct to do so. Do our worthy ticket-buyers go to flickers to see themselves? Nawp. Do they go for Ladies' Church Social goody-goodies? Nawp. They don't get to antic much, our worthy ticket-buyers, but deep down they want to, oh, they want to. That's where we come in—the desire of the *behaving* person to *misbehave*."

Marie Dressler, she claps. "Rivets here is deep, children. Do you know he started out to be an opera singer?"

"Marie, they don't need to hear this *every* day."

"Repetition makes for learning, I was told so in school, and that may be why I left home at thirteen and joined the circus. Well," she goes on grandly, "I was playing the legit in Hartford—that's the legitimate theater, for rubes who don't know—and a gangly tall sixteen-year-old shy boy enters my dressing room *with his mother*. He's tongue-tied, but not she. She asks me to help him secure employment in the opera. Says he can sing. I ask after his present employment. He's working sixteen hours a day in a steel mill—which is why I call him Rivets. As I recall, I said to you"—

"You said 'The theatrical profession is very uncertain.' But who are you working for now?"

"And very expensively, too, to bestow upon you the glow of *respectability* that shines along The Great White Way."

Charlie's back, in a brand new proper collar.

"Places, kids!" That's the Boss. Everyone knows where to stand. "Action! Make it move!"

And don't they move smooth!

What we do at the Keystone, be it ever so frantic, underneath it's so smooth.

The café that's always the Keystone café, it's narrow and long. This day there's one table up front, another behind it. Bandstand to the left—piano man's poundin, fiddler's fiddlin, a tall man plucks a wide string-bass, Chester Walrus bellows nonsense la-la's for a song. Waitresses in uniforms exit and enter through a door on the right, about mid-set. Couples dance, though there's hardly room, and men and women sit at tables that go back to the far wall and they gab and laugh and watch the dancers, and don't all of them instantly look like they've been at it for hours?

Then in comes Charlie Devil and Marie, they enter at the back of the set, and look at her hat! Decked with artificial flowers and a duck. No kiddin, on her hat's a rubber duck. Rubber-duck wobbles as Marie waddles. She plays a gal who's known only a farm, like me, and she's all awkward and gah-gah to see this nastiest and exciting'est place she's yet seen in life. Charlie's grim-embarrassed escortin such a hick, but there's a wad of bills in her purse that he means to flinch. Marie, she's all a'fluster, gigglin at the fiddle-player and makin eyes till Charlie tugs her to their table none too gently. And, durin all that, swift as sin, Charlie flirts with a girl at a table, negotiates somethin with the host, keeps his eye on Marie and tugs her and threatens to kick—it's all so alive, every actor doin somethin of their own, everybody active and purpose-ful, but not in each other's way, like it's all one thing, this café and everybody in it, all one burst of life. If a real café was this alive nobody'd want to be anywhere else. And Charlie and Marie makin their way through all that life, each with lotsa "precision," as they say, expressions and gestures and biz just so, durin just that little bit of an entrance— thirty seconds, tops.

"Cut! Everybody stay put. Ready out there to bring drinks."

"Well," says Marie, right in place like she's supposed to be, "look who's here."

Who's here is Miss Mabel, and she couldn't look more gorgeous, costumed to the nines for her entrance and lookin like the good'est bad girl that ever there was, and it ain't her clothes that does it so much as how she stands and flashes those big dark eyes.

Cept for one thing. She's holdin Sommie by the hand, and he, poor man, looks cowed.

"Why, Miss Normand!" greets Miss Dressler.

"That's what I ask myself, Miss Dressler: '*Why*, Miss Normand?'"

Sommie makes to step back, but Miss Mabel's grip won't let him, so he stands stiff as a wooden Injun, makin like he's not really there.

Says Marie, "I read in *Variety—Variety*, if you please!—that *you* are 'Queen of the Movies.'"

"I've read something, too, in our *Herald*, Miss Dressler, about how some big Mick lug, whom we'll not name, thought so little of his Queen of the Movies that he gave your good self his Queen's own dressing room. The reading public, Miss Dressler, believes we're at war, you and me."

"Good publicity, dear girl."

"You wait," says Miss Mabel. "It's gonna get better."

"No firecrackers, young lady. I've heard all about that. Remember, I'm bigger than you are."

"Lots. As for firecrackers, Heaven forbid. But I read how you're mighty proud of that Fiat you drive. A thousand bucks says my Stutz Bear Cat beats it."

"Two thousand, and we're on."

"You're off your rockers, both'a you!" That's Mr. Sennett. "My stars don't race cars till we finish the first feature-length motion picture comedy in all human history!"

"I wish people would stop saying that over and over," says Marie. "We *know*, Rivets."

"This is important to you, is it, Nappy?" says Miss Mabel sort of sadly.

"Fifty thousand dollars' worth, Mabel. Behave."

"I'll behave, Great Man. It's a date, then, Miss Dressler? When Napoleon, here, finishes his famous first what's-it?"

"Mabel Normand, my Fiat will eat your Stutz."

"Miss Dressler! Eat my Stutz? Eat my Stutz? Don't you dare talk dirty at me!"

Just for a sec that hung in the air as gals gasped and guys got wide-eyed, till all and each set to howlin, Miss Dressler posed in mock shock as Keystoners chorused every laugh twixt titter and guffaw, "Eat my Stutz," "Eat your Stutz," "I'll eat your Stutz alright!"

Everybody joins in but Mr. Sennett, who removes his skimmer, scratches his silvery hair and blushes red as red, while Sommie's still fastened to Miss Mabel's right hand tryin to look dignified.

"Ahem," says Sommie. And again, "Ahem."

The fiddler on the bandstand sets to with a fury, Chester joins in bellowin la-la's, and a mousy frail, plain as a post, takes to high-steppin an Irish jig. Miss Mabel, she tugs Sommie backwards to give the jigger room, and I'm by her, and people take to clappin time, and "*Look* at her!" says Miss Mabel, "she does it perfectly, heel-toe, heel-toe, back straight, head high."

Ends as sudden as it started.

"Sommie, Catch, stay close," Mabel says, "we need to pow-wow. Catch, take his hand." She hands me his hand like he ain't even stuck to it. "See that he heels."

And she's off to Mr. Sennett's side. They whisper fast and furious.

"Willie, I do not see that this hand-holding is necessary."

"Why's she got me doin it?"

"Seems I'm untrustworthy at the moment."

"Drunk."

"I prefer 'tipsy.'"

Mabel's back. "Just a sec, now, I want to see this. Then there's my entrance."

"See what?"

"Marie's next biz. She's *terrific*."

"But you hate her," says me.

"I hate that big Mick, I take it out on her."

"Kids," Mr. Sennett calls out, "the title card is THE EFFECT OF TILLIE'S FIRST DRINK. Make it move now!"

A waiter serves drinks to Charlie and Marie. She gulps hers and spews it, spits a wide splatter straight into Charlie's puss and both not showin the slightest hint that they knew what was comin.

"Mabel!" yells the Boss.

She's high-tailed round to the back of the set and now she enters, sees Charlie and Marie, goes into her biz, and it's like a dance, how they move, change places, complicated "blocking," as they say, but so quick, a bunch'a biz with lotsa bits to it, all in maybe a minute.

At the Keystone you get it in one take cause one take is all you get.

"Cut!" Mr. Sennett, he takes off his skimmer, fans his face, spits his wad without carin where and watch your feet.

"Rivets," Marie Dressler says, "really! We *know* you're proletarian. No need to prove it so."

He grins a grin that grin says, I've got the best movies in the world.

Mabel's back by us. "I'm done for now. Let's find us a quiet spot."

There ain't so such animal in the Ghost Building, but we grab three chairs in the center of it all and sit facin each other in a huddle. Two fellas in prison-stripes waltzin with each other almost run us down, while stagehands tote vases and moose heads and a brass frame bed and a portrait of George Washington, The Father of Our Country.

Miss Mabel's agleam. "Catch, you can let go his hand."

"I forgot I was holdin it."

Miss Mabel says, "I did a flicker with John Bunny back in Brooklyn at the Vitagraph. I was still a kid, fourteen or so."

"When did you become not-a-kid?" says me.

"I'll be twenty come November, is that not-a-kid? Anyway, this flicker I did—*The Subduing of Mrs. Nag*, I think they finally called it. John Bunny was Mr. Nag, and Mr. Nag's a lecher, so I'm a frail who wants him to hire me but I don't want him groping me—so I dress as a boy. Problem is, Mrs. Nag gets into the act and has a crush on the boy that's me."

"The relative and the absolute"—

"Sommie, quit it. So here's the gag: I'm a boy and Mrs. Nag is after me—first I was thinking Phyllis Allen, but Esther's just as big *and* pretty—and we pad it up with stunts and biz so it's not a one-reeler, it's two."

"You can't be a boy," says me. "You're—too beautiful."

"I can be anything. And here's where you come in, you're my sister who helps me pull it off, *you* disguise too as a boy, we'll do some cockamamie stunts, and in the end we're pretty girls again!"

"I don't want to," says me.

"It's great biz, sweetie, it's"—

"I don't want to!"

"Don't go teary on me, Catch. Jeez." She reaches out her small hand and strokes my wet cheek. "You're really young, still, aren't you. A young girl lost in the world. That's what I used to say to myself, 'I'm a young girl lost in the world.' Hokey, huh? *There's* that smile I love."

I blushed so hard. Grinnin, blushin, teary—scared.

Which is all I'm full of while they talk, Sommie and Mabel.

"Sommie, get us into some real trouble, hear?"

"I don't like to. Honestly, I do not."

"But you do it so well," says Miss Mabel.

"It's not my nature," says Sommie.

"Sigmund Freud might not agree."

"Bugger Sigmund Freud."

"You're not so much older than me, you know," says me. I'm still in a little sniffle and not even tryin to overtake the conversation.

"Only several eons," says Miss Mabel. "You'll catch on, Catch. Catch'll catch up and catch on, poor thing."

"Mabel," says Sommie, "Wally Beery for our Mr. Nag?"

"Great. That's great. I really want your Esther, Catch, if she'll do it. She's finicky. Hardly ever says yes when I ask her. But with you in it, bet she does."

I whimper up, "Does it gotta be Wally?"

"Does what gotta be me, na'ow?"

Into our huddle stepped the man himself. That's kind of his "touch," I don't know how.

"Big Wally," says she, "I'm tapping you for our heavy. Opposite me and Catch."

"Then it's me to play with the two prettiest ones in this here lot or even this here town, exceptin my Glow'ree. Well, na'ow, I call this a lucky day."

Wally Beery saunters away.

"Now, Som," says Miss Mabel, "what I want"—

"Please, no. Not Som. If you do it, Mabel, others shall. Please?"

"Sure. Sorry—Sommie. Started to say . . ." and she goes on, so excited, sitting pigeon-toed, tap-tappin her right foot to a beat only she can hear.

5

SOMMIE LOOKS SORRY TO SEE ME. He sits in a rocker by the prop shed. Waves me over with a handful of "pages," as he says, fresh from the typewriter no doubt. He smells of brandy and his pipe.

Says he, "You'll say if I've disappointed?"

"Sommie, that's not up to me."

"Entirely up to you, far as I'm concerned." Hands me his pages. "This activity raises in me questions religious in nature—the efficacy of penance, for one."

"You're talkin to yourself again."

"I quite enjoy your hat!" says he.

It's a wide-brimmed vanilla number that slopes with a never-a-care air.

"I'm pleased to please the only"—I whisper, "*not quite an*—Englishman I know."

He stands and bows slightly. "Shall you have the rocker?"

"Shall you go away? I ain't readin while you hover."

He stands, I sit, I make shoo-away-fly with my hands, he shoos. I read.

MABEL/CATCH VEHICLE—that brought me up some. "Mabel/Catch." Oh boy.

CARD #1: HEAVEN HELP THE WORKING GIRL—AND HER SISTER
Mabel/Catch vend flowers on busy corner. Biz/pedestrians who've no time for flowers. Biz/Red Car riders, also no time. Brush-offs build. Passing motorcyclist (HANK MANN? AL ST. JOHN?) plucks flowers from Mabel, thus knocking her into Catch, biz as both fall into path of oncoming Red Car, close call. Kop (GLEN CAVENDER? EDGAR KENNEDY?) comes to aid, flirts, Mabel/Catch mock him, he angers, biz, Mabel/Catch scooped on cow-guard of Red Car, expressions of oh-what-a-day.

CARD #2: "LET'S FIND US SOME EASIER WAY TO WORK HARD!"
Mabel/Catch on street, biz looking for work. Sign in store window:
'Want to Work Sitting Down? Learn to Type! (Females Only)." Brief
typing biz, flirty instructor (CHESTER). Mabel/Catch escape his
advances, discombobulate instructor.

CARD #3: EMPLOYED IN A PINCH BY A PINCHER
Bicycles in line in front of office, with boys, 12-to-18 in age. Boys
wear large cloth caps, jackets, close-fitting pants—messenger boys.
Biz of bike-boy pedaling fast to office, just missing Mabel/Catch.
Sign painted on plate glass: "Telegraphic Messages Sent and Deliv-
ered." Second sign, hung on door: "Secretary Wanted (Deportment
Counts)." Biz with Mabel/Catch regarding "deportment." Catch
shy to go in. Mabel enters office.

CARD #4: MRS. BOSSIE AND HER BOYS
Mrs. Bossie (ESTHER) bosses the bike messengers with kicks and
slaps and pinches, some suggestive. Directs Mabel to inner office.

CARD #5: MR. BOSSIE AND HIS GALS
Mr. Bossy (WALLY) bosses secretary/telegraph pool of young women
(CECILE ARNOLD, VIVIAN EDWARDS the principles)—flirting,
groping, pinching as he does so. The girls are annoyed but take it.
Mock him behind his back. Normal business day. Mr. Bossie taken
with Mabel, biz of turning on charm, Mabel tries to appease, biz
with his pinches, Mabel won't stand for that, bites Mr. Bossie's hand,
exciting Mr. Bossie more, biz, Mabel escapes office.

CARD #6: MABEL'S STRATEGEM
Mabel demonstrates her idea of cross-dressing to Catch.

CARD #7: GIRLS WILL BE BOYS
Mabel and Catch dressing as bike boys. Biz with clothes, shyness
etc., posing tough etc., bunching hair beneath cloth hats. Biz of
imitating boy-walks, walking behind various males and imitating.
Flash to boy-Mabel & boy-Catch outside office, biz of fight for bike
with messenger boys. They get job. In office Mrs. Bossie shoves and

slaps boy-Catch as she does the other boys. Catch ready to fight but Mabel restrains. Mrs. Bossie likes boy-Mabel, strong attraction. Flirtation biz. Sends Catch on job, others on jobs, all but Mabel. Explicit flirtation biz. Mr. Bossie sees, gets huffy, biz, orders Mabel out on a delivery job.

CARD #8: SITTING DOWN AT TOP SPEED
Biz with boy-Mabel and boy-Catch on bikes criss-crossing in traffic happy as larks making car Drivers unhappy.

CARD #9: MRS. BOSSIE'S GOT HOT NOTIONS
Mrs. Bossie's bright idea: Send boy-Mabel to her own address. Flash between boy-Mabel biking to destination and Mrs. Bossie driving. Pick up Mrs. Bossie arriving first and boy-Mabel arriving within moments. Butler (SLIM SUMMERVILLE) shows Mabel into ornate "library"—divans, love-seats, statues, etc. Enter Mrs. Bossie dressed for seduction. Play up seduction biz. Mabel escapes out the window and onto her bike. Mrs. Bossie pursues in car.

Flash on Mr. Bossie seeing them race by office. Mr. Bossie jumps into his car and is in pursuit. Boy-Catch sees, joins pursuit on bike, hangs onto a truck to catch up. Bike gets caught on something on the truck, truck goes to turn, Catch jumps to passing Red Car, climbs roof, surprised to see boy-Mabel driving a car, Catch tries to swing into back seat via Big Red Car's connective rod, cannot.

Mrs. Bossie's car goes by. Mr. Bossie's car goes by. (Open air vehicles, naturally.)

Boy-Catch jumps into Mr. Bossie's car, her hat falls off, hair billows in wind, Mr. Bossie delighted, biz pinching and flirting while racing after Mrs. Bossie.

Flash from boy-Mabel's car to Mrs. Bossie's to Mr. Bossie's, swerving skidding biz, pick up Kop (FRED MACE) calling STATION. Flash on "alert" Kops biz in STATION. Flash from boy-Mabel's car to Mrs. Bossie's to Mr. Bossie's, w/biz, and Kop's car pursues all (BILLY GILBERT, FRITZ SHADE, HARRY McCOY, JOE DEMMING,

RUBE MILLER). All converge at intersection in the middle of which is a Kop (MACK SWAIN) on platform directing traffic, biz, Kop spinning around. Flash to Maid (LOUISE FAZENDA? GLORIA SWANSON? DORA TAYLOR?) with baby carriage crossing street to Echo Park, dodges cars that spin the platform as they do their biz, tries to escape to curb, carriage bumps hard on curb, baby bounces out of carriage and flies into arms of Kop on platform. Kop, in surprise, flings baby up. Flash to Catch in Mr. Bossy's car. Catch sees baby in air, jumps from Mr. Bossy's car, catches baby mid-air as she lands on back seat (running board?) of boy-Mabel's car.

Mabel skids car into a 180 and faces pursuers, drives straight at them while they scatter all over. Flash on pursuers recovering. Mabel does another 180, scatters them again, hits bump, baby bounces into air, Catch leaps to hood to Catch baby, biz with how Mabel can't see past Catch, biz as Catch jumps into back seat with baby, tries to get out for baby's safety, somehow ends jump in back of Mrs. Bossie's (ESTHER'S) car.

All cars now are headed for Echo Park Lake as if in race for who'll plunge in first. Catch throws baby into the air as Catch jumps, lands on her back on the grass, safely catches baby.

Mr. Bossie now in Mrs. Bossie's car and they struggle for wheel, Mrs. winning. Mabel's car neck in neck with Mrs. Bossie. Mabel doffs her cap to reveal true identity to Mrs. Bossie. Mrs. Bossie horrified, drives her car into lake. Kops drive their car in too, to save her. Biz.

Mabel and Catch laughing, Catch with baby in arms. Maid runs up, takes baby.

Mabel and Catch ride away on bikes, their hair flowing behind them.

The End. A Keystone production, etc.

I wave the pages at Sommie, who's watchin from across the lot, and over to me he trots.

Trots, mind.

"Well?" says he.

"Couple'a things. Mabel's on a bike, then she's in a car—where'd she get that car? And how does Mrs. Bossie get in Mr. Bossie's car?"

"Easy to fix. And?"

"Too much Catch, not enough Mabel."

"And?"

"It doesn't have to make sense, right?"

"Of course not."

"Then we're fine."

"And you like it?"

"May even survive it. You're the best, Sommie."

Didn't have the heart to tell him I can't ride a bike.

Sommie did his fixin. Miss Mabel loved his pages. Next is to get Mr. Sennett's go-ahead. I figure that's up to Miss Mabel and Sommie, but no. Says she, "It'll help if you're there. He's impressed by you."

"Miss Mabel, it's awful of me that I haven't said"—they're waiting on me to say. "Ma'am, I never rode a bike in my life."

"Told you your first day don't call me Ma'am. Can't ride a bike? Don't tell Mack."

The first here-to-stay building at the Keystone is a four-story wood job, painted white, a switchback staircase up the side. Top of the staircase there's a landing and a door.

Just as we start up the stair, Miss Mabel tugs my arm. "I meant it, hon. Don't tell Mack."

"But I can't ride a bike."

"Didn't say lie. Said don't tell. It's nothing at all. I'll teach you myself."

"Mabel, dear," says Sommie.

"I absolve thee of all responsibility, my good man. Say two Hail Marys and tell the priest hello from Mabel Normand."

She's boundin up the stairs as we trudge after.

"This is a bad time," is Mr. Sennett's greetin.

That's on account'a there's a big hole in the wall, a big square got sawed away, and through that hole you see down into where the new hugest Ghost Building will be, and beside the hole is the largest of bathtubs. Seems that tub was hoisted up on winches and pulled in through the hole.

It, the tub, is maybe twelve feet long, a yard or so wide, shiny new and white, standin on eight sets of bright brass balls the size of a big man's fist.

"Like it?" says Mr. Sennett. "I've always wanted one. Plumbers and carpenters due back any time now to cut into the floor and rig the pipes. So whatever you want, want it later. I am in the midst of a dream come true."

"Whoa there, Great Man, not so fast. We've got a doozy for you. Will make Big Chief much wampum. But—Mack, a tub? In your office?"

"I mean to spend a good part of my workday in this tub."

"Doing what, pray tell?"

"Working. And watching. A floor-to-ceiling window will fit into that hole in the wall."

"You'll sit buck-nekkid in a tub looking down upon we who are your minions? Discuss scenarios from the vantage of your bath? Will you play with rubber ducks?"

"I might."

"There's a book by a Viennese doctor you need to read."

Mr. Sennett importantly lights a cigar. I say "importantly" cause he took his time cuttin the tip, lippin it, lightin it, puffin. Then he climbs into his tub and perches on its rim.

Miss Mabel, she plants herself, feet a little apart and pointed straight ahead like she's about to rise on her tippy-toes, which she does not.

Mr. Sennett puffs. "Very well, watchya got? What's it aboot?" He means 'about,' but he's from Canada.

"I have pages," says Sommie. He takes em from the pocket of his jacket, hands em to Miss Mabel. She unfolds em with care and reads em out like a teacher's pet at show'n'tell.

"The End," reads she gamely. "A Keystone production, etc."

Mr. Sennett's chompin his cigar, red in the face under his silver hair.

"That's not a comedy, that's a suicide pact. What's more, it'll take twice, three times as long to shoot as a two-reeler ought—and this in the midst of *Tillie,* in which you star."

"In which I what? Doesn't Marie Dressler star? She's got the star's dressing room, I heard."

"And you damned well know this thing of yours'd cost a fortune. My fortune."

"But it's good."

"Sure it's good. So it hurts to say no, but I can stand it. No."

Sommie says, "Then we are leaving?"

"We are not," Mabel says.

Mr. Sennett, he chomps his cigar. Starts to spit but it seems he don't want to stain his tub so he turns his head and spits on the floor and misses his—I finally learned this word!—cuspidor. Says, "Look what you made me do now. This masterpiece got a title?"

Sommie chirps up, "*What Do We Do About Mabel?* seemed apt."

"What *do* we do about Mabel?"

"You could marry her, Mack," says she brightly. "Seems you asked, seems she said yes—that was on a ferry, as I recall—or did I see this in a flicker? Two, no, three *years* ago?"

"Mabel… Oh, go, go, go spend my money. Get yourselves killed."

He scratches his chin, puffs his cigar, spits into his tub without thinkin.

"But," says he. "But."

"What but, you mutt?"

"You don't direct this one. Don't be giving me grief. Not a chance you'll change my mind."

"Watch me."

"Not this time. It's good and its damned dangerous—cars and bikes careening who knows where. No use to pout. Brick directs the action biz. He's good with cars. Or me, if I have time. Or Roscoe. Oh, hell—it'll be me. Damn."

"I can do it, Mack."

"You can do anything. We know that. But I direct the car and bike biz. If something goes wrong, it's got to be on me."

I swear, right then Miss Mabel looked like a little girl with how she gazed at him. Her big eyes, dark and sweet, they all but spoke, sayin, He does love me after all, doesn't he?

"But I can direct the rest of it, can't I, Mack?"

"I guess so. Alright. Alright, then."

Miss Mabel and me, walkin slow across the lot. We climb the steps of the Ghost Building and find ourselves two bar stools midst this day's commotions. She lifts a flap on her dress, fetches up a pack of Egyptians with a familiar flair remindin me of D'Varn. Bet D got that gesture from Miss Mabel. Now she puts the Egyptian to her lips as three men nearest compete to light her up.

"Like one, Catch?"

"Sure. Thanks."

Now they light me up.

"Hope D'Varn didn't mind my little pig stampede too much?"

"You hope that, do ya?"

"And you two . . . have distanced?"

"Miss Mabel, I don't talk about D'Varn, cept to D'Varn. And of course Esther.'

"And you're—with Esther now?"

"I don't talk about Esther either."

"You know what I like about show business, Catch, what I like best? I like how we've got all kinds in show business, *all* kinds. Maybe that's what show business is for—to give a home to people who haven't got it in them to feel at home anywhere. Know what we're doing right this moment?"

"Passin the time?"

"Me?! Just pass the time!? We are *rehearsing*. Gotta see what kind of boy you'll be."

I feel me blush. "Miss Mabel—what kind of a boy can *you* be? I just don't believe it."

"Suppose I'll have to convince ya. Follow me."

Up she stands and steps out of her shoes. Of a sudden somethin's different in her face. How her lips curl around the cigarette, maybe. Somethin.

"Come on, kid," says she.

And off we go for a walk across the Ghost Building. Passin Brick, she snatches the cap off his head—she so small and he so tall she tippy-toes to fetch it as he laughs. She pulls that cap down close near her eyes, tilts her head a little different, like it weighs more, and we're off to a clothes rack on the side wall, where she takes this-and-that, puts em back, takes somethin else.

Beside the rack there's a stairway to nowhere. She gets between the stair and the rack.

"Keep watch, Catch."

I got my back to her and I'm lookin all about like Injuns are fixin to ambush us.

Movies are liable to dress and undress just about anywhere, and but only three Keystoners keep it private: Miss Mabel in her dressing room, which she ain't got right now—Charlie Devil with his own room too—and me. I've made a little barricade to form a nook in Sommie's prop shed. That's where we, Es and me, do my changes now.

Miss Mabel didn't come out from behind the rack the way she went in. She fixed herself up and walked roundabout to face me.

It's Miss Mabel and it's not. In thin pants and flannel shirt tucked in, sleeves rolled like man-cuffs above the wrists, she takes a stance, still as still, lookin straight at me but more through me. She kinda shakes herself, eases her stance to a newsboy's cocky slouch, and the way she pulls the cigarette out of her mouth and holds it tween thumb and forefinger, and the way she puffs out the smoke, and the way she turns from me, slow, looks around, puffs again, shifts her slouch, and struts off, me followin behind, and how she holds her shoulders—she's a cocky tough newsboy to a T. I don't mean she looks like a boy to me. I mean I know how things look to the camera, and she'd look like a boy to the camera. Every move she makes says "boy."

She turns to me, flicks her cigarette down. Bends her head to spit on the cig butt.

"How'm I doin, girlie?"

"I can't do that, Miss Mabel. I can't get nowhere near to doin that. I see what you're doin, but you're Mabel Normand, you *can* do anything. I'm just me."

"Kinda scared to try?"

"Kinda."

"But we don't let that stop us, do we, the likes of you and me?"

"No, we don't let that stop us," says me.

"Keep watch now while I shed these duds. We'll give Brick back his cap and get to work."

We go to where she left her shoes. She steps into them and I remember when we compared our look-alike feet.

Then we're sittin on the steps of the Ghost Building. She gets out another one of her Egyptians, offers me one, a passin man lights us up. I'm followin her lead, so I just sit and smoke and stare like she's doin.

"Do you dream, Catch? Dream at night?"

"Yeah. Don't remember much. When I do, it's generally unpleasant."

"Dr. Freud makes a big deal of dreams. Sometimes I think I dreamed that ferry—the Staten Island ferry on a clear breezy night. But it happened. I didn't dream it. He proposed. I said yes. And there, with the breeze in my hair, he slipped upon my finger a dime-store ring. I love that ring. A month ago, to shut me up, he bought me a big diamond ring. I'm not a girl can love a diamond. Charlie says Mack's a fairy. He says Chester thinks so too. Do you think that? What do you hear? Mack's a Catholic, not a fairy—is what I think. He tries to be a good Catholic. I'm a Catholic too. And I try to be a good Catholic. Madcap Mabel, the good Catholic."

Papists is what Daddy calls Catholics. Hates em, naturally.

"Let's go find you boy clothes, Catch."

We stroll slow to the wardrobe shed.

"See how the boys eye us as we go?" says she.

"Everybody eyes you."

"Think they're eyeing only me? And when you strolled with D'Varn, think they eyed only her? And when you walk alone, who do they eye?"

"Not that I don't like bein noticed, but I don't think about it much."

"You'll think about it more when your chest fills out some."

"That's not gonna happen."

"Just as well," says she. "What we do, tits get in the way."

"You think boys give me the eye, *really*?"

"Oh, honey. You tellin me you don't get your ass pinched on the streetcar?"

"Sure I do."

"Well?"

Miss Mabel Normand is a disturbin person, though I don't believe she means to be.

In my little nook of the props shed with the ordeal of boy-clothes.

If Daddy's dead in Hell, where I hope he is, he's lookin up at me and laughin like t'die.

I stand behind the screen as Miss Mabel hands me this and that. I don't even care whether she steps behind that screen and sees me as I am. She don't do it, but I don't care if she would, I'm that mortified. Let her see! How dare she think she understands me.

My things are folded neat with my knife-rig amongst them. The boy shoes pinch. The boy pants feel like pajamas. The boy shirt and jacket feel like I'm tied up. The cloth cap, pulled down like she'd pulled hers, my hair bunched under it, makes my head feel too big. Miss Mabel's an angel and angels can get away with what-all, but what she's gettin away with now is, as Mother would say, "beyond the pale"—whatever that actually means. I'm mad as mad.

I swallow down my bile and step out to where Miss Mabel sees me clear.

"Come, laddie," says she. "Let's walk in the sun."

We do so and, "That's good," says she, "you're sullen and spitty like a boy. I knew you could act. Walk for me."

I do so.

She laughs.

"Oh, honey, I'm so sorry, I don't mean to, but"—she laughs more.

"Guess we can't do the flicker then, huh? I can't walk right and can't ride a bike."

"Listen to you! Gals like us, we can do whatever we have a mind to. There's nothing to it but to study. Come with me."

I do so, of course.

Back in the Ghost Building we sit, she in a rocker, me on a three-legged stool, hubbub all around us. Folks look at me and titter.

"Miss Mabel, this your day off or somethin?"

"What do you mean?"

"Ain't you got work?"

"You kidding? I'm working hard. We got a two-reeler on our hands, and it's a dandy, and we've got to deliver it on the money, and here I am working right now. Directing *you*. Study up. Look at the men. Don't stare. Look. See. That's what an actress does most of all, she *sees*."

"I'm not an actress."

"Just hush up and look. See. Watch the men."

I do so.

"Study how they move. There's a sadness in it. They move sad, every last one of them—cept maybe Chester, forget him. They walk heavy, men do, like they're pulling something behind them, or like they're wary that something may hold them back. Women, young women, don't walk like that. We walk like we're balancing something on our shoulders or on our heads—balancing, not pulling. Your walk, D'Varn's, very different, but you dance your walks, both of you. Me, I glide. But men—the good ones—they walk like maybe they'll have to fight. Not fancy gentlemen, they don't. Nor Frenchies, nor Englishers. Our kind, I'm talking about, our kind do. They walk like they fear a fight or want a fight, and that's so much in them you don't even notice, cause it's all-the-time. And they're tight—their shoulders, their arms, how they hold their arms, they're tight. They don't flow, not like us. You know? Can you see?"

I started to.

"Feel it in your skin, Catch, and *on* your skin. Don't move. Just feel it. If you feel it, the moves will come."

"I'm feelin it some. A little. And I don't like it."

"Remember what you're feeling. Spend the rest of the day working on it—like how you worked on Coy's stunt-car. Don't mind people looking at you. Just work."

"I know how to do that."

"I know you do. Bike lessons start tomorrow. See you then."

"You're leavin me?"

"The work you've got to do, *you've* got to do it. That's best done alone." Then, "Catch?"

"Miss Mabel?"

"You sure you want to do this flicker? Mack's not wrong—it's dangerous, more than usual. Don't do it because I want you to. Do *you* want to?"

"I do now."

"You didn't before?"

"Not a lick."

"Why now?"

"Cause when you just said I could back out, my feelin was it would be terrible to miss this."

"That tickles me. Cause I do the same. Sometimes the Keystone seems like a senseless dream I can't wake up from and I wish I had another kind of life—till I think how terrible that would be."

I worked all the afternoon. It was powerful strange. An actress is one unsettlin thing to be.

Later, wearin my own things—they felt so free, free as free as free, like as if my very garments were tellin me, "This is you *free*."

Sittin, sippin and smokin on the white bed. The only light's from the window, glare'ish, the new electric streetlamps in the night. Hopin to sleep before light, but I'm sure awake now. And I find myself doin somethin for the first time, a call to D'Varn through the telephone.

"Who the hell is this?"

"Auntie, did I wake you up I hope?"

"You. On the telephone. All sophisticated and 20th century, are we?"

"Ever so much. I just called to say I think you're right."

"Of course I'm right. About what?"

"Miss Mabel. I think she *is* a virgin."

NOT ALL DAYS BUT MOST DAYS how Miss Mabel comes to work, she drives one'a her cars through the gate, salutes Mr. Walker in his uniform and cap, he returns her salute, then she parks near the coffee-fire with a "Hiya, fellers!" and "Hiya, Mabel!" they chorus back.

I'm coffee-dunkin my donut in a tin cup, outfitted boy'ish like a snotty newsy.

Cookie pours Miss Mabel a tin of coffee. She sips and says, "Let's see the walk."

I hitch my shoulders and walk like I seen sand-lot baseball players step up to the plate.

"How'm I doin?" says me.

"That's something like a boy," says she. "Keep at it. And file those nails down."

"Do I gotta?"

"Not now. After we shoot the flower-vender biz." She laughs. "Maybe we'll do a flicker called 'The Reluctant Actress.' Not a bad idea. Remember what I said about how men walk?"

"I remember it all."

"Well, some men walk like they're wading through slush."

"Does *slush* mean like it sounds?"

"Just like. Show you." Miss Mabel hikes her dress above her knees—and don't that get attention from the donut-table?—and she walks in a trudge. Gets a laugh all around.

"Did I miss something?" That's Sommie, newly arrived.

"You meant did you miss something *else*?" says Mabel.

"That is precisely what I meant."

Spills and wobbles, wobbles and spills—that's me so far on this bicycle.

Miss Mabel is patience itself. Not me. When I get on the damn thing I wanna stay on.

Miss Mabel, she rides easy as you please—can steer the handle bars with her feet, or sit backward on the seat, or not touch the blessed handlebar at all and just lean back and peddle. Can even turn her bike no-hands.

"Catch, if you *try* to get your balance, you won't get it."

"You don't make sense, Miss Mabel."

"Do so make sense. You'll see."

After a bit, I saw.

She's clapping for me while she rides no-hands. "You're getting it quick. Don't *try* to do it, just do it. Like when you jump."

Of a sudden, I did get it. Your brain *can't* do it. But your body can find its pace and its place and just know. I'm happy now, wheelin around the lot with her like there's nothin to it but handlebars, peddles, and foot-brake. Says Miss Mabel, "I'm on *Tillie* all afternoon. Stay at it, practice biking and boy-walking—also practice stances, how you'll stand like a boy for this or for that. Don't look at mirrors yet. Feel it on your skin first. Look at mirrors tomorrow. Speaking of tomorrow, we shall bicycle together out into the great world."

I practiced all afternoon on the lot. On account'a what Miss Mabel said, I'm noticin how folks notice me. Oh, today, the looks I'm gettin at the Keystone, me with my boy-pants and long shiny dark hair, speedin up the bike and my hair spreadin out behind, then I hit the brake, turn the handle-bar just a bit and get a real good skid-to-a-stop that sweeps up and lets down my hair.

And here comes that Dora, costumed like a waitress for *Tillie*—gone from a Destiny to Background, not bad. Says me, "Congratulations, Mrs.— what is Brick's last name anyway?"

"Mrs. Taylor!" says she brightly. "I'm bucking to get the maid part in your bike picture, which my husband is set to assistant-direct." And she adds, "He liked you for a time, didn't he?"

"Maybe a little," says me.

"And you liked him? Course you did."

"Maybe a little."

"I got my eye on you. See you steer clear of what's mine."

I nod. She nods back sharp and goes her way.

Brick didn't tell her what I did on the Fourth, I'm sure now of that much.

Folks are walkin about doin what they're doin and I'm weavin in and out of em. Ain't hit one yet. I'm lovin this bicycle. All afternoon, back and forth and in circles, till I'm tuckered out.

I lean the bike against a shed wall and sit down beside it, huggin my knees. Hank Mann's passin. I see how he walks, from his shoulders and his knees, yep, like he's pushin himself through somethin, hands held always in loose fists. Says, "Catch, true you couldn't ride a bike this morning?"

"True as true."

"Nice work." Only he said it, "woik."

I'm somebody today. In pants. Look't me, I'm a boy! Wish Fred could see.

Next day I'm so excited.

Now, I don't feature walkin without my knife-rig but my rig don't go with boy-pants so I'm havin to venture into the great world armed with just a bicycle and Miss Mabel Normand. We're at the main gate standin by our bikes while Mabel jaws with Mr. Walker who's like always, a wide smile beneath his long moustache, spruced in his gray Confederate-like uniform and his Union-like stiff cap.

Mabel has *lots* of hair, dark and thick and curly and hangin in waves down her back. My hair's finer and lighter and straighter but wavy and just as long down my back. White shirts with boy-collars and cuffs. Plus boy-shoes. And, oh—suspenders. Mabel must'a mummied up her breasts for this biz.

"Gals in pants," says Mr. Walker. "Only at the Keystone."

At the north corner of the Keystone, Aaron Street, she turns right and I turn with her up that steep dirt road till it becomes a path just wide enough for two bikes and rises at too hard a slant to peddle, way up, to a hard-packed dirt road that follows the ridge-crest northwest-southeast.

"Which way, Catch?"

"That'a way," says me, and off we head northwest.

Our bikes kick up dust and rattle on the gravel as we peddle furious, then easy, then furious, hers rattlin more than mine cause she's got a handle-bar basket full of what-all wrapped in a blanket. Over Edendale's hills go we, stickin mostly to the crests, racin down the dips, slower up the rises, and all about us there's the great world, far as eyes can see. A toy-like world from up here. As the path twists we see the buildings of downtown or the wide Valley with its Angeles River shrinkin drier. Flowers to one side with slap-dashin colors, dry land and sagebrush the other. Houses and farms one side, streets and traffic the other. Groves of this and fields of that, birds above us, birds below us, dogs chasin us barkin and we kick at em laughin, and in the road-dust tracks of deer, coyote, and one cougar's paws. Bears don't come near anymore, but still did when I was little. Hawks ride the wind. A freight train down the Valley puffs black smoke.

We stop for a breather. Miss Mabel takes two canteens out from the blanket in her basket.

"We lost, Miss Mabel?"

"We're going nowhere special, how can we be lost?"

I've got used to her rehearsin ways. If we're gonna bike-biz in traffic, we got to know how we ride together—how we feel the pace and space between us, how we follow each other's signals that don't even look like signals, just nods and not even that, just kinda knowin from how one leans and not even that—just kinda knowin.

"It's wide and flat over there," she says, "let's try some biz. We'll synchro-nize our skids."

"Synchro?"

"Do them together—in unison—time them perfect."

In a few tries we had it down. Go fast, hit the foot break, turn that handle, lean into it, stop dead—the two of us turnin on a dime like birds do in the air.

Got so's we could skid a 180, syn-chro-nized.

Canteens again. Then she says, grinnin, "Let's find us some grass and try some falls."

When she really grins her lips rise above her teeth and show her gums and that's really cute—those top teeth goin rotten some on the sides, which just makes her cuter to me. I wanted to kiss her. I don't mean smooch her, just friendly-kiss her. Didn't take that liberty.

We got some falls down good. That wasn't hard.

"Try fallin in a heap together?" says she.

That's hard.

Now we race zig-zaggin like so—she races ahead, cuts in front of me, then I race ahead, cut in front of her. We get that down, first on a level path, then on the dips.

"Now, Catch, when we get to that curve—it curves to the right so we're gonna fall to the right. You're on my right, so you start the fall first, and you gotta fall clear of your bike good so I can fall over your bike and not on it."

"You'll be fallin on me?"

"Pretty much. So land on your back."

"Gotchya."

"Sorry in advance if I break anything. Race you to the curve."

"We ain't gonna do it slow first?"

"Slow is how you hurt yourself. You can't get clear going slow."

"Right, then. Race ya."

First time's a mess. Didn't break anything, just bruised.

"Sorry about my elbow, Catch." Her elbow banged my ribs.

Next try, I'm sorry about my knee. It was a little elevated for her fall, and that wasn't good.

"Third time's a charm," says she.

It wasn't.

But next time—we got the height and speed and the kind of pattern our bodies make as we're goin down.

Then we did it again, for fun.

She's sprawled on top of me and I naturally hug her. She pecks me on the nose.

"Perfect," says she.

"We ain't gonna do this on pavement, are we, Miss Mabel?"

"We'll jump a curb and hit a lawn. Let's find us a good bump to jump."

Time comes to head back and we're a sight. Shirts stickin to us with sweat. Dusty-faced. Torn pants. And our hair! Oh, brother, our hair. Brushin out the tangles shall be painful.

We're on the ridge crest sittin beside our bikes directly above the Keystone.

"There's Mack," says she. "His big man's walk and bright straw hat. Funny how you can spot someone by their walk even from so high up."

"Looks like a toy fort from here."

"And the people look as little as we *really* are."

"Think we can ride down a hill this steep, Miss Mabel?"

"You daring me?"

"I know better. I'm askin, is all."

"A body could have quite an accident going down that hill."

"We better not talk about it more or we'll hafta."

"We may have to already. Shoulda kept your trap shut. But let's just sit for now."

We sat. Lit up cigarettes.

"Miss Mabel, can I ask somethin?"

"Shoot."

"True what happened with Nick Cogley?"

"I am so bare-assed about that."

"Pardon?"

"That's how I say embarrassed, bare-assed. When I was little, how I pronounced embarrassed sounded like bare-assed—Ahm s'bar-assed! Dat bar-assed me! Don't bar-ass me! The grown-ups thought it was cute. You bet my ass was bared good with Mr. and Mrs. Nick Cogley. See, it's this way. Cogley is so dear and his Missus is so un-dear. And Nick's old, older than Mack, Nick's forty-four—and he's so sweet and he's so fucking easy to tease that I can't help myself.

"So I tease him. Some months ago he bemoaned as to how I get sacks of fan mail and his mail doesn't even fill his little mail-cubby, so I cut out every coupon in every paper and magazine I could find, and I sent them all in with his name and Keystone's address. Now he gets sacks of advertisements!" She's laughin. "Well, that old man should not, should not ever, do falling biz—but he insists, you know, to be one of the boys."

"Broke his leg last week," says me.

"Course Mack keeps him on payroll though his leg's in a cast. So he gets fixed up with his cast and I visit his home—it's a nice apartment in a court. I brought him a basket of fruit and a bouquet of flowers and his 'fan mail' in a sack. Well, how his Missus keeps house, everything sparkles, there's no dust anywhere, you could eat off the floor—and maybe they do. I go to light a cigarette and the Missus does not approve of Madcap Mabel, no sirree, she won't let me smoke. Says it stains the walls and ceiling. Maybe it does. Well,

I know when her shopping day is. While she's marketing I take a crew there and tell Nick that, since he's on payroll and laid up useless, we're using his place for a location. Nick howls protests, but he's in a chair with his leg in a cast, nothing he can do. We put smoke-pots all over, lit them and left. Meant to return real soon but on our shoot we forgot all about Nick. He came near to suffocating in the smoke. Don't you know the fire department came and hosed everything down, ruined everything, left the walls and everything coated with smoke-stain from my pots. You can imagine his Missus when she gets home with her purchases. I'm told her head exploded. Well, that's a prank that went bad and I was sorry, really, sorry enough to write them a check for a thousand dollars. Oh, I was bare-assed. Still am."

She's laughin fit to cry and me with her, but I keep my opinion to myself, my opinion bein that sometimes Miss Mabel is flat-out nuts.

She's rubbin laugh-tears outa her eyes. Dust-runnels all down her face. Down mine too.

"Anything else you want to know, missie?" says she.

"Yep. Why you read so many books?"

"Because nobody talks to me! Not really. Mack doesn't. Well, sometimes he does. But rarely. Sommie sometimes. Charlie sometimes. I mean really, really talk. About what's important. And you, why the hell don't you want to talk about what's important?"

"Maybe I don't know what's important."

"Really?"

"Maybe not."

"Sometimes I think I do and sometimes not. To be honest, the whole question rattles me."

She puffs her cig to a nub and snuffs it into the ground.

"Miss Mabel, maybe we should ride our bikes some more. That's what's important right now, right?"

"Ride straight down this goddamn hill, you mean?"

"It's pretty steep. Does that make it important?"

"Now you mock me!"

"We gonna do it?"

"We're already doing it," and she's up, and I'm up, and down we go, oh my dear, dear God.

We're down at the bottom and still alive.

Managed to stop before skiddin into Alessandro Boulevard's traffic.

We're laugh-cryin and takin deep breaths.

"Catch, honey, we're dangerous for each other."

"We really are," says me.

"That's wonderful! And—I do so know what's important. The meaning of life, goddamnit. The *meaning* of *life*. Am I the only one besides Sommie and Charlie who thinks about that? Am I the only girl? I feel like I am. I read, read, read"—

"So does Esther"—

"Then I get scared—cause what if it's not in the books, the meaning of life? And if it's not there, I don't know where. Not here at the Keystone, that's sure."

"I am not sure I agree," says me.

Jeez. Each word popped whole outa my mouth like I'd burped bubbles.

"Sister," says she, "if there's meaning-of-life at the Keystone, I am in trouble. We all are. Hail Mary, full of grace."

Went straight back to Hotel Hollywood and sprinkled perfume on the bath water, which got all brown with dust and dirt. Drained it, cleaned it, ran another bath, sprinkled more perfume. Washed my hair good, twice. It took a painful forever to brush those tangles. Robed myself proper. Ordered room service cause I can—made eighty dollars last week alone and I don't know how to spend that much money. A steak with the fixin's, cherry pie, coffee with cream. Lit into that food. Esther calls to say goodnight, which is what we do when she's for bein alone.

Then in my billowy new pretties I sip and smoke to beat the band. I'm hearin Miss Mabel say "the meaning of life," and how it ain't at the Keystone. I do *not* agree. If there is such a thing as the meaning of life, well, life is everywhere, so the meaning of it might be—must be—everywhere, even at the Keystone. So Miss Mabel is wrong.

But she sure is fun. Oh, that last steepness of a hill, that was some dare. What could we have looked like? Couple'a banshees, I'll bet, screamin, hair a'flyin, ridin near as fast as fallin.

7

HAZY WITHIN SLEEP some'a my toes felt wondrous warm and wet.

Stretched out that leg for the joy of it.

"Ow! You demon! Trying to kick my teeth out, you?"

Eyes snap open. D'Varn's rubbin her mouth.

Says me, "Wha?"

"I wake you prettily, licking on your toesies, you kick me for my trouble."

"Is this a dream?"

"No. Just dreamy, is what."

"You're drunk."

"And high. Want some?"

"What are you doin here?"

"Licking your toes. I have a key."

"Yeah, you do, don't you. Auntie—I'm with Esther now."

"Where is she, under the bed? In the closet?"

I tap my chest. "She's right here."

"My, my. Where was I?"

"You're in there too. But I'm with Esther now."

She sits on the bed, near my feet. Fetches a gold-tipped Egyptian from her very large purse that doesn't match her dress (which, oddly, isn't anything special)—lights her Egyptian with matches in the teenie vase on the vanity— looks into the mirrors where she's always found herself, and I know what she's gonna say before she says, "I'm still there," noddin at the mirror.

She takes a long drag, lets it out slow. "They'll be releasing *Ayesha* soon. *Ayesha—The Story Of SHE*. I'm already in some magazines."

"And on that billboard that's your favorite. I've seen. And you're even more beautiful."

"Thanks for noticing. Anyway, aside from being disappointed in fuckery, in these wee hours I have tales to tell."

She was, I don't know—"collected," Sommie might say?

Handed me her Egyptian to finish and lit another. I rose from bed, nightied in billows, and poured us brandies that I put on the glass table in front of the divan. Out of the bedroom.

"Oh, alright," she says from the bedroom and comes to join me.

We raise glasses. "To"—and she can't think of to what.

"Ayesha, of course."

We clink.

"Know what cheesecake is?" says D.

"Besides delicious?"

"Not that kind of cheesecake."

Gets up, pulls the floor-lamp closer to the divan, turns the switch up two clicks to brightest. Then sits, fishes in that large purse, pulls out papers—sheets of some kind—and lays em face down in a stack on the coffee table.

"Behold," says she.

One by one she turns over the sheets, which are photographs.

The first is D'Varn bare-backed, bare-shouldered, honey-colored hair a bright gray in the glossy photo and piled high on her head, and she's lit bright against a background of pitch black.

"That's me cheesecake. 'We suggest more than we show,' Douglas says. He takes the pictures—a sharp pansy, very la-la. This shot's just my back and shoulders and profile. Douglas says the idea is to make it seem I'm about to turn to the 'viewer'—and show all. Dirty but tasteful, says our Douglas, adding, 'That is Mr. Sennett's instruction.'"

"Keystone cheesecake?" says me. "Not Ayesha?"

"These are from a 'session' a week ago. Tonight's aren't developed yet. Behold."

"Miss Mabel!"

It's a front shot—Miss Mabel, turned a bit to the side, showing bare back, while her bare arms don't quite cover her breasts—you view her breasts slope but not where they slope. You kinda do, though, in your mind.

"The lighting is great," says me.

"High-contrast it's called. Mabel helped arrange the lights. Another."

"Oh, brother."

Miss Mabel lies on a pillow, face turned to you. Her expression's all dreamy, eyes half open, mouth half open, a look to melt you. What's crazy is what's on her. A cougar skin, the head posed fierce and growlin, a scary head that lies on her breasts, which again you don't see much of, except in your cheesecake mind. Stranger yet, the right leg of the cougar wraps round her neck like it's cradlin her head with its big paw, and the cougar's other leg embraces her too—all like she's sorta gently mid-screw with the beast. Lovin it, looks like.

"What think ye, missy Willie?"

"Wouldn't have imagined it."

"Apricot brandy, reefer, some nose candy, your Miss Mabel's all set for the naughty."

I drink my brandy kinda fast. D joins me in that. I pour us more.

Miss Mabel's dark hair blends into a black background like it's a part of the dark. She's clothed, sort of—gossamer over her breasts and round her shoulders, a ghostly air. Her face, that's really what's naked. A Miss Mabel you never see in a flicker. She's lookin straight at you, her head's turned up, her throat's exposed—very carefully lit it is, neck and face partly in slight shadow and partly too bright, and her look—mouth dreamy half-open, eyes starin out from her soul like they don't ever blink—and her hair, as I say, blends into darkness all round her. Oh, Miss Mabel.

D'Varn's face goes blank kinda. "Know what she said tonight? Said, 'Nothing can love you like the camera—if you're one of the people it loves— it sees you like you wish you were. So honest is the camera—and such a liar.'" A long snake of smoke lifted from D'Varn's nostrils and mouth. "I said what she said over to myself three times so I could remember. *She* called *me*, you know. Congratulations for my magazine feature. 'Star to star,' says she. 'Meet for a drink?' says she. I pick her up with my car and my driver."

"This is where I'm supposed to be impressed, auntie?"

"I didn't actually expect you to be. We go to that place they all go to, all the somebodies in pictures, Vernon's it's called. I thought at first she was putting the make on me. But no, or not really. She was pal'y, you know how she gets. And she invited me to a 'private session,' and next thing it's nose-candy and hash and we're posing half-naked for a fairy. And tonight we did it again. It's not because she likes me."

"She likes to dare. And you, Miss D—you like to study."

"Of course! Mabel's the best actress in pictures, better than anybody Griffith's got, including L. Gish." Then D asks, "What's a First Communion?"

"I'm not at all sure," says me.

"Mabel made some First Communion cracks. I laughed along, but didn't get it. Do you know she's posed for lantern slides that they show in burlesque when a tenor sings tween hoochie numbers? Mabel told me Sennett wanted Minta to come with, for cheesecake, but Minta, she hit the roof. 'Me, a married woman? Roscoe would kill me.' But isn't Mabel Sennett's fiancé? I don't feature a man asking this of his fiancé. And his fiancé agrees gladly? What's that, Willie? I wouldn't. I am a silver-plated slut, but I would not let my intended ask such of me."

"Can't put em up in theaters," says me. "Get arrested straight to the hoosegow."

"Where we all maybe belong," says D.

"Can't make postcards of em, not so's you could send them through the mails. They'd hoosegow you. Can't print em in the papers."

"Yep."

"What, then?"

"Smut. Big secret market out there for smut—so I am reliably informed. Star-smut. The male of the species pay dear for star-smut. Wouldn't they just, the swine? Anyway, that's my tale to tell." She's whoozin. "Willie, I'm too loaded to leave. Staying here tonight."

"You take the white bed, I'll be on the divan."

"You're with Esther."

"Right."

D'Varn, she busts out laughin like at a dirty joke. "Come on, you," says she. "Let's go, missy. We'll take a walk."

"No, we won't."

"A walk to the round room!"

"What round room?"

"It's circular."

"What is?"

"The round room. You are such a little animal. You have your territory and stay where you've sniffed and peed, don't care a damn for anything else even if it's just down the hall. Come."

She kicks off her shoes, takes off her dress, smooths her slip up and down her body, and she wears no underthings. My chest thumps. Says she, "You're with Esther?"

"I'm with Esther," says me.

"We must walk to the round room."

"As we are?"

"Dare ya."

"Oh, boy."

We peek out the door to see is the coast clear.

Course the coast is clear, it bein 4'ish in the mornin. Tippy-toe we go down the carpeted hall past potted plants and closed doors, past Esther's door—and I ain't never been past that door -- and past a wide stairway, till sure enough at the end of another hall there's a circular room.

LADIES' RECEPTION ROOM says a gold plaque on the open double-door, and inside there's writin desks with stationary and paper and pen and ink well laid out on em, and also comfortable chairs and nice end-tables and ashtrays on stands and landscape paintings on the walls, and one-two-three-four-five windows in a circular, and the shades are drawn so it's dim as dim. D'Varn, walkin wobbly, makes her way to the windows one by one and lifts each shade so there's light from Hollywood Boulevard's new streetlamps.

I open a window, we lean our arms on the sill, stick our heads out. The breeze kinda snaps us into more drunker.

"Lookee," says she, "not a soul and barely a sound. You won't even kiss me?"

"I really won't."

She laughs a soft real laugh.

Flowery scents of the night, reefer smell in our hair, and Egyptian smell, and a brandy-tobacco taste in my mouth.

D'Varn says slow, "Finally Mabel posed real risqué. Seated on cushions with not a stitch, arms crossed over her tits, legs crossed too, so's not to show her kitty. Dared me and I did too."

"Hoosegow for certain, I swear."

"We're all sad, really, are we all sad?"

"Hoosegow, is what."

D takes a pose. "See that dragon coming down the block, bigger than anything ain't it, isn't it, it is." Now D stands stiffly to her full height, arms at her side, pretty titties and pretty legs prettily 'defined' by her pretty slip. Says, "I'll do Uly."

She throws her right arm full out and points her forefinger. "'East ist dah desert!'" Left arm straight out, forefinger pointed. "'Vest ist dah oceans! In betwixt ist vat? The Dragon!' Then he speels, Uly does: 'Vat is The Dragon? Who is The Dragon? Dah Dra'gone ist *us*, us movies. Ist dah pictures. Motion pictures! Dah Dragon shall consume de vorld!' And Uly gets so excited that he has to excuse himself to take more drugs."

"Back to *my* room now, auntie."

"Cause if they catch us we're hoosegow? Let's us go. Ulysses speaks American cause he is one, he just likes accents." She stops cold. "My Billy topped himself."

"I know."

"He deserved it. Deserved what he got that day and *you* deserved what you got that day, you who are with Esther."

And we went, tippy-toe, back down the hall toward *my* rooms, and as we tip-toe D'Varn says, loud, "That hair of Mabel's! Thick as a forest and down to her waist!"

"Shhhhhhh."

"Shhhhhhh."

"Shhhhhh."

Then we're back. On the divan I need another drink and so does she. I need another smoke and so does she.

Says D, "Mabel told me about your bike ride. She respects you."

"Go to bed, auntie."

"No. Here. Sleep here just like we are—just like we used to."

"Pee first."

"Me first."

She goes and makes, I pop into the bedroom—well, not pop, cause I'm brandy'd and wobbly. I drag the comforter off the big white bed. Find her lyin on the floor. Tuck the comforter round her. Go pee.

"We gotta wake soon for work," says me.

"Silly," says she. "It's Sunday by now."

When a farmhand, I would'a knowed.

I feel myself passin out on the divan, but there's somethin—somethin.

"Hey, D?"

"Shush."

"Auntie D?"

"Shush."

"You believe in the meaning of life?"

"The which?"

"Meaning of life."

"Shush up," says D, "like a good girl."

When I wake she's not on the floor. Look to the bed. She's gone. I lay myself on that white so-soft bed and I'm wonderin is it so, what she said that time it rained—is it so that a moment of happiness, a moment of true happiness, goes on and on and on—"lives on its own," she'd said. You know, I'm bettin it is. Is so. *Can* be so. I just bet.

"You don't have to tell me D'Varn was here," says Esther. "I can smell her."

She slams open the window above the divan, then slams open the bedroom's double window, also the bathroom's small window that's paint-stuck shut but Big Esther manages.

I pointed to the glass coffee table: "Auntie left her key."

Esther looked at me with all the effort of not-askin.

"Esther! What you thinkin? We did *not* do touchy-feely or smoochy or S-E-X or goodbye kiss. I *was* glad to see her but does she have some nerve comin in like that? Oh, yes she does."

"Neither one of us would be here if she didn't," says Es.

Esther trembles, like her head's about to burst, then she rushes me, buries me under her on the divan, sob-laughin, "You chose *me*!"

Calms down. Gives me breathin room.

"It's just us now, Esther. I don't know how to tell you how much I'm likin that."

Esther stands up, walks about, stops. "How was she?"

"Like the Fourth—Ayesha, and at her ease. She's already in the illustrateds."

"I've seen. It's a pretty Sunday out there."

Which is how we got to the zoo in Griffith Park, best place for hot dogs on a Sunday. We dressed alike in bright summer shifts down to the ankles, no gloves, no stockings, bare feet in sandals, quite the walkin scandals! No make-up. And (apparently our new fashion) no hats. Hair shiny-brushed and loose for the breezes to play with. One purse between us, one of mine, small, latched, shoulder-slung, for cigs (not that we'd smoke at the zoo), matches, cash, and derringer. The only females dressed anything like us are lots littler, while their mothers sweat under layers of cloth and lace from toe-tip to bonnet and warily eye us. There's also how Esther's large and I'm slight, and that there's lots of pretty between us, lots to see.

And of course, hidden, my knife-rig, Esther's shin-holster.

Peculiar to see lions caged—and bears, and monkeys—after you've been with em up close for real doin biz. Then at the kid-park Esther stops to watch playmates on a teeter-totter—she calls it a seesaw—up-and-down, up-and-down.

"I was always too large," Esther says. "I would *promise* to go up-and-down, but couldn't resist letting my victims teeter up there, poor helpless things, until they'd cry, or jump, or climb down. Nanny would scold, in French, but I was a favorite and, anyway, sort of her employer. It's *my* money. All mine. PaPá died otherwise childless and left a spiteful will, as far as concerned MaMá. I give *them* an allowance—the so-called family. I cage them with opulence."

Small round tables in the shade, waiters in uniforms, the works—hotdogs on buns with two bottles of pop and a stack of napkins plus all the fixins, all held one-handed on a tray. One for Esther, two for me, and my usual silver dollar tip for a thirty cent meal. I'm dollin up my dogs with mustard, relish and sauerkraut in just-right balance when Esther says, "D'Varn won't touch those, says they look too much like you-know-what."

"What if they do? We don't have to talk about it while I'm eatin."

"She'd say, 'How can you eat those in front of me?' and I'd say, 'They don't remind me of anything.' "

"Esther?"

"For instance, that hot dog—doesn't remind me—of your you-know-what."

She dropped the subject until, back in my rooms, lounging in our billowies, we sat enjoyin breakfast-in-the-evening, my new favorite meal. The way we movies tipped, Hotel Hollywood's kitchen crews—in fact, any kitchen crew—would do anything for us. Two politely light knocks on the door, a silver dollar placed in a gloved hand, a tip of the cap while the bellboy tries to keep a straight face at the sight of Gals-In-Nighties (but ample nighties, not so untoward), and we roll in the table-on-wheels with its thick tablecloth and covered dishes and hot coffee pot and cream in its own spouted vase and soft cloth napkins and heavy silver utensils and a fruit bowl on a glass shelf midway twixt floor and table-top. Three bananas. Oranges, too, in a bowl. You can have all the oranges you want in this orange-blossom town.

We pull up two inconspicuous polished wood chairs we've had sent up, which are for nothing but eating room-service, and we sit at opposites of the wheeled table.

Eggs, sausages, porridge with pads of melting butter, and, of course, champagne—on a roller of its own, restin in a silver (real silver) bucket of ice. Esther pops the bottle, then pours into thin stemmed glasses. "To summer evenings," says she. We clink and drink.

I'm diggin into my food but Esther's runnin her forefinger, her right forefinger, up and down a sausage for to suck its grease off her fingertip. And again. And again.

I stop eatin and light a cigarette.

"My sausage," Esther says, "looks like a you-know-what that's had a difficult time of it. She did yours didn't she?"

"I told you, no sex last night."

"But before."

"I—didn't participate—when she'd do that."

"I may know what you mean."

"I'd be behind the white wall. Mother would say, 'When he beats you bad, just go behind the white wall, imagine the white wall and just go behind it and wait there for him to stop'."

"I do know what you mean," says Esther.

"Mother would say, 'It's there when you need it, the white wall.' Lord knows she needed it. Went behind it finally and never came out. When D wanted me in her mouth she'd usually slap me around a little first, then get to it. I didn't mind the slaps. They helped with the white wall. I think she knew that."

Esther begins to say somethin but I say, "Just shut up, ok?"

"It goes off sometimes anyway"—

"Oh Christ," says me.

"— it does, and it's"—

"It's just part of the act, Esther, my dick joins the show, does its biz, and doesn't matter, goddamnit. We slither on its cream, big fun. Mabel wants me to be a boy, now what do you want?"

"The rare creature that you are. And you've got a you-know-what. I want that dick in my mouth and told you as much the first time I saw you naked. But I'd want you to—participate. I need that. And if you don't want me to"—

"Get me a real drink, pleeeeeeeeeeease."

She poured me a glassful of pricy rye that I hadn't much liked but it sure is a real drink.

After we did what we did, she mouthing my thing, she moved to kiss my mouth.

"Let's wait a little on that," says me. "Let's drink some rye first."

She did so. Says Es, "Did I do it well? What did it feel like?"

"*Esther.*"

"But what?"

"Gettin thrown—not pushed, thrown—off the Palisades."

I woke in the night to a moment of not knowin where I was. Esther pulls me onto her, all the way onto her, so's I float on the generosity of her body.

8

MISS MABEL TAKES HOLD OF MY HAND as we walk across the lot.

"Seen D'Varn lately?"

"Miss Mabel, I don't talk about D'Varn."

"D'Varn tell you about our outing the other night?"

"I don't talk about D'Varn, Miss Mabel. Where we goin?"

"That new building there."

"What's it gonna be for, that building?"

"I'm not sure Mack knows. He gets a kick out of all this construction, sheds doing down, buildings going up. Makes him feel important. I suppose he is."

We stepped through a doorway that had no door. Smells of fresh lumber, fresh paint. The bareness of it. She pushed a button on the wall. The room lit up from a light on the ceiling. Then a hall without doors, with rooms of several sizes, mostly big. She hit a button and the hall lit up—ceiling lights down the length of it. Very fancy.

"I'll bet this is for the new labs," said she. "Developing rooms, drying rooms, editing rooms. In one building—not sure which—there's to be a cafeteria! No scattering for lunch. A cafeteria with radiators! No standing around the coffee-fire to stave off morning's chill."

We step into a room that's already lit and there's the man I like to avoid.

"Brickface," says Mabel.

"Mabel. Catch."

"Thanks for doing this, Brickface."

"Just doing my job." He tries to smile and fails. Hatless, his red mop unevenly cut, and heavier. Looks just like most cameramen now in the picture game. Light tan shirt buttoned at the collar and at the cuffs, dark tie, respectable trousers, work boots. His stained felt slouch hat hangs from a nail in the wall. Tends a hand-cranked projector that's plugged into a wall-socket.

"Wires in the walls!" says me.

"And insulated proper," says he. "Mabel, the opposite wall will have to do for a screen."

There are two folding chairs and two piles of film canisters.

"I've arranged them in sequence," says Brick.

"Thank you," says Miss Mabel. "Now you can un-arrange them—please. I think about scenes better when I see them out of sequence."

She and I sit and light cigarettes. Brick slides a canister-lid our way for an ashtray. No eye-contact with me. He hits the light, then he takes to crankin. The bright beam goes ghostly with our floatin smoke.

No piano. Just the rattle of that projector.

We've shot most of our story, savin the most dangerous stuff for last, which is where it goes in the story anyhow. That's when Mr. Sennett takes over, tomorrow. But Miss Mabel's cheated on that, as we—she and me—cooked up bike biz. She says, "Once it's in the canister he'll love it."

Brick's already loaded the first scene, so we started in sequence after all.

When a flicker opens with the title and, beneath the title, "Keystone—A Farce Comedy," you're set to laugh cause you've been kinda told to. But raw like this it's sad to see those sincere girls offer their flowers to folks who don't want them and who don't care a fig about sincere girls.

We are pretty, no mistake. Big and Little Sister should be stoppin traffic, as pretty as we are, but the Great World treats us like we ain't there. It's a flicker, and it's Miss Mabel, so you know the girls are important, but not when you see it this way. I've learned how you build comedy, commonplace-to-outlandish, still those two brave pretty girls are doing honest humble work and the world walks right over em.

As Brick changes canisters Miss Mabel, who's sittin close by me, she leans over to squeeze my thigh. "I told you, didn't I? You're an actress."

"I didn't know what I was doin when I was doin it."

"That comes later."

Now there's us as boys, toughies, standin slouchy midst the bike-boys, wearin stiff-brimmed messenger caps cramped down at saucy angles—we needed tight caps to bunch our hair under, braided and coiled, and the excess, lots of it, was hid clever by our collars and stuffed smooth down our backs under our white shirts, which all these bike-boys and newsies wear, and they turn up the collars to look rough. And we're all puffin cigarettes, makin lotsa smoke like all newsies and bike-boys when they slouch about.

Miss Mabel says, "Glad I junked our 'changing' scene. This way our worthy ticket-buyers may think we're really boys for moments until the camera irises in on us and we wink them."

These next two canisters are us as boys, doin this and that in the story, and I'm thinkin, That's what you wanted me to be, Daddy. Work the farm with you shoulder-to-shoulder. Sure, you wanted our farm to one day be your son's. All this time seeing how you hurt me, I never before seen how I hurt you. I ain't sorry, Daddy. All I knew to be was me. Cruel Daddy, silly Daddy, my Daddy, in all your accursed cussedness all *you* knew how to be was you— and that man was unloved. We none of us—Mother, Fred, me—could see our way to loving you. You were bad enough and we made you worse, didn't we? You won't see this flicker, cause you take it for unholiness, but there I am, on the screen, a boy, your boy. It ain't real, but there I am.

Wonder what you're up to. Wonder about Mother. Wonder will Fred call.

There's Mabel and me, dare-devilin on bikes in traffic. Brick on the camera-car was yellin, "Goddamn, slow up, you'll get us all killed!" So what did we do but dare-devil the more?

There's your son, Daddy. No "rare creature," as Esther'd have it. A regular little hellion is what. You'd like him maybe. But I bet you'd whip him plenty, cause that boy, you can just see he's got no use for Bible-learnin. Bet he'd run off to be a newsie or bike-boy, support hisself, gone on his own at fourteen or twelve maybe, like they do. Cause he would still be me, Daddy, see? Yeah, he would still be me. A pain in the ass for sure, but would you hate him? Bet not.

Of a sudden I'm all clammy. I fidget and Miss Mabel notices and I stop.

She had to teach me, but I learned fast, didn't I? Tomorrow I gotta be boy-me again. Tomorrow we do the real danger, the worst, all in one day, because Mr. Sennett wants it that way so's not to take more time away from *Tillie.* That boy—lookin at his face I see my face, he's pretty, that boy, like some boys are, pretty in the face. *Was* I supposed to be that boy? Was I that boy last night? It's only a flicker, *but not while we're doin it.* While we're doin it, it feels real.

Being a actress is a discombobulatin business.

Miss Mabel says, "You with us, Catch? You like it?"

"I'm impressin myself, I guess."

Now we're watching Mr. Wallace Beery flirtin up his secretaries.

There's Big Esther now, settin herself up to seduce Miss Mabel-the-boy, who she's lured to her home—this is just before Miss Mabel-the-Boy gets there.

It's somethin to see Big Es gussied up feminine. When she's just with D'Varn and me she's her real feminine, definite and strong and sad and smart and curvy and *big*. When she's playin lady-feminine, well, look at her, how she gussies, how she holds herself, dainty, sly, greedy for boy-Mabel.

"Take a gander at that," Miss Mabel says.

When they shot it I was ganderin alright. Standin to the side of the camera, on the set of a new Ghost Building, and there are boy-Mabel and Big Es alone together. Esther's shiny auburn hair is full out, hangin down her back in waves like a cape. Her great bosoms are half-exposed in a gauzy, layered thing that sweeps from her neck to her feet and is kinda see-through and kinda not, with wonderful lacey sleeves that finish at her wrists. She made quite the impression, stately and tall, walkin that Ghost Building in that get-up before they shot, puffin smoke on a cigarette in a long-stemmed holder. The looks she got! They see her mostly doin man's work in overalls and such, or drivin a stunt car, but "on set," as we now say, their eyes are poppin.

Es and Miss Mabel didn't rehearse. Just dove into it. Boy-Mabel sees what Esther Lady is up to and plays for time, they do S-E-X'y back and forth biz, all as Boy-Mabel maneuvers toward the window she'll jump out of.

How they're lookin at each other, titter-laughin, eyes a'gleaming, tastin each other with their eyes—and me, standin beside the camera, jealous!

Oh, I'm watchin. And I'm jealous. As far as I'm concerned it took forever for Miss Mabel Normand to jump out that goddamn window.

The scene is done and folks who've watched go to cheerin and applaudin. Miss Mabel and Big Es are huggin and laughin, and "That was fun!" says Miss Mabel—"It surely was" says Big Esther—and Esther does what she rarely does, she grins ear to ear.

Saunters on to me in her nightie-gown, still "in character," as they say, and twists a cigarette into that long-stemmed holder.

"Light me up, will you?"

I do so.

"You're too good for your own good," says me.

"And too large to be taken seriously. But I like that my carpenter buddies watched. Gotta go say hello."

"There's all of it, Mabel," says Brick as he puts the reel back in its canister. "I didn't see one wrong move in any of it."

"I didn't either," says she, "and I'm picky."

Brick hit the lights. Just as he did so I happened to be lookin his way—I'd stood up from my chair, see. He looked at me with—hatred. Which vanished quick.

"Your expression!" That's Miss Mabel to me. "What were you thinking? Just now, what?"

"If I could only say, Miss Mabel. If I could only say."

————————————

Esther's workin background on *Tillie*. Mabel wouldn't let me. "Save it all for us," says she. Sent me home after our rushes. And now? Don't they say think of a devil and there shall he be? Wasn't I just thinkin hard of Daddy? And didn't he just board this damned Big Red?

A Big Red trolley, you board at the front or the back. Conductor at each end, in uniform and cap, takes your fare, punches a ticket, you find a seat or stand. I'm sittin about three strides from the back. Daddy's up front occupied with the conductor. I study him.

Somewhat crazy in the eyes—probably always was, but we were used to it. An ill-fittin wool suit, too hot for the day, and it hangs on him. Shined tan-and-white leather shoes, why, Daddy, who'da thunk! Holds a Bible. Flat-brimmed hat. A preacher's look. His expression—solemn and somewhat disappointed, which I've noticed is a not uncommon look of folks while ridin trolleys.

Picks his place to stand—seats are all occupied—and there's four-five standin riders twixt him and me. I'm on an aisle seat. Ready to bolt.

Trolley's clunkin along and we all sway a little and bounce a little and Daddy's just lookin about, the way you do, and his eyes pass over me without seein me. Well, I ain't in a farm girl's housedress and my hat cost a pretty penny. But oh he now does see—it's like he can't believe his eyes, but then he believes and knows and his eyes light up bright with Daddy-hate.

Daddy's still Daddy and he can make me jump a foot as he thunders, "DAMNATION! DAM'nation on THAT sinner! That's my SON!" His long arm and long finger point at me, and the trolley folk are shocked at his fury as, screamin, he takes a step toward me, and another, and the Big Red sways as it rounds the curve where Hollywood Boulevard heads due west, by the Griffith lot, and Daddy loses balance on his bad leg, lands on a man's lap, still with his DAMNATIONS and blazin hate, and I heard a scream, felt that scream in my throat, surprised it's me screamin, animal-screamin, and Daddy's again makin his way toward me, pointin at the pretty young lady that is me while yellin, "That's my SON! Fetch a ROPE!"—and others sayin "Mister, you're loco," "The man's outa his mind!" The conductor in back and the conductor in front call for him to desist while they're comin to lay hands on Daddy midst "Fetch a ROPE!" and in this confusion is my opportunity to bolt to the rear and swing off the Red.

Damn.

I'm shaky, in a sweat. Maybe the conductors pin him down and call police or maybe he gets off a block west and doubles back. I cross the street dodgin cars against traffic toward the Griffith lot, then it's up six-seven steps to a gate. There's a guard this time, but I say, "I'm from the Keystone, come to see a friend, Karl-with-a-K." He lets me in.

Well. Family reunion. Thing is, I realize as I light my cigarette, fingers unsteady, that there was one itsy bitsy moment, before he screamed, when he was just my Daddy. Other thing is, if those on the trolley knew about me really, they'd hate me too? Most of them, probably. Mother'd say, "That's just the Lord's way of keepin things interestin."

I've had more than enough of bein a shaky creature standin about at Griffith's gate. Hotel Hollywood is some two miles west, and I mean to strut it. Let's see how many horns I can make honk and how many wolf-whistles and catcalls come my way as praise due my beauty in this world of fools, of which I am one.

ECHO PARK

INTERVIEWER
*How did you learn to control your body
during the many difficult stunts?*

BUSTER KEATON
*Any time you leave the ground
your head will steer you.*

1

THE DARK OF THE MORNING. A steady Santa Ana breeze out of the desert, warm'ish now, hot later. Early in the year for that. Farmers hereabouts, as they wake, they'll scent the wind and curse its out-of-season dryness. And these breezes shall bear stinks of Edendale's oil wells all the way west, past Hotel Hollywood to the sea—a general smell embroidered, as you might say, with flowers waking without much dew, if any.

Didn't think I'd sleep at all, what with what's planned today, but, well, Esther . . . attended to me . . . the lushness, Esther's lushness, and with how she did my nipples my ass *blossomed*, I felt it *open,* I wanted her inside me, not a wand, her hand, and when she went into me how I moved and what crazy joy it was, then she turned me and with what crazy joy did I cling to her as I'm coming (*going*) with my entire body . . . then deep sleep. Not much, but deep.

Mr. Sennett ordered all hands to show early and ready. "Come costumed!"

I'm in my bike-boy look. A neck-to-ankle mink gives Esther a bear-like quality, especially when weighted, as it is, with two large pistols in its inner pockets. She opens the coat to reveal the "suggestive" but not quite see-through neck-to-ankle nightie-gown of Mrs. Bossy. Of course that hair of hers has a way of blending with the furs.

We're alone in the world on Hollywood Boulevard, me scrunched against her in the wide front seat of her "touring" car, half an hour or so before first light. Bright in the glare of the new streetlamps a white box-like one-horse wagon turns onto Hollywood from a fresh and narrow dirt road that has no sign as yet. Lettered on the wagon:

Max & Ida's
Dairy'n'Eggs

The gent who holds the reins, white-uniformed and white-capped, may be the Max, cept beside him is not an Ida but a Mabel.

"Hiya fellas," says she, dressed as a fella. Introduces us all round, including the horse, whose name is Adelaide. "Sometimes I can't sleep so I help Max with deliveries." Max smiles shy, nods, and Mabel says, "Can we interest you in cow's milk, goat's milk, a wedge of butter, perhaps an egg?"

"Want a lift to the lot?" says Esther.

"Thanks. Bye, Max." Kisses his cheek. "My best to Ida. Bye, Adelaide."

First light. Esther's off with Mr. Coy Watson and his spanking new, very bright, five-battery Ever-Ready flashlight for to peer under her hood and beneath her chassis, the double-check on if her auto's up to snuff for stunts. Miss Mabel and Assistant Director Brickface yell, boss and bully folks to ready a Keystone convoy—for instance, an open truck full of bicycles and boys, and two buses of background actors so's we don't take unfair advantage of civilians. All the while Mr. Sennett's watchful. He stands by the coffee fire at the old Ghost Building with a gaggle of folk, a little apart from them, and they're careful not to mix with him. He watches my approach with unusual interest.

"Grab a cup of Joe and walk with me some, Catch."

I do so.

We stroll slow. The "Joe," as he calls it, heats the tin cup and my hands are grateful. He keeps quiet till we reach the old well from when this lot was a farm.

"Gonna keep this crank-well," says he. "Reminds me of home in Canada. When I was a boy my family grew, hunted, or traded for everything we needed. Clog or hide shoes. Fur coats from animals we shot or trapped. Trade for flour, sugar, coffee, cloth. Mother made our clothes. When she visits, she will be glad to see this well. The new stage goes up over there," he pointed. "Four times the size and three times as high as this old one."

"Why higher?" says me.

"Just thought I'd like it that way. We'll keep the chicken-coop. Not the pig-pen. There'll be ducks when Mother comes. She especially enjoys ducks."

This does not happen, Mr. Sennett and me like this.

He bit a wad of tobacco. "Last night I watched what you kids shot."

He lets that hang for a bit, so I get bold. "Like it or not?"

"Did and did not. You heard me tell our Mabel. No dangerous stuff. Told her to wait on me for dangerous stuff. You heard that?"

"I heard it."

"Thought so. Thank you. See, she's liable to swear I never mentioned that—and even convince me. Somerset was present as well, but he lies for her."

"Wish I'd thought to," says me.

Up scampers a girl who's all-over goose bumps cause she neglected to dress for dawn's chill. Her cute blue cotton blouse displays lots of shoulder. Her chest's not undeveloped and not too developed. A broad belt at her waist, nice hips, long legs under a swirly red skirt. Not a whit scared. Plants herself in front of Mr. Sennett and gives her head a shake so's he'll notice she's not bald.

"You are Mr. Sennett, aren't you?" She nods towards the coffee fire. "They called you 'the Old Man'."

"They'd rather you not tell me that."

"I'm an actress."

"Are you? She's an actress, Catch."

Girl darts me a look. I hope her bashful smile is cause my boy-costume works a charm.

Says she to him, "I wish to be a Daughter of Destiny. I'm not asking for much pay. At first."

Mr. Sennett chews his chaw.

"Show me your legs."

"Pardon?"

"Show me your legs. Girls in pictures need fair legs. What I say to you I say to every lass who wants to work here, don't I, Catch?"

"Yup." My boyish grunt.

"Sir," says she, "are you making sport of me?"

"Not at all. Promise. Show me."

He gives out a long spit. She watches wide-eyed as that gob lifts from his lips and lands in the dust.

Up goes her dress all the way to her business.

She endures his up-and-down, down-and-up survey bravely before she drops her hem.

"Choice legs," says Mr. Sennett. "How old?"

"Sixteen."

"See, if you're fifteen, it's a violation of law to hire you."

"That's why I'm sixteen!"

"You're not fourteen?"

"Sixteen."

"When?"

"In a few weeks. Months."

A pretty half-smile went with that.

"You've got the smick-smack, as I call it. Two dollars a day to start. Report Thursday, early. Be sixteen."

"Don't you want to know my name?"

"Tell me Thursday."

She beamed him a wide smile that I bet she'd practiced. "I'll be there."

Gave a curtsey—nice touch—and off she went, goose bumps and all.

Mr. Sennett spit again.

"Ever hear it said, Catch: Grab em young, treat em rough, tell em nothing?"

"I've heard that all my life, Mr. Sennett."

"Did I ask if you were sixteen?"

"You asked if I'd jump off a higher building. I am sixteen. But is Miss Mabel really only nineteen? She's so wise and all. How old was she when you met, if I can ask?"

"Old enough to be Mabel Normand."

"And when you gave her that ring on the Staten Island ferry?"

"Getting a little personal with the Boss? She told you about the ferry." A sigh. "Mabel was three months, not quite three months, shy of seventeen—if *she's* telling the truth about her age."

Then off he went, without a nod.

2

AT THE KEYSTONE YOU GOTTA CLIMB a roof or hike the ridge to see Los Angeles. At Echo Park just look east and there it is, the risin city, bustlin up a fury and proud as proud.

Echo Park is a pretty'ish place, gathered as it is around a lake. Tall palms, thick trees, park benches, gravel paths, flowers abloom, fountains, and high shrubs planted so's to make places of privacy. They got a sprinkler machine waters grass all by itself. A kiosk rents cozy boats and serves refreshments, and, as I noticed with Fred, two black swans patrol the lake and they got red eyes. But the star, as we would say, is a small island near the eastern shore, and you may step to that island across two wooden bridges, one from the east and one from the west, neither more than twenty yards span and each a thing of beauty. The east bridge is flat, the west bridge arches. Both are railed with cut and polished tree limbs, thick and slim, entwined somehow together, braided, as though some faery-tale trees took a notion to grow into bridges.

The waters by the island are faery'ish too, with flowers called lotus that Sommie says are holy in Asia. Gotta be two-three hundred of these holy lotuses, thick round green leaves larger than pie-crusts afloat on the water—floating flowers! On each leaf rests one pink-white bulb, some big as my fist, some big as Pasha's. Sommie says their scent has soothin powers. I don't want to be soothed, it's not good for what I do. I want to get to work.

We're all here, us Keystoners, but it's like we're on a picnic. Nobody's givin orders, so we dawdle about. Moseyin, I am, slouchy-strollin, boy-like, a newsie's cloth hat cocked to one side, hands pushed down into pockets— which are the one feature of this costume I've come to enjoy.

Esther sits "resplendent" (a D'Varn word) on a bench across the lotus pond, watchin me watch her, or vice versa, her shiny mink wide open, long legs crossed at the ankles, her layered nightie especially white as it's outlined by all that dark fur.

She's in what you might call our corner of the park. The Keystone has invaded. We got vehicles anywhere on the grass at the whole northwest corner—three cars for the chase, the Kops' paddy wagon, two camera cars, Miss Mabel's lavender Stutz, Mr. Sennett's gaudy six-seater, Mr. Coy Watson's two-seat Studebaker, and Esther's Cadillac tourer, plus the winch-truck for pullin cars out of the lake, covered trucks that stow gear, and an open truck with high sides and the tailgate down, truck-bed filled with film canisters and the two cameras that ain't on cars.

All around Esther, as though to guard her (though that's not the case), our Kops hang out in silly-fittin uniforms. They smoke, gamble, and chaw, awaitin direction. Brickface and his boys see to the prop boxes and cameras. Our background people huddle about our food-tables, amongst them Mrs. Brickface—background players are what we call a good step up from smick-smack Destinies, so Dora's doin alright for herself. Near the food-table, but shy about it, are "extras" hired for the day to play citizens we can run amongst and occasionally knock over. It goes without sayin that, being on location, Keystoners sport pistols stuck in belts and blackjacks half-hangin out of pockets. And there's hatless-as-usual Sommie, wearin clothes he slept in, his back against a tree, smokin his pipe.

When word's out that the Keystone has taken over the park, venders will swarm here, some with pushcarts, some with their fare on wood trays suspended from their necks by belts or ropes—hot dogs, ice cream, peanuts, donuts, licorice, tobacco, tamales, bagels, and flavored seltzers and ices, all hawked by Dagos, Jews, Mexes, and gypsies. By lunch this park'll look like a county fair.

Steppin toward me on the flat faery-bridge comes Mr. Coy Watson, his straw skimmer bright on his head and a fancy photograph-camera hangin from his neck.

"Fine day," says he.

"You mean fine day to stand around doin nothin as the light's gettin good?"

We weren't workin cause Mr. Sennett and Miss Mabel are havin it out on the arched faery-bridge since we got here. It would be fine if they yelled as usual and if, as usual, Miss Mabel hopped up and down and maybe kicked his shins. But she's stock still, he's stock still, and they're whisper-shoutin, if you know what I mean.

I nod toward them. "Us kids don't like it when Mommy and Daddy fight."

"Makes for an uneasy atmosphere," says Mr. Coy Watson.

He looks down at the viewer on his camera, sizes Mommy and Daddy up, clicks the shutters. Says me, "It ain't right. You don't wanna leave people like us idle." I wink Mr. Coy Watson.

"Here goes nuthin."

I almost tippy-toe across the little island with its tall trees and high brush, and take my stand at the foot of the arched bridge. My plan is to look this way and that, just within hearin range, until Mommy and Daddy get annoyed and ask me my business.

They're at it with, "We need gravel for the 180s and tarmac for the spins," Mr. Sennett says, and Miss Mabel says back to him, "As if I don't know what it takes for a 180!"

"But," Mr. Sennett barks, "you've never driven either."

"Haven't I, though? You don't know everything, Nappy."

"Only thing I have to know is I told you no, and you didn't care. It comes to that. And something else. Don't know for how long I'll let you direct or even if I'll let you direct once more."

"You—announced—to the press—from now on, I direct my own pictures."

"We never signed anything. Look at you, five feet and a hundred pounds of skirt, bossing big men. They don't like"—

"Who don't like? Gimme names!"

"Bossed by a skirt not yet twenty! You've got to see how that could grate on a grown man. And again, I can't let an employee violate my directives. I can't run this menagerie if"—

"Employee? *I'm* an employee?"

"Mabel"—

"Too late now, Great Man. I am paid by Napoleon but I did not realize I was Napoleon's employee. Thought I am his fiancé."

"Damnit, that's not what I'm talking aboot. I am talking aboot running this studio and"—

"*We're* talking about those terrific scenes I've been shooting all week, bossing them as don't want a lassie to boss em. Catch," says she, without lookin at me, "why are you standing by listening to this nonsense?"

"Nothin else goin on," says me.

They look around.

"Time to go to work," says he.

"I just wanted to show you I could do it, Mack. That was all."

"I know."

"Okay?"

"Sure. Sure. And—this is no day for Madcap Mabel's firecrackers and such-like."

"You think I don't know that?"

"I'm sure I don't know what you know or don't know."

Then it was like in a Keystone script where you read "Flash to girl hangin from tree limb and kickin," cause these two characters flashed into two different people who are suddenly all smiles and good fellowship toward a tall young man upon whose head sits the largest possible bowler hat.

Grinnin wide and wavin this gentleman near, Mr. Sennett says under his breath, "Are we still sure this is a good idea?"

"Comfort thyself," whispers Miss Mabel. "The man can handle a car."

Handshakes all around and I'm introduced as a "rising star," and, "Don't mind the get-up on our Catch, she's a real looker." Me, I take my cues from the grown-ups and hope for the best.

I get from their pleasantries that Miss Mabel and Mr. Sennett attend prizefights regularly, where, just last night, they met the lanky Mr. Lewis Jackson, race-car ace, who stands before us now under his out-sized bowler and in his checkered suit. Mr. Lewis Jackson last night announced himself keen to pilot a Keystone paddy wagon dressed as a Kop, and how, if he liked *that,* he might "take a swing at the picture racket," while Boss and Miss claim to be glad he showed up after all and there's always extra Kop costumes and we're all sure he'll perform splendidly.

Says our racing ace, after a breath, "If you won't think me presumptuous, Mr. Sennett"—

"Mack," says Mr. Sennett.

"Mack," says our ace. "Now, that's fine. Mack, then. And I'm plain

Jackson to my friends."

"Jackson, then," says Mr. Mack Sennett.

"That's fine," says Jackson.

"Mabel," says Miss Mabel.

"Jackson."

"Fine," says Miss Mabel, smiling like an angel, "Most fine. Very fine."

Jackson don't know she's makin fun, but, oh, he nearly chokes as Mabel lights a cigarette out here in public in broad daylight.

"I, uh," says he, "I guess these movie gals are pretty fast, Mack."

"You're fast," says Miss Mabel. "Fast is your profession."

"Fast, I trust," says Jackson, "but not rough."

"Well, I hope we don't shock you," says Miss Mabel, "cause around here we deal in rough."

"There were no dukes on the Mayflower," says Mr. Sennett.

"Nappy's fond of that, uh, formulation. But weren't you going to say something presumptuous, or that you feared might be presumptuous?"

"If you'd really like me to continue?" says Jackson.

"That would be very fine," says Miss Mabel.

"Well, Mack, and, er, Mabel—that Griffith fellow, I suppose you know him? I thought you might. *The Battle of Edlerbush Gulch,* I viewed it two weeks past. People innocently stupid—that's the root of the whole story, that's what the story is about. Innocent stupidity is presented as the basic cause of our humanity's dilemmas. Why, there's nothing but emotion in the story—everybody doing one thing or another from emotion only. If I drove a race on emotion only, I'd be dead. And"—

"Speaking of thoughtful notions," Mr. Sennett says, "here we think till we laugh and we laugh till we think, and right now we've got a dilly of a comedy to shoot, so let's have at it and get you your Kop uniform, whataya say?"

"Why," says Jackson, "that's fine. Just fine."

Mr. Sennett takes the ace by the arm and guides him off while Miss Mabel pinches herself on the ass so's not to laugh but we both laugh anyway.

"He's cute, Catch, don't you think? Lovable as a smiling dog. I think I'll marry *him.*"

"He wasn't surprised you're a boy," says I.

"We warned him at the prizefights I wouldn't be dressed like a lady."

"You like to see men punch each other, hey, Miss Mabel?"

"The spectacle is dear to me."

Here where Edendale meets Los Angeles the population stirred itself up, crowdin Big Red trollies, takin mornin constitutionals, nannies pushin baby-strollers, urchins and tidier boys playin this-and-that and fishin. Plus Sommie, lookin unwell.

"It appears we're finally being organized," says he.

I nod toward an old gent sportin a perfect white Buffalo Bill moustache-and-beard, gold-topped cane, and a wide-brimmed gray hat slanted cocky. "What do you think of that citizen?"

"That's a cavalry hat. A Confederate officer's. No doubt raised a glass at the veteran's reunion last year's Fourth at Gettysburg's fiftieth anniversary nonsense."

"My Daddy's father was a Confederate. That's all I know of that whole side of the family."

"Blood tainted with cruel sin runs ever in my veins. At least the sea, and the stars above the sea, taught me my place—gradually. Look at boy-Mabel on tiptoe to kiss Mack publicly!"

He's pushin her off, she's tryin the more—he knows how it looks from any distance at all. "Mercy," says Sommie, "she can unnerve one."

Her fun with her fiancé concludes and Miss Mabel hollers like a steve-dore, "Catch! Get over here, Missy Actress, we're working. You, too, Sommie. Brickface!"

Jackson, in Kop get-up, was cool toward us as we gathered round them.

"It's as I've explained to Mabel," Jackson begins, "it may be 1914 and all, but they haven't yet made an auto that brakes worth a darn at over 20 M.P.H. Many streets hereabouts remain unpaved, and that's what we'll need for our 180s."

Mr. Sennett joins the gaggle.

"So," says Jackson, with a nervous nod to the Boss, "I shall take, uh, Mabel, take Mabel out and show her how it's done, and thus we'll leave nothing to chance."

The Boss spits a wad.

Jackson registers that, and proceeds. "Now on the first 180, Mabel, you watch my feet. On the second, watch my hands." Mabel's lookin at him grinnin with those big eyes. "Then, Mabel, watch my feet for when I gun it, when I brake, and when I quickly gun it again. You have control when you gun it, not when you brake. You gun it again to regain control. Then watch my hands for how I hold the wheel on the turn and for when I shift gears. Timing matters. You watch, and, while you're watching, feel it on your, uh, bum—if you'll excuse the reference."

"The reference is fine," says Miss Mabel.

"I'm not being vulgar," says Jackson.

"Why, you wouldn't know how," Mabel gushes. "Mack, Jackson has a college degree!"

Jackson blushes. "It's just the truth that your bum will know when to turn that wheel and hit that gas. Happens pretty quick. You follow me alright?"

"She follows you fine," says the Boss.

"It'll be a nifty, Mabel," Jackson says proud, "let me tell you, a nifty."

But Mabel now, she turns to Mr. Sennett like a different person, all business.

"Mack, I want that downtown skyline as background for this biz."

Him, too, all business. "I know a place."

"And I'll want tarmac for the close shots."

"On a 180? I thought we said"—

"When we do our close-shot biz with the camera car, we do it on tarmac. Pour a few barrels of soapy water on the street—we've brought that, right?" she says to Brickface. He nods. "And we'll spin and *spin the camera car,* turn that 180 into a 360 and a half, you see what I see?"

"Mabel, Madcap Mabel," says Mr. Sennett, "I don't know"—

"You do know," says she, "cause you see what I see. Brick'll adjust the tripod so the camera's lower on the close-shots, pointing slightly up, and that spinning camera car with a downtown background—our worthy ticket-buyers will see this city sway in circles! Talk about a nifty."

"Mabel," says Mr. Sennett, "I said I don't know."

"Ever see a shot like that before?"

"No."

"Anybody else? Sommie, get over here!" She tells him the shot. "Ever see that?"

"I wish I had."

"We've got to do it, Nappy. If none of us have seen it, nobody's done it. We can't think of something this good and not do it. Napoleon, we'll beat Griffith to it. You know you like that."

For reply, the Boss turned to the racer: "Teach her that 180 real good, Jackson."

Miss Mabel jumped up and down then linked arms with Jackson. Jackson got red and so did Mr. Sennett.

Mr. Coy Watson appeared from somewhere, for the whole crew saw that a Big Talk was happenin and that it would likely ricochet on all and sundry.

Mr. Sennett explained to Mr. Watson. "Can the camera-car take it? Spins—that's a lot of torque on that platform."

"We learned lessons on the Palisades, Skipper. We're rigged. The camera's clamped down steady, we've got hand-holds on the rails, the platform's bolted solid to the frame, and there's enough give in the wood so that the it'll sway without breaking—I think. I'm almost sure, Brick."

Brick's hangin on every word (and has not met my eyes once). Mr. Sennett steps close to him. "We've never done this. I still know how to grind a camera, you don't have to."

Brick grins. "Can't wait, Boss." That's the guy I once liked.

"Pardon," says Sommie, "but what if it's not a first? Maybe somewhere it's been done. Haven't I concocted sufficient violence?"

"Don't spoil things." That's Mr. Sennett, who winks Sommie a stagey big wink. He spits a great tobacco wad and gestures to the others with a nod of approval, then watches his fiancé and Jackson walk off arm in arm and surprises the lot of us by thinkin out loud.

"A nice white kid, this Jackson. That shanty-Irish vixen wants me to do something appalling, like knock his teeth out, so she makes with the big eyes. Just loves it when I appall myself." Spits another wad. "Let's make this happen, kids."

And off folks go to their jobs. Everyone's gotta be carted to that location, we gotta shoot, and be back for lunch.

Then Sommie, low voiced, to me. "That man Sennett was play-acting all along about our scenario being too this and too that, too expensive, too inter-ruptive, too dangerous. Look at him today—needed no convincing. A subtle sod, in his way. Wants everyone to be quite certain that if we kill ourselves it's our own bloody idea and he is absolved. But he'll be happy to facilitate the risks, the more the better—all for profit, all of it. He's supposed to love that woman, and look what he allows! With you, too! The two best people in the world, and for what?"

I blushed.

Sommie's on with, "Don't think for one instant that I am hypocrite enough to feel superior. I take the man's money, don't I? And I want to see the damned 360-and-a-half as much as anyone, don't I? I am a bloody movie, aren't I?"

"Catch! Hey, Catch!" Miss Mabel's bellowin again. "Here with me, girl! Ride the back seat while Jackson gives me lessons."

She made sure her fiancé heard that.

I run up to them.

Says Mabel, "You gotta get the feel of the 180's too, girlie. We won't rehearse your biz. You just get the feel and be ready to play with the feel when it's camera time."

I understood every word and was proud to.

Between you and me, I don't believe Miss Mabel Normand needed any racecar driver's pointers. If I'm any judge, she's been off on her own in her Stutz every chance, gettin the feel, as she says. She's been stirrin things up, is all, like she always does.

So we 180'd around some with Jackson, me thrown side to side in the back seat as the city of Los Angeles spun and spun about us, and then it's Mabel and me alone, me with her in front, spinnin and shootin that biz for real, so by the time we're set for the 360-and-a-half we're dizzy-silly fools who hit that soap slick and spun fast-and-faster, Brick's on the spinnin camera-car's platform hollerin for pure joy, same as we're hollerin, same as the whole damned crew's whoopin and yodelin, all of us movies, we know how it'll seem on the screen, a great big modern city swirlin and spinnin with us round and round past all reason.

LUNCH TIME'S GONE ON TOO LONG. We shouldn't relax this much, it's makes me nervy. Nervier. Timin's everything in how we do, and I say that includes timin lunch. Too little, we're frazzled. Too long, feels like no one's in charge.

Lookee there, three actual police officers sit on the grass with our Kops smokin and laughin. Some Kops gamble at cards, but those officers don't mind. Our women smoke in broad daylight. It's ok with these police. The City Fathers may exclude us from their brochures but "the department," as it's called, knows Keystone makes many a personal donation to its constabulary.

Echo Park is in full swing and Keystoners have pretty much taken over its northwest lawns, benches, and tables. The rest of the park is, well, park-like; not crowded, just populated. Respectable people behavin respectably, gloved and bonneted ladies carry parasols, gloved and bowler'd gents sport walkin sticks, and workin folk are clothed to their station. One circle of ladies on the grass passes a book around and each takes her turn to read aloud. Two old whiskered fellows fish from a peddle-boat in the middle of the lake. It's fair to say—and it doesn't speak well of us—we movies don't care much for our fellow citizens except for how they do-or-don't suit as picture background. Background they are, and background they'll always be. We couldn't live like them or we'd be doing it. Is it only me that thinks it's strange, how more and more they line up to see our pictures?

Then there's Mr. Coy Watson, bent under the hood of the winch-truck. Somehow he steps from us movies to those others and back again without strain or change.

I turn round and there, on the island, on a park bench, sits resplendent Esther readin a book. We tend to keep our distance on this shoot out of respect for Mr. Sennett's wishes and mostly his hawk eye and that way he has of suddenly showin up. But I don't feel like distance, so I step out onto the flat bridge that's above the lotus pond, where barefoot boys sit on polished tree-limb railings and fish with polls whittled from branches. One kid under a worn straw hat and wearin faded overalls, he fishes with just a string. Several wear quality leggins and jackets, and a kid with a skimmer sports a bow tie. Not one is older than eleven and I bet any of them could be the son Daddy wanted. They don't notice boy-me cept to look away. I'm a newsie, rougher and older and lower-classed, so they pretend I'm invisible but haven't the sand to pull it off and don't meet my stares. As for the respectables, I'm not worth lookin at, a no-account who'll always be no-account.

Hey, I'd pulled it off. Bein real boy-lookin, I mean. I'm foolin these boys. Like I'm showin Daddy I coulda done it, I had it in me somewhere. It just wasn't strong, Daddy. There wasn't enough of that boy. He got swept away by everythin else in me. I like him, I see now—the little enough there was of him. But there wasn't enough *him*, Daddy, and there was a whole lotta me.

It's warmed up with that desert wind and Esther's gotta be sufferin in that mink, though it's as open as can be. But even a Keystone movie can't walk about Echo Park in lingerie.

"Didn't you bring overalls, Es? It's gotta be hot under there."

"This is probably the only day ever that I can walk about like this in daylight. It's worth a little suffering. And why, may I ask, are you walking around so boyish? We revealed your hair several set-ups ago."

"Somethin like you—this is the last day I'll look this. What you readin?"

She showed me the cover. *The Iron Heel—Jack London*. "Mabel gave it to Sommie who gave it to me. It's a man writing a novel as though he's a woman keeping a journal about the destruction of the working class. The working class really gets it in the neck. Makes me delighted I'm rich. And you! You are a subject of gossip amongst us. Seen this morning in conversation with Sennett. Had the gall to interrupt Sennett and Mabel in the midst of their argument. You're Mabel's favorite, they're saying. Meaning, Watch-out,-Esther!"

"But Esther knows better?" says me. "Burns to do unspeakable things with only me, right?"

"That is so very true."

"I can't kiss you here."

"I know."

"Bye."

"Bye."

The island is little and heavily shrubbed and there's tall thick palm trees and it's an *island,* first of my life! Still and all, I'm antsy we ain't workin yet. It don't help that I step around a clump of high brush and here are the Beerys at picnic. I hear it before he says it. "Well, na'ow." He goes on with, "Here we meet again in an idyllic-like settin, and we're peaceful colleagues na'ow, you and me, and nobody's pointin pistols. Told Glow'ree all about that, didn't I? And where are my manners! Glow'ree, this here is"—

"Everybody knows who she is."

She stuck out her hand for a shake.

"Hello, Willie. Anywhere else I'd introduce myself as Miss Swanson, professionally, or Mrs. Beery, in actual life, but here at the Keystone it's Gloria. Not, may I mention, Glow'ree."

"Na'ow, that's my cute name for ya, is all, and only mine."

We shake hands firm, she and I.

"Pleased to meet you, Gloria."

"Likewise."

"What are you doin with this lug?"

"Learning all about life, can't you tell?"

She's a little thing, no older than me and maybe younger, with a strong chin, strong nose, frank eyes.

"Na'ow, Glow'ree, don't Catch here look like a very boy?"

"Of course she does not. Not to me."

"Might not to you, dearie, on accounta you seen her as herself—and I'll grant you a point that in close-up she would not look a boy. Queer thing."

"Willie," says Gloria, "I may call you Willie? Thank you. Don't mind my husband. He means well, but his notions of charm are—what word am I searching for?—unique."

Beery gives himself a stretch that puts him a little behind her, and from there Beery gives me such a look. Like he's measured me for sale and knows my weight.

Sommie is smart in his way, Miss Mabel and Esther are smart in theirs, and Mr. Sennett surely is smart, but Beery—Berry's smarts are like Mother's.

"Dear, what's wrong?" That's Gloria.

"Somethin I ate, of a sudden, I suppose. See you two in front of the camera, hey?"

"Fetch yourself a bicarbonate'a soda, na'ow," Beery says after me. "Can't have you dizzy on a day we're out to pull the devil's tail."

There it is again, how that man knows all about me and has told no one, I'll bet, not even his Glow'ree, but always he manages to let me know he knows.

And listen to him sing!

"And he HUNG his hat upon the FLOOR'RRRR!
WHAT an af-ter-NOOOOON!"

"Wallace, pipe down!" says Glow'ree.

"Sor'ree, Glow'ree. Hard to contain myself. But you love that bout me, don'tchya?"

"Hush," says she.

There's Miss Mabel on the arched bridge. Her hair's down and her newsie cap sits atop it.

As for my hair, I didn't have to wear this cap this way today. Es is right, we shot the last of Boy-me yesterday—I'm on the bike, I grab onto a truck to keep up with the chase, a what's-it on the truck hooks the bike, I jump to a streetcar, swing on the rod, hang down from the rod as Miss Mabel's car and Esther's fly by, doin biz like I'm surprised they went by so fast—and I land in Beery's car, flop into his front seat, which knocks the cap off my head, my hair flows out and he's happy tryin to goose me and drive (and he did, for the picture—it's not really us, it's the picture). By the time I'm in Miss Mabel's car doing 180s and 360s-and-a-half, my girlish nature has been exposed. So—I took off the cap and pins and all to do this morning's biz, which kicked up lots of dust, and I was thinkin it'd be a long night of hair-washin and brushin, and then—pinned up my hair again kind of without realizin. Saw myself doin it and just kept on doin it.

Miss Mabel's on the arched faery bridge, tappin her fidgety feet as her fidgety hands pat the railing. Looks at me harsh. "What are you wearing that thing for?" Takes the cap from my head, side-swipes it into the lake, and pulls out my hairpins with, "You shoulda done this at lunch, Catch, I'm surprised at you," and takes a brush from her belt and takes to brushing through the knots, ouch, and as she does so she talks fast.

"Napoleon received a big important business telegram about a thousand words long and he's urgently at the Western Union making a big important business reply. 'No help for it, Mabel,' he says, 'back in a jiff.' A jiff has come and gone and I've waited as long as I'm gonna. What were you wearin that cap for?"

"Whimsy," says me.

She brushes hard and harder. "Your hair is a prop. It's gotta fan out. Keep this brush close and brush every chance you get. And we are done with this waste of good light."

So sayin, she strides like a captain onto the island. "Beery! Swanson! Let's go!" Passes Esther's bench. "Big Es, saddle up." And as she's crossin the flat bridge to where the Keystone's sprawled about on lawns and benches she yells out, "Brickface, where the FUCK are you?"

The fishin boys damn near fall into the lotus pond.

Every face in sight is wiped clean of expression.

She's on the east shore, has everyone's attention, and what with those lotus flowers fannin out behind her on the waters and how the waterfall of her hair flows down to her bum with Miss Mabel in boy-pants and boy-shirt, Mr. Coy Watson's delighted and stiflin a laugh, Brick's at attention with a crisp salute, Big Es beams with pride at her captain, and poor Racin Jackson in a Kop costume looks like a child slapped for no reason.

"Are there grown men here who mind a boss who's a woman, raise your hands, I want a look at you. No hands. No balls. I like that in my men. Actually, I don't. Anybody here remember what this picture's about? Wally, Esther, me, and the Kops drive into the lake after Catch saves the baby, and the last shot is she and me riding into the distance on bicycles that apparently come out of nowhere cause in the scenario our bikes are long gone, but not to worry, every scene has to make a kind of sense but the picture doesn't. Very like life, I regret to say. Now listen good. We've got a lot to do and we're late but I chose great locations, the shadows will be on our side as the sun heads west. Dangerous biz today! Don't do anything you're afraid of or you will FUCK IT UP."

Civilians scatter, cept the fishin boys, who don't know whether to pee or throw rocks. The real cop who's been pal'y with our Kops, he beholds this tiny pretty woman bellowin the forbidden word loud as loud—he'd arrest a man for that but what's he gonna do with Miss Mabel Normand? Just stand there, is what, and look the other way.

"Positions in fifteen minutes, and I mean fifteen. Brickface and George with the cameras, follow me." And to me, soft, "That was fun. Nappy's gonna get so many complaints from every church! Keystone won't be allowed to use any park in this town for a month, no matter whose hand Mack greases. Sonofabitch strands me to show me who's boss, hey? Bet he won't do that again."

We'd shot the skid-and-spin scenes this mornin, plus closer shots while spinnin. Yesterday, we shot "inserts," as they call em here—other lots are callin them "close ups"—plus close biz in the cars, "reaction" shots, they call em. That's not really how you'd want to. You'd want to shoot the big action so as to place your reaction-shots once you see how your action plays, but today's schedule is not normal cause Mr. Sennett wanted to direct the finale himself on his personal schedule, not the picture's. If that's confusin, it oughta be—confused the daylights outa us.

So anyway we're done with givin the baby to Gloria and done with Miss Mabel and me bike-ridin into the distance. What's left is the really hard stuff.

The scene now, Gloria has already dodged the cars and bumped the baby stroller on the curb, and the baby's flown out with the bump—which we shot backwards, lobbin the baby *into* the stroller at the bump. Run the footage forward, it looks like Baby got bounced high out of the carriage. Baby, of course, is a doll.

Just a doll, but the character I play don't know that. She's dead set on catchin Baby no matter what. That's where I am right now. I have to catch Baby, it's all I can think about.

The biz is on tarmac so we don't kick up dust. This one's too dangerous for dust in our eyes.

Here's what's mine to do: Grab the top of Wally's windshield, hoist myself up, right foot on Wally's seat to left foot on Wally's passenger-side door, push off from there into the air, catch the baby, twist in the air, and land in Mabel's rear seat on my back— and it's all shot by the camera car that's right behind us, about ten feet behind. Naturally the three cars gotta be "in sync," as they say.

Brick's on the camera-car platform, grindin. Hank Mann'll throw Baby at just the right instant for me to catch it cause, next to Roscoe, he's the most accurate thrower of pies, babies, knives, whatever needs throwin.

Sommie's on the camera platform too, grippin two hand-holds. He's makin himself do this cause he thought it all up and needs to suffer for it. He'll probably throw himself under the wheels if anything happens to me.

Roscoe said one time, "Doin the things we do, your mind's gotta be fourteen feet ahead of your body if you want to stay in one piece." Just as the biz is about to go I see that we didn't think hard enough, but in a heartbeat the baby'll be in the air and there's nothin for it but to do it.

What I just seen is that Miss Mabel's gotta look ahead, drivin pretty fast, which means she can't see me, she can't know exactly when I'm jumpin. She's gotta keep her car perfectly timed with Wally's and not fall behind or get ahead even a bit or I'll land on her car and not on the seat. Wally's gotta do the same, cause the only way Miss Mabel stays steady is if outa the corner of her eye she's got Wally to go by. And me, when I jump my eyes gotta be on that baby, to catch it clean, so I can't look at Miss Mabel's car, I can't be sure where I'm landin. If I hit her trunk and roll off the back, Brick's camera car shall run right over me.

Mabel and Wally can't see me. When I'm in the air catchin Baby and twistin round and coming down backwards, I can't see them. This is crazy.

Is anyone else seein what I'm seein?

You may not believe all that went through my mind in a blink but it did. You do some serious stunt biz, you'll see what I mean.

There's just this one sliver of a moment when I could call it off but I don't.

Mabel's signal to throw Baby is she'll swerve the car just a little—and now she does, Baby's in the air, I do what I do, I'm in the air, twistin some as I make my catch like Baby's a football and—in what I do, you learn how much can happen in the blink of an eye and how much you can feel and how deeply you can feel it durin what is really no time at all. I am terrified. So terrified.

But gotta catch Baby.

I've caught Baby and I'm goin down backwards with my eyes full of sky.

I hit smooth as silk. We were perfect, all of us. But the terror didn't go nowhere. Stayed tight inside me.

Miss Mabel veers off away from Wally, slams on the brake, we skid, she looks back at me with those big eyes afraid—"You're alright!?"

"A-ok, Miss Mabel, and let's don't ever do anything like that again."

"What were we thinking?"

"I realized just when it was too late," says me. "Did you?"

"I did," says she. "Seemed too late to call it off. Did it seem that way to you?"

"Pretty much. But Miss Mabel—Brick better've got that shot, cause if he didn't—I'm no coward, but I can't do that again."

"I wouldn't let you." She looked up. "Brick's giving us the thumb's up! Sommie's puking over the side. Alright, then. One more and we're done."

Oh. Right. We ain't finished yet.

"Next one's not so hard, Catch. For one thing, we'll be able to see each other. I will *never* do biz again with my back turned to what's really going on." Then she adds, "I wonder if there is such a thing as 'never' in our business."

"Well, na'ow, you ladies." Wally Beery's standin there holdin his hat and, I swear, his eyes are wet. "This hat's off to ya, I'm all admiration, and if there's any man anywhere more brave than you, why, I hope I never have to face him."

"Thanks, big guy," says I.

We grinned. Then his hat's back on his head, and with a touch to its rim he goes off singin once more about the man who hung his hat upon the floor.

In minutes we're ready for the next thing.

"Nothing to this one, right?" says Miss Mabel.

"Miss Mabel, who was it told me every time you leave the ground you better believe it's important?"

"*Moi.* So this biz is?"

"We're gunnin for the lake, I don't want Baby to drown, I toss her in the air, jump after her, catch her—she's in my sight the whole time—I twist as I catch, land flat on my back on the grass, so's I skid, roll with the fall till I rest on my back like I've done more than once."

"All I get to do is drive into a lake," says Miss Mabel. "You'll have all the fun."

She smiles at me with that particular smile that makes you just know she's an angel.

Here's Brickface. "Mabel, my camera can stay tight on Catch from when she jumps to when she's at rest on the ground and holding up the doll—that way you don't have to drive into the lake today. We did that master shot yesterday. So—we don't need your close lake shot."

"That does make sense, Brickface, but—I kinda need to drive into that lake."

When I'm goin good I just think it and my body does it. I tossed Baby into the air, leapt at her—Baby's a her, of course—caught her like a football about eight feet off the ground, twisted, straightened—straight but not stiff, never stiff—straight so's my weight hits even—and landed flat on my back on the grass easy as you please, landed so good there was no need to roll cause the arc of the fall sent my laying-down body on a grassy skid. Not that bruises won't swell up and not that I won't ache in places, but not very much and anyway you don't feel it when you're goin good, not till next day. When it's goin good all you feel is the good.

I didn't see no reason to move. My work was done, the grass was sweet, and this is silly but Baby felt good cradled in my arms all safe.

It'll look great on screen, my hair fannin out behind me on these jumps. Lookin straight up all I see is sky and a little bit of tree off to my left. Clouds pass high with nothin to do but be clouds. On this lawn I got nothin to do but be as I am.

I hear children splashin as a Red Car clangs by on the Alessandro line. I hear Keystone voices callin out this and that. They're spreadin two barrels of soapy water on the northwest corner of the park, sorta on my left, and that's so's the Kop paddy-wagon can spin and skid with Kops hangin off all sides. Mr. Sennett says you just about have to stick a skiddin paddy in a Keystone picture now, people expect it. Next time I'm a boy I want to be a Kop and do just silly biz. Maybe a picture about a gal pretendin to be a Kop? Two Kops? Mabel and me? Not a bad notion.

You know how in dreams one thing changes into another just-like-that? Happens all the time in life too.

Just-like-that, screech-sounds so terrible—people screechin, metal screechin—crash sounds, screams, and somethin blows up and as I turn to look my left side gets hit so hard it knocks the breath out of me and as I gasp somethin . . . somethin slams my head.

Felt like nothing but surprise at first. Then there's hammerin in my head, lights flash behind my closed eyes, then—terrible pains in my side.

Hard to breathe, hurts to breathe.

It comes to me like a strange message from a far place—I'm injured. I'm hurt. And there's nothing for it now but to hurt.

Oh, dear.

Doesn't occur to me to move. Don't know can I or can't I. Just want to lie still. It's two pains to breathe, one pain breathin in, another breathin out. Pains announcin themselves all over now. In my head—I never felt such.

Open my eyes and look straight up like before. Blurry. The movin clouds, their movin makes me wanna puke. The puke comes up and I swallow it down and I cough, swallowin and coughing hurt me so inside.

What could the puke be? I don't eat when I'm workin, but some ice cream if there's ice cream around. Shut up. You're a hurt person that's never been hurt before, not like this, so shut up.

I know what it's like to have two minds. This is more like three. Four. Cause it's like I split up inside myself. There's one of me that can hear real clear—through the tinny-buzzy sound that I also hear and that is very annoyin. There's one of me who is very scared. There's another of me sayin, Hold on to yourself, it's really not so bad. That voice, she with her Hold-on-to-yourself, she's who I'm tryin to listen to.

I suppose the part of me that's listenin is still another part.

Hold on to yourself.

I wonder if I'm bleedin. Can't tell. You'd think I'd know.

Nobody's noticed me.

Wait, now someone has.

"They're calling for help. You lie still, little girl."

I'm not a little girl, don't call me that. I'm a big girl. Who can't say anything.

"I seen what happened to you. That paddy-wagon, it just blew apart, in all directions. The pieces that hit you, well, just be glad they landed yards away and skidded at you—if they'd hit you direct, you'd be dead. Curved part of a fender—it's right here"—I guess he knocked it, sounded like a dull bell—"it landed hard over yonder, skidded a good ways, conked your head just at the end of its skid. Can't figure what hit your side, it's all twisted up—I suppose by the explosion. I was looking at you cause I thought you had to be one of these picture people. I was looking already, so I saw."

Didn't open my eyes to see him. Tried to say "Thanks" and must have managed it cause the voice said, "There, that's good. If you can hear me you'll probably be fine eventually."

Eventually. I thought that was funny and chuckled but chucklin was not funny, it hurt.

Now I'm hearin one—two—more—several more—ambulance bells clang-a'clang-clangin, hoof beats of their horses on packed ground and tarmac, bells of fire wagons, a heavy engine, now a strong voice with, "Clear the street! Give the engine room!" A fire-wagon that's a truck?

More horses. Different hoof beats. They're carryin riders. Police, must be.

"I'm going now to tell an ambulance crew you're hurt. Cause it looks like you're just lying here peaceful—and you're a little far from the baddest trouble so they won't know to come to you. Then I'll be back."

My heart froze up. I wanted to yell for him to come back but no yell came out.

Ambulance means hospital. Oh, oh. Oh, please God, please, please God not a hospital. They'll take my clothes off and they'll see and they'll make it awful. I just wanna be Willie. Let me be Willie some more. Not a hospital, please God.

Either that or let me die. Right now.

You know my heart, Lord. You know I mean it.

Amen.

And there's that one part of my mind that is infuriatin in its certainty and keeps sayin, Hold on to yourself, girl, you hold on to yourself now.

How did I get in so much trouble just lyin peaceful on a lawn?

"Ok, now, little girl." It's that same voice. "Ok, now. Ambulance men are coming. I see them come, they know you're here and hurt, and now I must go. I have my duties. Good luck."

I moved my fingers like to wave him bye-bye to that kind heart who is ruinin my life.

More clangin. More horses. Excited voices. But not the voices of Esther—Miss Mabel—Sommie—I don't hear them—oh please be alright.

Young man's voice: "Lie still, girlie. We're gonna pick you up, we're gonna put you on a stretcher. Can't see what's wrong, but a Park Attendant told us what happened to you. I don't see much blood. Hold real still now."

Hospital. I'm bawlin like a baby and it hurts so bad to cry.

"Don't touch that girl, you two. I mean it."

Esther!

"Who'ah there, lady. Put that thing away."

"I am in dead earnest. This girl is my private patient."

I turn a tad, which is expensive in pain, and, fuzzily for me, there's Very Big Esther, mighty in her nighty get-up, a head and some taller than two gents she's facin, pointin her *pistola*. Someone grind the camera.

"I am Doctor E.H. Heinz, M.D., Ph.D., this girl is my responsibility, under my protection."

"A lady doctor? A giant undressed lady doctor with a gun?"

She rattles off a mouthful of twenty-dollar-gold-piece words about my "condition."

"Have it your way, lady doctor."

"Leave the stretcher."

"We got a job to do, lady doctor. There's lotsa people hurt. You're not gonna shoot me. We're taking the stretcher."

Her blurry face fills my eyesight as she leans down.

"I didn't do anythin, Esther, and I got hurt."

"I know, sweetie, I see that. Just lie still."

Very lightly with those big hands and strong long fingers she touches my head all over. Some spots hurt lots.

"You surely have a concussion, and likely a fracture. You've got to lie still."

"Really a doctor, my Esther."

She's feelin me all over lightly.

"Move your hands from side to side, just a little. Wiggle your fingers. Move your feet from side to side. That's all very good. Your pulse is fair. Not erratic or thready. Good sign."

Puts her ear to my heart. Feels around my chest and I scream. Presses my stomach.

"Does that hurt, your stomach?"

"Everything hurts. It hurts bad, Es."

"But when I press your stomach, does your stomach have a special pain?"

"No."

She pokes and asks the same here and there.

"Cracked or broken ribs, probably both. If you were bleeding inside you'd be very pale by now. Could have been very bad, but I don't think it is, not very. Open your eyes. I've got to leave you for a few minutes. I'm coming back with my car. Everything's crazy, there's fire equipment and ambulances, crowds gathering, so it may take a little time. You look nice and peaceful. You bled a bit at the head but it's stopped and I've arranged your hair over it, no one should notice. Ambulance men should leave you alone. If they don't, don't worry, I'll find you and get you home. I promise. You're under my protection. Remember that. And lie still. Just lie still. Gotta find something to pillow your head." She was gone only a little bit. "Here's somebody's picnic blanket."

"You stole it. They'll think I did."

"Remember. Lie still but—this is very important—don't fall asleep. Understand?"

"D'Varn got under your protection too?"

"She did. And what did I just ask you to understand?"

"Get some good sleep, right?" I winked her.

"You are impossible. Just do what I say. Back soon."

I'm still holding Baby. I'm gonna keep her. Daddy broke all my dolls that Mother had made when I had my fifth birthday. Now I have a doll again.

"On my mother's grave, Mabel, that's how it was." It's Mr. Sennett's voice.

"Nappy, I'm so sorry, did your mother die? Why wasn't I told?"

"You know what I mean."

I don't let them know I can hear. I'm so ashamed I got hurt. Don't want them to know.

"Some Western Union kid, uniform, cap and all—maybe ten years old— hands me a disaster, a thousand-word telegram from New York. Panic— they're struck dumb with panic at *Tillie's* over-costs. I had to nip that in the bud. Couldn't give them even one afternoon to think. I needed a renewed commitment to *Tillie* and I needed it today. You won't believe what I had to promise them. But Mabel—you gotta believe how sorry I am that this happened to you."

"Didn't happen to me, Mack. Happened to Jackson, and to George, and to a woman buying a flavored ice from a Dago pushcart. A piece of flying paddy-wagon got her. Nobody's fault. Couldn't be helped. Paddy-wagon's front tire blew just before Jackson hit that soap slick. Skidded all over that soap slick on the axel and the front end just collapsed into itself. I saw the steering column jam Jackson the moment before the engine blew apart. George was still grinding film when the whole smoking mass of wreckage barreled like a steam-engine toward us both. I made it out of the way. George didn't. Jackson—he met us last night and because he met us he's dead today.

That's fine, isn't it? Very fine."

"Mabel."

"We're not good for people, Mack."

"He caught a bad break."

"The Kops got out alright, I don't know how. Some sprains and breaks, nothing terrible. I don't know how many civilians got hit by this and that. Are we in trouble with the law? Am I?"

"There are no laws about bad luck. You're going about your business and get struck down by a piece of bad luck. What's the law got to do with that?" Then: "George, Jackson, that woman—let's find her name. We'll give the families five thousand a piece. As the decent thing. Two thousand. Three— three thousand. Let New York write me more telegrams."

I opened my eyes. Mabel's eyes, they were closed. She was on her knees making what papists call the Sign of the Cross.

"I like your teeth, Miss Mabel." She opened her eyes. "Small and even in front, then two big dog-teeth, like they're for a taller person."

"Catch! I swear, there's so much going on I didn't even see. You alright? You sleep through all this?"

"Big Esther is a doctor."

"Cause if you're ok, there's a great piece of biz I thought we can do, and we can do it right now—a terrific ending, better than the stuff we shot yesterday. We ride bicycles down that sloping side-street straight at the camera! Getting bigger and bigger on the screen as though we're riding straight into the audience! We zip by the camera, you and I, on either side. The end. No one's done that, that I've seen, not on bicycles. Up to it?"

"Course."

"Mabel!" says Mr. Sennett. "That's not how we honor the dead."

"Mack, it's a great shot. We spend the rest of the week splicing at night while we shoot *Tillie* days, put *this* negative on the train to New York, they get it early next week, a great new picture, full of thrills and ahead of schedule— and they'll shut the fuck up."

"That's my Mabel," Mr. Sennett says. "That's my girl."

"Brickface! Brickface!" she's callin out. "The camera, pronto, loaded. Send somebody for a couple'a bikes. Buy them out from under folks if you have to. Pay em anything."

I'm thinkin kinda dreamily how Es isn't gonna like this.

Mabel extended a hand and I took it and fixed a smile on my face and she pulled and I stood. Oh, my God. The pain. But I keep my smile. I'm split into pieces again, cause the pain is over there and I'm over here. It hurts very bad, but I'm not where it hurts, though I can feel it. My left side's stuck full of knives. My head's hammerin. Vision's fuzzy. I blink some, it comes back, it goes away. But it's all like it's happenin to somebody else, like I'd loaned somebody else my body and I was just off somewhere watchin. Somebody in me faintly warns that Es is gonna be pissed, you shouldn't do this, but nobody listens to that somebody.

It's better when I can hang on the handlebars of the bike and walk. The pain happenin to this other me is awful, but it's not happenin to me who's walkin a bike.

While Mabel and her Mack yak about the shot, Brick positions the camera about half a block away down a steep-sloped side street. We'll ride at him. There's an ambulance near where we're waitin—it's harnessed with such fine horses. All I can think is, "What fine horses." They're loadin a bloody mangled man on a stretcher and I'm thinkin how pretty are those white horses.

Now the part of me that's watchin is sorta alarmed that I'm actually gettin on this bike. Then sorta surprised I can. Then sorta amazed, cause I'm ok on the bike, we're ridin side by side, Miss Mabel and me, and all of a sudden nothin's hurtin, we're pickin up speed, our hair's fannin out behind, it's easy—looks easy—I'm sorta watchin—we speed by either side of Brick-face crankin that camera, Miss Mabel's got the shot she wants, but now the damnedest thing—I sorta pass out with my eyes open. I'm headed straight for the broad side of a four-horse haulin wagon. Somebody's screamin my name. So is someone else. I am gonna hit that wagon. I'm kinda not seein it and I kinda am. I'm goin straight for it and I kinda don't mind.

THE NIGHTINGALES

WILLIE DIED. I didn't.

When I woke I knew not a yesterday, not my name, not a thing, not for a while—knew nothin cept the feel of bein cared for in a small clean room in Hotel Heaven. Soft voices nearby spoke sounds I couldn't place. Woke after that, now and again, in a floaty kind of way, then woke for real to feel small strong hands rub damp towels the length of me. Two bronze-skinned faces topped with white wing-tipped hats, white sleeves rolled up to tend me. They see I'm lookin. Faces radiant now, both small women, one in tears, sayin what sounded like, "Sammie! Sammie!"

There appeared above them—behind them—a taller white-faced woman garbed the same.

All three makin the Sign of the Cross several times apiece.

"Welcome, you," said the white woman. "Oh my. Such an event. I am Sister Joan. These are Sisters Alma and Maria. Do you understand me?"

I nodded.

"Don't try to speak. You haven't in years and it will probably be painful. We must get you stronger, now you're awake. Our vocation is to care for infirm nuns, so you're something of a unicorn here. Forgive my breathlessness, but it isn't every day our prayers are answered with a yes."

Days and nights more. Watchin green lizards scurry sometimes up or down the bumpy white-washed walls. Massages. Gruel. They were well used to cleansin what my body put out, but I wasn't, and I guess embarrassment was the first actual feelin I had, apart from dulled gazin. Of course they'd seen the all-of-me for some time, hadn't they?

To be told the year, 1922, the desert mild in November. To realize my right foot got lopped off above the ankle "quite a while ago, before you came here," Sister said. To be told I arrived at this St. Vincent's, in the Mojave

Desert, outside Vidal—arrived three years ago, my breaks old but my burns fresh—"You shouldn't have been moved, but no one thought you'd live so . . ." To begin to remember, and then to remember and remember—oh, God, that was peculiar. And to begin to feel, to have feelins within, was just awful—at first. To be told Sisters Alma and Maria were of a tribe in the hills that would tell no white person its actual name, nor translate its talk for whites, but that my burn-scars would have hardened, crippled me up twisty-like, but that Sisters Alma and Maria made a salve from desert plants they'd not reveal, and that's why my scars are soft and leathery. Sister Joan explained I'd been coma'd out, she didn't know how long, at the St. Vincent's "in that far city," as she enjoyed callin it, and it was a four-story hospital that burned and fell down upon me.

"You're tellin me a burnin building fell down upon me? Serves me right."

With that came my first sorta laughter. Which hurt, but couldn't be helped. Sister Joan was so happy I laughed that she cried, and Sisters Alma and Maria cried, then so did I cry.

Sisters Alma and Maria called me "Sah May," it sounded like, and would not say what it meant, only that it was good, and Sister Joan made it "Sammie." I'd got used to Sammie by the time I full-on remembered Willie. Wouldn't be fair to trap Willie in such a body as this, so I kept Sammie. They added Doe. Sammie Doe. Sammie the Gimp, I say.

In coma my hair turned silvery white—like Mr. Sennett's!—before I was brought to the desert, but whiskers never grew on my face, and only fuzz grew anywhere else, like always.

I couldn'ta weighed but sixty'ish pounds. Didn't ask for no mirror and they didn't offer.

Took a while to sit up in bed on my own. Took most of a year to walk, after a fashion, with aid of crutch or cane. When I asked Sister Joan what work I could do to help out, she said, "Mercy! I suppose you *are* well."

Find some way to be useful is the least a person can do—but, to be honest, I generally made a mess of tryin till I remembered I could sew.

My hands had made it through alright. The burnin stuck my left pinky to its neighbor, but my left hand worked passably regardless, and I'm anyway a righty. Worked to sew slowly, gradually, till my fingers remembered. Hems, tucks, pleats . . . embroider, knit, sew a seam that ain't obvious and won't split . . . needles and thread, iron and board, scissors, pins and an ancient fine Singer machine. Saint Vincent's needs in the way of sewin, soon I could do it all, and did.

Vidal was a smudge on the map, barely a village, but in the cooler months, and with Sister Joan's blessing, I set up the Singer and sew-kit on a little stand under Vidal's one shade tree, to earn nickels, dimes, and the occasional quarter for Saint Vincent's Of The Desert, its small clinic and smaller chapel, where I lived and where old nuns died and a priest outa Blythe celebrated Mass and heard Confession at irregular intervals. First I'm a movie, then a Catholic. Daddy's loss again.

Now and again I'd wonder of my sister Fred, trustin that, if she's alive, now and again she'd wonder of me.

Of course, I thought of Esther and D'Varn. Oftener, as time passed. "What am I?" I once asked them. They gave out a word and it made Willie glad. I imagine they'd be hard put to find a word for Sammie.

It was at my sewin stand I met Jo Earp. Jo for Josephine. This was late in the year 1925. Jo was in her sixties, I'd say, and carried herself like the beauty she'd been—garbed and coiffed for desert life, but there's the slant of her hatbrim, not to mention her cigarette, or how weekly she played poker with men at the general store where, Prohibition or no, she partook with them of locally distilled spirits. Proud, she was, of the small newly painted Vidal house she and her husband just bought —"The Marshall," as she always called him. "Together forty years and more," she'd say, "and that's the first place of our own," gesturin toward her home.

Jo Earp wasn't much for chorin. Hired out for housecleanin and laundry, I did their darnin, but she had to cook, this bein Vidal. The Marshall was, I'd say, pushin eighty, but six feet tall, ramrod straight, steady-eyed. One look was all it took to believe the tall-tales about him. Bein around them, I felt somethin like a movie again—cause they reminded me of how we movies was.

The Marshall mostly worked his mine claims up in the hills, made camp up there days on end. Jo liked campfire life, liked even to cook campfire style, but spent half her time in Vidal, lazyin about or readin newspapers and illustrateds sent her through the mails—publications which, without my askin, she'd pass on to me. First I'd seen since I woke. Sister Joan allowed none such at St. Vincent's Of The Desert and right off I could see why, especially the illustrateds. Page after page of every temptation. And I thought of tough newsie kids hawkin papers they got from newsstands and carried in shoulder-slung sacks, and of how, as Willie, I'd enjoyed to browse those stands.

When the desert burned hotter in the spring the Earps returned to that far city. When it got hotter yet, I put away my outdoor stand. Started it up again, under the shade-tree, late October. A week after I did so, the Earps returned. Sister Joan knew what was on my mind before I myself did. "Sammie, our Sammie, do you long for the world?"

"I do," I heard myself say. "I like it so well here but . . ."

"But you long."

"If you don't want me to go . . ."

"Only a free will can find God."

"A Rosary every day, Confession and Mass every week, I promise." I didn't believe or not believe, but I'd sooner cut off my one foot than break a promise to Sister Joan.

I'd picked up their lingo last winter, so, without invitation, I knocked on the Earps' door and asked straight out, could they "stake" me to a news-stand? In Los Angeles? With enough for me to clothe myself and rent a single room with its own bath? And, if they'd go that far, let's make our newsstand in a wonderful location! They'd own it and get all profits beyond my room-and-board and a monthly donation to St. Vincent's Of The Desert until I pay back the stake-plus-a-half, after which we'd split sixty-forty, with them on the sixty side.

The Marshall smiled with his eyes only.

"I guess you leap right in, don't you?"

"You might say that," says me.

"Sammie—I've taken poorer chances with lesser men. Josie, let's throw in a wood foot on the deal, what do you say?"

"To go with his hard head," she said.

The Marshall spit into the palm of his hand and stuck it out to shake. I did the same. Then me and Jo did.

The wood foot clomps good. Need a strong cane anyway, or a sling crutch, depending if there's rain. As for that far city—seems there's ten times the buildings, ten times the people, ten times the autos, and ten times fewer flowers and trees. Streets all paved. Air not near as sweet.

Back in the world where mirrors count for somethin. Broke nose. Jawline altered with a break, and cheekbones too, which makes my eyes set not quite right. Missin teeth. Not ugly, understand. I like to think of this face as . . . interestin. Slight of build as ever. The burn-scar on my face ain't bad, the pinky stuck to its neighbor don't look awful. My awfulest scars are out of public view. A silver head of hair is my finest feature, barber-shop cut. It's a shame to wear a hat upon it, but who's ever heard of a newsie without his newsie hat? Your store-bought shirts come with cuffs and collars now, fastened permanent. Jacket, tie, work-smock. Sammie the Gimp makes a noticeable, interestin impression, or so I prefer to imagine.

Course, there's pain always—but it moves around, this limb or that joint, and I manage. Wake in the night with pain, but I manage. You might say I'm dedicated to managin.

Now that I've had instruction as to what temptation actually means, I see that on a farm you gotta kinda make your own but in this far city it's bright in the open in all directions. So I wondered would the S-E-X stir again in me? Well . . . I recall fuckery sweetly, but like it happened to someone else. Some other body. That old S-E-X has been busted, crushed, burned and coma'd outa this body. Funny deal is, I don't miss it. I miss *them*. Esther. D'Varn. Sommie. Miss Mabel. But the Keystone ain't even in Edendale anymore. It's gone past Hollywood's hills out to Burbank.

Sammie the Gimp works the newsstand on the southwest side of Windsor and Melrose, catty-corner to the Paramount gate—a studio with a graveyard behind it, real handy. *PARAMOUNT PICTURES* is boldly carved upon the arch above the gate, which is what Famous Players moved and turned into, a walled city within the city that goes for blocks and blocks east-west-north-south, cept for that boneyard. Hundreds and hundreds of folks work behind Paramount's walls and hundreds of those hundreds step off the eastbound trolley right in front of our newsstand where it's, "Hiya, Sammie," from lotsa em as they buy "the trades" for "industry" news—they call picture-making "the industry" now. I've got tough newsie boys, a cigarette in every mouth, workin from this stand and hawkin the mornin, afternoon and evenin daily editions for blocks around. If there's a dispute amongst em, I am Judge and Jury, trusted to be fair to all parties. Since the Crash it's Hard Times, and they say how even mighty Paramount might go bankrupt. "We'll burn that bridge when we get to it," scrawls Josie Earp on a postcard from San Francisco, livin with her people, who are Jewish, and where she's buried the Marshall's ashes in a cemetery of her religion. He died last year.

Miss Mabel died last week. Of the tuberculosis, so they said.

Each daily, this Monday morning of March 3, ran the same photo of her casket on its way into the Church of the Good Shepherd, Beverly Hills, with her "honorary" pallbearers, whatever that means. Hard to make them out in the photo, except for Mr. Sennett, taller than the rest, tall as the Marshall. There's Devil Charlie, famouser than ever. Mr. Griffith, down on his luck, and Roscoe, whose luck crashed years ago. I guess they don't allow lady pallbearers, even honorary ones, but it says "attendees" include Marie Dressler, Mary Pickford, Douglas Fairbanks, Marion Davies, Wallace Beery, Gloria Swanson (they're no longer married), and, sure, D'Varn. At that name my chest got tight and got tighter. Had to ask Spider to take over, cause weekdays this newsstand ain't a one-man job. Spider's a newsie since age eleven, now he's a man grown, knows every quirk of our racket, and I pay him what I pay me. Told Spider I needed to take a walk. Around the block. He looked down at me from his height—"spider," I suppose, is for his long legs and arms—and he asked no questions cause you don't in our little world.

The "block" means south on Windsor to Clinton on the corner, east on Clinton to Plymouth on the corner, north on Plymouth to Melrose, turn right, and the next corner's our newsstand. It's a ways, with cane or slingcrutch—I use the crutch on my right, but it's slung around my left shoulder. I find that easier, not having to grip hard every step. It's a decent stroll for an able body, a hike for me. It's just . . . I need to breathe and you breathe deep crutch-walkin. It's just . . . those memories are where I want them, quiet but there, or in my dreams sometimes when I wake from doin some biz . . . I have a life, I don't need Willie's . . . I loved her life so much, but I love this one enough, it's lively in its way, it'll do, it does fine . . . Whoa there. I think I'm frightened. And so, so sad Miss Mabel's dead.

I'm comin up on Melrose, turnin right, I've gone far but my breath's even, lookin forward to water from the big clay jug Spider keeps filled in our newsstand's hut. He's parcelin out the afternoon editions to our newsie kids, they go forth in all directions, the ones comin my way touch a finger to their caps and some say, "Hiya, Sammie," and I put a finger to my cap as reply, and there *he* just is. Hatless as always. Hair grayed and thinned. Tailored clothing, high grade. A toff's cane. Maybe I fell and passed out on this walk and I'm dreamin. But no. This day of all days, it's him. I'm a little behind him. I say softly, "Sommie?"

He turns, a little alarmed, but he's got himself in hand: "Pardon me, did you say . . ."

He's lookin at me so hard while holdin back at the same time.

"So tell me," says me—"continuum or no continuum, betchya those absolutes still can't abide their relatives."

He's lookin.

"It's me, Sommie. It's me, I promise."

"Oh. Oh, my dear God. Willie."

Hearin the name was like . . . like nothin I knew ever.

Spider said, "Sammie? You back? Cause I gotta go soon."

"I know. Right with you, Spider. Gimmie two minutes."

Says Sommie, "We must speak, Willie . . . Sammie . . ."

"There's a restaurant, The Nickodell—see that big sign, cross the street, west down the block? Past the Paramount wall?" I'm pointin.

"Not quite, without my glasses, but I trust you."

"After the evenin edition, I'm usually there for my meal of the day, bout seven. If you're early or I'm late, tell em you're waitin for Sammie the Gimp, they know me, they'll get us a booth."

"So. Sammie the Gimp. The Nickodell. Under my nose. We have business to conduct, you and I."

"Biz?" says me.

"Business."

In the old way, no formality, he turns and hails a cab.

A waiter directed Sommie to my booth. As he slid in he said, "It's rather dark in here, isn't it? American restaurants are so often too bright." Swept his hand across the back and seat of the booth. "Red leather. Not likely to age well but, for now, how welcome. I am stunned to see you, cannot believe it, have not believed it all day since. It is you, I can see that, but . . . what? How? They told me you were dead. We've thought so since, naturally. D'Varn and I, I mean. Esther never knew. She'd been killed by then. Oh. I'm so stupid. Sorry."

I'd ordered welsh rarebit with a side of medium rare steak. I pushed both plates away.

"Killed?" says me.

"In the Great War," says he.

The waiter's here with, "Sammie, what's the matter with the food?"

"Hey, Hector, food's great. My stomach."

"I'll get you bicarbonate."

"Thanks, pal." Then, to Sommie I say, "The war?"

"Just as well I start there. Your accident—August 17, 1914—a date I do recall too well. Mabel was so wound up with the shoot she neglected to report you won. Her Panama Canal lottery of the Fourth? You picked August 15th. Which turned out to be correct."

He took an envelope from his vest and pushed it across the table. Upon it, "Willie" was written in swirly letters. Sommie says, "Open it."

I do so.

"Whew. Sommie, there's more than two hundred dollars in here."

"Three hundred thirty two. It was agreed that I'd be the one to keep track of you—after Esther left for the War—so Mabel gave me your winnings. There you are. The fire in that hospital happened after Esther's death. Many patients, many staff, dead. Injuries, confusion. You were listed as missing. And missing and missing. And from missing to dead. I kept your winnings. Certainly wouldn't spend it. And Esther's bank draft, though there were complications. Her instructions were, 'If Willie wakes up tell her I'm coming back and give her this.'"

Another envelope.

"It contains rather more than the first."

"What the hell, Sommie?"

"Five thousand, exactly. It was a bank draft, but she couldn't leave such a document to 'Willie,' as banks are rather persistent about last names. Thus it was in my name. But in late '27, 1927, D'Varn—whose financial acuity is as surprising as it is impressive—warned me a Crash was imminent. I cashed it to keep for—you, your ghost, I don't know. Her warning panned out. That bank has failed, like so many others. You will take a cab home, please? We can't have you robbed."

"Esther. Is dead, you say."

"I was beginning to say, but one's tangents have a way of . . . Yes. I started with your accident? Yes, and the European war began in earnest that very month. Esther was maddened by your situation, your coma, amputation— you slid under that huge wagon after you hit, fully loaded was the wagon, and a steel-rimmed wheel crushed your ankle. That first month she lost at least fifty pounds. I feared for her medically. She began building a house in the Hollywood Hills where you two would live—happily ever after, I presume. But she became obsessed with casualty figures in Europe. From early September to late October that year, '14, in just two battles, massive battles, more than three quarters of a million dead. History never saw such madness."

"Sommie, how—why—how did she die?"

"Overcome with an urgent need to be of use. You were beyond help. Please don't be impatient with me, it's . . . I'm telling my Willie the tale of our Esther's death, my God . . . Willie, Sammie, is here again, I'm talking to her, him, my dear God . . . With Esther's unexpectedly impressive resources, she outfitted a squad, as she called it, of ambulances, twelve, to be precise. A driver, doctor, and nurse per ambulance, all females."

Says me. "I wouldn't have let her do that alone. She was teachin me how to drive. I'd've gone with her and with her and with her."

"I daresay. Of course. Willie would. So. Esther was granted an officer's commission of major with the French, and of course she spoke French—and she was given more or less complete autonomy. By January Esther's reckless squad patrolled the Western front, wherever it was hottest. Got away with it for better than a year. Direct hit. Artillery barrage. Awarded quite a medal, posthumously."

"Hang on a minute, Sommie—I saw that picture."

"I wrote that picture. *The Nightingales.* That's what the troops called her squad, The Nightingales."

"I just thought D'Varn was bein sweet, playin a character named Esther. She was good, too, D'Varn. Not youthful anymore, harder eyes, better smile. Still real good. And oh, brother, you and Auntie D let Esther—in the picture—fall in love with what's-his-name!"

"John Gilbert. On loan from Garbo, in more ways than one."

"Esther woulda ripped auntie's hair out."

"Of course, Hollywood had changed with sound. We'd made the picture silent. Then the Warner Brothers gummed things up. Had to add a 'soundtrack,' music and gun effects. I did like the sound-scene we reshot, the soldiers entrenched, singing a song very popular during the war. *There's a long long trail a'winding . . .* I liked that."

"Hollywood," I said soft. "We remember when they didn't call it that, there wasn't a word for that, Hollywood was just a neighborhood. We made pictures, now they make movies. Used to be we were the movies."

"'God help the movies on a night like this,' Mabel would say in broad day. Do you go to pictures much?"

"Not much," says me. "What's so great about people talkin?"

Sommie suddenly goes pale, shaky, holds his chest, fishes in his pocket, downs some pills.

"That didn't look good," said me.

"It's not," said he. "Soon, it seems—but not this evening. I don't believe in God but I sometimes believe in Grace. What a gift this is. You and I, a conversation." Then, "I'm still admitted to D'Varn's presence—and she keeps me on salary, very good of her. Not that I haven't earned my way, but still. We've a ritual, and have had for some time. Sunday she sends a car to collect me, ten-forty-five A.M. I am delivered to her mansion in the hills for brunch, catered specially for her by Musso's, delicious food served at an unfailingly proper temperature. I am forbidden to speak of the past, but that's why I am there—so she may look at it, in my person. We talk of this and that. After perhaps two hours she calls me 'a good egg.' My cue to be dispatched."

"You won't tell her"—

"About you? No. Best not to overdo this gift, I think you'll agree. She had—a breakdown --playing Esther. Serious, actually. Not so tough as she was. Oh. I'm afraid I am very tired."

I paid our check out of my Panama Canal envelope.

"We'll talk again, Sommie?"

"Here! Tomorrow night. It shall be your turn to tell the tale."

We stood outside awaitin cabs to hale.

He looked me up and down.

"I never saw a wild thing sorry for itself."

"Sommie?"

"A small bird will drop frozen dead from a bough without ever having felt sorry for itself."

"Sommie!"

"David Herbert Lawrence, an unrhymed po'em."

A cab pulled up. Sommie got in. "Goodnight, Willie. And just so you know—yes, my relatives still fuss with my absolutes within that self-same continuum."

"Never doubted it," says me.

"Mind how you go."

THE FOURTH–1970

D'VARN'S BIRTHDAY. She's still up there, one of them lights in those hills. I've never cared to know which light. It's best that way. The hills are D'Varn's as long as she manages to live and why shouldn't they be? And me, I'm not so far down those hills in Hotel Hamblin here, on Flores, just below Hyperion. Got a third-story room with kitchenette and bath, where nothin blocks my view uphill north. Also got a east-facin view to a far horizon, where, as evenin darkens, I watch Dodger Stadium's fireworks, flashin colors ablaze over what once was Edendale, a name that's disappeared.

Echo Park, Silver Lake, Los Feliz, Chavez Ravine—they're where Edendale was.

That money Sommie gave me—I tried givin it to Sister Joan. A kind of expedition, hired a car and driver. She sat with that money-sack all night. Over breakfast gruel she was quiet, finished her bowl, then softly said, "God is our greatest gift. And then each other. And then poverty."

She separated a Jackson bill from the rest and said, "Thank you very much," and pushed that money-pouch back across the table. "Sammie, dear man, we must each know our place or find it."

Sent Sister Joan a Jackson a month for years, until one came back with St. Vincent's address crossed over and a thickly printed message on the envelope—*No one is here anymore.*

Esther had staked me to choose my own life.

Jo Earp was happy to be paid back and bought out, and Spider took my deal. He gets the newsstand and sends a check to a West Hollywood postal box address, ten percent of profits per month till he decides he's paid me fair. I spit in my hand and offered it for a shake. He did likewise.

See, I'd developed a plan. Stand on a busy corner all day for several years, you notice how people approach, with or without confidence, with or

"](

without an *eye-to-eye*—what they pick up and put down before they buy what they came for—and who looks at who gettin off the trolley, gettin on, passin in the street, and what's in the look. Learned from Auntie D to "study," study faces, postures, my own and others', and I'll tell you who's invisible in this world: older women—they look at each other, but folks pass them by and don't pay best attention.

I could be an older woman.

Took the train to San Diego, rented rooms near the depot, purchased everythin needed for sewin includin a new Singer—all from the Sears catalogue, all door-delivered. Patterns, materials, hats, bonnets, scarves. Dresses. Pretty shoes. Nice-lady canes. Practiced whittlin. Kept myself to myself. Finally ready, I carved down my wood foot so's to fit it into a nice-lady shoe. A little make-up. Primpin my hair some. Kept the name Sammie Doe. It was Sammie got this notion and deserved the name. People didn't keep track in those days, no Social Security numbers or anythin like that. Like I say, people don't look hard at white-haired women.

The Singer folded into its own case. Packed my clothes in a wicker valise. I'd tested out canes and settled on a strong, thick'ish model with a silver top. Sammie the Gimp, he'd get from here to there any old way. Miss Sammie Doe, maiden lady, she's one to walk straight, with a slight limp. Spent days in that little house walkin room to room to room—dayroom, bedroom, kitchen-dinette, till Miss Sammie Doe's posture got second-nature. Finally made arrangements by telephone. Boarded a train for Union Station. Took a cab to Hotel Hamblin. Tipped the cabbie a silver dollar. In those Hard Times, that was a real good tip.

Cab-fare was my biggest expense at first. If you showed up every day at MGM sooner or later an Assistant Director or Casting Director or Costume Designer, somebody or other, would pick you. If they picked you once, they'd likely pick you again. Show up and show up, sooner or later you're a regular. An extra. Background. In a year's time I worked whenever I wanted to, which was every day I could. Comfortable in my skin like I'd never hoped to be again. And some kind of a movie.

I took to extra- and background-actin real well.

When *Gunsmoke* went from radio to television, I walked those board sidewalks and across that one street I don't know how many times. I liked the Westerns especially, but maybe the last Western I'll ever do is *The Wild Bunch,* last year. Mr. Peckinpah, he picked me himself, as he knew me from his work on *The Rifleman* and *The Westerner.* Course, by then I had to limp a little more. I didn't have to play old cause I'd got old.

They shot that picture near Saltillo down in Mexico, where there ain't many old white ladies, so us extras got bussed down there to sing "Gather At The River" and limp along in the Temperance parade, where I supposedly get trampled by the Bunch, and I woulda done that stunt, I pleaded on it, but no, no, no, I'm not in that union. Probably just as well I wasn't allowed, but I'd never been stunt-doubled so I sulked some.

My God it was hot. Actors ate in a tent with an air conditioner powered by the production's generator. "Grunts," as they called us, found what shade we could, which was hardly any. My pal Bessie and me, we're sittin on the ground with our backs against a hot wall takin advantage of a foot or so of shadow, our boxed meals on our laps.

"Sammie, is he headed for us?"

"Seems so," says me.

William Holden smiled at us, a smile that could and did charm Audrey Hepburn right out of her panties.

"Ladies," says he, "may I interrupt?"

"I daresay, Mr. Holden," Bessie blushes, "I daresay."

"You *are* Miss Bessie Love, am I correct?"

Bessie couldn't make a peep.

"And who am I?" says I.

"A tough customer, I'd say," he smiles.

"You bet. Sammie." I stick out my hand.

He kisses it!

"And yeah," says me, "this here's Bessie Love."

"Miss Love, you worked with D.W. Griffith, didn't you?"

"That is correct, sir."

"Please, call me Bill. You played in *Intolerance.*"

"Bill—I was the Bride at Cana. Our Savior and His Mother were my family's guests."

"Miss Love"—

"Bessie, to you!" says she.

"Bessie, I am here on behalf of our cast to invite you to please join us and take your meals with your fellow actors."

With just the right glisten to her eyes, she tells him, "I'd be proud to. But Sammie too!"

"We'd be honored," says William Holden.

Bessie Love wasn't one to stay intimidated long. She had a tall-tale to tell for every meal.

Met Bessie Love twelve years back on the set of a "remake," in Cinemascope, with that deep velvety color you hardly see any more—Ava Gardner and Stewart Granger in, of course, *The Nightingales,* directed by Mr. Nicholas Ray, eyepatch and all. Miss Gardner's the only talkie actress who reminds me of D'Varn and handles her stuff like D'Varn—more beautiful than anyone, smarter than everyone, more go-to-Hell than a man can handle. D'Varn played Esther in '28, and now it was like D was playing her again in '58. There was a dizziness about it as far as I was concerned.

Stewart Granger, of course, he's the flier Esther supposedly falls in love with. He's already swooped her into Paris in a two-seater biplane and she's fired the spotter's machine gun at Bosch biplane fighters. We're at a boulevard café like you've seen in a hundred pictures, and Mr. Ray *likes* my busted nose, so I'm gonna be the flower-seller with my wood tray of flowers hangin from my neck. First I'm performin like any background while Stewart Granger smiles at Ava as his flier-friends, at a sidewalk table, sing *There's a long long road a-winding into the land of my dreams—where the nightingales are singing—and the bright moon beams . . .*

The land of my dreams is in the direction no one can go—and while I'm lost dreamily in that thought, they're movin stuff around as Mr. Ray instructs the next set-up. I seem to be ok where I am so I just stand there. Miss Ava's saying, "So, Nick, I take the rose, like this," and she takes a rose out of my box—is when I know I'm smack in the next shot, foreground.

Mr. Ray's sayin, "What would she do with it, Ava?"

"Esther isn't easy. She'd"—and don't you know Miss Ava flipped that flower over her shoulder like D'Varn done long ago that first day in front of the Keystone. I got the tingly chills.

"It's Sammie, right?" says Mr. Ray. "Sammie, I want that expression that you just this moment had. Can you do it and keep it?"

"Sure," says me.

"Ava, you stand so," he places her. "Then take the rose, smile as you take it, but smile-without-smiling." Turns to the camera guy. "It's going to be a two-shot, then a slight pan to Ava, focus, a beat, pan to Sammie, focus, hold for a beat."

"Beauty and the Beast," says me.

Soft chuckles, with a nod of approval from Miss Ava.

Make-up runs over to fuss with my face a little. Camera and crew are in place.

Quiet-on-the-set, roll sound, picture, "Action." Ava Gardner, she selects her rose, smiles at me with her eyes, a beat, I look at her with everything . . .

"Cut. We'll fade it from there. That's a wrap."

WORKPOINTS— NOTES ON SOURCES

TITLE

Edendale was a Los Angeles district that, circa 1900–1940, encompassed the neighborhoods now called Los Feliz, Silver Lake, Atwater Village, and Echo Park. A 1916 map shows that Edendale included much of Griffith Park to the north, several miles of the Los Angeles River to the west, and reached Elysian Park to the southwest. In 1909 Selig-Polyscope and Bison built the first West Coast film studios in Edendale, followed in 1912 by Mack Sennett's Keystone. In 1914 D.W. Griffith set up his Edendale shop roughly where Sunset Boulevard crosses Vermont; it was a large lot where he filmed most of *The Clansman* (aka, *The Birth Of A Nation*) and *Intolerance*. "Edendale" now exists as an official name only at the U.S. Post Office on Glendale Boulevard, "Edendale Station."

DEDICATION AND TRIBUTE

Ginger Varney's roles in my life as colleague, friend, and the great flame of my overextended youth, culminate (but do not end) in this dedication. Varney taught me movies could be a study as well as a passion and showed me where to look. Always a great adventurer, she taught me something about adventure too. It is said that in 1978 Ginger and I, with Jay Levin and Joie Davidov, founded *LA Weekly*; it was more complicated than that, but I'll let it stand. In those days we lived on Ewing and then Duane, two of those impossibly steep streets in the Los Angeles neighborhood where Silver Lake and Echo Park blend. Directly below Duane on Glendale Avenue, on a fenced lawn, a plaque upon a stone declared itself the site of Mack Sennett's Keystone studio. We took to calling our block "Sennett's Hill." In the spring of 1979 Varney discovered Dorothy and John Hampton's Silent Movie Theater on Fairfax in Hollywood. We included its schedules in *LA Weekly*'s film section, which we edited. Dorothy and John purchased their two-story building soon after World War II. They lived upstairs; the first floor was their theater. They sought out and bought silent films whenever possible. Their weekly lineup always opened with a Keystone Chaplin followed by a one-reel or half-reel "actuality" [documentary] from as early as the 1890s, followed in turn by one or two features. Many Silent Film Theater showings—for instance, Mabel Normand's 1927 *The Nickle Dancer*—were absent from even the most erudite film studies and catalogues circa 1979. The Silent Film Theater, as it existed while Dorothy and John Hampton lived, was the find of a lifetime, and you might say that this novel, *Edendale,* began there, and on Sennett's Hill, for that's when the notion gripped me that Ginger could have been a stunning silent film actress, with her sashaying array of gestures and expressions. However, *Edendale's* D'Varn is in no way Ginger Varney's portrait. Ginger's tastes are not D'Varn's, Ginger is far more complex and intellectual, and a better fighter; also, so far as I know, she was not brought up in a brothel. When I warned Ginger Varney she might see some of herself in a character in this novel, she said, "So long as she is beautiful" (or words to that effect). Ginger knows better than anyone that I'm not good enough to portray the actual Ginger. In fact, it is impossible for a fictional character to represent an actual person. Not Shakespeare, nor Dostoevsky, nor anyone else, ever invented a fictional character that could exist apart from the context of its fiction, whereas actual people must be themselves and survive (or not) in context after context not of their choosing. No imaginary character is complex enough to do that. Imaginative writing attempts somehow to create an entertainment applicable to reality that, if it goes far enough, may redeem reality and perhaps even forgive reality for being the thing it is.

HISTORICAL FIGURES IN ALPHABETICAL ORDER OF FIRST NAMES:
Al St.-John—Alice Davenport—Ava Gardner—Bessie Love—Billie Bitzer—Cecil B. DeMille—Charles Chaplin—Chester Conklin—Coy Watson—Coy Watson, Jr.—D.W. Griffith—Gloria Swanson—Hank Mann—Henry "Pathé" Lehrman—James "Big Boy" Medlin—John Bunny—Josephine Marcus Earp—Karl Brown—Lillian Gish—Louise Fazenda—Mabel Normand—Mack Sennett—Mack Swain—Marie Dressler—Minta Durfee [Mrs. Arbuckle]—Nicholas Ray—Phyllis Allen—Phyllis Haver—Roscoe "Fatty" Arbuckle—Stewart Granger—Wallace Beery—William Holden—Wyatt Earp.

CHAPTER 1—THE KEYSTONE
- The Keystone crew shows up at Willie's fire in timely fashion because in the studio's early days "Sennett had a direct link to the fire department" (*Hollywood— Episode 8—Comedy: A Serious Business,* documentary written and directed by Kevin Brownlow and David Gill, PBS 1980). [**Note:** The Brownlow-Gill 13-part *Hollywood* remains the most exhaustive visual source concerning USA silent

cinema. In 1980, when decent prints of silent films were hard to come by, it was a godsend, and had a lot to do with the original instigations of what, forty-two years later, became *Edendale*. Since the advent of the DVD, hundreds of films unknown to Brownlow-Gill have become available. Given what we've learned since, their groundbreaking doc, still immensely valuable, requires major revision.)

- *My sense is that Mother and Daddy came from different Southern classes, possibly in Missouri or Tennessee, she of a merchant, modestly middle-class family, he of share-cropper stock. They wouldn't meet socially anywhere but at, say, a county fair. Impregnation was probably violent but also probably not premeditated. Daddy wanted to "do the right thing," when all was said and done, so they married; however, it seemed a good notion to go where they might buy a plot of ground free of past associations. In the 1890s the Wild West was largely tamed and many headed for new starts to California. Given their upbringing and young dreams, both trying to make the best of it, Mother and Daddy couldn't resist a settlement called "Edendale," where the climate was perfect and, in the 1890s, land was cheap.*

- That Keystone plaque on Glendale and Duane got it somewhat wrong (and is no longer there). At its economic peak in the 1920s, Mack Sennett's studio did indeed stretch from Effie, on Alessandro Avenue (since renamed Glendale Boulevard), all the way to Duane, on both sides of the street. Most extant photographs date from Sennett's post-1916 plant. The Keystone that Willie discovers was crudely slapped together from September 1912 to February 1914 and fit snugly on one block between Effie and Aaron, on both sides of Alessandro. Sennett's first expansions were straight back up the west slope from Alessandro. Nothing of the earliest Keystone lot survives. The only remaining Keystone building (on Effie and Glendale) dates from 1916 and at present serves as a U-Haul storage facility. The entrance to the Jack-In-The-Box on Glendale, west of Effie, is just about the exact location of the main Keystone gate.

- Two years into *Edendale*'s composition I learned from Brent E. Walker's exhaustive *Mack Sennett's Fun Factory* (2010) that one Ray "Brick" Enright (1896-1969) worked his way up to director for Sennett, beginning a long career that included directing John Wayne and Marlene Dietrich in 1942's *The Spoilers*. This coincidence tickled me too much to change my Brick's name, but no resemblance to Mr. Enright is intended or even possible, as I've seen only Walker's single-paragraph bio.

- *March 2008—Driving west on I-10, New Mexico, L.A.-bound, maybe an hour from the Arizona line . . . Willie suddenly showed up, strong, in my "mind's eye"—I knew right away that she was the "star" of my long-intended silent movie novel. At the*

California border I detoured to 29 Palms Inn. They remembered me there. The place was packed but they let me stay in a house on the property. By then, D'Varn showed up beside Willie, but had no name so I spent all night working it out. By the time I reached L.A., Esther had joined Willie and D'Varn in the back seat of my '69 Chevy.

- Letting just about anybody into the "dailies" or "rushes," as they're called now, was common practice. Agnes DeMille (Cecil B. DeMille's niece, daughter of director William DeMille): "Whenever they finished a picture, which would be roughly every week, they'd run it, and ask everybody, all the families, all the children, all the cousins, neighbors sometimes, 'Come in, come in, see our picture, we're running it!' And then they'd ask everybody what they thought. I cannot believe that it was that simple, but it was. And I think some of that simplicity, and some of that fervor and excitement, is in the films, and that's why they're valuable and lovely." (*Hollywood—Episode 2: In The Beginning*, Brownlow-Gill, PBS 1980).

- *Sommie, Esther, Brick, Mother, Daddy, Fred, they appeared to me as firmly and confidently as if they'd been announced, after I realized that Willie could exist only at the Keystone and only in 1914 and could come only from Edendale.*

- Films screened: *A Flirt's Mistake*, directed by George Nichols, performed by Roscoe "Fatty" Arbuckle, Minta Durfee [Mrs. Arbuckle], Edgar Kennedy, and Cecile Arnold, *not* Virginia Kirtley, who's listed in the cast as "girl on the sidewalk" on IMDb, in the notes of *The Forgotten Films of Roscoe "Fatty" Arbuckle*, and Brent E. Walker's *Mack Sennett's Fun Factory*. In *Edendale*, D'Varn takes Ms. Arnold's roles. The film in which Willie discovers "Devil Charlie" is *Kid Auto Races At Venice*, directed by Henry "Pathé" Lehrman, performed by Charlie Chaplin. This was Chaplin's third Keystone picture, and his second outing as "Charlie" or (Chaplin's phrase) "the Little Fellow." *Kid Auto Races* was the first "Charlie" picture to be seen by the public; it was shot after, but released before, the much more elaborate *Mabel's Strange Predicament*, where the familiar "Charlie" first appeared, directed by Mabel Normand.

CHAPTER 2–GHOST BUILDING

- The recording Sommie plays is "Nobody," sung by Bert Williams (1874-1922); written by Williams and Alex Rogers; recorded by Williams in 1906 and 1913. Williams was the first African-American to star in a Broadway production and is believed to be first to star in a motion picture.

- The incident of the pickle barrel is straight out of my Bronx kidhood, circa age 4.

- *I collected research material for* The Dragon (Edendale) *from 1979 on. Willie didn't show up to constellate that research until 2008. At first I didn't realize how close I am to her, though she kept insisting on it. Suddenly, as though I did not will it, in the summer of 2009 she decided to open our story by setting her house afire. Ok, I went with that. When she got to Keystone there was still the question of what she would do there. Sketch chapters though I might, I had no idea, except that I never saw her as an actress. She decided to climb that roof. Nothing surprised me more than her leap into Pasha's arms. I have a note on yellow paper that I intend to frame, dated 1/22/10:* How does 'Catch' change the other chapters?

- *My intent: to present people of a certain profession, in a certain time and place, as these people experienced themselves, without exaggeration or suppression, and through them, to close in on what Conrad called "that glimpse of truth for which you have forgotten to ask."*

- Henry "Pathé" Lehrman (1886-1946) was an excellent comedy director, almost universally disliked. Earned his nickname "Mr. Suicide" for purposively putting actors and crew at risk of their lives. Left Keystone soon after Chaplin arrived. Famed also for giving fabricated testimony in the Roscoe Arbuckle manslaughter/rape trial.

- The scenes shot in this passage—performed by Mabel Normand, Charlie Chaplin and Chester Conklin—are from Chaplin's first picture as "the little fellow," *Mabel's Strange Predicament,* directed and written by Mabel Normand.

- Mabel was infamous for cursing like a man, when she remembered to do so; her informal "girls' cursing club" probably went through various names, depending on the day.

- *Hollywood—Part 8—Comedy: A Serious Business.* At 3:44 into the opening montage, two lions appear in almost exactly the situation I describe. The lions are clearly not controlled and, just as clearly, the performers are surprised and terrified. Documentarists Kevin Brownlow and David Gill didn't bother to credit their clips, so, for now, the perps go unaccounted for.

- *For a long time, Edendale disguised itself as another novel with the same char-acters called* The Dragon, *based on my thought in 1978-L.A. that "Hollywood," where American cinema* **became** *American cinema -- the Hollywood that included Edendale and Culver City and North Hollywood—the Hollywood that is not a place but a state of mind, located and rooted in Los Angeles—that Hollywood was in fact the Dragon between the desert and the sea, the Dragon of the old tales, the one Archangel Michael never killed quite dead enough. Later I learned that Edison's first nickelodeon on Broadway in 1894-95 sported a neon dragon in its plate-glass front.*

CHAPTER 3—THE PALISADES

- The *National Geographic* with the Tunisian large gals dates from early 1914. Mabel had a passion for geography.

- The rooftop chase of Willie's first shoot is based on a similar rooftop chase in Keystone's 1914 *The Rounders,* directed by and featuring Roscoe Arbuckle, with Chaplin in a supporting role.

- In the early days of Los Angeles filmmaking, many directors (Alan Dawn and Cecil B. DeMille among them) sported side arms. Not Sennett, six feet tall and exceptionally fit, who (like D. W. Griffith) occasionally settled on-set disagreements with his fists. There were many cowboys about who often went armed. On location, gun-toting was *de rigor,* though the threat was probably exaggerated. Mack Sennett and Mabel Normand loved prizefighting and he made a point of hiring former boxers, wrestlers and strongmen among his "background" people. In those early years if Sennett had to leave L.A. for any reason, he put a big guy— Roscoe Arbuckle or Mack Swain, for instance—in charge.

- Coy Watson's technical prowess is as recorded by Coy Watson, Jr., in *The Keystone Kid—Tales of Early Hollywood.* Junior was a Keystone child-actor who became a noted Los Angeles photo-journalist.

- *Hollywood—Part 8—Comedy: A Serious Business.* At 3:23 into the opening montage, a car (plus driver) goes over the Palisades cliff and hangs by a rope or cable. In a 1917 Sennett production, *Her Torpedoed Love,* directed by Frank C. Griffin and performed by Louise Fazenda, Ford Sterling and Wayland Trask, the concluding chase includes a large "police patrol" car full of Keystone Kops that skids over the cliff and hangs from the Palisades. In both these specimens, there's no doubt that live players are in those imperiled cars and that the Pacific Coast Highway is way down below.

- Lottie and her mother are loosely based on Lucille Rickson and her mother. Rickson was cast in adult parts at age 12 and died during childbirth not very long after.

CHAPTER 4—HOTEL HOLLYWOOD

- In the Brownlow-Gill documentary it's often called the Hollywood Hotel, but in photographs from the hotel's heyday its sign reads "Hotel Hollywood."

- *If I hadn't been born in 1945 . . . if a certain toughness hadn't been necessary for the survival of a boy's dignity on the meaner streets of New York City circa 1945-1972 . . . if "trans-gender" had been a concept prior to the inception of this novel in 2008 (though lesbian friends would casually say, "Michael is a lesbian in a man's body.")—if, if, if . . . I would have gotten into very different kinds of trouble but would I have had Willie's courage? As it was, I was in my sixties before my sensual nature became clear.*

- The picture shot in Echo Park is *Those Love Pangs,* direction and scenario (supposedly) by Chaplin, performed by Chaplin, Cecile Arnold, Chester Conklin and Vivian Edwards. I say "supposedly," because it's a mistake to take Keystone documents too literally. Intentions were written down, records were kept, but anything could happen on a Keystone set, including casting changes, and anyone might contribute to the scenario.

- The usage "special friends" dates to the late 19th/early 20th century; in circles more tolerant than most, it was a courteous way to refer to a lesbian couple.

- Charlie tells Willie about a scene from *The Face On The Barroom Floor,* direction and scenario (supposedly) by Chaplin, co-starring Cecile Arnold. It's significant that Chaplin's two outings with Arnold as co-star are his most lecherous films by far. I have no proof, but I'm fairly sure Ms. Arnold had something to do with that; however, I'm responsible for the liberties D'Varn takes with Charlie.

- At Medlin's Eatery, Charlie refers to *The Rounders,* performed and co-directed by Chaplin and Roscoe Arbuckle.

- In later years Chaplin dissed Keystone, pooh-poohed his early films, and was condescending toward Mabel Normand, but observers at the time (Robert Sherwood among them) noted that Normand deeply influenced Chaplin's basic attitude toward the camera—the very attitude upon which his later work was constructed. In Chaplin's first Keystone, *Making A Living,* we see a music-hall performer, playing broadly; in his second film, directed by Mabel Normand, *Mabel's Strange Predicament,* she puts Chaplin in confined, one-on-one situations in which he must perform more delicately, closer to the camera, encountering people more personally. As Chaplin's year at Keystone progressed, he caught on to Normand's techniques and they became his own. Letters to his brother Sydney prove that, during his Keystone year, he believed he was doing the best work of his life to date. In later years, as the greatest cinema star of his or any day, when he intended a one-on-one scene and needed someone really good, Chaplin, in effect, went back to Keystone: Mack Swain in *Gold Rush,* Hank Mann in *City Lights,* Chester Conklin in *Modern Times* and *The Great Dictator.*

- In *The Extra Girl* (1923), produced by Sennett, directed by F. Richard Jones from a story by Sennett, and performed by Mabel Normand, Mabel shares a cage for a few moments with a male lion, then leads that lion by a thick rope where it's reluctant to go. Her protection, off-camera, was director Jones with a pitchfork. In the first take the lion went for Normand, knocked her down, and Jones, in his excitement, stuck Normand's bum with his pitchfork, after which they shot Take 2. As the *Extra Girl* sequence continues, the lion runs loose;

Mabel Normand and her colleagues are then in uneasy proximity of a grouchy, impatient beast. Also: About eleven minutes into *Hollywood—Part 8—Comedy: A Serious Business,* a large male lion leaps onto Mack Sennett's desk and Sennett calmly gives it room. He sat with that lion on his desk for publicity photos. In *Swanson On Swanson,* Gloria Swanson describes how, when filming Cecil B. DeMille's 1919 *Male And Female,* DeMille had her lay down while a male lion placed his paws on her bare back and sniffed her hair and neck, "and then when he roared it was like thousands of vibrators all over me."

- I've taken liberties with a 1914 Keystone half-reel "actuality," *Our Largest Birds,* shot at an "ostrich farm."

- Ulysses' "My lords and my ladies" comes straight from Lord Buckley. A tribute.

- D'Varn's audition owes something to Betty Blythe's description in Kevin Brownlow/*The Parade's Gone By* (1968), an invaluable book of interviews.

CHAPTER 6–ESTHER

- Esther's experience at Vassar is rooted in Nancy Milford's *Savage Beauty— The Life of Edna St. Vincent Millay.* Millay, whom family and intimates called "Vincent," made no secret of her buoyant and bisexual promiscuity from her time at Vassar to the drunken night she fell down a flight of stairs and died, age 58. What did you think *My candle burns at both ends* meant? The verse goes on:
It will not last the night;
But ah, my foes, and oh, my friends,
It gives a lovely light!

- I did not make up rumors about Mack Sennett's libido. Decades later Keystone veterans recalled that Chaplin and others speculated on Mack Sennett's preferences. Rumors aside, the historical record is clear: Mabel Normand was the one and only person with whom Mack Sennett was ever seriously involved.

- Christina Rossetti's "The Goblin Market" (1862) doesn't describe sensuality; rather, her poem reproduces sensuality in an enmeshment of words. Her brother understood in his illustration:

- *D'Varn knows what she wants. Willie loves what she has. It's Esther, the most solid of the three, who's really the most lost. Stenya's "Long, long periods of indecision and suffering, when you don't know which life is your own."*
- *And . . . unless the playwright is Shakespeare, the play and even the cinema are confined forms. Theatre and cinema are confined by budget first of all, but also by time—cinema determined even more so by the unalterable condition that the camera changes what it sees, sees selectively, and is mysteriously effected by its supposed masters. Of all art forms the novel is most unconfined—and is the most merciless as to what it reveals of its author, for every single detail, every character, every action, every taste, scent, sound, sight, and every word, is a fluid artifact of its author's psyche, combining and interacting and alive, often behaving as independently of its author as a child of its parent. An author cannot hide from this creation—and that is what the author of a novel must seek: to be as unhidden as possible.*

CHAPTER 7–GRIFFITH

- The cop and the apple—a tribute to Nell Shipman.
- D.W. Griffith's on-set behavior is described in Lillian Gish/*The Movies, Mr. Griffith, And Me* and Karl Brown/*Adventures With D.W. Griffith*.
- In this period D.W. Griffith didn't work from screenplays or scripts—at least, not anything that would be recognized as such today. (Title cards were written after shooting.) For *The Clansman* (aka *The Birth Of A Nation*), Griffith followed the Thomas Dixon Jr. novel (subtitled *A Historical Romance of the Ku Klux Klan*). He had absolute control and worked very freely. He'd assign his "department heads," as we might call them, what he wanted in sets or props or costumes, then left them to do as they pleased, after which he nayed or ayed. Precious few records were kept. Griffith commonly told his cinematographer Billy Bitzer to shoot such-and-such in this or that way, Bitzer would say, "That's impossible," to which Griffith would say, "That's why we'll do it," or words to that effect.
- Sommie's "Take your lover in the ring" sing-song is remembered from a 1968 TV episode of *The Outcasts* of the same title, scripted by Anthony Lawrence and starring Don Murray, Otis Young, and Gloria Foster.
- *When we meet Willie she's what we would call an "adolescent," but that concept was still new in 1914; at 16 Fred would have been considered a "woman grown," and Willie? It would take a century for Willie to be called anything, but she presented as a woman grown and, in that society, was taken at her word and invited to take her chances like all others. What Fred and Mother knew, and what Willie and Daddy didn't, is that Willie and Daddy are the determinant factors of their family. Willie*

and Daddy are the fixed points, equally stubborn, equally willful, equally fierce—and either one is certainly capable of killing the other. Willie always imagined Fred to be the stronger of the two. Of course, Fred was following Willie's lead the whole time; when forced, by Willie's action, to face society, she sought protection in a show of normalcy.

CHAPTER 8–THE FOURTH

- In the early years, Sennett made a big deal about the Fourth, a hearty party at the lot.
- In April, 1912, five months before Sennett and Normand left Biograph to form Sennett's Keystone company, he directed her in *Oh, Those Eyes!* and *The Brave Hunter.* In both, Mabel rejects handsome male suitors and chooses instead to play with, ride, and cuddle a large adolescent bear, the mere sight of which is enough to scatter her terrified suitors. Beautiful, flirty, demure, playful, brave, Mabel Normand, aged about 17, turned over all the tables not in protest or to make a point but as a matter of course. Of course. (Nell Shipman also deserves mention in this regard, especially when it comes to bears. Nell Shipman/*The Silent Screen And My Talking Heart.*)
- Wallace Beery in blackface performs Bert Williams' 1913 hit "You Can't Get Away From It," lyrics by William Jerome and Grant Clarke, music by Jean Schwartz. I have taken the liberty of placing Beery and his teen wife Gloria Swanson at the Keystone a year-and-some before they actually arrived.

CHAPTER 9–MISS MABEL

- I've seen a silent-era "still" of a woman performing this fire-escape-downtown biz.
- *Tillie's Punctured Romance,* world cinema's first feature-length comedy, premiered on December 21, 1914, a smash world-wide hit, produced and supervised by Mack Sennett. Keystone being Keystone, it's probable that Sennett directed most of Marie Dressler's scenes, while Roscoe Arbuckle, George Nichols, and various others directed as needed. During the shooting of *Tillie,* Sennett's studio still had to meet its contract of two finished one- or two-reel pictures per week. In September, for instance, Keystone released 11 films; in February, 12; in June (while *Tillie* was shooting), 12.
- Many Keystone half-reel and one-reel comedies were made up on the spot, but (contrary to legend) many were not, especially those with multiple locations and elaborate situations. In the most thorough history to date, Simon Louvish/ *Keystone—The Life And Clowns Of Mack Sennett* (2003), the author reproduces typescript scenarios of several pictures, including 1914's *Mabel's Strange Predicament.* MABEL/CATCH VEHICLE follows the style of those scenarios, in which

"biz" is indicated but not spelled out, details to be concocted on-set by director and performers (and any crew person with a fresh idea).

- MABEL/CATCH VEHICLE owes a little to Vitagraph's 1911 John Bunny-Mabel Normand *The Subduing Of Mrs. Nag* (directed by George Baker, written by Van Dyke Brooke) and more to Keystone's Mabel Normand-Fred Mace-Alice Davenport 1912 *Mabel's Stratagem* (directed by Mack Sennett, writing uncredited). That said, beyond some plot-points, MABEL/CATCH VEHICLE is on its own. *Edendale's* Mabel credits the Vitagraph film to honor the almost universally forgotten John Bunny (1863-1915), American cinema's first comedy star.

- The biz of Mabel/Catch scooped onto the cow-guard of a Big Red trolley is flinched from the ending of Chaplin's first Keystone, *Making A Living*, directed by and co-starring Pathé Lehrman. The trolley-stunt is my tribute to Gene Kelly doing the same in *Singing In The Rain*, Kelly playing a silent film star adapting to talkies.

- *Hollywood—Segment 2—In The Beginning.* At 30:22, in a montage, there's a brief sequence of Mabel Normand on a bicycle performing an extremely dangerous stunt involving a galloping four-horse fire-wagon. Not credited, of course, as is Brownlow-Gill's practice, but it's definitely Normand, possibly from one of her lost features for Goldwyn in the late 19-teens, shot beside her personal triangle-shaped studio on Effie and Fountain. An example of how far she'd go, on a bicycle or anything else, to do something on-camera no one else would dare.

- The soft-porn shots of Mabel Normand that D'Varn shows Willie are actual, and can be seen reproduced in Betty Frussell's *Mabel.* To my knowledge, there is no commentary about their existence anywhere.

CHAPTER 10—ECHO PARK

- Mabel and Mack loved auto races and went out of their way to befriend winning drivers, several of whom appeared in early Keystones. Sennett recognized the importance of the automobile as a culture-altering medium all by itself; from start to finish, cars, trucks and motorcycles figured largely in his cinema.

- Such an accident as I describe actually happened, though details varied somewhat. The real-life casualty count was higher. The city thereafter barred Sennett's filmmakers from shooting in Echo Park, though other parks remained open to them.

EPILOGUE—THE NIGHTINGALES

- See Ann Kirschner/*Lady At The O.K. Corral—The True Story of Josephine Marcus Earp.* See also, impressions of Wyatt Earp from various Hollywood figures such as Adela Rogers St. John. I base my presentation of Earp on them.

- "God help the movies on a night like this" is borrowed from Nell Shipman, in tribute.
- Bessie Love (1898-1986) worked in talking pictures as "background," credited and uncredited, in features and on TV. Her final appearances were in *Reds* and *Ragtime*, 1981. Several silent stars did the same for decades after their era.
- "There's A Long Long Trail A-Winding," music by Zo Elliot, lyrics by Stoddard King, was an enormous favorite among British and American troops on the Western Front of the Great War (1914-1918). I learned it from my friend Naunie B. and she learned it from her father, a veteran of that war, who sang it all his life.
- And how has such a thing as *Edendale* come about through this Willie? Who does she speak to? Has she "written" it somehow? How is she speaking? Through the novel's enchantment as a form.

FROM THE BOTTOM
OF THE WELL

THANKS from the bottom of the well to Jazmin Aminian Ventura—Steve Erickson—Dave Johnson—Rocco LoBosco. To James "Big Boy" Medlin for our misadventures in Hollywoodland and for Medlin's Grub & Suds. To Chuck "Shark" Rosenthal, Gail Wronsky, Ash Good, and Giant Claw. And, along the way, Kip Hargrove—Jessa Zarubica—Joseph Leahy—Jane Morton—Simon Baril—Evann Marie.

www.ingramcontent.com/pod-product-compliance
Lightning Source LLC
Chambersburg PA
CBHW022020300726
48970CB00003B/980